He got out of bed, quite naked, and taking her
in his arms, kissed her. She was dressed for
work in a suit and stockings.

"Whatever, else, Paolo, you must keep painting.
I'm willing to live through what you must do,
but you must do this for me."

He kissed her again, but she pulled away. She
would be late for work.

"Just give me some hope that one day we can
have a normal life." She touched his face.
"That's all I ask."

Also by Barrie King
Published by Ballantine Books:

CONTESSA

Julia

Barrie King

BALLANTINE BOOKS • NEW YORK

Copyright © 1994 by Barrington King

All rights reserved under International and Pan-American Copyright Conventions. Published in the United States of America by Ballantine Books, a division of Random House, Inc., New York, and simultaneously in Canada by Random House of Canada Limited, Toronto.

Library of Congress Catalog Card Number: 93-90860

ISBN 0-345-37864-4

Manufactured in the United States of America

First Edition: April 1994

10 9 8 7 6 5 4 3 2 1

For S., remembering Italy.

Chapter One

April 1930

"THERE YOU ARE my dear, a complete transformation, and the work of an artist, if I do say so myself."

Julia Howard studied her image in the mirrored walls. Her eyes seemed larger, her cheekbones more prominent, her neck longer. She looked in the mirror into the eyes of the man behind her chair, standing with his hands on his hips.

"It's terribly short, Victor."

"It's perfection, that's what it is," the hairdresser said. "Short bobs were all the rage in London and Paris this winter. Rome is always a bit behind the times, but you'll be right up to the minute. You've the perfect head for the boyish look, and with that boyish figure of yours I almost became aroused myself."

Julia laughed. "I rather fancied myself a female."

She looked down at the locks of dark hair that Victor had amputated with a few sure strokes of his scissors, lying in a coil on the floor like a small sleeping animal.

"Oh, you'll have the men panting after you, never fear." He turned the chair slowly, so that she could see the cut from every angle.

"It's very nice, but I think it makes me look older."

"Which is what you want at your age. And what would that be? Twenty-one?"

"Twenty-two . . . today."

"Well, happy birthday. And remember that I created a new woman for the occasion."

"A new woman for a new life. That's just what I want."

"Good luck, my dear. I used to start new lives all the time, but it never seemed to work for me. I've had an unhappy time." Victor looked sorrowfully at himself in the mirrors. "I'll never leave the ships again. It's safe here, and I make so many friends."

He was talking to himself now. Julia got up and smoothed out her dress.

"Thank you, Victor."

"You'll be a sensation tonight."

Julia gave the hairdresser a large tip and went out on deck. The time between tea and cocktails was the dead period on shipboard, and the promenade deck was empty. Most people were in their cabins, already packing trunks. Europe in the morning. Julia stopped and looked at her reflection in a porthole. A new woman for a new life, and anxious for it to begin.

She strolled onto the stern and leaned against the rail. The ship's wake cut a path of icy green in the blue of the Mediterranean. Gulls glided along effortlessly above the stern, and the Union Jack snapped in the breeze. Julia looked down at the gray-green water being churned up far below by the ship's propellers and shuddered. The sea seemed so deep and cold. She drew back, her hands tightly gripping the rail. For a moment she had been almost overcome by an old fear.

"You're looking very thoughtful."

"Oh." Julia started. It was Francesca Danieli. "I was thinking about tomorrow."

"Excited?"

"Scared." It was a more honest answer than she had meant to give, more honest than she had been with herself.

"Why?"

"There are . . . so many possibilities. I can, well, do almost anything I want."

"I envy you. How about a drink?"

Julia looked at her wristwatch. "Well. . . ."

"Oh, come on. Let's get tight tonight and make a spectacle of ourselves."

Francesca hooked her arm in Julia's and led her to the little glassed-in bar in the stern. Julia was flattered that someone so worldly sought her company. She and Francesca had become close friends, she felt, in the few days since they had sailed from New York.

The bar was deserted except for the barman polishing glasses, who silently brought two martinis to their table.

"What have you done to yourself?" Francesca asked, eyeing Julia's hair and taking a sip from her frosted glass.

"It's awful, isn't it?"

"It's gorgeous. I wish somebody could do that for me, but then one must have something to work with."

"Why do you say that? You're so attractive."

Francesca snorted. "That's what you beautiful ones always say to us plain ones. Either that or 'you have an interesting face.' "

Julia held her tongue. Anything she said could be twisted by Francesca to mean what she wished. Francesca was plain, but she was attractive to men. Anyone could see that.

"What could anyone do with this?" Francesca ran a hand through the mass of red curls that encircled her face. Then she opened her handbag, took out a cigarette, and put it in the ivory holder she used. As Francesca leaned forward to light her cigarette she exposed deeply shaded eyelids and long, mascara-heavy eyelashes. She never wore any other makeup. Why was she attractive to men? Francesca's body was long and awkward, her limbs wiry, her creamy skin covered with freckles. She had a narrow, muscled jaw that thrust out and a turned-up nose. She raised her head and opened wide her china-blue eyes.

"Your eyes are beautiful."

"My best feature." Francesca snorted again. "My only feature. Why are you scared?"

"I've burned all my bridges."

"Odd. So have I."

"How so?"

"I've been home to 'face up to responsibility,' as Mother calls it. I told her I couldn't manage that, but I went home anyway, since she paid, first class—and round-trip—I insisted on that. It was just as I expected, lawyers, lectures, threats, promises, ultimatums."

"What does she object to?"

"Oh, everything. My being a sculptor, living in Rome, and worst of all, 'living in sin.' I pointed out that she went to Rome at my age and married an Italian. I refrained from suggesting that they slept together before they were married, but she got the point. However, she thinks Father's part of the problem. He's a bad influence—now that they're separated. No divorce in Italy, of course. Bad influence! I see the old boy maybe once a year."

"Your father's in Rome?"

"Oh, yes. The famous Danieli, maker of the most god-awful movies in the history of the cinema, but it's not all his fault. What else can he do under Mussolini? Anyway, to make a long story short, I was told either to come home and lead a useful life or be disinherited. So I've been disinherited. It's a pity. I could have used the money."

"You did that for James?"

James Morrison was an American artist with whom Francesca shared a studio in Rome, and Julia supposed that was what was meant by "living in sin."

"Not for James. Well, for James in a way." Francesca made a circle in the air with her cigarette holder. "For freedom. I would have done it anyway." She smiled. "But having James makes it easier."

"I envy *you*."

Francesca raised a thin line of auburn eyebrow.

"I mean, it was for freedom that I burned my bridges, but I haven't had much of it yet. At home one has to be careful. I don't have to go home again if I don't want. I could live in Rome, too." The idea had just occurred to Julia.

Francesca drew on her cigarette. "You aren't a virgin, are you?"

"At my age, and in these times, that would be pretty unlikely, wouldn't it?"

Francesca looked at her through narrowed eyes. "Well,

it's better to have that kind of thing out of the way if you're going to live in Rome, that's all."

There was an awkward silence. Francesca's typically blunt question had taken her by surprise, but Julia thought she had turned it aside rather nicely. It wasn't that she had any qualms about going to bed with a man. She fully expected to have a passionate life, and it was perhaps for this reason that she had disdained to begin it with any of the college boys she knew. There had been that time on the sofa with her English professor. She would have done it then, but he had begun declaring his love.

"Julia, I didn't mean to embarrass you."

"You didn't. I was thinking about some things that are past now. I want to be free. If you get too involved, well, you lose your freedom, don't you? . . . Tell me, Francesca, are you going back to Rome for good?"

"I guess so. I certainly couldn't live in New York again. But I enjoyed the trip, and especially meeting you."

Julia didn't know what to say. Almost everything that Francesca said put her off balance, shook the poise she was trying to maintain.

"If it weren't for you," Julia said, "this would have been a dreadful voyage. I didn't realize that first class would be filled with nothing but doddering old millionaires."

"Aren't you forgetting Angelo Morosini?"

"Except, of course, for Angelo."

Was Francesca jealous that she was being pursued by Angelo? Julia wondered. The phone rang.

"It's for you, Miss Danieli."

"Hello. . . . You've been calling everywhere? Well, you should've tried the bar first. . . . No, I'm not going slumming. It was your decision to travel third-class. You come up here. . . . Suit yourself, but you really should meet this ravishingly beautiful friend of mine I've been telling you about. . . ." Francesca winked across the room at Julia.

"Who was that?" Julia asked when Francesca returned from the bar.

"My brother."

"You didn't tell me your brother was on board. You

didn't even tell me you had a brother," Julia said, feeling somehow betrayed.

"Oh, yes, I have one, but I was just teasing him about meeting you. He wouldn't be your type. Very serious. The big thing with him is principle. For example, he won't travel first-class. I suppose if they still had steerage he would be sleeping out on deck. That, of course, didn't keep him from cashing in the first-class ticket Mother gave him and pocketing the difference."

"Then he lives in Italy, too?"

"Very much so. In fact, he's become Italian. No matter how long I live there—and I'm as much a half-breed as he—I'll always feel American. Paolo chose Italy a long time ago."

"Is he coming up here?"

"I don't think so. He said he wanted me to look at a drawing he's working on."

"A drawing? . . ."

Julia was suddenly aware that a shadow had come between her and the brightness of the sea. A tall, muscular sailor in canvas pants and a black turtleneck sweater was standing in the doorway of the bar. As he stepped out of the glare and into the room Julia drew in her breath at his extraordinary good looks—Mediterranean: dark, unshaven, with long hair curling over his collar. His features were perfect except for a crooked nose that looked as if it had been broken, and somehow made him even more handsome.

"*My!*"

"What?" Francesca swiveled in her chair.

"That seaman over there. If you were going to have one of those shipboard romances we've been joking about, you couldn't do much better than that."

"I'm afraid he wouldn't do for me."

"How can you say that?" Julia whispered as he came closer. "He's gorgeous."

"He's also my brother," Francesca said with a laugh. "Well hello, Paolo. So you decided to come up after all."

He was standing directly over Julia, who could feel herself blushing.

"You made it sound interesting."

Julia turned even redder then, but decided that his voice was as exciting as his looks.

"My ever tactful brother, Paolo," Francesca said, a touch of annoyance in her voice, "who I haven't seen since we left New York. We communicate by telephone. Paolo, this is my friend Julia Howard."

He nodded to her and she returned the gesture. Neither of them spoke. Francesca looked at Julia and then at her brother.

"Paolo, you look like a bum. How did you manage to get into first class?"

"It wasn't easy. I had to crawl up a ladder."

"*Buffone.*"

Julia was trying to bring what she had thought was a rough seaman into focus as Francesca's brother. This was the serious man of principle? He bore no resemblance at all to Francesca.

"Won't you join us?" Julia finally managed to say.

"Thanks, I will," and Paolo Danieli pulled up a chair from another table. He looked at her with a directness that she found unsettling.

"Your description wasn't far wrong, Francesca."

"Paolo, *caro mio*, Julia heard what I said to you on the phone."

His eyes met Julia's.

"And you should have heard what she said about you," Francesca added, and she threw back her head and laughed in her characteristic way.

"I thought you were a member of the crew," Julia got out before Francesca could say anything more.

"He's an artist actually, and a damned good one, aren't you, Paolo?"

"I don't know. I used to think so."

Julia and Paolo continued to stare at each other. She couldn't quite take in this presence with dark unruly hair that merged into the dark stubble on his face.

"You have a studio in Rome?" She was still almost tongue-tied.

"Yes."

Francesca broke the silence that followed. "Julia is visiting her aunt in Rome."

"You'll be staying long?" he said then.

"I don't know. Without quite knowing why, she added, "I might stay in Italy for a long time. It's up to me, I guess."

She turned her eyes away from him. "Oh, dear," she said, almost with relief, "there's that old bore, Oxley."

"Major General Sir Neville Oxley, retired," Paolo said dryly. "We know each other."

A heavyset man in a tweed jacket and plus fours came up to the bar and ordered a scotch. Turning around, he saw them and said in a loud voice, "No ice, understand, no ice," as though the barman might be influenced by some Americans across the room to fill his glass with ice cubes. He looked at them more closely and then came across and glared down at Francesca's brother, his ginger mustache bristling on his florid face.

"You've no business here, Danieli."

Paolo sprawled in his chair, a big hand around a glass of red wine. He didn't change his expression and he didn't move. He was not unlike Francesca, in the set of his eyes, though his were dark, and the strong jawline.

"Mr. Danieli is here as my guest," Julia said quietly.

"I'm sorry," Oxley said in a shaking voice, turning to her, and apparently only then remembering that they shared the same table at meals, "but this man does not have a first-class ticket, Miss Howard, and is not allowed into first-class facilities."

"Oh, really!" Julia said under her breath, and then to Oxley, "But surely, on the last night out . . ."

"There has to be some kind of order. That's why the world's in the state it's in." He turned and went back to the bar.

The barman came over to their table and said apologetically, "I'm terribly sorry, Miss Howard, but I'm afraid the gentleman must leave. Normally we look the other way, but when a passenger makes a complaint . . ."

"I'm going," Paolo said, getting up, apparently not in the least concerned.

"No." Julia was immediately on her feet. "George, we're all going up to my suite. Would you please take everyone's order for drinks, and have them sent up with a nice tray of canapés."

"Yes, Miss Howard. Right away."

An elevator took them to the uppermost deck, where Suite *A*, with its oil paintings on wood-paneled walls, Oriental carpets, and a small deck of its own, occupied the forward section.

"Posh, would you say?" Francesca looked at her brother.

"Louis the Fourteenth would have felt right at home."

"I didn't realize it would be so elaborate." Julia didn't know what else to say. She had foolishly told the Cunard Lines office that she wanted the best available accommodations, anticipating her very special twenty-second birthday. She had had no idea that "the best" would mean this.

"If it's what you like, no need to make excuses," Paolo said with a shrug.

"I'm not," Julia replied, lowering her eyes to light a cigarette. "You made quite a commotion down there."

"That was Francesca's fault . . . and yours, of course."

"An innocent lured into first class by two depraved women?"

"I . . ."

Francesca laughed at her brother's loss for words, sauntered over to the baby grand piano, the focal point of the furnishings in Julia's suite, and began to play.

"Good day, anyone at home?"

Julia turned to find Angelo Morosini standing in the doorway.

"The door was open, so I thought I'd just look in, but I see you have guests."

He bowed slightly to Francesca at the piano, but she ignored him.

"No, no. Please join us."

Angelo came into the room. He was wearing white ducks and a navy blue blazer. With his neat brown mustache, reg-

ular features, and soft brown eyes, he was almost too good-
looking. He smiled at Julia, and then the smile faded. His
gaze was fixed on something behind her. She turned. It was
Paolo Danieli.

"Angelo, you could have stepped right out of a fashion
magazine," Julia said in a slightly louder voice than she had
intended. "What a smashing blazer."

"Oh, this," Angelo said, fingering a lapel. "Had it made
up in London, a tailor my family's used for ages."

Out of the corner of her eye, Julia saw that Paolo was
watching them with an amused, slightly mocking grin.

"Come on, Angelo," Julia said, "join the party."

"Any particular occasion?"

"We had a row with General Oxley in the bar and had
to flee here for our lives."

"Really. What happened?"

Paolo stepped forward. He was half a head taller than
Angelo.

"The row is with me, not with Miss Howard. General
Oxley objected to my presence in first class. Now, if you'll
excuse me, I must go."

"Nonsense, Danieli," Angelo said. "Oxley is a fool."

"Oh, dear," Julia said, "I forgot to make introductions.
But I see you know each other."

Paolo smiled. "Count Morosini and I met briefly in New
York."

There was a knock on the open door.

"Come in."

The purser, a big, pink-faced Englishman bustled into the
room, directing two stewards in white mess jackets, one
carrying a tray of champagne and glasses, the other a crystal bowl of caviar packed in ice.

"Terribly sorry, Miss Howard," the pink-faced man said.
"My sincere apologies. I hope you were not too inconve-
nienced."

"If you mean General Oxley, I rather enjoyed it."

The purser shot a hostile glance at Paolo. "You may, of
course, have as guests whomever you wish. Again, my re-

grets." He gestured toward the champagne and caviar. "With the compliments of Cunard Lines."

"Thank you."

"That was a nice gesture," Julia said, as the purser and stewards went out.

"One that is included in the fare," Paolo said.

"What do you mean by that?"

Angelo turned and walked away from them out onto the private deck.

"It comes with all this," Paolo replied, including with a sweep of his hand the mahogany and teak and Bokhara carpets and Francesca at the piano.

"Well, I'm not sorry about it." I'm a coward, she thought. I didn't mean to have this grand suite. Why don't I tell the truth? I borrowed the money for this trip against my inheritance.

"I wasn't asking you to apologize. All I meant was that pursers and stewards don't bring me caviar and champagne."

"Poor dear."

Their hostile stares dissolved into laughter. God, she thought, he's beautiful. She took a chilled tulip-shaped glass of champagne from him and their hands touched briefly.

"You are, you know, rather beautiful . . . Julia." He lifted his glass to her.

"Why, thank you . . . Paolo."

"Now, what did you say to Francesca about me?"

"Oh, really!"

She turned and walked over to where Francesca was playing snatches of Broadway show tunes on the piano.

"I see you and Paolo are already getting along famously."

Julia sat down on the bench next to her. "He can be rather difficult."

Paolo was standing in front of a bookcase full of leather-bound volumes, pretending to study one that he had taken out. How oddly everyone was behaving.

Francesca lifted her fingers from the keys. "Difficult? I warned you. And leave it to Paolo to create a scene."

"I think it's rather amusing."

"More amusing than you imagine. I suppose it's time I told you what's going on."

"What do you mean?"

"Well," Francesca said, reaching for a glass of champagne, "General Oxley is head of a Fascist party that's been formed in England."

"My goodness, I didn't know there was such a thing there."

"That's the problem. People don't know. The Fascists could take over everywhere. Germany is already headed that way."

"Is fascism all that bad? People say Mussolini has done a lot for Italy."

Francesca frowned. "That's not the point. Mussolini is like General Oxley. There's no room for anyone else's opinion. And if you don't do what he says, he uses violence to make you do it. I'm sure Oxley would, too, if he could. The only difference is that Mussolini is clever and the general is, as your friend Morosini says, a fool ... but a dangerous fool. My brother is also a fool ... an idealistic fool. He is one of the leaders of the opposition to Mussolini. Oxley has been in New York trying to drum up support for Il Duce. He spoke to a big Italian-American rally, and I guess Paolo caused some trouble. He's good at that. I'm sure the general will have a lot of things to say in Rome about Paolo."

"But they can't do anything to your brother. You're American citizens."

"Maybe they can and maybe they can't. The Italian government considers us Italian citizens." She shrugged. "Anyway, just be glad you're not half-Italian."

Francesca looked carefully at Julia. "Come to think of it, you're the one who looks Italian. I'm the one with Italian blood, and I just look like an Irish tart. My luck to inherit my mother's looks. Hasn't anyone ever told you that you look Italian?"

"Caviar?" Julia held the bowl of gray fish eggs in front of Francesca. "The best Beluga."

They both had a heaping spoonful on toast.

"Actually," Julia said, on a sudden impulse, "I'm not, but my mother had an Italian, well, lover." That didn't sound quite right in describing Gus Bramante. "My mother moved in with him and took me with her. I lived with them until I was eleven."

"Why didn't you tell me, *carissima*? We have something in common."

"I've never told anyone before."

"And after you were eleven?"

"My mother accidentally drowned, at Rehoboth Beach—that's near Baltimore—and I went to live with my Aunt Agnes and Uncle Charles at Branwood, that's their place, also near Baltimore. They have a daughter, Victoria, my age. My aunt sent me to boarding school, and then to Goucher College."

Francesca was obviously reassessing her, interested now.

"And your real father?"

"Oh, Tim Howard, I don't even remember him. He left my mother when I was very young, died of typhoid in some village in Mexico, before drink could do the job."

Julia, already a little light-headed, refilled their champagne glasses. What a strange turn this last day at sea was taking. She couldn't seem to stop talking. Were the two men listening? But Paolo continued to pretend to read and Angelo stood at the rail, looking out to sea. She had planned on spending the last evening out with Angelo, but now, if only . . .

"What's going on with them?"

"They won't have anything to do with each other, and each is hoping the other will leave first."

"What's the problem?"

"Politics, I imagine . . . or you."

"You don't like Angelo, do you?"

"Let's say he doesn't excite me. But let's get back to you. What about the Italian?"

"Oh, he's still down on the waterfront in Baltimore. 'Agostino Bramante, Fine Art Restorations.' We lived in a loft above his shop."

"Do you see him often?"

"I used to. After my mother drowned, Aunt Agnes was going to get a court order to take me away from him, but she needn't have worried. He knew the advantages I would have at Branwood, her estate. He wasn't welcome there, of course, but I used to sneak away from boarding school and spend weekends with him. And then . . ."

Unexpectedly Julia could feel tears welling up in her eyes.

"Land ho!"

Julia and Francesca ran out onto the deck.

"Italy," Angelo said, pointing. They stood with their hands on the rail, straining to make out some landmark that would tell them where they were, but the point of land on the horizon faded away again. When Julia turned away from the rail, Paolo had disappeared.

Julia finished dressing for dinner, and stepped back from the mirror. She saw with satisfaction that the plum-colored silk gown with narrow shoulder straps clung to her figure in a flattering fall to her ankles. She was lightly tanned from long hours beside the swimming pool, and the combination of the silk, her dark hair, gray-green eyes, and the single strand of pearls against her bare skin was perfect. No wonder Francesca had thought she looked Italian. But why had she told Francesca about Gus?

Frowning, she looked into the gray-green eyes in the mirror, her mother's eyes, the color of the deep cold sea beneath the ship's stern that afternoon, the color of the sea that day her mother had dived into a wave and never come up again. With such a small key was the door opened that she had closed behind her when she walked into the entrance hall at Branwood, and once open, the memories poured through in a flood that she could not hold back.

The entrance hall was dark and smelled of floor polish, and Gus hung back as Julia went forward to meet her Aunt Agnes. He had not wanted to come, but there were papers to be signed, not that he had any legal rights over Julia, as Aunt Agnes made very clear. The only rights he had over her were those of love, a love for her mother that had encompassed Julia from the day they had moved into the loft. She had thought them the handsomest couple in the world, and as Gus held her mother in his arms on the sofa while Julia played on the floor, she had seen what love and affection between a man and a woman could be. Oh, Gus, Gus, how could you have done it? *All for the best. Assure your future. Your inheritance.* Well, tonight she would come into that inheritance, but what was it worth if . . .

She looked down at the white knuckles of her hands grasping the back of the dressing chair as tightly as they had the rail on the stern. Julia, get hold of yourself! The flood subsided and the doors of memory closed. She sighed with relief.

She turned her head to study herself again in the mirror. The cut was a bit extreme, the dress too daring. The silk revealed the exact form of her thighs and stomach and small round breasts. It was not the kind of dress one could wear with a brassiere, and the shape of her nipples showed all too clearly through the fabric. Well, let it be too daring. Tomorrow they landed in Naples, and a new life would begin for her, a life in which she would do many things she would not have dared at home. She fitted a pearl earring into her newly pierced and still tender ear. There was a light tapping on the cabin door.

"Oh, hello Forbes."

"Evening, miss. Compliments of the captain."

The steward held out a silver tray on which a tiny yellow orchid nestled in a bed of shredded cellophane.

"How beautiful, and it goes perfectly with my gown."

"Happy birthday, Miss Howard."

"How'd you know?"

"They take it off your passport, miss, the purser does. You'll be having a small party this evening, I shouldn't doubt."

The cathedral-like doors of the main dining room were open wide. Julia passed through them and up the center aisle that led to the captain's long table. She had waited until the meal had begun, and every eye was on her as she made her way to the far end of the salon, to the accompaniment of the orchestra in the balcony above. She had deliberately overdressed for this last night when, by tradition, evening clothes were packed away. It was her night, her reward for having the courage to break free.

She made her way around the table to the empty gilded chair. The captain and Angelo rose on either side. A waiter slid the chair under her, and slipped a napkin off the table into her lap. There was a cold lobster on every plate but Julia's, which was empty except for a small brown envelope.

"I like lobster, too," she said with a pout.

"Too late, Cinderella. Yours has turned into a telegram," Angelo said, touching her arm.

"There's champagne, though," the captain said.

Julia took a sip from the offered glass and tore open the envelope:

MISS JULIA HOWARD—SS VELONIA AT SEA—TODAY 7 APRIL 1930 PROCEEDS TRUST FUND TRANSFERRED TO YOUR ACCOUNT MERCHANTS AND FARMERS BANK IN AMOUNT OF FOUR HUNDRED EIGHTY ONE THOUSAND THREE HUNDRED TWENTY NINE DOLLARS AND SIXTY NINE CENTS STOP HAPPY BIRTHDAY—ELMER J. THORNLEY JR.

Julia looked up at the captain. His pale blue eyes beneath bristling black brows gave him away instantly. The wireless operator had shown him the message.

"Good news?" he asked.

"Yes, good news." And sixty-nine cents. How like Thornley. Well, she wouldn't have to be nice to that unctuous banker anymore. She was on her own. The orchestra began to play a slow fox-trot.

"You haven't asked me to dance this entire voyage," she said to the captain, wanting to get away from the table full of people, to bask in the knowledge that she had the means to do whatever she wanted.

"Why, that's right," the captain said. "What luck, they're playing a slow number."

He folded her into his giant arms, the masses of gold braid on his sleeve scratching her bare back. She looked up into his red, weather-beaten face. The captain was a good six feet four, and at least sixty years old. His idea of dancing was to walk stiffly around the circle of polished teak. Moving automatically to the captain's simple steps, Julia was free to consider what it meant to be a rich woman.

Eleven years at Branwood, at boarding school and Goucher, waiting to be independent, on her own, so anxious to be that she had simply walked out of Goucher a few weeks before graduation and begun preparing to sail for Europe. As of her twenty-second birthday she was . . . what? Free? Free to do what? To indulge herself? To have affairs with men? To drink and smoke and drive fast cars and dance until dawn? Banal.

She realized why she was scared, what she couldn't express to Francesa, to herself earlier. She was afraid she would come home from Europe in a year or two, like the daughters of Aunt Agnes's friends she had so often met, talking endlessly about adventures and escapades and Count this and Baron that. Then, one by one, she had seen them settle down into the routine of marriage—the right husband, children, country clubs, steeplechases, charity balls. She would rather cut her throat than do that. An image arose before her, the same image, of her mother in Gus's arms on a broken-down sofa.

"You're not having a chill, are you?" asked the captain.

"No," Julia said, suppressing the shudder that ran through her body, "I'm fine."

The tempo of the music had quickened, and the captain led her off the dance floor. Angelo rose and seated her.

"Oh, you found some lobster for me after all."

The telegram, which had been removed to make way for the lobster, had been folded and tucked under the edge of her plate. She looked closely at Angelo, who only smiled.

"We wouldn't let you go hungry just for being late, Julia."

After they finished their lobster and more champagne was poured, the others got up to dance, leaving Julia alone at the table with Angelo.

"May I pay you a compliment?"

She turned to him, smiling. "Why, Angelo, how old-fashioned. Of course you may."

"You are the most beautiful woman I have ever seen."

"Flattery will get you everywhere."

"Julia, don't tease me," he said in a low voice, almost a whisper.

Well. Things had taken a serious turn.

"It's just my new haircut," she said lightly. "You'll find me quite ordinary tomorrow morning." Now that she had him, she couldn't resist playing with him a bit.

She put her hand on his and leaned over and kissed him lightly on the lips.

"Don't be so serious," she said.

He laughed, showing his perfect white teeth. Wouldn't the girls at Goucher go mad over him, Julia thought, with his soft brown eyes, mustache, and brown silky hair that kept falling in his eyes. Handsome, a diplomat, with the most gorgeous clothes she had ever seen on a man, and rich. Must be. Francesca said he has a huge estate outside Verona. And I have him wrapped around my finger.

"Tell me what happened in New York," she said.

"What do you mean?"

"General Oxley and Francesca's brother had some kind of fight. Francesca says you know all about it."

"She said that?" Angelo's face hardened.

"Were you there?"

"Well, yes. . . ."

"Whose side were you on?"

"I was in New York to meet with leaders of the Italian-American community, so naturally I had to go to this meeting in support of the Italian government."

"But Francesca said it was a Fascist rally."

"My dear Julia, Italy has a Fascist government."

"But you said General Oxley is a fool."

Angelo smiled. "Of course he is."

"I don't think I understand. But, anyway, what happened?"

"Oxley was giving a speech, and Danieli and his friends started shouting from the balcony, there was some scuffling, somebody called the police. Nothing serious. Actually it was quite amusing. Too bad Danieli didn't travel first-class. We could have had great fun watching those two."

"You still haven't told me which side you're on," she said.

"Does one have to be on a side? You certainly don't let on how you feel about . . . things."

The music had stopped and people were coming back to the table.

"Italy tomorrow," the middle-aged man named Tate, sitting across from her, said. "I'm looking forward to that. I haven't been there since my college days. I suppose there've been lots of changes."

"And all for the good," General Oxley put in, from the far end of the table.

"Tell us about Mussolini, General." Everyone turned to stare at Julia. Angelo looked amused.

"In my opinion," the general said, drawing in his breath, "if we had the equivalent of Signor Mussolini in every country of Europe, we would soon have things back on course, and have the Bolshies on the run to boot."

"Including England?"

"Most of all in England. The society's rotten clean through, clean through to the bone. Believe me, I know."

"I'm sure you do, General."

People were beginning to move from table to table, and Francesca chose that moment to drop into the empty chair beside Julia.

"May I join you?"

"Indeed, you may," Julia said, barely suppressing a smile. "Mr. Tate. General Oxley you know from this afternoon. But I don't believe I made introductions. Miss Danieli. The general was just telling us what admirable things Mussolini is doing."

"Just what do you find so admirable in Mussolini, General?' Francesca Danieli asked, nervously flicking her painted lashes, her eyes all fire beneath the mass of red curls. Oh, dear, thought Julia, Francesca has had too much to drink. We're in for it now.

"I want to dance," Julia said, turning away from the brewing storm to Angelo.

"You're a coward," he said after he had maneuvered her onto the dance floor. "You started that and then you ran away."

"I don't know why I did that. I don't like scenes."

"Neither do I."

Yes, she thought, we are alike in some ways. The music changed to another slow fox-trot, and she held him closer, feeling the roughness of his jacket against her bare arm. His hand was farther down her back than was really proper, but she only pressed closer still.

"And what do *you* think, Count Morosini?"

"About what?"

"About Mussolini."

"I work for him, you know."

She looked up at him. "You don't have to be careful with me, Angelo. I won't tell."

He only smiled.

"Well? Is he good for Italy like the general says or is he a monster like Francesca says?" She didn't really care what Angelo thought about Mussolini, she just enjoyed teasing him, upsetting his pose of amused cynic.

"I think judgments are old-fashioned. Il Duce is there, and that's that. And I do not think he will go away soon."

"Spoken like a diplomat."

"Spoken like an Italian. We learned centuries ago to accept things the way they are. Such as me on this dance floor with you in my arms."

"Except that I *will* go away. Tomorrow morning."

"I think not."

"No?"

"I won't let you."

Julia looked into his eyes but said nothing. She rather believed he meant what he had just said. She put her head back on his shoulder. He was, of course, a perfect dancer.

When they got back to the table, both Francesca and Oxley had disappeared.

"Where's everybody?" Julia asked, looking out across the darkened dance floor, where colored lights from a revolving mirrored ball played over the turning couples.

"Gone for a walk on deck," the captain said. He was looking subdued. "Well, never mind. Here's something to cheer you up." He motioned to the cake that had been put at her place. There had obviously been a row between Francesca and Oxley. So, Francesca was as reckless as her brother.

The steward lit the candles and Julia blew them out. In the upset over what had just happened, they forgot to sing "Happy Birthday."

"Cut us all a piece and have some more champagne," the captain said. The steward filled her glass. "Did you make a wish?"

"No," Julia said. "There is nothing more I could wish for."

"May it always be so," the captain said, lifting his glass. But it seemed to Julia that his old eyes saw things in the future that were hidden from her.

Chapter Two

AFTER DINNER JULIA strolled out on deck with Angelo, as she had expected. They took a turn around the promenade deck, neither of them speaking, her arm in his, each waiting for the other to make the first move.

"Look," she said, freeing her bare arm from the rough tweed of his sleeve, "there's land again."

A string of lights was barely visible on the horizon, beneath an almost full moon, hanging low and red in the sky.

"Italy," he said.

"I can't imagine what it will be like. What will I do there?"

"See lots of me, of course."

They were leaning against the rail in the shadow of a lifeboat. She turned her head toward him.

"Will I?"

"Won't you?"

What was he waiting for? Perhaps she really was an enigma to him. But then he must have seen the look in her eyes. He put a hand on her shoulder and drew her to him. She put her arms lightly around his neck, and when he kissed her, she half opened her mouth to his. He kissed her on the neck and shoulders, and she shivered with pleasure. His hand stroked her back.

"Nice," she said.

"Are you that smooth all over?"

She laughed and put her head on his shoulder. "More champagne," she whispered in his ear.

"Will you tell me then?"

"Maybe."

While he was gone she drew a deck chair into the shadow of the lifeboat and curled up in it, pulling her shawl around her shoulders. Angelo was back in minutes with a bottle of champagne and glasses.

"And a blanket."

When he brought the blanket she moved over so that he could squeeze into the chair with her. She pulled the blanket over them and kissed him lightly.

"There, that's better," she said.

Sitting there together in the moonlight, they kissed and drank champagne. When his hand moved from her back beneath her scanty evening dress, she let him caress her bare breasts. She let his hand follow the curve of her stomach, but when his fingers grazed the edge of her pubic hair she twisted away and sat up. She didn't want him to feel the wetness there, and know how much she wanted him.

"I'm sorry," he said.

"Nothing to be sorry about. I liked it."

"Then come to my cabin."

"That's the problem, Angelo. I'm not sure that's what I want to do." She took a comb out of her handbag and ran it through her hair.

"Julia, I want you. I want you more than anything I've ever wanted before."

She turned and looked into his face, half-hidden in the lifeboat's shadow.

"I'm not just a piece of candy you're asking for."

"What do you mean?"

"It wouldn't be something I gave you. It would be because I wanted to."

He laughed nervously. "And you don't?"

"I didn't say that. You're a very attractive man, and I've had too much champagne."

She stood up. "Let's take another turn around the deck."

When Angelo saw her back to her cabin an hour later, Julia had soothed his ruffled ego by promising to be in touch with him as soon as she settled in Rome—once again with her Aunt Agnes. She gave him the telephone number of the Palazzo Rosalba and, just in case, Uncle Charles's number at the American Embassy. She was surprised at Angelo's reaction to this routine information.

"The Palazzo Rosalba? Your aunt lives in the Palazzo Rosalba?"

"She rents it, I believe. Why? Does that mean something to you?"

"The Palazzo Rosalba? If you're from Rome it does. And her husband, Charles Pemberton, he's with the American Embassy?

"Yes."

"What exactly does he do?" Angelo seemed intrigued but also a little suspicious. How quickly his passion for her had switched to interest in the Pembertons. Perhaps that was the way European men were, and why not? It made her feel sophisticated.

"Charles? He's the counselor of the embassy, that's second to the ambassador."

"Yes, I know. He's in your foreign service, then?"

"No. Aunt Agnes gave some money in the last election."

"Ah."

And then, suddenly, all of Angelo's attention was focused on her again. His long, passionate kiss was, she knew, meant to lead them into her cabin, but she slipped out of his arms and through the door with a breathless "Good night."

As the cabin door closed behind her, she almost called Angelo back. She was ready to say that she wanted him, then and there, in her cabin. But she struggled with her indecision, biting her lip in frustration, until when she opened the cabin door again, the passageway was empty. She sighed in relief, closed and locked the door, and leaned back against it.

In the mirror behind the vase of exotic flowers she saw her face, pale and tense. What had she been thinking of? To go to bed with Angelo? That was not how she wanted to begin her new life. What she needed was a shower and bed. She crossed to the bathroom. Her still-damp red bathing suit and white rubber cap hung from the shower head. Even better, a hard swim in that elegant pool three decks below reserved for first-class passengers. She stripped off her gown, slipped into the clammy wool suit and threw a robe over her shoulders.

The bronze doors to the indoor pool, decorated with a stylized design of seashells and underwater life, were closed. She should have realized that the pool wouldn't be open past midnight even for first-class passengers, though they expected to be able to do anything they wanted at any hour. But when she pushed at one of the doors it slowly swung inward. The long room, tiled in waves of blue and green, was brightly lit but empty; the only sound was that of water lapping against the pool sides with the roll of the ship. The *Velonia* was surging ahead at full speed on this last night, as the captain hoped to break the transatlantic record to Naples.

Julia tossed her robe on a bench and tested the water with her toes. Pulling on the cap, she reached back to tuck under the long tresses that were no longer there. Julia sighed. Her first day as a modern free woman hadn't been all that successful. Ah, well. What she needed was to swim a few fast laps to calm down, and then go straight to bed. She leaned forward, her arms drawn back to dive.

"The pool's closed, you know."

"Oh!"

She was thrown off balance and would have fallen head-long into the water if a hand hadn't grasped her arm firmly. She spun around. The hand belonged to Paolo Danieli.

"Oh, it's you," he said, letting go of her arm.

"You scared the hell out of me. What are you doing here?"

"Trying to work in peace and quiet. Usually after midnight the swimming pool is ideal."

His eyes were the darkest eyes she had ever seen. He had shaved, and his jawline was clean and straight and hard, but the dark hair still curled in disorder over his collar.

"Work?" she asked in confusion, turning away from those eyes. Then she saw that he held a fistful of brushes, and the old shirt he wore was splattered with gold paint.

Her eyes moved beyond him to a large glass panel in the far corner, on which a life-size mermaid, all in gold, swam amid waving golden seaweed among a school of golden fish.

"What are you doing?" She moved away from his too-close presence, her heart still racing from the fright he had given her. She walked toward the mermaid, feeling his eyes on her bare back and her low-cut tank suit. He came up beside her.

"It's beautiful," she said.

"It's trash, nothing but slick decoration."

"Is that so bad?" she asked softly, sensing the unhappiness in him.

"No, I guess not. It paid my bar bill." He dipped a brush in a can of gold paint and like magic a striped fish appeared on the glass and a stream of bubbles in the mermaid's wake. He moved back and forth along the panel, bobbing and weaving like a boxer, jabbing with his brush at the painting.

"Don't you ever make a mistake?"

"I can do this kind of thing with my eyes closed. I've painted sets."

He stopped and stepped back from the painting. She could see the dark hair on his chest through the half-open shirt, as he squinted at the painting. He looked at his wristwatch.

"Nearly two o'clock. Naples in four hours. I finished just in time. . . . Oh, there's one last detail." He dipped a tiny brush in gold and wrote something along the edge of the mermaid's fin. "There."

Julia came closer and looked at it. "For J. H.?"

"I'm dedicating it to you."

"What?" She tried to read his face. "Why?"

"Well, because . . ." He seemed about to say something, then changed his mind. "Because when we get to Naples this is going to be installed above the bar where we met. Our first meeting will be immortalized."

"Our first meeting . . . Oh, yes, it's called the Mermaid Room."

"And this is the mermaid, the last piece of decoration to be finished. For Julia Howard." His eyes looked her up and down, as she shifted from one foot to the other in her tight red bathing suit.

"Well, thanks . . . I guess. Now, I'd better do a couple of laps if I'm going to get any sleep at all before we arrive."

Before he could reply, she ran to the edge of the pool and dived in, swimming the whole length under water. She came up and held on to the edge of the pool, panting. That, she said to herself, is the first time, Julia Howard, you've ever run away from a man. She did a crawl back, and when she grasped the edge of the pool with her red-tipped fingers, he was standing above her.

"Help me out."

He reached down and caught her under the arms and lifted her in one smooth motion, setting her on her feet on the pool's edge. They stood looking into each other's eyes, neither of them smiling.

"Could you get me my robe?"

She walked away from him, pulling off her bathing cap and shaking out her hair. She stood before the golden mermaid. Coming up behind her, he draped the robe over her shoulders, his hands brushing her lightly. She turned away from him again. She had never felt awkward with a man before. She pretended to look at the sketch for the mermaid that was taped to the wall. But it was not a mermaid. The pose was the same, but the sketch was of a nude woman lying on her stomach on a ship's bunk, her breasts peeping over the edge, her legs lifted in the air—transformed in the painting into a mermaid's tail.

"Who posed for that?" she asked. The drawing was obviously of a live model. "You can't call that trash or slick decoration."

"No, it's a rather good sketch."

"When did you do it?"

"On shipboard."

She glanced out of the corner of her eye at him. "Anyone I know?"

"Yes, as a matter of fact."

"Oh." He obviously wasn't going to say who. Probably done in his cabin after they had ... or before ... well, it was no business of hers.

"Would you like to see the mermaid lighted?"

"Lighted?"

"Just stand right there."

He plugged in a string of lights on the floor beneath the glass panel.

"In the bar it will be lit from below and, of course, it will be pretty dark there."

He turned a switch on the wall and the entire room was plunged into blackness. In the dark, the mermaid on the glass seemed almost alive, her golden body shimmering in the depths of some sea.

"I don't care what you say, it's beautiful." Her voice was small and tense.

"For Julia Howard." And in the dark he took her hand, quite casually, and she let it stay there. But then she thought of the naked woman sprawled in an abandoned pose across Paolo's bunk, and drew her hand away.

"I really must go now."

Later in her suite, after a hot shower, drifting off to sleep, an image floated through her consciousness. She was lying on a chaise longue by the sun deck pool in her red tank suit, flipping through a magazine, her legs lifted above her in the air. . . . She sat bolt upright in bed. There had been a man across the pool in dark glasses and a fedora, sketching. . . .

She turned on the light and picked up the phone.

"Yes, madam?"

"Operator, I want to speak to Mr. Danieli. He's a passenger in third class."

"Would he be awake at this hour, madam?"

"Never mind that. Just ring him."

"Yes, madam."

"Hello," a sleepy voice answered.

"Paolo?"

"Yes?"

"Julia."

"Julia? What is it?"

"That's me, isn't it?"

There was a long silence and then soft laughter.

"And I had on a bathing suit. You took it off!"

More soft laughter.

"And now I'm going to be hanging over a bar for—well, forever—like that! How could you?"

"Who'll know but you—and me?"

"What has that . . ." and then she broke into laughter herself. She couldn't stop. She put the phone back on the hook. What more was there to say to that crazy man? Lying back on the pillow, tears of laughter running down her face, she knew her twenty-second birthday had been magical after all. And there was no other woman in Paolo's bed. . . . No other woman? What did she mean by that?

"Six o'clock, Miss Howard." It was Forbes, tapping on the cabin door.

"Thank you, Forbes. I'm awake."

"Very well, miss."

After she had stood under a cold shower for a minute or two, she really was awake. One good thing about her new cut, she thought as she rubbed her head with a rough Turkish towel, by the time they landed her hair would be dry. My God! She had completely forgotten why she had asked Forbes to wake her at six. She threw open the silk curtains at the porthole. And there it was. She stood motionless, naked and dripping on the cabin rug, tense with excitement. Beyond the wide sweep of the Bay of Naples was Vesuvius with a plume of smoke rising into the clear spring sky, and beyond that, ranges of mountains of the palest lavender. It was Europe, Italy, the Old World.

Somehow, it was not what she had expected. It seemed fresh and new, and she knew in that first instant that this was where whatever was going to happen to her would happen. Already she loved Italy and yet was afraid of what it held for her. In a way, it was home, and fleetingly her mind went back to Gus's studio. Somewhere in those mountains behind Naples, Gus's mother still lived. . . . They were rapidly approaching land, and she was not ready. She picked up the telephone.

"Forbes, I know breakfast isn't served in the cabin on the last morning, but things are in such a mess. Could you possibly? . . . You are a dear. . . . Yes. Raspberries and cream, toast and coffee." Julia surveyed the disorder of the cabin. Her steamer trunk stood with underwear hanging from half-open drawers. "And Forbes, if you could possibly pack my trunk for me. I just can't manage everything." After all, she would make it worth his while. She could afford that now.

The main dining saloon, where the remains of breakfast were being cleared away, still showed the effects of the night before. Tattered paper streamers hung from the ceiling, a balloon was caught in the fronds of a potted palm. The captain's table was vacant except for General Oxley, once again in plus fours and a tweed cap, his nose buried in a red Baedeker. Julia veered away from him and toward the small table where Francesca Danieli sat alone, in the same green knit dress she had worn the night before, a cigarette holder clenched between her teeth.

"Sorry about last night."

"Why sorry?" Julia slipped into a chair beside her, checking the seams of her silk stockings.

"For breaking up your birthday party. But then it was a pretty dreary affair. I'm sure you would rather have been off somewhere with Count Morosini."

"Actually, I was off with your brother."

Francesca's eyes opened wide. "You're not serious?"

"I am. At the pool . . . at two in the morning."

"You work fast."

"Oh, do you think . . . I mean . . . why, he treated me like a sister."

"That surprises me. In that case what were you two doing together?"

"He was showing me . . . a drawing. He's very good."

Francesca shook her head in disbelief. "He hardly shows anyone his work." She stared blankly at Julia as if she was reassessing both her and Paolo. "Yes, he's very good. He could be one of the most successful artists in Europe—if it weren't for his politics."

"I think he just wanted someone to talk to." That, of course, was not quite the truth.

"I suppose that could be. He has a few political chums, but people avoid anyone who is known to be an opponent of the regime. On the other hand, maybe he's fallen for you." She took Julia's hand in hers. "Seriously Julia, I do love him, but don't get involved with Paolo. Women do."

"Why not? I mean, I don't plan to, but why not?"

"He's headed for disaster. He should never have come back to Italy."

"But you're going back to Italy, and you're opposed to fascism."

"I keep my mouth shut."

"The captain said you called General Oxley a Fascist last night."

"I don't know why he got so upset. He is. And besides, he called me a Communist. I'll bet he doesn't know how right he is."

"Let's see your party card."

"We don't carry them. If they find out you belong to the PCI, it's jail, or worse. Oh, politics is such a bore. Sometimes I wish the whole thing would just go away."

I really like this woman, Julia thought and said, "Angelo thinks Mussolini won't go away."

"I imagine the count has reasons for hoping he won't."

A steward struck the big gong by the bronze doors of the dining saloon. The purser was making an announcement.

"Ladies and gentlemen, we will be docking in Naples in one-half hour, four hours ahead of our schedule from New York, and two hours and twenty minutes ahead of any other liner in maritime history."

Although everyone already knew, there was clapping and some cheers and even a "Rule, Britannia!"

Francesca put out her cigarette in the ashtray.

"The Italian immigration and health officials will soon be coming aboard. Please assemble with your passports in the aft lounge, I repeat, the aft lounge." Julia felt a thrill run through her. It was all about to begin.

"Listen, Julia, I really hope I didn't spoil your evening. And I hope this turns out to be more than a shipboard friendship. It is, as far as I'm concerned."

"For me, too."

Francesca lit another cigarette, tore the lid off the box and wrote something on it.

"Here's my number in Rome. Give me a call whenever you want. It's still possible to have a good time in Italy."

The beautiful white vision of Naples that she had seen from the deck turned out to be, as the tugs brought them alongside, a mass of tenements with washing hanging from rotting balconies. The customs house was a cavernous shed in which thousands of people pushed and shoved and shouted. Julia realized that after being pampered and waited on for more than a week at sea, she was now very much on her own. She had neglected to buy any Italian currency on board and had no idea how one went about getting to the Naples railway station.

She saw Francesca ahead of her in line, but just as Julia reached the head of the line herself, Francesca ran across the hall and threw herself into the arms of a tall blond man. That would be James Morrison. He took her bag with one hand and with the other arm around Francesca's waist led her through the doors to a small open car. As they drove away, Julia felt a pang of jealousy. She stood with her passport in her hand. She had no idea what she was supposed to do next.

"Could I be of assistance?"

She turned and looked into a pair of soft brown eyes.

"Oh, Angelo, I'm glad to see you. It's all so confusing. Where do I find my bags?"

"Not to worry," he said, taking her arm. "Just follow me."

Outside, her bags were neatly stacked beside a long, black official car, and a man in a uniform was strapping her steamer trunk to the luggage rack on the rear. So everything had been arranged. She should have known. It reminded her of the end of a hunt weekend at Branwood. The cars of important people lined up at the entrance, baggage strapped to the rear of touring cars, doors open to receive the departing guests, drivers and attendants standing almost at attention. As she slipped into the back of the official car, Angelo went around to the other side, and the two heavy doors slammed shut together. Money and power, in that at least Europe was the same.

They drove through incredibly crowded, dirty streets, the driver continually honking the horn. The squalor was incredible, and yet the old buildings turned into tenements had once been palaces. The flow of ox-drawn wagons and laden donkeys and porters pulling handcarts had probably not changed in ages, but where once they had had to make way for gilded carriages, now it was for their long black Fiat.

"What do you think of Naples?" Angelo said.

"First impression? Well, it's strange to see, set in these great crumbling walls, such fine shops of jewelers and couturiers, and coffeehouses with marble counters and bakeries with fresh baked bread."

"I'm afraid Rome's not much better."

She looked at him in surprise.

"I meant, Angelo, that I like it."

"Oh. Yes, it does have its charm."

"Anyway, it was awfully nice of you to see me to the station."

"My pleasure. I only wish I could see you all the way to Rome, but I have some business to take care of here."

At the station, Angelo proved a whirlwind of efficiency. He bought her ticket, an English-language newspaper, a small box of chocolates, and a bouquet of spring flowers. He saw her suitcases into her compartment and her trunk into the baggage car. By the time she was settled in her compartment, the train was ready to depart. He stood outside on the platform, smiling.

"I can't thank you enough," Julia said. "I would never

have been able to do it on my own. And I do want you to call me when you reach Rome. You will, won't you?"

"Of course I will."

The train whistle blew and she leaned out of the window to kiss him good-bye. As she did so she saw over his shoulder, at the far end of the platform, two policemen pushing and shoving a man in a black turtleneck sweater toward the stairway.

"Angelo, look! That's Paolo Danieli."

He turned his head.

"You must be mistaken."

"No, no. It's him, I'm positive."

"I do think you're right, but I'm sure it's nothing serious. They're probably just checking his identity papers. I'm afraid there's a lot of that here."

"Then why are they pushing him? Angelo, do something!" she said, her voice rising. She was on her feet, trying to open the door. How did the damned thing work? There were several short blasts of the whistle, and the train lurched forward, throwing her against the window frame.

"Please, Angelo, help him!"

"I will. Don't worry. I'll call you. . . ." But the rest of what he said was drowned out by another whistle blast as the train pulled swiftly away.

Chapter Three

THE TRAIN SLID into the Rome station with squealing brakes and clouds of steam. As soon as it came shuddering to a stop, compartment doors flew open and people began passing out their bags. Everyone was shouting for porters: *"Facchino!" "Facchino!"* Julia pulled her bags out onto the platform, but the blue-smocked porters were already disappearing, their iron-wheeled trolleys piled high with luggage.

Suddenly a brass band struck up, the sound reverberating from the vast iron-and-glass vault. A column of black-shirted young men poured down the platform, not marching but jogging, chanting in unison. A black boot kicked aside her two bags, knocking her against the compartment door. The Black Shirts formed two rows, and down the corridor they made strutted a little man in riding breeches, black shirt, and military cap. A child came forward and thrust a bouquet of flowers into his arms. He grinned, showing a wide row of white teeth above a goatee. The Black Shirts gave the Fascist salute she had seen in newsreels, formed a column again, and marched away behind their leader into the main station. Julia was left, shaken, almost alone on the platform.

"Ciao, Julie," a familiar voice called.

Her cousin Victoria, thank God. She wore a burgundy-colored pleated skirt, a diamond-patterned gray-and-burgundy sweater, and a beret also in burgundy; the color, Julia remembered from a magazine on the ship, was the rage in Europe that spring.

"You look great, Vicky," Julia said, throwing her arms

around her. What a good moment. Years ago they had both
sworn they would get to Europe. Victoria had made it first,
but then she was Agnes's own child, not a niece taken in on
charity; and when Vicky insisted on going with her parents
to Rome, well, that was that.

"Welcome to Italy. You don't look so bad yourself."

"I've had quite a reception already. Who was that?"

"Italo Balbo, a big Fascist. Are you all right?"

"I'm fine. They nearly knocked me off the platform,
though."

"Not that. Did something happen to you in Naples?"

"What do you mean?"

"Someone named Angelo called me just before I left for
the station. He said the trouble with the police was nothing
but a case of mistaken identity."

"Thank God! What a relief!"

"You certainly don't waste any time," Victoria said with
a puzzled smile.

"I'll explain it all to you later."

"Come on then, let's go." She took Julia's arm.

"I have a trunk."

"All taken care of. The stationmaster is on Mother's
Christmas gift list."

"Is that the way things are done here?"

"That's the only way." And they sauntered down the
platform arm in arm.

"I see you've gotten rid of all that hair."

"Does it look all right?"

Victoria laughed. "Remember, Julia, I was here first.
Don't take all my men away from me, please."

Aunt Agnes's old Dusenberg stood squarely in front of
the station. An Italian chauffeur with a pencil-line mustache, wearing a uniform, patent leather boots, and a billed
cap pushed down low over his eyes, held open the door.

The car slid off into traffic. "Now, let's hear everything,"
Victoria said. "Did you meet any men on the ship? Other
than Angelo, that is."

"Wait, Vicky, wait a minute. I just want to look at
things."

She felt her throat tighten. This was it. The first wave of feeling had come when she had looked out the porthole and seen Vesuvius hanging like a lavender stage cloth behind Naples. Then she was drawn into the scene herself, as the Naples-Rome express raced through the green fields of the Campagna, the hillsides heavy with pink-and-white fruit-tree blossoms, alongside the ruins of the Roman aqueduct, past flocks of sheep grazing under the vine-grown arches. And now she was at last at center stage: Rome itself. It was as if she were coming home.

As they drove through the streets of Rome the feeling became overpowering. Everything was timeworn, every building a work of art, the whole more beautiful than any of its parts. There were tall palaces painted orange and ocher, with flower-laden balconies, corner restaurants with striped awnings, waiters with white aprons waiting for customers under the mottled shade of the plane trees, nude statues diving through the spray of ancient fountains, crooked bell towers, and golden domes above the narrow shaded streets through which they sped. She felt as if she had returned to Gus's studio; as if something she had thought lost forever had been restored. It was as strong a revelation as she had ever experienced.

"Like it?"

Julia turned on the plush seat of the glassed-in compartment of the Dusenberg and faced Victoria, pink-skinned and bosomy, but still with that slim, supple waist. How could she say all she felt?

"I am going to make it mine."

Victoria tossed back her head and laughed. *"Buona fortuna."*

"It is good to have you here," Aunt Agnes said, stirring her drink with her finger. Branwood was grand, Julia thought, but this was so much grander and marvelously old. The library of the Palazzo Rosalba was the first room in Europe that she had been in. It smelled ancient and European, a smell that seemed composed of dried rose petals, leather, and wood-smoke. Sitting in a high-backed brocaded chair, even Aunt Agnes looked small. Julia gazed up at the timbered ceiling. A fire burned in the marble fireplace beneath a tapestry depicting men in armor on rearing horses. Higher up on the wall, niches held marble busts of men who looked like bishops and cardinals.

"It's magnificent," Julia said.

"It's cold," said Victoria, tossing her burgundy-colored beret on a refectory table next to a huge bowl of roses. "You'd better be glad you weren't here in January. You'd have frozen your tail off."

"Of course, Julia, we weren't expecting you until June," Agnes said. Julia gave herself time to compose a reply by taking a drink from the tray offered by a young man in a tailcoat, white tie, vest, and gloves. She had said she would have the same as Victoria, which turned out to look like cherry soda and taste like cough medicine. The young Italian was eyeing her. She had expected Aunt Agnes to have a butler, but this handsome young man was her own age.

"I decided that I'd had enough of school," Julia said. Just as well to get the storm over with. Agnes was twisting her red-painted mouth in a way that usually meant trouble.

"Dean Winship wrote me. She was completely mystified and, frankly, so am I. You would have been the third generation. Mother was a member of the very first graduating class at Goucher."

Nothing, Julia noticed, was said about Agnes's own daughter, Victoria, who wouldn't have gone to Goucher on a bet.

"An honor student, too. . . . I hope you brought some evening dresses with you."

"Yes, I did."

"We'll put you over the jumps right away then," Agnes said, and smiled. "We're having a formal dinner tonight, and Princess Orsini has come down with the flu."

Victoria, taking Julia up the marble staircase to her room, whispered, "Princess Orsini no more has the flu than I do. She's teaching Mother a lesson for putting on airs."

"Anything to change the subject. I thought I was going to get scalped over quitting Goucher."

"Goucher has done its job, dear."

"It has?"

"The purpose of college is, of course, to produce ladies, and Mother looked you over and decided they've done their job. So why continue? Besides, the spring social wars have begun, and she would rather have a *numero* like you on the front lines than back in training camp."

"Still, I got off lightly."

"What can she do? You have your own money now. Mother's no dummy."

They passed into a high-ceilinged room where the walls were covered in red cut-velvet and hung with the largest mirrors Julia had ever seen, all spotted with age, and framed with gilded cupids, Venuses, and swags of flowers and fruit.

"It isn't exactly cozy, but nothing here is."

A maid was taking clothes out of Julia's steamer trunk and hanging them in an elaborately carved armoire. Julia walked out onto a balcony and rested her hands on the balustrade. Across from the palazzo stood a piece of crumbling Roman wall, beyond that a park where people were riding horseback. Farther on, she saw the skyline of Rome and a great dome against the evening sky, where April clouds were piled up like scoops of orange sherbet.

Sitting on the balustrade, Victoria lit a cigarette. "I'm glad you've come, Julie."

"I can't believe it, it's so beautiful."

"Like a movie set. The Borghese Gardens, St. Peter's, the works. Mother's arranged everything. Best view in Rome, Bruno says."

"Who's Bruno?"

"Bruno Bronzini. He's the big thing in my life at the moment."

A church bell began to ring, and soon bells were ringing all over the city.

Victoria stretched and yawned. "Time to go. You've the big formal dinner at eight. I pity you. They're terrible bores." So Victoria wasn't going to be there.

Victoria turned on a dresser light, which was reflected all over the room.

"What a lot of mirrors," Julia said.

"I stayed here when we first came, until I heard that Cardinal what's-his-name, who built this place, had this room fixed up so he could enjoy a romp with a girl or two. It gave me the willies when I undressed at night to see myself from nine different angles."

"Oh, stop it, Vicky."

"You think I'm kidding, don't you? Rome ain't tidewater Maryland, you know."

"I submit," Charles Pemberton pronounced, "that if there were a Mussolini in France and England and Germany, the situation in Europe would soon right itself."

My God, Julia thought, General Oxley's very words. She would have given anything to have had Paolo or Francesca Danicli at the table. The dinner had been even worse than Victoria's prediction; a white-tie affair with long gowns and jewels and seven courses and people who all seemed to say the same thing. There was a scraping of chairs. Aunt Agnes, at the far end of the enormously long table, rose. She was wearing a diamond tiara in her hair, like royalty.

After dinner, Julia slipped away from the gossiping women, Italian nobility, and ambassadors' wives. But the men had formed a tight circle over brandy and cigars, where Uncle Charles continued to preach the virtues of fascism. She wandered into the library and found the funny little man from the American Embassy, who had been seated across from her at dinner, reading a book.

"What are you doing here, Chester?" She had forgotten his last name.

"I'm filling in for someone who came down with the flu."

"So am I." Julia sat down beside him. "What I meant was, what are you doing in the library all by yourself."

"I couldn't take any more of Pemberton's garbage. What an ass."

"I'm his niece, you know."

"I know. But you look like a good sport. I figure you won't report me."

"He is an ass, isn't he?" Julia opened her beaded evening bag and took out a cigarette. "Tell me, Chester, are all diplomatic functions this boring?"

"Absolutely."

"Then why are you in this business?"

"Somebody has to tell Washington the truth. Our exalted counselor-of-embassy, Charles Pemberton, sure won't."

"Soon to be Ambassador Pemberton," Julia said.

"You're kidding?"

"Maybe even to London, Paris, or Berlin. Aunt Agnes now realizes that this is a minor position he's in. But it's been good training for Charles, who isn't all that bright. In '32 she's planning to make a whopping big contribution to President Hoover's reelection campaign. Or so Victoria says."

"Well, then our only hope is that Hoover doesn't get reelected."

"Fat chance of that. Maybe I should write an anonymous letter to the President and tell him what a dope Uncle Charles really is."

They laughed together.

Two days later Angelo Morosini showed up on the doorstep of Palazzo Rosalba. Julia was pleased, but still she couldn't help thinking how much she would have preferred it to be Francesca's strange, attractive brother. But she couldn't call Paolo, that would have been gauche, even had she known how to get in touch with him. The only way she could do that was through Francesca, and she felt awkward about making the first move to renew their friendship. To Julia's disappointment, Francesca had not called her. So Julia began a whirlwind of social activity and sight-seeing with Angelo Morosini, always, and barely, keeping his amorous advances within bounds.

The last week in April, Angelo invited Julia to the wedding reception of a friend of his in the foreign ministry. Not until they were on the grounds of a villa in a suburb of Rome did Julia realize that it was the wedding that everyone had been talking about since she had arrived. She found herself shaking hands with Benito Mussolini, the father of the bride. Julia thought him comical-looking in winged collar and striped pants, with his bulging eyes and perspiration trickling down his shaved head; and he was inches shorter than she. So, that was the famous dictator. He looked like any father of the bride worrying about how much it was going to cost. Mussolini and Angelo exchanged a few words in Italian.

"What did he say?" she asked as they moved down the line.

"He said you're beautiful."

Then she found herself shaking hands with the groom, a rather short, strongly built man, handsome in a coarse way, with black hair and dark, hard eyes.

"Galeazzo, I would like to introduce Miss Julia Howard, a friend of mine. Julia, Count Galeazzo Ciano, my colleague in the foreign ministry, and now Prime Minister Mussolini's son-in-law."

The groom gave Julia an overtly sexual going-over from head to foot with those eyes, while his bride stood beside him. He embraced Angelo and whispered something in his ear. Both men laughed.

"Now, what did *he* say?"

"He said I was very lucky to have found you." Julia knew that Angelo's friend had said something cruder than that, and she was annoyed with Angelo for having laughed.

"Get me some champagne, Angelo." Julia sent him away so that she could regain her composure. Victoria had said that Italian men looked upon women as animals, pieces of property that were also sexually useful. Angelo had just made her feel like that; and instead of growing calmer she became more angry. Still, she wasn't going to let him see that he had hurt her.

"Champagne and something to eat." Angelo handed her a plate with tiny sandwiches on a pink linen napkin.

"My heavens, watercress sandwiches. It's just like a society wedding at home. Who would have imagined?"

"What were you expecting?"

"Oh, I don't know," she said, and took a bite of sandwich.

"Perhaps you thought Mussolini would serve pizza when his only daughter was married." Now he was angry.

"I assure you, Angelo, I find everything most elegant." And it was. Hundreds of guests were scattered over the great sweep of lawn, the men in tailcoats and striped pants, the women in spring dresses and little hats, and here and there the red and purple robes of monsignori and bishops, archbishops and cardinals. It was a perfect day for a wedding; a string quartet under the trees was playing Schubert, the music punctuated by the popping of corks.

"Funny champagne," she said.

"It's Asti Spumante. Italian champagne."

"Oh."

"You don't like it?"

"It's different," she said, and took another sip. "Isn't that General Oxley shaking the great man's hand?"

"Yes."

"Aunt Agnes will be furious. She didn't get invited, and she and Charles are almost as good Fascists as the general."

Angelo said nothing.

"My cousin Victoria says your friend Ciano is quite a skirt chaser. I suppose now that he's married the boss's daughter, he'll have to reform."

"Galeazzo has always been attractive to women, and I doubt marriage will change that. Given Mussolini's reputation with women, however, there won't be much Il Duce can say."

"Nor much any Italian male can say."

Angelo looked at her, puzzled, as handsome in winged collar and gray silk tie as Mussolini was ridiculous. 'What's the matter with you today, Julia?"

"Nothing. Nothing at all. What's the matter with you? Don't you like women to have opinions?"

"My heavens, Julia." He laughed. "All right, then, what do you think of Mussolini and the newlyweds?"

She looked at the wedding party. Galeazzo Ciano was standing with his hands behind his back and his chin stuck out, in an obvious imitation of his father-in-law.

"Your friend and Mussolini look like a couple of gangsters."

Angelo laughed uncertainly. "Galeazzo wouldn't mind if you called him a handsome gangster."

"Oh, he's handsome enough, but he's so short."

"Perhaps it's just that you're so tall," Angelo said with a trace of irritation in his voice, having to look up slightly into Julia's eyes.

When Julia returned to the Palazzo Rosalba, there was a message for her. Francesca Danieli had called with an invitation to dinner that evening, to meet James. A welcome change, Julia thought. She and Angelo had been seeing too much of each other, and he was beginning to get on her nerves. She picked up the receiver of the odd-looking Italian phone that looked like a candlestick with a mouthpiece.

"*Pronto.*"

"Count Morosini, please."

"Speaking."

"Don't you recognize me, dear?"

"Julia?"

"Angelo, I'm going to take a rain check on tonight, if I may."

"A what?"

"Something has come up."

Silence.

"I said, something has come up."

"You're angry with me."

"Of course I'm not."

"Julia, if I've done something to offend you, please tell me."

"Damn it, Angelo, you haven't done a thing. It's just that I've had a dinner invitation from Francesca Danieli, and I feel like going."

"Julia, she and her brother are well-known radicals. You should be aware of that."

She tried to suppress her anger. The whole world was hers as long as she remained emotionally detached, and now she could spoil everything by screaming into the mouthpiece of a ridiculous Italian telephone.

"Angelo, I know that."

"I don't want you seeing her."

"Angelo Morosini, you don't own me. What you want has nothing to do with it." She slammed down the receiver. Angelo could go to hell.

There were three people at the table. Julia hesitated and looked back at the Dusenberg idling under the streetlight. The chauffeur stood beside it, his cap under his arm. He had insisted on waiting because, he said, the neighborhood of Trastevere was unsafe. She looked down at her evening dress. Why hadn't Francesca told her that the address was not her apartment but an outdoor restaurant? Three young people sat staring at her across the little cobblestone square—and at the Dusenberg and driver. They were all casually dressed. Well, make the best of it. She put her arms in the sweater she had thrown over her bare shoulders and buttoned it down the front. Then she went back and told the driver to take the Dusenberg home. She would find her own way back.

As she drew closer to the tables set out on the cobblestones, she saw that all three of the people sitting there wore turtleneck sweaters, a kind of uniform. Francesca had on a tweed skirt, the men corduroy jackets with leather elbow patches. Francesca looked the same as on shipboard, the dark makeup around her eyes, the mop of red curls, the cigarette holder clamped in her teeth. There was James and there was . . . Paolo.

"You already know my charming brother, Paolo. And this is James Morrison." Tall and thin, blond wavy hair and pale blue eyes, a crooked smile.

"Hi, Julia." Pure American accent. "Where did you get the motorcar?"

"It belongs to my aunt. I didn't know . . ."

"Haven't seen anything like that in Trastevere since the Bulgarian ambassador came slumming . . . looking for boys, of course."

"No, no, James, it's the Rumanian ambassador who likes boys," Francesca interjected. "Well, Julia, how are you finding Rome? I saw your picture in the papers."

"Oh?"

"With your cousin and one of the Bronzini boys and Count Morosini. What would you like to drink?"

"A *Punt e Mes*," she said, taking the name from an advertising sign over the bar inside. What she got was dark brown and even more like cough medicine than the other things she had been drinking in the last two weeks.

"How is Morosini?" Paolo asked, speaking to her for the first time. She had not even looked in his direction.

"Oh, he's fine. He took me to the Mussolini-Ciano wedding reception this afternoon."

"Did they serve castor oil cocktails?"

Julia looked at him in astonishment, and when she did she saw that one of his eyes was swollen and that there was a piece of adhesive tape across his cheekbone.

"Oh, stop it, Paolo," Francesca snapped.

"I don't understand."

"Paolo's being his usual funny self. You know about the castor oil treatment?"

"Let me tell her," Paolo said. He was unshaven again. "They hold your head, put a funnel down your throat, and pour in a liter or so of castor oil. It's supposed to cleanse you of anti-Fascist poison. But I don't suppose anyone at Edda's wedding needed his insides washed out."

"No, I don't suppose so. . . ." She was too shocked to know what to say. "How did you hurt yourself?"

"Now I will explain," Francesca said, glaring at her brother, "and then, Paolo, we will not continue this discussion." She turned to Julia. "They did it to him, just as soon as he got back to Italy. I warned him."

"But why?"

"For what he did to them at the Fascist rally in New

York. Oxley must have gone to them as soon as he got off the boat."

"Unless," Paolo said, "it was your friend Morosini."

Francesca turned to him. "Paolo, if you can't leave her alone, then get out of here!"

"All right, I will." He stood up.

"Wait!" Julia said, standing up, too. "Was this something that happened to you in Naples? Because if it was . . ."

"No. If you're interested, the police picked me up there, but for some reason they let me go. It was on the way to Rome. Some Fascist thugs stopped the bus and pulled me off."

"I'm sorry."

"Thanks a lot. Maybe now you can understand why I don't care for your friends."

"They aren't my friends."

But Paolo was already walking off into the night. Julia's eyes stung with tears.

"I don't see why . . ."

"There's nothing to see with Paolo." Francesca put an arm around Julia's shoulders. "He's so bloody rude. . . . James, goddamn it, don't just sit there. Order some pasta and get some wine on the table."

While they ate, Julia looked around. The tables under the strings of lights were full of gesturing, laughing people. There was a fountain playing in the square beyond the lights, and beyond the fountain, lighted candles glowed through the windows of an ancient church with a leaning bell tower. It was all so wonderful. If only . . .

The maid came through the door, wheeling a white, rubber-tired breakfast cart and making a lot more noise than was necessary, Julia thought. She opened one eye and looked out from the pile of lavender pillows, as from a cave.

"The signorina is awake?" The trim, young shape in a black uniform, starched apron and snow-white cap was lighting a spirit lamp under a silver-covered dish, noisily arranging the blue-flowered breakfast service on the tray. Julia opened the other eye.

"With your help, yes." She smiled. A very pleasant dream, the erotic details of which were already escaping her, had been stolen away.

"You can't sleep all day." More clatter of china and silver, an omelet sliding out of the pan onto the Meissen plate.

"That's my business, Gina." Julia yawned lazily, stretched in the hugeness of the four-poster. "I don't need a nanny to tell me when to get up."

"Perhaps you do. And when to come in. If I had not waited up last night with the key you would have had to ring the bell, and you know what the signora's rules are."

Julia's heart sank, and the last wisps of her hot romantic dream were burned away in the cold bright light of a Rome morning, as the maid threw open the shutters. In one day she had upset first Angelo . . . and then Paolo, the same evening. . . .

"Gina, did you know your seams are crooked?"

"Oh, *grazie*." The maid turned and checked the seams of her black silk stockings, stooped and twisted them back into line. However mean-spirited Aunt Agnes might be, Julia thought, she didn't stint on money: silk stockings even for the maids. Gina put the breakfast tray across Julia's lap after she pulled herself up in the bed. On the tray with the eggs and coffee was a bowl of strawberries set in ice, and a bunch of spring wildflowers in an antique glass pitcher: the kind of thing that Aunt Agnes picked up in twos and threes on shopping trips along the Via Veneto.

"*È bella, no?*" the maid said, gesturing at the tray and smiling.

"Yes, it's very pretty."

"*Buon appetito,*" and Gina went out the door.

Julia looked down at the strawberries and cream, the wildflowers, inhaled the aroma of black Italian coffee. She wasn't hungry at all. Why had Paolo attacked her, humiliated her in front of his sister and her boyfriend? What kind of man was this? Angrily she whipped the shell-pink linen napkin off the tray, and an envelope fell out of the folds: "To J. H."

She looked at the handwriting in amazement and tore open the envelope. A nugget of gold fell into the empty porcelain coffee cup. She lifted it up by its fine gold chain into the stream of spring-morning light that poured through the open window of the palazzo: it was a tiny gold mermaid, swimming back and forth at the end of its chain in a sea of light. All at once tears sprang to her eyes, and the dome of St. Peter's and the pines of the Borghese Gardens through the window became a blur.

Swaying back and forth in the bed, she clutched the gold mermaid in a tight first. He cared after all! The mermaid fell out of her open hand. She quickly wiped her eyes with the napkin and felt in the envelope. Yes, there was a note: "Sorry for everything. Truly. Would you have lunch with me at the Ristorante Foro Antico? I'll be waiting there at noon. If you don't come, I'll understand why. P." She let out an involuntary sob, crushing the note in her hand, as Rome became a rainbow in front of her eyes.

Julia, Julia, get ahold of yourself. He's just a man you barely know. What has come over you? Remember that you were going to be cool and careful; remember that the world is yours if you play your cards carefully; remember that . . . She looked at her frowning image in the mirror, but it just laughed back at her. There was no use giving herself a lecture, because she wasn't going to listen. That was obvious. All she could think of was that she was going to have lunch with Paolo Danieli.

Julia looked at the bellpull on the table, with ivory buttons for maid, laundress, bootblack, and Aunt Agnes's social secretary. She rang for the maid.

"The signorina is finished?"

"Not quite," Julia said, and spooned down the last of the strawberries, so ripe they melted in her mouth. How hungry she was!

"Where is the Foro Antico restaurant, Gina?"

"Overlooking the ruins of the ancient Roman forum, Si-

gnorina Julia. There are terraces outside, one above the
other, *molto bello*. You wish to go?"

"I'm going," Julia said, wiping her mouth with the napkin. She looked at the antique clock on the night table sup-
ported by porcelain cupids. Eleven o'clock. Just time for a
bath and to dress carefully, to look her best. What to wear?

"I'll want the Dusenburg."

"I'm sorry, the signora has taken the car to go shopping."

"Oh. Well, never mind. I'll take a cab."

"They will be difficult to find, signorina, and the streets
will be very crowded. There's a rally today."

"I'll find one," she said, leaping out of bed as the maid
removed the tray. "Run my bath, please." She threw her
nightgown over her head and saw out of the corner of her
eye the maid turn away, embarrassed, into the bathroom.
The water roared out of the bronze sea-serpent spigots into
the marble tub that had, Victoria said, once been used for
watering the cardinal's carriage horses. The maid was saying something.

"What is it?"

"Bath salts?"

"Yes, please." But Julia's mind was far away, as she
gazed at herself in the many mirrors, no longer seeing herself as beautiful, but as naked and defenseless. A shiver ran
through her body.

What nonsense! It was eleven o'clock on a spring morning in Italy and, as Browning had said, "all's right with the
world." She was going to have lunch with an interesting
man, and there was nothing more to it than that. She got up
onto the bathroom stool, climbed into the green marble tub,
and sank down into the bubbles. There is, she said to herself again, nothing more to it than that. But it was no use.
She wasn't going to listen. Oh, God, all I want at this point
is to be with him, to talk, for there to be no unpleasantness.
That's all I want . . . for now.

At twenty before twelve the white-tied, tailcoated young
Italian butler cast an appreciative eye over Julia Howard as
she swept out of the doors of the Palazzo Rosalba in a

spring creation that, after three fittings, clung to her body like another skin. Gina had been wrong about the taxis. There was a whole row of them, many more than usual, parked alongside the curb at the top of the Via Veneto. Julia called to the old man in the front cab, half-asleep.

"You know where the Foro Antico restaurant is?"

"*Si*, signora, but . . ."

"Well, take me there."

"Much traffic."

"Then hurry."

Over Rome a black thunderhead was building. Julia got in before the man could say anything more and slammed the door. The driver shrugged, started the engine, and pulled away from the curb. Julia leaned back in the leather seat. She loved Rome taxicabs, big and square inside and always highly polished, with headlights the size of dinner plates, and deep, resonant horns. How good life was! Halfway down the Via Veneto big drops of spring rain began to fall on the tarred canvas roof, and steam rose from the pavement. By the time they reached the Piazza Barberini with its fountain of stone tritons blowing on seashells, the rain was coming down in sheets. They started down the Via Tritone, but it was blocked by cars and buses. Horns blew from every side street, and nothing moved. Behind them traffic was piling up.

"What's going on?"

"As I told you, Signora, much traffic today."

Julia looked at her wristwatch. Already five to twelve.

"Well, turn around."

"Not possible."

"Take a side street."

"I try," the driver said, looking doubtfully at an empty side street that ran straight up a steep hill to the left.

"Okay, I go," the driver said, turning violently to the left with screeching tires, between startled pedestrians, and up the empty street, empty because it was one-way—the other way. Blowing the horn continuously, he made it to the top without having an accident. It was exactly twelve. Bells rang and clocks chimed. The rain had stopped as quickly as

it had begun. They were at a crossing that looked down in
every direction on Rome, and at each corner of the crossing
was a fountain, old and moss-grown, and two small
churches.

"Quattro Fontane," the driver said. "Four fountains."

"Yes, I know. But where is the Forum?"

"Forum down there," the old man said, waving his arm.
"Too many people. Better you stay here. This church for
marriage. I show you. Fine people they marry here, *nobili*."

Yes, she remembered that it was a place for society weddings. But why in heaven's name couldn't they just go
down to where Paolo was waiting for her, had been waiting
for her. . . . "If you don't come, I'll understand why. . . ."
She knew, of course, that he was referring to his behavior
last night. But it implied something more: If you don't
come, I'll know you don't want to see me again.

"Never mind the people. Go down!"

"Okay. But double fare. Too many people."

And down they went, until they were at the Piazza
Colonna, where all the streets were blocked by barricades
and blue-and-red uniformed police. What was going on?

"Mussolini already begin to speak. Piazza Venezia."

"Why didn't you say so?" she said in a shrill voice.

"Everybody knows that, everybody in Italy, everybody in
the whole world."

Except me. Gina had been trying to tell her.

She gave the driver a large bill, too large, and jumped
out of the cab. No need for panic. Paolo would wait, and
if he didn't, what of it? It wasn't as if she was chasing after
him. . . .

"No." A burly man in a black shirt and black riding
boots and pants, a tassel from his black cap falling across
one eye, blocked her way. *"Via fermata."* The street was
closed. She didn't know enough Italian to explain that she
just wanted to get to the Forum.

"Foro Antico."

"No Foro Antico. You go home." He stood with legs
spread wide and his arms crossed, not moving. Then he
said something rapidly, and the only words she understood

were "dress" and "*puttana*"—whore. The white-gloved policeman at the other end of the barricade laughed. Furious,
Julia pushed past the Black Shirt and walked rapidly on.
Who did he think he was? And that policeman just standing
there laughing . . . A hand seized her by the arm with such
force that her high heels went out from under her on the
cobblestone street and only the iron hand of the Fascist
thug held her up.

"I say go home . . . Italian women . . . modest . . . children . . . home."

And then he pulled her toward him and looked down her
low-cut spring dress.

"I'm not Italian," she said in a loud voice. "I am American. Let go of me." She was scared now. The policeman's
smile faded. He said something to the Black Shirt and the
hand was released. Julia stumbled and would have fallen if
she hadn't grabbed onto the lamppost.

"These streets are closed, miss," the policeman said in
English. "You'll have to go the other way. Il Duce speaks
today."

"Did you see what he did?" Julia said in a shaking voice,
pointing at the Black Shirt. The policeman pulled the visor
of his white helmet down over his eyes and looked the
other way, as if he hadn't heard her. The Fascist bully
laughed. She turned and walked rapidly back and down a
narrow side street, humiliated, angry—and still frightened.

The dark street led out after a few blocks into the big
square in front of the Victor Emmanuel memorial, which
everyone quite rightly said looked like a giant wedding
cake. The square was deserted, but beyond it she could see
the back of a vast crowd packing the Piazza Venezia.
Mussolini's amplified voice rose and fell and his black-clad
figure could be seen far in the distance, striding back and
forth on a balcony as he spoke. Arms were raised in sa-
lutes, and the movement swept across the crowd like wind
across a field of wheat. The cries of "*Duce! Duce!*" echoed
back and forth across the empty square in front of her. She
remembered that the Forum was just beyond. She was halfway across the square when the rain began to fall again in

big drops, and she ran. By the time she reached the far side
and the shelter of a bus stop, she was soaked. The rain
pounded down on the metal roof, and suddenly she was
cold. Goose bumps ran up her arms. She looked at the red
marks on her arm where the Fascist had grabbed her, and
shivered. Then she looked at her watch. Twenty-five past
twelve. Paolo would be gone by now, thinking she didn't
want to see him again. Just as well. She couldn't go there
looking like this. He would be gone by now . . . gone for
good. . . .

She stood there, hugging herself, wet, cold, and trembling. You can't, she told herself, give up that easily.
Maybe he was caught in the rain, too. She imagined him
sitting by a window in the restaurant, looking out into the
rain, glancing at his watch. And then, as if on command,
the rain stopped and the whole great empty square was
ablaze in sunlight.

The restaurant was empty: rows of white tablecloths,
starched napkins stuck in wine glasses, bottles of wine lined
up on the tables like rows of soldiers. The headwaiter was
reading a newspaper in one corner of the dining room. He
looked up at Julia. With the downpour and the Fascist rally
blocking streets all over Rome, it was no wonder the restaurant was empty. She stood hesitantly in the doorway.

"The signora is expecting someone?" He came toward
her across the empty dining room.

"Yes, I am. . . ." She looked around the room. And then
she saw, as she had in her imagination, a table for two by
a window, an empty coffee cup on it, an ashtray with a
half-smoked cigarette stubbed out in it. She stood over the
table. Beyond the window, below the descending brick terraces, where waiters were sweeping away the rainwater, the
ancient forum of Rome spread out, white columns, archways, walls and towers, deep-green umbrella pines: *molto
bello*—as Gina had said—in the sunlight after the rain.

"There was someone here?"

"Yes, a gentleman."

"When did he leave?"

"Only a short while ago, when the rain ended."

Beside the ashtray was a matchbook cover with the number of Palazzo Rosalba written on it. He had even tried to call her. She looked up at the headwaiter and realized, with annoyance and embarrassment, that he felt sorry for her. She must look a mess in her still-damp dress, with her ruined hair and makeup.

"Thank you."

She walked slowly out the door and down the long flight of stairs through the terraced gardens to the street. At the curb a Rome taxi was just pulling up. She started toward it, waving, when the door opened and Paolo Danieli got out.

"Julia."

"Paolo, did you just . . ." She was confused.

"I nearly missed you a second time. I was here at twelve, and when you didn't come . . . but after I left, I thought maybe I hadn't waited long enough, so I took a taxi back, and just in time. We both would have thought . . ."

There was no need for him to finish the sentence. Comparing his voice to the voices of other men she knew she realized his was like that of a cello among the high-pitched squeals of violins and the deep rumbles of double basses in a symphony orchestra, coming through warm and rich and sure of itself. Sure of himself. That was what he was, most of all. "I forgot about Mussolini's speech. Me, of all people." His smile flashed. "That's why you were late, and the rain."

"Yes." And now she smiled. "I knew about the rally, but I didn't take it seriously."

"You didn't have a problem?"

"No, well, not much of one." She could still feel the grip of the Black Shirt's hand on her upper arm. There would be bruises there in the morning.

"Paolo, let's go somewhere else," she said on an impulse.

"I know just the place. Come on, get in."

As they passed through the Piazza Venezia, they saw that the rally was over and the crowd had dispersed. The doors of Mussolini's balcony were closed. Banners and bunting lay sodden in puddles in the empty square.

"I thought you weren't coming at all. After last night . . ."

"Oh, that . . ." She turned her face and looked out of the window. They were in dark, narrow, crooked streets now. Neither of them spoke and she turned back to him. The adhesive on his cheek was gone but a neat row of black stitches remained.

"Are you all right now?"

"Oh, fine. It's not the first time," he said. He grinned and rubbed his crooked nose. "I'm beginning to think the Fascists don't like me."

"Be careful," she said, and an electric spark passed between them. What right had she to say that? She was ashamed to tell him of her own foolhardy encounter with the Black Shirts.

"I tell myself to be careful all the time, but then . . . You got caught in the rain."

"Oh, I must look awful." In the excitement of losing him and finding him, she had completely forgotten about her appearance, which had been so important to her when she left the Palazzo Rosalba—ages ago.

"I like you better a little mussed up, not so . . ." A long pause.

"Well?"

"So perfect."

Julia raised an eyebrow. "Perfect?" she said lightly, "That's a serious charge."

He suppressed a smile, but in that smile she had seen the possibility of the chasm that still separated them being bridged.

"How can I put it? The greatest masters of Chinese painting, when they had completed a work that seemed perfect, always did something to make it a little flawed—a drop of ink spilled, a smudge, a clumsy last stroke of the brush. That was to fend off the wrath of heaven that descends on those who aim too high. Fortunately, by getting caught in the rain you have avoided that fate."

They both laughed, as if all he was talking about was his image of a young, beautiful, and rich American girl, a shade too calculating, who had come to make Rome hers. But she read something else into his remark about those who aim too high, and she shuddered and rubbed her arms, as if she were still chilled from the rain. What she felt he was saying, whether he knew it or not, was that if they got involved it would be at great risk.

"Piazza Navona, signori."

Paolo paid the driver and they got out in a tremendously long, open piazza, enclosed by churches and the striped awnings of restaurants and bars. The fountains were even larger and more ornate than the others she had seen in Rome, water cascading down, pigeons whirling overhead.

"Do you know the Piazza Navona?" he asked, linking his arm with the utmost naturalness in hers, as they began to walk.

"No." Just, dear God, let this go on, she thought. "I've never been here."

"I'm glad. I thought on the ship how much I would like to show you Rome, my Rome, the old neighborhoods. The Piazza Navona, for example; it's shaped like this because, a couple of thousand years ago under the Roman emperors, it was a racecourse for chariots. It's been full of Romans day and night ever since. There, right beside Bernini's fountain, is a favorite restaurant of mine. And I did promise you lunch. Would you still like to?"

"Oh, yes. Yes, I would like to very much."

"Let's take that table there under the awning," he said. "I think it's building up to another shower."

Toward the end of a meal that had begun with tiny artichokes and progressed as far as pears stewed in red wine, the rain did begin again, falling in big drops on the striped canvas over their heads, increasing in intensity until even Bernini's fountain was half-obscured and they were enclosed in a private grotto surrounded by falling water, alone on the empty terrace. Paolo had taken off his coat and tie, and she had kicked off her shoes under the table.

"This has been wonderful," she said, reaching out and

touching his hand, something she had been wanting to do all during lunch, as she had listened to him talk about Rome and his art and politics and . . . she didn't remember what else. She had been too much in the spell of his presence, his voice, his looks . . .

"Has been? You're not planning on leaving now?"

"Well, I really must—"

"Things are just getting started in the Piazza Navona."

"It's pouring rain, Paolo."

"All the more reason to stay. By the time we finish the last of the wine," he said, filling her glass from the majolica pitcher, "I promise you the sun will be out again, and then . . ." He squeezed her hand that was still resting in his.

"All right," she said, "I'll stay if . . ." She was just tipsy enough from the wine she had drunk not to care. "If you'll tell me about yourself." She withdrew her hand from his.

He looked surprised. "There's not much to tell."

"I don't care. I want to know."

"You do?" They looked at each other, not smiling now.

"Yes."

"I'll tell you if you'll go to the circus with me tonight."

"The circus? Where?" She remembered with uneasiness that she hadn't seen Aunt Agnes and Victoria in nearly twenty-four hours.

"Right here in the neighborhood."

"It's a deal." To hell with Aunt Agnes. "Now tell. Starting from the beginning."

"All right. In the beginning there was Mama and Papa. Mama was rich and lived in New York. Papa was a poor artist and lived in Rome. Mama, like all the rich, wanted to create something. Papa, like all artists, wanted to be rich. It was a natural combination."

"And they both got what they wanted."

"No, they didn't. It never works that way." He leaned back in his chair, a reflective look coming over his face.

"My mother wanted to be a great opera singer, my father wanted to be the man who breathed life back into the Italian theater."

"And?"

"And my mother came to Rome to study for the opera. Her voice wasn't as good as she had been led to believe in New York. My father was doing something around the stage, and she settled for him instead of a career. By the next year he was an independent theater producer . . . which takes nothing in Italy but money. The following year I was born; three years later, Francesca. By the time the 1914 war came along it was all over between our parents. Mother sailed for the States and got a divorce."

"I thought there was no such thing as divorce in Italy."

"It isn't recognized here, not that it makes any difference to my father. He's completely absorbed in developing the talents of all those fresh, young country girls he puts in his third-rate Italian films, such as *A Neapolitan Tragedy* or *My Soul Is Not For Sale* or *Flower of the Alps*."

"At least he's able to work."

"Oh, I can work, too. Few artists, denied the right to work, can fall back on *My Soul Is Not For Sale*. It's right there in the film credits—'Sets by Paolo Danieli.' "

"Paolo, I'm sorry. But I know a talent like yours will win out in the end."

"Well, thanks for the moral support anyway." He smiled and looked into her eyes. "And you see, the sun is coming out. I'm glad you stayed."

"I am, too," she said, lowering her eyes from his intense gaze.

"Where else in the world," Paolo said, leading Julia down the wooden steps into what seemed a dark pit opening up in the night streets of Rome, "could you see a circus amid two-thousand-year-old ruins?"

It was true. In the midst of broken columns and smashed statues and remains of Roman walls, a modest tent had been set up.

"It's a family circus. The tightrope walkers, the trapeze artists, the knife thrower, the clowns, all from one family. Somehow they keep going . . ."

"Paolo!"

"Signora Orteo."

"Where have you been?"

"I've been on a visit to America."

"You should have stayed. Things are getting even worse here." He turned to Julia.

"Signora Orteo, my friend, Julia Howard. From America."

The light from under the circus tent fell on a silver-haired woman, dressed in a suit covered with sequins.

"Come here, into the light." The old woman motioned to Julia, who stepped forward.

"Well, Paolo, you waited a long time, but I see it was worth it. Bravo. A real beauty."

Embarrassed, Julia shot a glance at Paolo.

"It's not what you think . . ." Paolo was blushing.

"How do you know what I think?" the old woman said, and laughed. She was at least sixty-five, but her eyelids were painted with blue glitter. "Never mind. Come with me. Tonight you are going to see something special. My granddaughter Antonia, Franco's daughter, is making her debut."

Seating them at ringside in the tiny arena, Signora Orteo refused to hear of their buying tickets.

"I'm sorry about Signora Orteo's remark about you," Paolo said when they were alone.

"I'm not. I was flattered. How do you know her?"

"The theatrical world. She used to be . . . my father's mistress."

"Signore *e* Signori!" the silver-haired woman cried through a megaphone, standing in the center of the single ring. On the platform above, her twelve-year-old granddaughter waited, wide-eyed, and then at a cue swung out into space to the roll of a drum and somersaulted across space into the arms of her partner on the other trapeze. Applause.

What a different world I have entered, Julia thought.

"It's a different world," Paolo said. "A long way from estates in Maryland and embassy parties."

"Do you always read women's minds?" And what had

Signora Orteo meant when she said, looking at Julia, that Paolo had waited a long time?

It was two o'clock in the morning before she got up the nerve to ask him. They had gone back to the Piazza Navona after the circus performance and watched fireworks set off for some saint's day; and then he had taken her to a dark and elegant club on the upper floor of a Renaissance palazzo where they had danced, and he had kissed her once, tentatively, because it would have been absurd, at that hour and after such a day, to not have; but they both knew that they were still poised on the edge of a precipice.

Waiting for a taxi in the dark, empty piazza, she finally said, "What did that woman mean, you have waited a long time?"

"It's a long story." It was too dark to see his face.

"There's a story, then?" He was silent.

"A woman?" She had to be bold.

"Yes. But she's dead now."

Julia gasped. "I'm sorry. I didn't mean to pry."

"It's all right. It was, as Signora Orteo said, a long time ago."

Julia awoke late the next morning feeling worn out. She had breakfast in bed again, took a bath, painted her nails, wrote some letters. Before she knew it the afternoon was half-gone. Too late to go out, really, she thought. Instead she took a book out on the balcony overlooking the Borghese Gardens and tried to read, but it was only words. As the sun was going down behind St. Peter's, Bruno's car drew up in front of the Palazzo Rosalba and Victoria got out. She came straight to Julia's room.

"Hi, Julie. Where've you been all this time?" Victoria plopped down on Julia's bed and lit a cigarette. "I covered for you last night with Mother. I told her you had gone to bed early. I know you'd do the same for me."

Julia laughed. "Of course."

"You weren't out with Count Morosini."

"No. That's finished. He tried to play the Italian male with me and I told him where to go."

"He must not have heard you. He called last night. That's how I knew you weren't out with him. It's the other one, isn't it?"

"The other one?"

Julia walked to the open doors and looked out at the park.

"You met two men on the ship. I knew from the beginning it was going to be the other one, what's his name? Paolo?"

"I don't know what you mean by that."

"Of course you don't. Sit down, Julia. You're nervous as a cat."

"Give me a cigarette," Julia said, sitting down next to Victoria on the bed.

Her cousin squinted at her through bleached lashes. "He hasn't called you today, has he?"

Julia just stared at her. Had she been waiting, hoping for a phone call from Paolo?

"You've been here in your room all day, waiting, haven't you?"

"I was tired, Vicky," she snapped, annoyed.

Victoria blew smoke at the ceiling. "You don't have to talk to me about it if you don't want. I'm just a little surprised, that's all. You were so cool; you were going to play the field, not get involved."

No, she didn't want to talk to Victoria about it. They had always gossiped about men, but not this time. There was only one person she could talk to about Paolo.

"Look, Vicky, there is something going on, but I don't want to talk about it right now. I'm very confused, and I'm going to have to work things out."

"I understand."

Julia reached out and squeezed Victoria's hand. "Thanks. I'll talk to you about what's going on later . . . if there's anything to talk about."

What was going on was that she had fallen hopelessly in love with Paolo Danieli, and there was nothing to be done about it. She had done exactly what she had said she would never do: made herself vulnerable to rejection and humiliation. She had chosen—though chosen was not the word—a man with whom the risk of being hurt could not have been greater. Here I am, she told herself, madly in love and miserably afraid.

The next day, Sunday, Julia was drawn, as if by a magnet, to Trastevere. She had no idea where Paolo lived and only a vague idea that Francesca's studio was somewhere near the church of Santa Maria in Trastevere. She found Francesca on the same café terrace facing the church, with a cup of coffee and a pile of Sunday papers.

"Well, hello," Francesca said, and smiled. "You came back. I wasn't sure you would."

"Paolo's apologized, if that's what you mean." She felt strange saying his name.

"Oh?" Francesca looked surprised. "Well, join me. Would you like a *caffè latte*?"

"Yes, thank you."

"I've just been reading Il Duce's latest pronouncement on the place of women in Fascist society. What a joke."

"It's not funny, you know. A couple of days ago, right in the center of the city, a Black Shirt stopped me and told me to go home and put on modest clothes befitting an Italian woman. When I tried to get past him, he grabbed me by the arm. It scared the hell out of me. But now I have an idea of what it must be like for an Italian woman living in Mussolini's Italy."

"It's suffocating. Listen to what the great man says now." Francesca picked up the newspaper lying in her lap. "I quote—'Intellectual women are *contra natura*,' against nature, if you please. 'Higher education for women should be limited to subjects that the female brain can grasp, such as household management.' What tripe!"

"But a lot of men think like that."

"Not any of my friends."

"Your friends are all artists and journalists and professors."

"Paolo doesn't think that way about women," Francesca added, giving Julia an opportunity to say more.

"Paolo is half-American, and I don't know how he feels about . . ." She couldn't finish the sentence.

"About women?" Francesca looked puzzled.

"About me."

"Oh, dear."

The waiter put the cup of foam-topped Italian coffee down in front of Julia. She fumbled for change, giving herself a moment to think. She felt Francesca's eyes on her.

"*Grazie*, signora," the waiter said, dumping the small coins from the saucer into his jacket pocket.

"You see, I'm in love with him." She would have revealed her feelings to no one else, not even to Victoria. Why then to this tough Italian-American redhead with the china-blue eyes? Someone she had known only a few weeks, someone who was, for God's sake, *his* sister?

"Oh." Francesca brought the look of astonishment on her face under control. "I guess it's too late then to remind you that I warned you."

"Warned me?" It was not the reaction she expected or wanted from Francesca.

"On the ship. I told you women always fall in love with Paolo. It could lead to problems."

"Why?"

"He's too involved in the Resistance movement." Francesca looked out beyond Julia, into the square where the fountain played. "Once, I would have said you were lucky, very lucky. . . ."

"There was a woman who died."

"You already know about Bianca?" Francesca shook her red curls, laughing. "You keep surprising me."

"I need to know."

"You *need* to know?" She searched Julia's face. "Yes. I suppose you do. Well, she was a woman—a girl, really, nineteen or so. He was very much in love with her. She was a dancer with the La Scala opera ballet in Milan, very talented. In those days Paolo didn't give a fig for politics. But there was a plot to kill Mussolini, or at least they said there was. A lot of people said it was cooked up by the

Fascists to win sympathy for Il Duce, who at that time seemed to be losing his grip.

"In any case they put the finger on Bianca's father as the man behind the plot. He was tried by a Fascist court and sentenced to death. Mussolini commuted the sentence to permanent exile, on a tiny island—it's called Levanzo—off the coast of Sicily, and Bianca and her mother chose to go there with him. That, as you can imagine, tore up Paolo. There was a big scene with Bianca. But in the end she went. Paolo couldn't understand why anyone would make such a sacrifice for a political cause, least of all the woman he loved."

"That's the way I felt," Julia said. "When you told me on the ship what Paolo was doing, I thought, well, it's just Italian politics. It's all a joke."

"That's what Paolo thought, too. But then Bianca was sent off to Levanzo. I guess conditions weren't too good, and she wasn't a strong girl. The end of the story is she contracted TB. They wouldn't let her leave the island for treatment. He tried to send food and medicine but it never got to her family. She didn't live long."

"Ever since then Paolo has been fighting the Fascists?"

"Yes. Not a very equal fight. But . . ." Francesca paused; she seemed to be considering just how to phrase what she was going to say. "I don't think anything . . . or anyone . . . can turn him aside. He's already thrown away a very promising career."

"What you're really saying is I can't turn him aside either."

"That's right, Julia." Francesca looked steadily into her eyes. "Even if he's in love with you."

"That won't stop me from trying."

"No, it won't. But don't say I didn't warn you—twice."

Chapter Four

HER HANDS GRIPPED the rough stone balustrade as the breeze that sometimes rises at dawn along the Tiber whispered through the dark pines in the Borghese Gardens below, and whipped the light silk nightgown around her body. Poised there on the balcony, she watched the first light of another day appear.

The first rays of sun grazed the edge of the dome of St. Peter's. How much time did she have? A few days before Paolo realized that someone had come to take Bianca's place, to turn him aside from his doomed crusade against fascism before it was too late. Francesca was no fool, and she had said that it was impossible, that not even love could turn him aside. We'll see, Julia said, turning back into the darkened bedroom, closing the glass doors behind her.

"I'm sorry, signora, the theater is closed."

"Lambretti," she said brusquely. "New York."

"Ah. Si, signora. Lambretti."

The guard stepped aside and she passed into the darkened theater. Lambretti was the name of the producer of the play that was to open in two weeks. She had read it on a poster outside. The theater was empty, the stage dimly lit. She slipped into a back row seat.

"What do you think, Paolo?" A voice came out of the dark below the stage. "Busoni's sets are a disaster. Can they be fixed in two weeks?"

"Oh, sure, I can do it. I'll start tomorrow."

A tall dark-haired figure disappeared from the dim stage and in a few moments came up the aisle toward her. He

66

walked slowly, his hands in his pockets. His voice had not shown much enthusiasm for the job he was taking on.

"Paolo."

"Julia. What are you doing here?"

"They said I might find you here."

"Is there something . . ."

"I wanted to see you again, that's all."

"I was just on my way home."

"Good," she said, lifting herself out of the plush theater seat, "I'll go with you."

They did go to Paolo's apartment, but it took them most of the day to get there. They strolled along the banks of the Tiber, first on one side, then on the other, beneath ancient plane trees now in full leaf. They lingered at bookstalls in the shade of the trees, stopped at a sidewalk café for coffee and at another for Campari-soda. They wandered in and out of cool, dark, incense-heavy churches. But mostly they talked.

They had a late, late lunch on the terrace of a restaurant in the Jewish quarter, almost in the shadow of the synagogue. From there, Paolo pointed out his apartment on an island in the Tiber. The island was joined by bridges to each bank; one bridge as old as Rome itself. His studio was on the roof of a crooked pile of pink-stained buildings that seemed to lean against each other for support, with flowers and vines cascading from balconies.

The terrace was now deep in shade, the other tables stripped of their white cloths.

"What would you like now?" Paolo asked.

"For this to go on forever."

He looked at her thoughtfully with those dark, serious eyes. She held her breath.

"Why don't we go to my place for a while. Would you like to see it?"

"I'd love to."

Standing on one of the tiny terraces that jutted out from various levels of his studio, nearly buried in green plants, they watched the sun set into the Mediterranean, a fine line of blue on the horizon. From another terrace, they looked down in the opposite direction toward the point of the island, which seemed like the prow of a ship steaming upstream into the Roman night. Paolo put his arm around her.

"It feels right to have you here."

"Yes."

"I wasn't sure it would."

"I know." She leaned against him, let him pull her closer. "But I was."

"You don't know much about me.".

"I know enough." She freed herself from his embrace and turned, leaning back against the balcony railing.

He folded her in his arms and she closed her eyes, so that when he kissed her on the lips, gently and for a long time, it was as if they were on their own small planet of stone and tile and geraniums, sailing through space. When at last she opened her eyes, it was night. She turned and grasped the railing, trembling. The Tiber cut a dark swath through the lights of Rome.

"Oh, dear," Julia said quietly, just what Francesca had said when she had told her that she was in love with Paolo.

"Is it all right?"

"Oh, yes, very much all right," she said. "But where do we go from here?"

"What do you mean?"

"Well," she said, drawing herself up straight, brushing back her hair, "we haven't seen everything. I want to see where you work."

Where he worked was a big room with the warm brick and old beams exposed, a wall replaced by glass. He had done the work himself, created this magical place up among the tile rooftops, a greenhouse in the sky, sailing up the Tiber. There were paintings everywhere, on easels, half-finished, stacked against the walls, brilliant colors, alive, vibrant: the skyline of the city, the green of the parks, the color of the Tiber winding through the city, the ivory-and-pink tones of female flesh. Among them there was one of a dancer, young, slim, poised on the edge of some darkness. Bianca.

"So many paintings, so many marvelous paintings."

"They pile up."

"But why?"

"The Fascists won't let me exhibit, and that makes everyone afraid to buy."

She put her hand in his. "I'm sorry." What else was there to say?

"You do care, don't you?"

"Yes."

He took her in his arms again, and with such force that her feet almost left the floor. This time his kiss was anything but gentle, and she responded with her whole body. They parted reluctantly, and he led her by the hand out onto yet another balcony.

"Rome," she said, "is so lovely, and I feel like it belongs to me."

"Almost everyone who stays here for any length of time feels that way."

"Do you?"

"I love it . . . and I hate it. . . ."

"Go on."

"On that side of the Tiber is Trastevere and freedom, art . . . even love. On the other side is official Rome, the Fascists, Mussolini strutting around on his balcony. One chooses either that bank of the river or the other. It is my curse not to be able to choose."

"What will you do?"

"I don't know." Paolo's profile was outlined against the lights of official Rome, strong, steady, beautiful. "Until recently I thought I knew, but now . . ."

"Does 'now' have something to do with me?"

"Yes. On shipboard I was attracted to you as to only one other woman in my life, but at the same time I could see— forgive me—what you were, what your background had made you."

"Cool and superficial?" She could have passed the same

judgment on herself, and preferred to say it herself than have him say it.

"Then I saw how wrong I was. I was the one who was superficial, and only gradually I realized how shy you were, how you were keeping yourself hidden from me."

Shy? Hidden from him? Why, she had absolutely thrown herself at him.

"Paolo, what are you trying to say?"

"That I don't want you hurt."

"There are worse things than being hurt."

She came to him then and he held her, once again gently.

"I think I should go now," she said.

"I will call you, Julia. I will call you . . . soon."

For the first days after that evening Julia was very steady, determined not to break down and try to see him. He needed time and so did she. By the end of the week her resolve not to get in touch with him until he called her was weakening; by the middle of the next week she was frantic. She could go on no longer. Aunt Agnes thought she was ill, and Victoria treated her as if she were a mental case. How could Paolo leave her dangling like that? Didn't he know what agony she was going through? Perhaps it was because he wasn't going through the same thing. Perhaps he had already decided that it wouldn't work, and his silence was his way of saying so.

Julia had been sitting for hours at a sidewalk café, at a table that gave her a good view of Paolo's apartment. It was growing dark, but the lights in his apartment hadn't come on. He wasn't even there. About to get up, on the verge of tears again, she saw him coming out of the door of his building. They met in the middle of the ancient bridge, where some great event in Roman history—she had forgotten what—had taken place.

"Julia!"

"Paolo."

Could he have grown even better-looking in a matter of days? Could his image already have begun to fade in her mind so that she didn't remember him exactly? She searched his face. Only a white trace of the scar beneath one eye remained. He was wearing a pale blue shirt and his long dark hair curled over the collar.

"Julia, are you all right?" He took her by the arm.

"No." She felt dizzy, almost ready to faint.

"What is it?"

"I haven't had anything to eat, that's all."

"Well, come on then. We'll go to Trastevere, to Sabatini's."

"No." She planted her feet firmly on the bridge.

"And why not?"

"Why haven't you called me?"

He held her now by both arms. "How many times have I called you? You were out, you were away for the weekend, you had gone to Florence. I thought you didn't want . . ."

"What? That's not true. I was always there, always waiting. Who told you I wasn't?"

"Whoever answered the phone, the butler, the maid. . . ."

"Aunt Agnes. I might have known."

"I'm sorry, but I don't understand."

"My Aunt Agnes and my Uncle Charles are great admirers of Mussolini. Word must have got to them that we'd been seen together. . . ." General Oxley? Angelo Morosini?

"Well, now that we know, let's go get something to eat. You look as if you need a good meal."

"Oh, Paolo, please, let's."

It was all a misunderstanding. But then her soaring spirits fell again. What had he been calling to tell her? Perhaps that it wouldn't work? That they shouldn't see each other again? She didn't dare to ask.

And all through dinner at Sabatini's she didn't dare. She made herself bright and cheerful. They laughed and talked about their pasts again, like two people who are on the verge of becoming lovers. Was he as fearful of talking about the future as she? But at least for now they were together again, and the hours flew by. She could have stayed all night, but the restaurant was closing and she must face facts.

"Well, I guess I'd better be getting home."

"I'll take you, if we can find a taxi at this hour."

"Couldn't we walk?"

"It would take a couple of hours."

"Oh." She didn't try to hide her disappointment. They were standing beside the fountain in the square, and the moon was sailing over Rome through fast-moving clouds. His dark shape in the moonlight turned to her.

"Paolo, could we walk anyway, even if it takes hours?"

"There's another way," he said after a long pause. "We could walk up the Janiculum Hill and down to the Vatican, across the Tiber and through the Borghese Gardens."

"I'd like that."

There were stairs that seemed to wind forever up from the streets of Trastevere. As they mounted the Janiculum through groves of pines black against the moonlit sky, the lights of Rome spread out in an ever-wider arc below them. Paolo's arm was around her waist, her head on his shoulder; they fit together well. They had reached the crest of the hill and all of Rome was now visible below them, the lights like strings of pearls thrown down on black velvet. They stopped there, drawn to the edge of a terrace where a dark equestrian statue seemed to gallop off into the sky over Rome. From the pine woods came the sound of night insects and the scent of night-blooming flowers.

"I think nothing could be more beautiful than this," she said, leaning against the stone balustrade.

"No, I suppose not."

His voice was tense. He put his arm around her, and she let his hand move hesitantly over her body. Love, at last. It had been a long time in coming, so long that she had begun to wonder, at age twenty-two, if there wasn't something wrong with her, some deep-down emotional block to giving herself to another person.

"You're trembling, Julia."

"I know. In a minute I'll begin to cry."

They were both silent then. He understood. But how

could he know that for the first time since she was eleven years old and was brought home in a police car from the beach where her mother had drowned, to fall wailing into Gus's arms, that she was letting down her defenses? And then she did begin to cry and fell into Paolo's arms.

"Julia, Julia." His voice was deep and warm. She could feel it reverberating in his chest.

"Paolo." She lifted her mouth to his and responded to his embrace with her whole body. He kissed her on the mouth and eyes and neck, and the lights of Rome spun around and around like a fireworks wheel. Their hands were under each other's clothes. They kissed and touched each other until she was rubbing and twisting against the hardness of his body, frantic with desire, her torso moving rhythmically.

She pulled loose from him and began unbuttoning her damp blouse with trembling hands.

"We can't," he said hoarsely, "not here. Not now."

"Don't you want me?"

"I want you so much." He was kissing her on the neck again. "I've wanted you since the moment I met you."

"Then, for God's sake, why don't you . . . I can't stand it any longer."

He took her arms from around her waist and held her by the wrists. "If we did, it would be for good."

"And you think I would mind that?"

"It's not too late to turn back."

She stepped back from him, the perspiration of her passion cold on her skin in the night air. "What do you mean by that?"

"You and I. Why did it have to happen?"

She searched for his face in the shadow.

"Paolo, don't."

"It's true. We'll bring each other nothing but misery. We were born at the wrong time."

"Oh, Christ!"

She turned away and went to the balustrade and put her hands flat down on the rough stone. The lights of Rome were an ugly blur through her tears. She wiped her eyes on her sleeve and went back to where Paolo sat slumped on a bench.

"Light me a cigarette," she said. Across the Tiber the siren of a police car screamed. He lit a cigarette and put it in her mouth. The smoke filled her lungs. She exhaled.

"Paolo, tell me. What is it?"

His silhouette against the sky was as still and as enigmatic as the unknown hero memorialized behind them in bronze.

"I know it's going to sound pompous," he said after a long silence, "but I feel I have a mission in life."

"And what is this mission?"

"To oppose fascism until it is brought down, or I am."

Her thoughts went to Bianca, of whom she could not speak, and she thought, too, of the craziness of standing alone against the Fascists, but all she said was, "And I could not be part of that ambition?"

"It's not an ambition but an obsession . . ." He took her cold hands in his large warm ones. ". . . and no one can have two obsessions."

She heard a rooster crowing. For God's sake, did they keep chickens in the capital of Italy?

"Paolo . . ." She flicked the glowing cigarette over the balustrade. ". . . do you love me?"

"I have since the beginning. That's why I say two obsessions."

"Well, I did ask you to be honest." She stood up and fastened her brassiere and buttoned her still-open blouse.

"Oh, God!" He put his head in his hands. "I didn't mean it that way. I can't let you share the life that I'm going to lead. Things are going to get much worse, danger, hardship. You were meant to have a happy life . . . and it can't be with me."

She sat down beside him and put an arm around his shoulder. "Suppose I want to share that life?"

"It's impossible, for so many reasons."

"Then give it up . . . for me. As you said, it's not too late."

"I can't. There are people who believe in me."

"Let them believe in someone else. It doesn't have to be you."

"It does. I don't know why, but it does."

He put his head on her breast and she held him close.

" 'I could not love thee, dear, so much, loved I not honor more.' I always thought that was just a poem, and here it's happening in my own life. Oh, Paolo, it's all so bloody sad."

They talked on, but she knew that it was no use. Then, as if by agreement, they rose and continued down the dark, tree-shadowed path. By the time they reached the foot of the Janiculum and came out into the vast empty square before St. Peter's, the sky was turning pink behind the great dome and the crooked, ancient skyline of Rome. There were still no taxis, but one of the old men who put out their ancient carriages to hire by tourists was grooming his horse beside a fountain. He took them back across the Tiber, the slow clip-clop of the hooves on the cobblestones the only sound in the still-sleeping streets. They passed through the silent Borghese Gardens, beneath the ancient umbrella pines, her hand resting lightly in Paolo's. It should have been the most romantic of dawns.

The carriage passed through the Pinciana gate and came to a stop before the entrance to the Palazzo Rosalba, just as the first rays of the sun were touching its dark Renaissance facade. Paolo helped her down from the carriage and kissed her lightly. He looked very tired and as emotionally worn out as she was.

"I'll never forget this night," she said.

"You'll forget."

"No. And I'm going to tell you something, Paolo. I'll never give up hope."

"If you mean between us, Julia, you must. There have been many hours, days, when I thought that it might be possible. There on the Janiculum I almost convinced myself that it was possible. I could have made love to you then. . . ."

"Yes, you could have," she said, not without some bitterness.

"Never was anything so difficult to resist, but then . . . I'll doom us both, I know, not just myself. . . ."

She felt there was something she had to say, even though she knew it would not keep them together now. Gus had left her, too, for equally "admirable" reasons, and though afterward they pretended it was not so, she had never forgiven him. She would not make that mistake twice in her life.

"Paolo, listen to me. Whatever you may say, I will not accept that we will be apart forever. You're going to have to live with that wherever you go, whatever you do."

He started to speak but she stopped his mouth with her hand. Then she turned, in tears, and ran to the door.

Julia let herself in with her key, took off her shoes and tiptoed up the stairs. A single night-light glowed beside her bed. She threw off her clothes, pulled back the heavy red satin bedspread and fell across the cool sheets. Before she could raise an arm to turn off the light a great wave of physical and emotional exhaustion swept her away into sleep.

"What did you do last night?" Victoria drew back the curtains and flooded the room with light. "Lying across the bed as naked as the day you were born!"

Julia rolled over and pulled the sheet up. "What time is it?"

"Noon. Want to go to Tivoli?"

"I don't want to go anywhere."

"Why not? It'll do you good. The night maid said she waited up till four for you. She almost woke Mother to tell her you had been raped and murdered. You'd better get out of here before the grand inquisition begins."

"Go where?"

"To Bruno's place. But you'll have to hurry. We're leaving in half an hour."

Thank God for Victoria—and distraction, the more unusual and the more intense the better.

* * *

After a hair-raising drive from Rome the three Alfa Romeos came roaring down the cypress-lined drive to the Bronzini's "place" at Tivoli, braking and sliding to a stop, one by one, in the marble chips in front of the columned entrance. The crowd of shouting, laughing young people poured down the path and out onto a great lawn. Formally planted terraces led down to a quarter-mile-long pool, and beside it, in the shade of ancient oak trees, stood a long table covered with white linen and laden with food. Waiters in jackets trimmed in gold-braid filled plates and brought them to the guests at small tables under the trees.

"Funny uniforms," Julia said, digging into a plate piled high with cold shrimp and lobster, salami and mortadella, green and black olives, mushrooms and mozzarella, and red and yellow sweet peppers.

"They're from the Chief of Air Staff's mess."

"How does Bruno rate that?"

"He builds the engines for their planes, doesn't he?"

Victoria was proud of her slack-jawed lover whose hair was as fashionably shiny as patent leather and parted down the middle. His picture was always in the society pages. Bruno's family might be arms merchants, but he himself seemed to believe in nothing but what he termed "café society."

"Merchant of death."

"That's Bruno," Victoria said, and she laughed uncertainly. "Can you imagine? Bruno Bronzini, merchant of death."

After lunch the women sunbathed beside the reflecting pool while Bruno and his male friends, in bathing trunks and striped tops, tried to start a motorboat. But something was wrong with the engine, and they fought over it like children. Like loud, vulgar children, Julia thought, sitting alone under the oak tree, puffing on a cigarette: that's what these Italian men are like. The women were all the same age, uniformly good-looking, their hair dyed blond and cut identically: country girls who had made it out of the villages all over Italy on their looks, the kind Paolo's father recruited for his movies. *Paolo*. Even thinking his name hurt, and she pushed him out of her mind.

"Who's for a sky ride with Bruno Bronzini, ace of the airways, the Milanese daredevil?"

Four men in mess jackets were pushing out from behind the trees a silver biplane with the red, white, and green bull's-eye of the Italian Air Force on its wings and tail.

"You first, Julia." Bruno, still in his wet bathing suit, had put on a leather aviator's helmet with goggles.

"You're kidding, Bruno." He had already had too much to drink, and she couldn't imagine that his invitation was anything but a joke.

"We'll be over Rome in five minutes, looking in the Pope's bedroom."

"Absolutely not!" She wouldn't have gone up in that plane with Bruno Bronzini, drunk or sober, for anything.

"Fine. But I know who will. Giovanna!" One of the blond, lithe young women came running. "Going to say hello to the Pope. Want to come?"

"Sure, Bruno, but no loop-the-loops."

"No loop-the-loops, I promise."

Bruno and Giovanna, in bathing suits and aviator's helmets, climbed into the two cockpits. One of the airmen turned over the polished wooden propeller, and the plane moved down the green swath, gathered speed, and lifted off, just clearing the trees at the end of the lawn. Bruno waved as they disappeared over the hills toward Rome.

"Aren't you afraid?" Julia asked, turning to Victoria.

"Bruno knows what he's doing," Victoria said with a shrug.

The whine of the plane's engine had barely faded away before it was replaced by the sputter of the motorboat that finally came to life in a cloud of smelly blue smoke. And then two handsome young men began racing up and down the shallow pool, the boat loaded with the look-alike young women in tank suits. The rest were dancing to jazz music blaring from the horn of a windup phonograph. It was a beautiful afternoon. Great, white fluffy clouds were piled high in the sky. The magnificent piece of Renaissance architecture that was now the Bronzini's "place" stood darkly, in the shadow of a cloud, far above the noisy vulgarity going on around the pool. Couples were being pushed into the water with screams of laughter. One of the dark young men leaped out of the pool holding aloft a woman's bathing suit. He ran along the edge, taunting the suit's owner, who came out of the water after him, the black triangle of pubic hair exposing the real woman behind the cheap dyed image. She snatched away the suit and pushed him, legs flailing, into the pool. There was a round of applause.

"Bravo," Julia said quietly to herself, stubbing out another cigarette on the ground beneath the tree.

The girl put back on her wool bathing suit with an awkward dignity. And then all eyes turned upward as the biplane came zooming in, turned a loop, and glided down as lightly as a feather onto the lawn. Giovanna stood up in the cockpit and gave the Fascist salute.

"One-two-three-four." The big black man in winged collar and black bow tie stamped his foot and music flowed out of the alcove like cool ferns and vines running along the walls and flowing over the twisting bodies in silk pajamas. Victoria's pajamas were overlarge and embroidered with the initials "B. B." over her firm, swinging breasts. Julia still sat alone, hugging her knees, wearing the same skirt and sweater that she had worn in Trastevere.

"Would you care to dance?"

"Chester! What are you doing here?"

It was the funny little man from the American Embassy who she had met her first night in Italy. He took her hand and pulled her to her feet. They danced stiffly while the insistent, sensual wail of the saxophone rose and fell.

"Well, what are you doing here, Chester? And please stop stepping on my toes."

"Sorry. The question is what are you doing here with all these Fascists?"

"Fascists? Surely not. Not Bruno." She was glad to have someone so normal and ordinary close to her.

"The big money is what got the Fascists where they are.

The Bronzini family was financing Mussolini when he was a journalist with frayed cuffs and a dirty collar."

"That's nothing to me, Chester," she said, taking him in hand and walking him around the edge of the dance floor.

"It should be. They're scum."

"Then why are you here?"

She maneuvered them away from the wriggling mass of bodies in the overheated room and out onto the cool dark terrace.

"To observe," he said, letting her go with relief. "I am an observer of the decline and fall of Mussolini's empire, the only person in the American Embassy who thinks it's coming."

"Chester, have you ever heard of a Paolo Danieli?"

"Oh, sure. He's skating on thin ice, that one."

"How so?"

"There are only about two dozen Italians right now who have the nerve to stand up to Il Duce. There might be more later, if, that is, there are others like Danieli to rally around. But knowing the Italians, there won't be."

The notes of the saxophone floated out across the lawn and down to where mist now hung over the reflecting pool.

"Julia, let me take you home. I'm leaving now. You don't want to be with this crowd."

"Thanks, Chester, but I'll stay."

Yes, she would stay. She wanted to see for herself these depraved monsters that Paolo was fighting, these phantoms that stood between her and the man she . . . loved.

"Okay. That's up to you. See you again sometime."

Chester went down the garden stairs, his footsteps crunching on the drive, and disappeared into the night.

A hand took her roughly by the arm. "I arrest you for being improperly dressed."

"Let me go," she said. What did this lout in an ill-fitting electric-blue suit think he was doing? The hand dropped from her arm.

"I think dancing in pajamas is rather stupid," she said, looking past him.

"You're American, aren't you?" he asked in heavily accented English.

"I am."

"It is America that is decadent." He moved up very close to her and grasped her arm again.

"I didn't say decadent, I said stupid. But I see you dance to an American band."

"Clowns, entertainers. We Romans have always had them. I am Farinetti."

She removed his hand and looked into the man's very ordinary face. "Is that supposed to mean something to me?"

"Head of all Fascist youth organizations in Italy."

"Good for you."

"Let's be friends. Dance with me."

She shrugged and let him take her onto the dance floor, not wanting to give him the satisfaction of knowing how frightened she was.

"You dance well for an American," he said, pressing his body against her. He smelled of cheap cologne.

"Don't hold me like that."

With an exaggerated movement he released his hold on her and held her at arm's length.

Through doors opened by servants Julia saw a long candle-lit table on which dinner was laid out.

"I think I'll get something to eat," she said, breaking away. He moved to go with her.

"Alone," she said, turning away from him. His hand gripped her arm once again and spun her around.

"All right, go." His face was close to hers. "I know who you are. But if it were not for Bronzini I would make you dance to another tune tonight."

"Oh, are you afraid of Bruno?" Her voice was trembling.

"That playboy? Ha!" Nevertheless, he let go of her arm. She walked unsteadily into the dining room. Victoria was standing by the table, eating hungrily from a heaped plate.

"Hi. Having fun, Julie?"

"Some of your Fascist friends could use a few lessons in manners." Her heart was still beating fast.

"Crude's the word," Victoria said. "Not our friends.

Bruno has to do it for business. Forgot to tell you to bring pajamas."

"It doesn't matter. I'm not much in the mood for dancing."

"Well, if you change your mind, just slip into your nightgown."

She gestured with her fork to Giovanna, the young woman who had gone up in the plane with Bruno, dancing in the other room in a nightgown so transparent that she might as well not have had anything on.

As soon as she could, Julia slipped away to her room and locked the door. Lighting a cigarette, she went out onto the balcony. I'm smoking too much, she thought. She was turning to go back into the room when she glimpsed through half-open curtains the girl who had lost her bathing suit that afternoon, naked again. She was speaking to someone. Then the man she had pushed into the pool came into view and pushed her down on the bed. He turned and closed the curtains on the image of a girl's frightened face.

I'll never come to a place like this again, Julia told herself, without an escort, someone who knows how to handle these awful people, to look after me. Yes! To look after me. Someone, after all, like Angelo.

There was such a tremendous din that night that she couldn't get to sleep until nearly dawn, and then just as she drifted off the music began again. She got up and went out onto the balcony in her nightgown. The big black man was sitting on the edge of the pool, his bare feet dangling in the water, still playing his saxophone as the sun came up over the Alban Hills. It was the second Roman dawn in a row she had seen. Couples were dancing drunkenly around the pool. The men had shed their pajama tops, the women the bottoms. Some of the blond girls had taken off everything and were splashing naked in the pool. Nobody seemed to care. Certainly not Victoria, who was among them.

Julia and Victoria arrived back at the Palazzo Rosalba late in the afternoon. There had been many calls from Angelo. The next call from him Julia took. His voice was calm and relaxed. She needed that. To imagine that she had considered *him* an impossible Italian male. How sane his voice sounded. Yes, she would see him again—after she had slept twenty-four hours.

"Whenever you wish," he said. "I'll be there."

The next evening Julia was standing at the top of the Via Veneto, her arm in Angelo Morosini's, Rome spread out before them. The last lavender glow of twilight was fading in the sky, and the streetlights had just come on.

"What shall we do?" he said.

"Nothing."

"Nothing?"

"Nothing. No drinks. No dinner. No dancing. No shows. I just want to have a quiet time. To walk, maybe."

"Where?"

"Where our feet take us."

"All right. Come on then." And they began slowly to descend the Via Veneto, arm in arm. She felt burned-out, but peaceful, almost happy. They walked in silence past sidewalk cafés and lighted windows filled with dresses and shoes and furs and antiques, her arm lightly in his.

"I've learned some lessons in the past weeks," Julia said. She owed Angelo that much.

"I learned one good lesson at the Mussolini wedding," he replied. "I'll treat you like an American woman from now on. All right?"

"It's a deal."

She wondered whether he had really learned how American women were different from Italian women or whether it was simply an act.

"What a beautiful color," she said. "Midnight blue."

They were standing in front of the Fiat showroom at the foot of the Via Veneto. A long, low sports car glowed, a deep dark blue, under a spotlight, surrounded by bouquets of cut flowers. A salesman with a red carnation in his lapel leaned out of the door.

"Come in, come in. Just the car for the beautiful signorina."

They went in.

"Brand new model. The 525SS. Curved windshield, leather fold-back top and upholstery," the salesman said, caressing the little car with his hands. "Two spare tires on the rear, wire spoke wheels. And—a real innovation—two sets of instruments on the panel. That's so the man can drive while his companion watches the speed, the fuel, all of those things for him, or vice versa, of course. A car for lovers!"

"I don't know about that," Julia said, "but I love the color. Midnight blue."

"And white leather seats," Angelo added.

"Midnight blue," the salesman said, looking at the car dubiously. "Yes, I suppose so. But the performance . . ."

Angelo squeezed her arm. "Buy it."

She felt as if a devil were tempting her. And at that moment the reflection of a tall, dark-haired man passed in the glass of the showroom window down the Via Veneto. Paolo, or her fevered imagination?

"I'll take it," Julia said.

Chapter Five

ONE MORNING IN September a whole packet of letters arrived with Julia's breakfast tray. A boat from America must have come in. There were two wedding invitations from classmates at Goucher and a letter from a third who was starting a career in New York. Julia opened her financial statement and looked at the total. There was more money than before she had bought the car. Oh, yes, interest and dividends. Wasn't that nice. You could spend and spend and never have any less. There was also a letter, addressed in pencil, from Mrs. Agostino Bramante. Why on earth would Gus's wife be writing to her? She was a quiet little Italian-American woman who Julia hadn't seen since she had gone to Gus's wedding when she was sixteen.

Gus was dead. He had known that he was dying when he had taken Julia for a farewell luncheon at the Lord Baltimore, the letter said, but he had not wanted her to know. In the days before he died Gus talked about his mother and he took consolation (the word was spelled wrong) in the fact that Julia would meet her, if she hadn't already. Julia sat motionless with the letter in her hand. In front of her eyes she saw an eleven-year-old girl standing in a doorway; she saw the bewildered look on Gus's face turn to pain as she told him that Claudia was dead. She had adored Gus then—and now? What she was feeling was guilt, and it was very unpleasant.

She got out of bed, lit a cigarette, and began rummaging through dresser drawers. Finally she found the business card that Gus had given her during their last meeting. On the back was written simply "Castel del Monte." When

Gina came for the breakfast tray, Julia asked her if she knew where Castel del Monte was. No, she didn't. "Please, could you find out," Julia asked, "because I'm driving there today."

The maid came back in a few minutes. The chauffeur knew where the village was, high on the Gran Sasso, the highest mountain in central Italy. It was wild, the road was very bad, a woman could not go there alone. He had to drive for the signora today, but if the signorina could wait until the weekend he would drive her there. No, she couldn't wait. This terrible feeling of having betrayed Gus couldn't be endured until the weekend. She wanted to be able to write to Gus's widow right away to tell her that she had done her duty.

Julia picked up the phone and was about to give the operator Angelo's number. But then she hung up the receiver. That wouldn't do. There were certain things that Angelo didn't need to know. The thought of Count Morosini driving her to some remote village to meet Gus's old mother was ludicrous. How could she explain what Gus had meant to her? However, Paolo would have understood.

Paolo. Why not? She had had too much pride to try to see him again after that wonderful, awful night and he had certainly made no effort to get in touch with her. He felt it was finished between them, that was clear. But they were both adults, after all. Why shouldn't she ask him to take her to Castel del Monte? It would have been easier, of course, if her last words to him had not been that she would never give up hope. . . .

A few hours later Julia was sitting on a terrace beneath oaks and chestnuts, their leaves already touched by the first faint yellows and reds. A chill wind blew through the mountain pass. The waiter put a cup of black Italian coffee down on the marble table, a pitcher of warm milk, a bowl of sugar. She spooned sugar into the cup, stirred it. Below, Rome was no more than a few tiny, faraway domes rising from the sunlit plain. She slowly turned her head and looked into Paolo Danieli's eyes.

"It's chilly."

"*Si, fa freddo,*" he said, echoing in Italian her first tentative words. On the way up into the mountains she had driven with the top down, making it almost impossible to talk. She hadn't known what to say, anyway. Constantly watching the narrow road, so steep and winding and full of bumps that she was afraid her shiny new car would be shaken to pieces, Julia had only been able to steal an occasional glance at Paolo. Now she was trapped. The radiator had boiled over and they were obliged to stop to let the engine cool off.

"Italians always seem to put a place to eat and drink at every point in the road where there is a beautiful view."

"Clever Italians," he said.

"You've turned all brown," she said. Months since she had seen him, and then, just by picking up the phone, they were together again, high in the Abruzzi mountains, as if by magic. The sight of him was like clear, cold springwater brought to someone dying of thirst: dark long hair, dark eyes, harder and leaner looking, and very brown, with only the fine white line of a scar beneath one eye.

"I worked all of August on a farm, cutting hay."

"But why?"

"I was out of money."

"Surely that's not a very good way to make money." She sounded so stilted to herself.

He raised his open hands in the Italian gesture that means one does what one must, adding: "And to take my mind off things."

Off things, or off her?

"And you?"

"Oh, I've been awfully busy." Yes, she had been awfully busy. With Angelo. Shopping, restaurants, tea dances, concerts, the races, museums, nightclubs. An occasional visit to Francesca's studio, alone. The summer was a blur. Somehow, through it, she had kept Angelo's fondling and kissing down to a level she could control. But she thought of his hands on her bare breasts with distaste, remembering the night when she had bared her breasts for that touch of other hands that had never come.

"What are you thinking?"

"I . . . I was thinking that it's pretty nervy of me to ask you to come with me today, after all this time. . . ."

"I don't have anything better to do." White teeth shone in his sunburned face. "The hay's all in."

"Oh, Paolo. But what about your painting?" Careful, she thought. You're just going to get hurt again. She sipped the coffee, which was already growing cold. A yellow leaf fell on the table between them. He shrugged.

"Tell me again," he said, "who is it we're going to see? The mother of?. . ."

"The man my mother lived with, Agostino Bramante. I called him—everyone called him—Gus. You see my father, my real father, ran away to Mexico and died there. He was never anything to me but . . ."

"But the fortune he left you."

"Yes."

"And Gus was like a father to you." Paolo was looking intently at her.

"How did you know?"

"Francesca has told me a few things."

"She tells you everything?"

"We are very close."

"Oh. Yes, my mother and I lived with him in a loft on the Baltimore waterfront—he restored paintings and furniture and porcelain. Those were the happiest years of my life. When my mother died, he thought it would be better if I was brought up by my Aunt Agnes. And then . . ."

"Yes?" He leaned forward toward her. A gust of wind blew across the terrace, and she pulled the tweed jacket draped over her shoulders close around her.

"People grow apart. You know how things are . . . and then Gus and my Aunt Agnes. . . ."

"So why are you in such a hurry to see his mother today?"

"I had a letter from Baltimore this morning reminding

me that I had promised to." She wasn't going to tell Paolo that Gus was dead.

They both looked out to the plains and Rome below, thinking their separate thoughts. She had begun to tell Paolo the truth about herself, as she would have to the man she would hope to spend the rest of her life with, and there was no point in going on.

"There's a waterfall near here. Would you like to see it before we leave?"

"Yes. Yes I would."

On the way back from the waterfall, through the autumn woods, their hands touched, awkwardly. They held each other's hands for a few moments, and then, just as awkwardly, let go.

Beyond Aquila the pavement ran out, and they met no more cars on the rough track, only men on foot and donkeys. When they reached the rocky crag on which Castel del Monte perched, they had to leave the car and walk the last mile. Julia was shocked. Most Italian villages were pleasant and cheerful. Castel del Monte, in the shadow of the ruined medieval castle that gave it its name, was not only desperately poor, it was a village that had given up hope. The narrow streets were filthy, the houses crumbling, many of them abandoned. The only paint the village had seen in years was a slogan in huge black letters on the side of a café in the little square: *"IL DUCE HA SEMPRE RAGIONE"*: Mussolini is always right. The only food in the tiny market was potatoes and onions and a piece of meat that looked as if it was days old.

"Goat," Paolo said. "Too bad they can't eat Fascist slogans. That's all they get from Rome. Let's find out where the Bramante house is."

The house stood at the top of the village, at the end of a narrow lane that was more steps than street. All the houses were of rough fieldstone, once whitewashed, dilapidated now.

"It should be somewhere around here," Julia said, suddenly wishing very much that they had not come. Then she spotted a number on the house.

The doors and windows of the little house were dark, gaping holes. They walked through the courtyard overgrown with weeds into a single empty room. Even the window frames had been ripped out, and the cold wind gusted in from across the valley, where the bare high mountains stood in silent beauty.

"Signor, are you looking for someone?"

They turned around. A little old toothless man, in a cloth cap, was standing in the empty doorway.

"Signora Bramante?"

"Dead."

"Dead? What happened?"

"Old. Very old. Very sick. She die."

"When?"

"Last month. Now they take all the wood from her house for firewood. Winter coming again."

The old man shuffled away, shaking his head. She and Paolo went further into the empty room. Whatever furniture there might have been had been taken away, too. But hanging over the blackened fireplace was a hand-tinted photograph in an oval frame of a handsome man with a mustache.

"That would be Gus, of course," Paolo said.

"Yes." The strangest feeling came over her. The photograph was certainly of Gus, but there was something she had never seen before in the eyes that stared out at her from the wall. She felt as if she had never really looked at Gus. Something was stirring in the back of her mind, some dim memory from early childhood . . .

"There are some letters here."

"Letters? Where?"

Paolo held out a bundle of yellowed envelopes tied with string. She reached out and took the packet with trembling hands. Why was Paolo looking at her in such a strange way?

"They were in a pile of trash in the corner."

The letter on top was addressed in Gus's hand. She broke

the string and opened the thickest envelope. A photograph fell out. The photograph was of her mother, Claudia, beautiful and smiling, and herself, a skinny, unsmiling girl—taken at Rehoboth Beach. How was it possible?

And then it came back to her in a flash. There had been a photographer on the beach. He had taken their picture and given them a ticket. An hour later her mother had drowned. What a shock it must have been for Gus when the picture came in the mail from the photographer's shop. And, dear Gus, he had kept it from her. She took the letter out of the envelope, fascinated, fearful. It was written in Italian. She handed it to Paolo.

"Could you tell me what it says?"

Paolo took a long time to read the letter, which was seven or eight pages. Then he looked up at Julia and said nothing.

"Well?"

"Well, it tells about Claudia's death. He calls her his 'wife' and 'a good Catholic.' Was she Catholic?"

"No. Does he say anything about me?"

"Yes. Do you want to hear it?"

"Yes." She was trembling all over now.

Paolo leafed through the letter. "It says, 'Every child needs a mother, and so, Mother, I have sent our daughter to live with her aunt, who is a very rich lady who will give her every advantage. That way she will grow up an American, but since I named her Julia after you, she will always remember that she is also Italian.' " Paolo looked up from the letter. "He spells Julia the Italian way, G-I-U-L-I-A."

"I don't feel well." She got up and bolted through the door. When Paolo came out to her in the courtyard, where dead weeds rattled in the wind, the feeling that she was going to throw up had passed.

"Are you all right?"

"Yes. But let's go."

They walked down to the car in silence, and Paolo drove back to Aquila. She was too upset to drive.

It was market day in Aquila, and the central piazza was filled with stalls and tents. Big rough-faced farmers with the complexions of heavy wine-drinkers stood behind mounds of fall vegetables, red and green and purple globes glistening in the September sun. Mountain women sold homemade quilts and handmade chairs. There were bins of walnuts and hazelnuts and chestnuts. Julia and Paolo walked across the crowded piazza, making their way past the roasting chestnuts, the stalls of local cheeses and farm sausages, to a shadowed arcade almost too elegant and citylike for a mountain town.

The more prosperous farmers were packed into a bar at the corner of the piazza, talking and gesturing and drinking wine. Julia and Paolo sat down outside under the arcade, at a round marble table still in the sun. She ordered a double shot of the local brandy, and downed it in two gulps.

"I needed that," she said.

Paolo said nothing. He was looking beyond her, somewhere into space, into time. Then his eyes focused on her.

"It's too bad you didn't come to visit your grandmother earlier. You might have been able to help." His face was hard, as it had been that night at Sabatini's when she had casually mentioned having met Mussolini. "Didn't you understand the letter I read you? All you have to do is look at Gus Bramante's picture."

"I don't understand."

"Have you ever looked in a mirror? You aren't Julia Howard, the heiress, you are Giulia Bramante, the daughter of an Italian immigrant."

The tears she had been holding back began to run down her face.

"What's wrong? Are you ashamed to be that old Italian peasant woman's granddaughter?"

"It's not that at all."

"If you weren't, you would have gone to see her when you first came to Italy, and then she might not have . . ."

"Shut up!" She leaped to her feet. "Just because your precious Bianca . . ."

"What do you know about Bianca?" Now he was on his feet, too. "Yes, she died . . . but *I* tried."

"Well, Paolo," Julia said, wiping away her tears, now

strangely calm, "once again you have been completely honest. And you couldn't possibly have hurt me more, if that gives you any satisfaction. When we get back to Rome," she said, trying to keep her voice cold and steady, "I suggest we never see each other again."

"I'll make it easier," he said, his voice trembling. "I'm taking the bus back to Rome."

Paolo turned and walked away down the long arcade, his hands in his pockets and his dark head lowered. When she was sure he could not look back and see her, Julia put her head down on the cold marble table and cried silently.

She felt a hand on her shoulder and looked up. It was the waiter, a middle-aged man with a pencil-line mustache and sad eyes with bags under them.

"*L'amore,*" he said. "It's never easy."

"It is not a question of love," Julia said in her best Italian. "Bring me another double brandy."

In a little while the afternoon light was golden on the stone facades around the piazza. The farmers began taking down their stalls. The smell of hot olive oil and garlic filled the air. The brandies had gone to her head, and she realized that she hadn't had anything to eat all day except a roll for breakfast. She crossed the piazza in the lengthening shadows. The smell of cooking came from where a farmer was frying country bread in olive oil. She asked if she could buy some. The farmer picked up two pieces of fried bread and handed them to her in a scrap of newspaper.

"For you, *bella signorina*, it's free."

When she got back to Rome there was a message from Angelo on her night table. Was she free for lunch on Saturday?

"It's against the rules," Julia said, arching her body against his dinner jacket and kissing him hungrily all the same. A bell was ringing in the distance.

"Closing time," he said, and then, looking at his wristwatch, "Midnight."

"Let's hide," she said.

"No, let's move on. The rain is over."

"Go where?"

"Where do you want to go?"

He kissed her on the neck, bit her lightly. It had been a good evening. They had gone to the best supper club in Rome, dressed to the teeth; then Angelo had had the idea of going to the museum on the Capitolino, which was open late at night once a week. They had had to run from the car in a sudden rainstorm so heavy that no one else had come out in it, and they were alone in the vast, dimly lit palace full of ancient marble statues and long rooms packed with Greek vases in dusty glass cases. They hadn't looked at a thing. Every time they were out of sight of a guard they slipped into the shadows and embraced until they were frantic, their senses heightened by the flashing lightning and peals of thunder that shook the tall windows.

She held him at arm's length and said, "Well, let's see, Morosini. Why don't we go home?"

"Whose home?"

"My home."

"Don't want to see Charles and Agnes."

"They're in Florence."

"Don't want to see Victoria, either."

"She's in Tivoli."

"All right, then."

There was a fire in the library and the usual hothouse roses on the refectory table. The cardinals and bishops, or whoever they were, looked down benignly from the walls. Angelo went over to the sideboard and poured two snifters of Charles's oldest cognac. He handed one to her, and she sank down on the overstuffed sofa. He stood with his back to the fire, and they regarded each other silently.

Julia's invitation to Angelo to come to the Palazzo Rosalba that evening had not been as spontaneous as he might imagine. They had been lovers for three months, and he was beginning to take her availability for granted. She had decided that the time had come to bring matters between them to a head, and all that she had been waiting for was an evening when both Charles and Agnes—and Victoria—were away.

Her affair with Angelo had begun the day after the disastrous trip to Castel del Monte. She had accepted his invitation to lunch that she found on her return to Rome, as well as his suggestion that they go somewhere special. It was a perfect September day, and they drove in her little car, with the top down, north along the Via Salaria. They had no particular destination in mind, but followed the Tiber as it wound through the countryside. All she required, she told Angelo, was the perfect spot, and they found it: a little inn with flower boxes in the windows and a terrace near the river shaded by an old willow tree. They laughed a lot as they lunched alone on the terrace, and what a pleasure it was to be in the company of a man who was steady and sane. Even Angelo's predictability was comforting.

As they lingered over coffee, Angelo playfully said that it would be a shame to leave such a beautiful spot, and they really ought to take a room at the inn for the afternoon. He often said things like that, and she responded as she usually did by laughing and saying nothing. And then she thought, why not? What am I waiting for? Why should I deny myself any longer? When she finally said yes, he had no idea what she was saying yes to; and when she explained, at first he thought she was teasing him.

Even that first time she liked sex. She liked it from the moment she began removing her clothes in front of him until they were lying on the bed, fully satisfied, holding hands. Her response was so immediate, so eager and uninhibited, that he would not have thought her a virgin until it was no longer possible to conceal the fact. He was, of course, delighted, but Julia would have preferred not to have given his male Italian ego that gratification.

They went back to that little inn and to that room many times. It was a kind of ritual. They made love there, and only there, always in the daytime and when the weather was good, with the windows open to the sky. Julia wanted it that way. The sameness added an element of stability that she very much needed. The only thing that changed was that with experience the pleasure that she got from sex grew, until sometimes it was almost overwhelming. But at the same time she realized that her affair with Angelo was leading nowhere, that the pleasure she now enjoyed was an opiate that dulled her sense of the aimlessness of her life.

Julia took a sip of cognac, put the glass on an end table and beckoned Angelo to the sofa. She gave him a long, hard, and openmouthed kiss, and then lay back passively on the cushions and let his hands and mouth do anything he wished.

"I can't take much more of this, Julia."

"There are ways of getting relief."

He looked down at her, the firelight twinkling in his eyes.

"Do you mean that?"

"Most men don't have to be asked twice."

"What about the servants?"

"I don't give a bloody damn about the servants."

She led him up the marble stairs to her bedroom, pulled the covers off her bed onto the floor, and walked over to her dresser. She turned on the two lamps. and the room came alive with the soft glow of mirrors. She took off her bracelets and strand of pearls and dropped them on the dresser.

"Unbutton me."

While he unbuttoned the back of her green silk evening dress, she took another sip of cognac. Then she slipped the gown off her shoulders. She was wearing nothing underneath but the sheerest of Italian brassieres and step-ins. She unsnapped the brassiere and let the step-ins drop around her ankles. He was looking over her shoulder at her body in the mirror.

"You're so beautiful," he said.

Before he could do or say anything else she walked over to the bed and threw herself across it. She watched him undress and studied both their bodies in the mirrors around the room. He was beautiful, too. He reached for the lamp.

"I don't want the lights off."

He went over to the bed and sat down next to her.

"Julia, I . . ."

"And I don't want to talk. I want to make love."

She had never been so cold-blooded with him, and she found it excited her sexually, as it did to watch what they were doing in the mirrors. When she couldn't stand it any longer she pulled him down on top of her.

"Now."

He tried to speak.

"Quiet," she said through clenched teeth. When he was inside of her, she made him be still. Then she made him move very slowly, holding him back mercilessly until there was no holding back the eager rhythm of her own hips.

"Come," she whispered. She was not asking. She was giving a command as if he were one of her horses at Branwood, and her legs were locked as tightly around Angelo as if she were taking a fence. Coming down to earth together, she left him wet and limp on the bed and herself, despite the completeness of her release, strangely unsatisfied. After a while she thought he might be asleep, and she got up, took another swallow of cognac from the glass on the dresser, and lit a cigarette. She saw him in the mirror raise himself on one elbow.

"I will never let you go," he said in a husky voice. It was the first thing Angelo Morosini had ever said that she was sure he actually meant. She felt as triumphant as the golden Venus reclining atop the largest mirror.

Chapter Six

LATE IN THE spring of 1931, Julia Howard signed the marriage register in the little church of San Carlino at the Four Fountains, as Contessa Giulia Morosini. The small church barely held the wedding party, which, at Julia's insistence, had included Francesca and James. Charles and Agnes were in fine form, and afterward there was a reception at the Palazzo Rosalba to celebrate the second marriage in the family within six months. Shortly before Christmas, Victoria had married Bruno Bronzini, now head of Bronzini Industries, and a changed man as a result of his new responsibilities.

There had been no more wild parties after one September afternoon when Bruno's elder brother had taken the biplane up and it had stalled as he went into a loop, then crashed in flames in the pine grove at the end of the lawn. The reputation of the girl who died with him was such that her name did not appear in the papers. Bruno took to parting his hair on the side, and his picture no longer appeared in the scandal sheets. But an Italian son-in-law? Aunt Agnes had put it to Charles: Why not? After all, there were a lot of voters of Italian extraction in Maryland. That having been accepted, Julia's marrying Angelo was a minor matter. Aunt Agnes even offered them a honeymoon trip. Julia said no, Angelo was arranging a surprise; and Bruno was providing a company plane to take them wherever they were going. The next morning Angelo carried her from the dock at Ostia into a silver-and-blue seaplane that skittered along the water, rose into the air, and headed south.

* * *

"Will you be sad to leave?"

She opened her eyes. She had almost drifted off to sleep to the sound of the cicadas in the olive trees.

"You know I will."

"It was a good choice, then?" Angelo had asked her that many times and still took a childish delight in hearing her say that it was so. As he sat up in the canvas chair, the light through the vine leaves played over the hairs on his chest. He was wearing only sandals and an old pair of white duck trousers cut off at the knees. Julia wore nothing but a transparent shift meant to be slipped over a bathing suit on the beach, but she had no bathing suit underneath.

"I would like to come back some day," she said.

"We can stay longer, if you like."

"No, it has to come to an end sometime. Already it's becoming unreal."

"In what way?"

"I've never been alone for so long in my life."

"You're not alone."

"All right then, I've never been alone with a man for so long."

"Sure?"

"You know everything there is to know about me, Angelo. Besides, if we stay here any longer they will think in Rome that you brought back a bride from North Africa." She let her brown arm dangle over the side of the chair until her hand found the bowl of water on the ground between them. She brought up a pair of cherries, bit them off the stems, sucked on the pits, and spit them into the dust. "I already look like a Sicilian peasant."

"You're too beautiful to be Sicilian, but with that tan you do look almost Italian."

She looked down at her body. She did tan beautifully.

"Are you sure there wasn't an Italian in the bushes?"

"Oh, who knows?" She glanced over at him. "I suppose I could have worn some clothes, but I like it like this."

"You're a sensualist, Julia."

She smiled and shrugged and ate some more cherries. "Get me some wine."

When he had gone to the house, she stood and stretched. Thank God she had had the good sense to get some advice from Francesca and Victoria on what Italian men expected. Actually, it wasn't all that difficult. When he came back with glasses and a pitcher of wine she kissed him and let him run his hands over her sun-warmed body. Then she took a glass of the harsh local red wine and walked to the end of the grape arbor. Some evenings they brought out the old brass telescope they had found in the house and looked at the moon and the lights, far below, of Agrigento. Once they had driven down, on a night of full moon, to wander among the ancient Greek temples. Everything was so romantic. It would have been the most perfect of honeymoons . . . if she had been in love with Angelo.

Now the temples of Agrigento were lost in the midafternoon haze. Beyond, the Mediterranean was as smooth as a blue skin stretched over the earth. She walked to the other side of the little porch and put her glass down on the railing. The spur of the mountain on which the house was built was like the prow of a ship jutting into space. Below, on one side was the sea, and on the other the heat-blasted plain of Sicily, where the wheat had already been harvested and dust devils played across the empty brown fields. On the mountain above the main house, the "palace", seemed to sleep in the shimmering heat waves, a great crumbling pile of masonry with all of its shutters tightly closed.

The estate belonged to some distant cousins of Angelo's who never visited it from year to year, but the small eighteenth-century guest house on the promontory, surrounded by olive trees, was kept open. Angelo remembered it from his childhood and had wanted to bring his bride there. Odd to think of herself as "the bride." She would go back the young wife, one day she would be the middle-aged wife . . . then, the old wife of Angelo Morosini. She realized, in a rush of panic, that the door through which she had passed of her own free will was sealed forever behind her.

Angelo came up behind her and put his arms around her,

one hand cupping a breast, the other over her dark mound of pubic hair.

"I can't get enough of you."

She twisted around. "Do you want to?" She looked him in the eyes. In her bare feet she was still slightly taller than Angelo. The immediacy of her response still seemed to shock him. "But I want a shower first," she said. "Go see if there is any mail."

The bathroom was like the rest of the house, with high ceilings, heavy peasant furniture, whitewashed walls and cool tile floors. There was a giant bathtub on clawed feet over which someone in recent years had rigged a shower. They had made love under the shower once, but where hadn't they made love? That was almost all they had done except sleep and eat and walk in the gardens. She had brought two thick books but had not made it halfway through the first. She had not seen a newspaper in weeks. There were times, she had told herself, when your mind should be blank. She walked into the bedroom dripping wet, her hair plastered to her head. The shutters were closed and Angelo was lying on the bed. She stretched out on the bed and then rolled on top of him.

"You're wet."

"That's right and I'm going to get you wet."

They wrestled silently until he was on top of her and they were moving together. They both came almost instantly, the tight knot inside her suddenly slipping loose, letting those delicious, impersonal shudders run all down through her body.

"Julia, you're crying."

"Don't be silly. Why should I cry?"

Why, indeed? Except that it was not Paolo Danieli who had made love to her . . . and it never would be.

She got up and dried her hair in front of the mirror.

"You're beautiful, Julia," Angelo said from the bed.

She kept combing her hair.

"You like it, don't you?"

"What?"

"You know."

"I adore it." That much was certainly true.

"Scandalous."

She looked at him in the mirror. He was propped up against the pillows. "Aren't Italian women supposed to enjoy it?"

"In Sicily I hear they beat them if they do," he said.

"Well, each to his own. Was there any mail?"

"It's on the table in the other room. You have several letters."

She went over to the armoire and took out a light robe. Of the twenty outfits that she had brought with her she had worn only three or four. She threw open the shutters. The sun was disappearing into the sea.

The first envelope she opened was an invitation to the American ambassador's Fourth of July reception in Rome.

"What day is it, Angelo?"

"The sixth, I think."

"This was sent two weeks ago."

"This is Sicily."

"This is Italy, *Fascist* Italy."

"Write a letter to Mussolini."

"I will. And I'll tell him the trains don't run on time, either, no matter what they say."

Angelo laughed. "You can't do that now. You are the wife of a government official, a minor official—for now. One who has only a tiny bachelor's flat to offer his new bride."

"I'll manage."

"Rome is not an easy city to live in, you know."

"It belongs to me."

"What do you mean by that?"

It was dark outside, and the cicadas' din had finally stopped. A moth flew in the open window and beat itself against the chimney of an oil lamp.

"The first day I saw Rome I made a vow to make it mine."

"Good luck."

"That's what Victoria said—'*Buona fortuna.*' But I'm going to do it."

"Several emperors have said they were going to make Rome theirs. A couple of them managed it, but nobody holds Rome for long. Even the popes lost it year before last."

"Julia Morosini isn't going to sign any Lateran Treaty with Mussolini."

Angelo put down his magazine. "You're amazing. And you're going to do all this from my tiny flat."

"That's right."

The second letter was from Victoria, from Milan where she and Bruno had gone to live now that he was head of Bronzini Industries. It was a letter full of gossip and slander. She threw it, with a laugh, to Angelo to read. The third envelope was addressed in pencil. Gus's widow was answering the brief note Julia had written after that dreadful trip to Castel del Monte that had cost her Paolo. She had written to discharge her duty and was grateful that there had been no reply. Now why was she writing? Because Gus's soul would rest easy now that he knew that his darling Julia had seen his dear mother before she died. Julia winced at reading the lie she had told. She hoped there would be no more letters from Gus's widow. All she asked now was to be left alone.

"Is something wrong?" Angelo asked.

"No," she said, putting the letter into the pocket of her robe. "It's only some tedious business from Baltimore."

They returned to Rome a few days later. Julia was not pregnant as Angelo had hoped. That fall and winter she began the process of making Rome hers, as she had sworn she would. She had learned a great deal in the eighteen months since she had stepped off the *Velonia* an American innocent. By the time that she had decided to marry Angelo Morosini she had a pretty good idea of what she was getting into. Later, she would wonder how she had closed her mind for so many months to what was going on in the world and inside herself.

In the autumn of 1931, however, Julia thought only of making a success of what she had committed herself to that stormy night she had agreed to marry Angelo Morosini in her mirrored bedroom on Via Pinciana. Once the decision had been made, her course was set.

As soon as they returned to Rome, Julia dressed her tanned body in the best clothes that money could buy—her money, after mild protests from Angelo. Her fittings at the *botteghe* of the top dress designers in Rome were sandwiched in between Italian lessons and riding on the grounds of the Villa Borghese. It was there that the young hard-eyed wives and mistresses of the rich and the powerful first took note of Contessa Giulia Morosini, as their boots and the knees of their canary-colored breeches rubbed together while their horses pawed the earth, breathing steam in the morning mist, waiting to take the jumps. Julia's skill as a horsewoman only confirmed what they had begun to say: Morosini's American bride has style. Those who had slept with Angelo said with harsh laughs that he'd obviously married her for her money. Those who hadn't, smiled and said that that was just sour grapes.

If Julia's days were full, her nights were continuous movement. There was no question of staying home. Angelo's apartment was even smaller than she had imagined, and the only time Julia and Angelo were alone together was on the wide bed they had bought and crammed into the tiny bedroom. And then they were either making love, or falling into an exhausted sleep from the constant social activity. The days were becoming a blur, and she noticed pale blue circles under her eyes when she made up in the evening.

Some evenings Angelo did not get home from the ministry until after nine, and on one such evening in early December Julia had had a couple of scotches out of boredom by the time he arrived. They ate alone that night, smoked salmon canapés and scotch in the Excelsior bar; and although they were alone together they hardly spoke. Later they went dancing on the roof of the Eden and she found herself dancing with men she only vaguely knew. At a break in the music, after a very fast set, she went to the bar, damp with perspiration, and ordered a scotch. A crowd came in, making a lot of noise. Then the lights went down and the musicians returned and played something with a very slow beat; the liquid notes of a saxophone floated out across the floor. She had no idea where Angelo was. Someone asked her to dance and she didn't even bother to look up and see who it was.

"Now you're stepping on *my* feet, Julia."

"Huh?"

"Remember me?"

She looked at the man she was dancing with. It was Chester what's-his-name.

"Why Chester, I thought you were . . . what are you doing here?"

"That's what you said last time, remember?"

"Still observing?"

"No. Just getting drunk. I've been fired. No need to observe anymore. I'm being sent to Iceland."

"To Iceland? Do we have an embassy there?"

"Apparently. That's what my orders say."

"What happened?"

"Your Uncle Charles did me in."

"I'm not surprised. He's a shit. But why?"

"He said I'd been meeting with members of the underground opposition to Mussolini."

"True, of course."

"Of course. As I told the ambassador, I thought my job was to find out what's going on in Italy. But Charles scared the old man. His Fascist buddies had him pass the word that if they didn't get me out of here, the embassy was going to have a lot of trouble. Charles said I was sending biased reports back to Washington. Biased! Can you imagine that? I expect to see Charles come to work any day now wearing a black shirt."

"I'm sorry, Chester."

"It's okay. Let's talk about you. I see your picture in the papers all the time."

"We go out a lot."

"Are you happy with Angelo Morosini?"

"Why, Chester, what a thing to ask."

"Well, are you?"

"Look . . . there's Bruno."

"Yes, and look who's with him, Mussolini's rotten son-in-law."

Bruno and Galeazzo Ciano stood in the doorway in evening dress, looking very much like two bachelors out on the town. Chester moved her firmly in the other direction.

"I like you, Julia, and I'm just drunk enough to give you some advice."

"What's that?"

"I'd slow down if I were you."

She laughed. "We have to go out every evening until we find an apartment big enough to sit home in."

"Well, I'm not trying to be . . ."

Julia was taken out of Chester's arms. Ciano had found her. As they danced away Chester called, "Come visit me in Reykjavik sometime, Countess."

"You should be more careful with whom you dance."

"Sometimes I think so, too. In any case he's leaving, as you know."

"Is he? Too bad." Ciano's dark eyes never left Julia's face. He smelled of cigar smoke. "You look more beautiful every time I see you. What's your secret?"

"Being happily married."

"Ah, so the dew is still on the rose." Ciano laughed. "Well, remember, my little place in Viterbo is really beautiful in the fall. I keep hoping you will come see it."

"Sorry, Galeazzo, my weekends are fully booked until Christmas."

"Still, one mustn't give up hope. The offer stands."

"No thanks."

"You're not offended?"

She looked down at his hard, smiling face. "Why should I be offended? Now if you will excuse me, I want to have a word with Bruno."

She left Ciano standing in the middle of the dance floor. She had had far too much to drink, and she wasn't sure she could control her temper much longer. She went up to Bruno, who was talking to two women.

"I want to dance, Bruno."

"My charming cousin, it would be a pleasure." He moved her smoothly back onto the dance floor.

"You're looking particularly beautiful tonight, Julia."

"Thank you. Bruno, what am I going to do with Count Ciano?"

"He's quite an admirer of yours."

"That's what I mean. He has been making propositions ever since Angelo and I got back from Sicily. Tonight I almost slapped his face."

"I wouldn't do that."

"I know. But what am I going to do?"

"The difficulty is that Galeazzo has always thought himself irresistible to women, and now that he is Il Duce's son-in-law he finds it strange that you do not throw your body at his feet."

"He handles me like a piece of merchandise. What makes him think a newly married woman is going to throw herself at him?"

"In the set you move in such things are not unknown."

"I am the wife of someone who is supposed to be his friend. I can't talk to Angelo about him because of that. I find Ciano repulsive."

"He is rather."

"Then why are you out with him tonight?"

"Business is business. I must think first about the stockholders of Bronzini Industries, of which I am the largest."

Julia smiled and put her head on Bruno's shoulder. "It's nice to be able to talk to you. You're not a bad sort, you know. I can get a straight answer out of you, Bruno, and that's more than I can say for most Italians."

"Ah, cousin, an Italian never exposes the truth in front of a stranger. The only way you can get what you call a 'straight answer' is to marry into the family."

"How is Victoria? Why isn't she here?"

"I couldn't get her to leave Milano. We've bought a new house, and it's full of decorators and painters. She is becoming quite domestic, if you can believe that."

"Maybe that's what I should do. I feel as if it's been one

long party since we got back from Sicily. But I wanted to make a mark on this town."

The music stopped and she sat down at an empty table with Bruno. Across the darkened room Angelo was laughing at something a tall aristocratic blonde was saying.

"I think, Julia, you've already made your mark. People say you can do anything."

"Except get rid of Count Ciano."

"Ah, I was coming to that. Within every problem is the seed of its solution."

"Yes?"

"Well, it seems that Galeazzo's chasing after women is very annoying to Edda. She's complained to Papa. Now Il Duce is annoyed because Edda won't stop whining, so he's going to get rid of them both."

"What do you mean?"

"Count Galeazzo Ciano is being sent as Italian Consul to Shanghai, China."

Julia laughed out loud. "Get me a drink, Bruno. That calls for a celebration."

"Anything else I can do for you?"

"Yes. Help me find a large, comfortable apartment."

"The easiest thing in the world. I'll have my agent call you in the morning."

"Bruno, you're a darling," and she kissed him. "No wonder Victoria married you."

"Well, that's that," Julia said. "My dowry." She and Angelo had just come out of the lawyer's office in the Via Condotti. It was one of those warm winter days for which Rome is famous. The late morning sun was like golden honey poured over the rooftops of Rome, and before they reached the Piazza di Spagna Julia had to take off her new coat with the fox collar. They sat down at an outside table across from the Spanish Steps and ordered an *aperitivo*. Julia stretched in the sun, closed her eyes and listened to the splashing of the fountains. What a perfect day, and what a good decision. She reached into her handbag and took out the big brass key to their new apartment, her new apartment, and put it on the table.

"Happy?" Angelo asked.

"Yes."

"Well, now that you've made Rome yours, what worlds are left to conquer?"

She looked at Angelo through half-closed eyes. "I want to be crowned empress in St. Peter's."

He laughed. "And I think you would be, if you decided on it."

"But for now I'll settle for the Via Giulia."

She had chosen the street at first because of its name, but found it to be the most charming in Rome and also, she was told, the most fashionable. Its elegant sixteenth-century houses ran in a straight line from the Palazzo Farnese to the Tiber. The amount of the check she had just signed had taken her breath away for a moment, but there was still plenty more where that came from. Elmer J. Thornley had taken her funds out of the stock market just before the '29 crash, and he still seemed to know how to make the shrewd investments that kept her money growing faster than she could spend it.

Out of nowhere, a small plane came roaring over the rooftops. It seemed almost to climb up the Spanish Steps in front of them, the sun flashing from the pilot's goggles. Pieces of white paper floated down.

"My God, he nearly took the roof off that church!" she cried, sitting up straight. "Why do they allow such crazy advertising stunts."

One of the pieces of white paper landed at their feet. Angelo picked it up.

"It's no advertising stunt."

"What is it?"

"It says 'Death to the Fascist tyrant Mussolini. Romans arise and free yourselves. First Rome and then all Italy. The great Resistance struggle has begun. Down with Fascism. Long live the Italian people.' "

Angelo laughed and put the leaflet in his pocket. "I

would hate to be the head of the air force tonight. Il Duce will eat him for supper."

"Is it serious?"

The plane made another pass over the rooftops and more leaflets sprinkled down.

"This is really funny," Angelo said.

"Whose side are you on?"

"Mine."

"I'll bet you don't tell Ciano you think it's funny."

"Oh, he'll get a big laugh out of it. He's very angry at Mussolini at the moment for ordering him to China."

Perhaps, Julia thought, but she had noticed that Angelo never made fun of fascism except when he was sure of his company. And he carried a Fascist Party card.

The plane made a third pass, and that time there was an Italian air force plane close behind it. Angelo put out his cigarette.

"Let's get out of here before one or the other of those idiots comes crashing down on our heads."

The next morning the papers trumpeted that the traitor had been shot down in flames. But when they discussed it, after Angelo came home from the ministry, he just laughed. The plane had completely evaded a whole squadron of Bronzini's best, but by nightfall it had gotten lost over the Mediterranean, run out of fuel, and crashed on Sardinia. The pilot, who had been killed, was some idealistic kid who apparently had never been in a plane in his life until two weeks before. So much for Il Duce's air force. The pilot's name was in the papers the following morning. Julia could see his face quite clearly. Yes, he was an idealistic kid, quite probably the most idealistic of the group of Paolo Danieli's friends that she had met at Francesca's. It seemed a long time ago.

By the new year, the Morosinis had already moved beyond the fashionable set they had partied with that fall. The invitation cards fell on the table in the entryway of their apartment like snowflakes, gilded with coats of arms, embassy seals, and the crossed keys of the Vatican. Julia had attracted the attention of the real leaders of society. She had worked hard for that. She had decorated the new apartment with Morosini family heirlooms and the best modern pieces. She paid calls and received at tea. Her small dinner parties soon included cabinet ministers, foreign ambassadors, and the upper nobility.

One spring evening, surveying her guests after a particularly successful dinner to honor her father-in-law, Julia decided that she had achieved the goal she had set for herself.

"How on earth do you do it?" her cousin asked. "Now Bruno's going to expect the same of me."

Julia regarded her own image in the mirror. She wore a sheath of black silk that fell to the floor but almost exposed her breasts. She wore more makeup than usual for the occasion; her lips full and scarlet, her eyes heavily shadowed. The pearls that Angelo had given her for Christmas hung from her ears. I have never looked better in my life, she thought, and probably never will again.

"Well, how do you do it?"

"Do what, Vicky?"

"You haven't heard a word. You've been admiring yourself in the mirror, and with good reason."

"No, I was thinking I will never look this good again. From now on we are going to get old, Vicky. We are already what they call 'matrons' in Baltimore."

"Well, we certainly aren't the skinny kids who used to go crabbing in the mud of Chesapeake Bay with rotten chicken necks."

Angelo's father rose to leave. The elder Morosini had been abroad as ambassador to Brazil when the young couple had decided to marry, and Angelo had had to get his permission by telegram. Having returned to Italy upon retirement, the elder Morosini would leave in the morning for his estate in Verona. As soon as he made his farewells, the others began to say good night.

"Contessa, the food was divine. You'd better keep your cook under lock and key. I'll steal him."

"You're too kind, Princess Orsini."

When the Orsinis left Victoria said with a giggle, "Do you remember? That's the woman who always had the flu when Mother invited her."

"I know. That's why I had them together."

Aunt Agnes and Charles were putting on their coats.

"Marvelous party, Julia. I'm so proud of you. I feel I should take some of the credit."

"You should, Aunt Agnes," Julia said and kissed her on the cheek.

"Where *did* you get your cook?" Victoria whispered.

"Good night, Excellency. I'm so glad you enjoyed the evening."

"I don't have one," Julia whispered back. "One of the best restaurants in Italy just happens to be around the corner. They cater all my dinners."

Victoria shook with silent laughter, her eyebrows bobbing up and down as they always did when she laughed.

"If you tell, I'll cut your throat."

Julia curtsied to the scarlet robe. "It was our privilege, Your Eminence."

When the guests had all gone, Julia, Angelo, Victoria, and Bruno sat down around the fire and had a nightcap.

"Congratulations, Julia."

"A fantastic party."

"All Rome was at your feet."

Julia sat on the rug in front of the fire, her back against Angelo's knees, soaking up the praise.

"Oh, I almost forgot," Victoria said. "Did you see Cicero's column this morning in *Il Tempo*?"

"No. I never read him."

"Well, you should." Victoria opened her sequined evening bag and took out a clipping. "I quote. 'Let the Orsinis and Colonnas continue to fight over Rome. What counts is elegance, and everyone agrees that the most elegant woman in Rome this season is Contessa Giulia Morosini.'"

Julia closed her eyes. She had done all she had sworn she would do. Yet there was no joy in it.

* * *

After what she had done to bring the Angelo Morosinis to the pinnacle of social success, Julia was all the more stunned one Sunday morning when a woman called and asked for Angelo, apparently thinking Julia was the maid. The first time could have been a mistake, a misunderstanding. But when it happened a second time there could be no doubt. Both times, the call came when she would normally have been out riding. Her first feeling was one of outrage. She had brought a man she didn't even love money, beauty, and intelligence. What was more, half the men in Rome who counted for anything wanted to get her into bed, and Angelo had every reason to know they would not have been disappointed if they had. It was not *he* who was unhappily married—as she must be with any man who was not Paolo. How dare Angelo be unfaithful to her!

That night as they were dressing for dinner she said lightly, "Are you happy, darling?"

"What a question. Of course I'm happy. I'm always happy."

"I mean are you happy with me?"

"In every conceivable way."

"There's nothing wrong with our marriage?"

"Of course not. What are you trying to say, Julia?"

"It's just a feeling I have that perhaps there's something not quite right, something missing. At least that you might feel that way."

"I can't imagine what you mean. We want children, of course."

"I'm doing my best. Does it bother you?"

"No. But Father is quite ill. It would be nice if he could see an heir before he died, a new Count Morosini."

"You want a son, don't you?"

"Naturally, I'm an Italian man. It's part of my role to want a son."

"And part of the role I have accepted in becoming an Italian wife is to produce one. I've sworn to do my best to play my role, in all respects but one. There's one thing I will not do."

"What's that?" he said, smoothing back his soft brown hair with a silver-backed brush.

"Permit you to play around."

He turned, a startled look in his brown eyes. "That's one thing you won't have to worry . . ."

"Just a minute, Angelo."

His look confirmed his unfaithfulness in a way that could not be denied.

"I told you before we married that I didn't care what women there had been in your life. But I won't have another woman now."

"Julia . . ."

"Don't say anything, because I'm not accusing you of anything. But as long as you sleep with me, that's the way it's going to be."

In April of 1932, Julia went to a doctor who her society friends told her was absolutely the best in Italy for her kind of problem. She had expected someone quite different. The doctor was a small, wiry man with a Sicilian accent, blunt in his speech and not very sympathetic; but he seemed to know what he was doing. She left Dr. Saraceno's office assured that there was nothing wrong with her.

As they were having coffee that evening after dinner she said, "I was at the doctor's this morning."

Angelo put down his cup. "What's wrong?"

"Nothing, nothing at all. I'm fit as a fiddle, he says. No reason at all I can't have children."

"Oh, that."

"I know it's important to you. So, I thought I'd better find out."

"Did you have an examination?"

"Complete."

"That probably wasn't too pleasant."

"Oh, I wouldn't have minded so much except for his nurse standing there watching."

Angelo laughed. "Required by law in Italy to protect public morality. Well, what did he say?"

"He said it's probably just a matter of time. He got a bit

peeved when I told him we had been married for eleven months. He said I was a woman, not a rabbit, and just because I hadn't gotten pregnant in less than a year didn't mean there was a problem."

"Is there anything we need to do?"

"The only thing we need to do he says we should do at least once a week."

"What's that?"

"Angelo, dear, it's usually done in bed, and I think the doctor would have been shocked if I had told him how much more often than once a week we do it."

"Just that? That's all?"

"Just that. But he did say that if we are really anxious about it, you should come see him."

"Me?"

"He said that sometimes it's the man who has the problem."

"There's nothing wrong with me."

"I'm sure there isn't—"

"There's nothing wrong with me, and I don't want to discuss it anymore."

Well, well. She had even been willing to have a child to give this marriage a chance . . . and to give herself some scrap of happiness, she had to admit . . . but this man who wanted an heir so badly wasn't willing to have his precious masculinity questioned.

After Angelo had left for the ministry the next morning, Julia got out of bed and went into the dressing room where all of the elegant clothes she had had made in the last year were hanging. In one of the storage drawers she found what she was looking for: a black turtleneck sweater and a tweed skirt. An hour later she drove her little sports car across the bridge over the Tiber, muddy and swollen with the spring rains, and down the boulevard, where the first leaves were coming out on the plane trees, to Trastevere.

"It's menacing."

"Don't you like it?"

Francesca took off the welder's mask that made her look

like a creature from another planet and sat down on the wooden bench beside Julia. The studio hadn't changed at all in a year's time, except that the windows badly needed washing and James's paintings had all disappeared.

"I like it, but I liked it better when you were working in wood. It looks like a war machine."

"Maybe I could sell it to Bruno."

"Why does your sculpture have to be so sinister?"

"What else can one do in such times?"

"It's cold in here. Could I have a drink?"

Francesca brought a bottle of grappa out of the closet-size kitchen, poured two shot glasses of the clear liquid, lit two cigarettes, and passed one to Julia. Francesca looked tired. She was far too thin.

"Francesca, I need help," Julia blurted out.

"Don't we all."

"Is Paolo likely to come in?"

"He's in France, with James."

"Oh. Why?" Julia tried not to sound too interested.

"You remember the plane that dropped leaflets over Rome last winter?"

"I saw it. I met that boy here, you know."

"I know. Well, after he died, Paolo and James thought they had better get out of sight. They're safe."

Julia downed the alcohol and stood up. She walked over to the grimy skylight to look out at the fluffy clouds being driven along by the spring winds.

"You know about Paolo and me?" Julia waited.

"All I know is that you went off to the mountains one day and had an argument."

"What did he say about me?"

"Nothing. He usually tells me things. But that time he said nothing."

"Nothing at all?"

"Just that you wouldn't be seeing each other anymore. Why've you come here, Julia?"

Julia turned and faced her. They were the same age, but she felt so much in need of the wisdom that Francesca seemed to have.

"I'm sorry."

"Sorry about what?"

"I haven't called you since the day of the wedding."

"I understood. Angelo doesn't want you to see me. I would have done the same if I were you."

Julia sat down on the bench beside her. "The truth is, I need your help."

Francesca blew out cigarette smoke into the air, poured two more glasses of grappa, and leaned back on her elbows. She was so thin, her breasts were like two small apples tucked under her sweater.

"I'm flattered you came to me for help. What's wrong?"

"Angelo."

"I thought you were the happiest couple in all of Italy. That's what the papers say."

"There's another woman." Julia let out a high-pitched laugh. "Could anything be more banal than that?"

"Actually, I'm rather shocked."

"You needn't be, Francesca. You know the kind of crowd we run around with."

"It isn't that. What surprises me is that he's strayed so soon. I figured you would know how to handle him."

"Oh," Julia gestured in the air, "I've handled everything. As you say, it's all in the papers."

"Problems in bed?"

"If there are, I'm a lot dumber than I think I am."

"Do you love him?"

"No." Well, finally, she had said it to someone, and who better than Francesca.

"Then why not let him have a girlfriend or two?"

"I won't accept that. I told him."

"Why not?"

"I'm going to make a success of this marriage."

"Julia, Julia, what are you talking about?"

"I . . . I don't know."

"Are you all right?"

"Yes, I'm all right, as all right as one can be living in hell, a hell that I made for myself."

Francesca looked stunned. "If you didn't love Angelo, why did you marry him?"

Julia shook her head, smiling. "You haven't the slightest suspicion?"

"Ah . . . Paolo. How stupid of me not to have seen."

"Hell is a place that you can't get out of. It's easy enough to get into. Pride. Jesus, what a fool I was. I was going to hurt Paolo, and, of course, I didn't hurt him at all. He saw me for what I am—cheap, shallow, and hard."

"You poor darling."

"Oh, I've shut it out for a long time. There're all kinds of ways—sex, drink, social success, but in the end they all run out. But what I've done, I've done. There's no divorce here. I'm married to a man I despise . . . for the rest of my life. . . ." Her voice quavered and broke. "I'm so much worse off than whatever woman Angelo is running around with. How . . . how did this happen to me?" Tears were streaming down her face. "You remember on the ship? Everything was going to be so wonderful . . . I had everything . . . and now I have nothing."

From that day on Julia had one consolation. Her friendship with Francesca grew stronger than ever, both because it gave her someone to share her sorrow with and because, in some small way, it brought her closer to Paolo. Many mornings she found herself drawn to Francesca's studio, either to talk or sometimes just to sit quietly and watch Francesca work.

One morning, wearing the usual black turtleneck and tweed skirt—her statement that her old self was not dead—she found Francesca painting one of her iron sculptures a bright red.

"What a good idea. It looks just right."

"Does it? I wasn't sure." She turned and looked at Julia. "My God, I don't know how you do it, Julia."

"Do what?"

"I don't understand how anyone who is as unhappy as you say you are can continue to look so beautiful. In fact, I think you're even more beautiful than when we met on shipboard."

"Beauty can be a curse."

"Maybe, but don't, my dear, try to convince a plain woman of it."

"On the ship you said I looked Italian. Do you still think so?"

"Even more so. You look like that new movie star, Gina Franco."

"Well, I am Italian, or at least—like you—half-Italian. Maybe I always suspected, deep down. But now I know. I found that out the day Paolo and I broke up."

"Do you want to tell me what happened, since Paolo won't?"

"Yes, I'd like to."

Francesca put down her paintbrush. "I'll go make some coffee."

They sat on the bench together with cups of strong Italian coffee and Julia told what had happened, and in a way she was telling herself for the first time.

"Now I see that asking Paolo to drive with me up to Castel del Monte was a last desperate attempt to get him back. I could not have made a worse move. What I did was wipe out any possibility for the future. The little house was abandoned and stripped of all its furnishings, but there was a portrait of the young Gus and some letters. One of the letters and the photo made it clear that Gus was my real father. I had promised Gus I would visit his mother and I didn't. Then Paolo said that if I had . . . if Gus's mother had had food and medicine . . ."

"Like Bianca."

"Yes, and I threw that in his face, and that was the end of everything."

"That is unforgivable!"

Julia was shocked at the anger in Francesca's voice.

"I know. It's all my fault."

"I'm not talking about you. How dare he! I am so sick and tired of his high-minded principles . . . and how could he hurt you like that. God!"

"Francesca, I love him."

"I know."

From that morning on, Julia saw things in a somewhat different light. While she still had no hope that she and Paolo would ever be together again, at least she was able to begin to put aside her self-hate.

In May, when the muddy roads had dried, Julia and Francesca drove up into the Abruzzi mountains to see if they could locate any of Gus's relatives—her relatives—so that she could put them in touch with Gus's widow. They started early in the morning, as soon as Angelo had left for the ministry, so that they could make the journey in one day. She remembered every inch of the way to Aquila and every word that had passed between her and Paolo.

When they reached the foot of the crag on which Castel del Monte perched, they found that help for the village had finally arrived from Rome. The road had been scraped and they could drive right up into the little central piazza. And then, as the stares of the old people sitting in the sun followed them, they went up the stone steps to where the ruins of Julia's grandmother's house stood, at the very top of the village. The snow-covered mountains towered above them on all sides, but big pieces of snow were breaking loose and crashing down the slopes. Spring had come.

"Pretty forlorn, isn't it?" Julia said. They went inside the empty room. The picture of Gus and the letters were gone.

"Why didn't I take them when I could have?" She stamped her foot in frustration. "Oh, I know why, I know perfectly well why." She sighed deeply. "But why am I always late, always missing the opportunity, always the cause of misunderstanding, always . . ." And then angrily, "And why would anyone want to take my—my father's—picture. And his letters?"

Francesca seemed taken aback by this display of emotion from her once cool and elegant friend.

"Why, I suppose they took the picture for the frame and, in a poor village like this, the letters to start a fire with."

"Now I'll never know so many things about Gus and my mother and . . ."

Another bank of snow broke loose and rumbled down

the mountainside. A flock of crows, disturbed, rose cawing from the trees.

"You know the important things, and maybe that's enough."

"Yes, I suppose so. And there's no use wishing I could live my life over again. But I would have behaved differently. Why is it, Francesca, that when you know what you should do, it's always too late?"

"Let's go, Julia. This is a depressing place."

Francesca suggested having lunch in Aquila, at the restaurant-bar on the corner by the market. Julia said nothing about it being the very place where she had broken so emotionally with Paolo that she was propelled into Angelo's arms. Even the waiter who served them was the same one who had patted her on the shoulder after Paolo had left her and had spoken of the difficulties of *l'amore*. He didn't seem to recognize her. Julia turned to Francesca, who had spent a half hour in the registry office, searching for traces of Gus's family, while Julia was asking questions of old-timers in the market.

"Any luck?"

"Oh, they know the family," Francesca said. "Gus had two brothers. Both killed at the Battle of Caporetto in '17. No other known relatives. And you?"

"Same story. I feel like an orphan."

"Julia?"

"Yes?"

"Is something more wrong?"

"This restaurant is the place where Paolo and I had that awful row and broke up."

"Oh, dear. I wouldn't have suggested coming here if . . ."

"Of course not. Oh . . . how I despised myself."

Francesca frowned at the veal cutlets that were put down in front of her, pushed them about with her fork.

"That was obvious, but surely not still?"

"It's not just the monstrous thing I did in marrying Angelo to spite Paolo. It started—I realized—a long time ago. When Gus took me to the Pembertons, I said I would never let Agnes's and Charles's money and fine things and their idle life seduce me. But somehow, over the years while I was growing up, I was seduced. By the time I met Paolo—who had nothing else to offer but love, you know—well, by then I was too self-indulgent to share the kind of hard life that he leads, whatever I may have said. I think he saw that."

"And now?"

"Now? Francesca, there is no now."

She looked bleakly at her friend. Neither of them had touched the food on their plates.

"You shouldn't blame yourself. The world of money and social position is a tough place to live. I know."

"But you broke away. You have James."

"Your life isn't exactly behind you at age twenty-four."

"The only thing that will ever matter to me is lost."

"Paolo?"

"Yes."

"He's not too far from here, you know."

"What do you mean? He's in France."

"No longer. He's hiding out with some friends in a village about twenty miles from here. Since we're this close . . ."

"Oh, I couldn't . . ."

They had both given up any pretense of eating their lunch.

"It's wicked of me, I know, and besides it's none of my business . . ."

"I couldn't."

When they reached the village where Paolo was staying, Julia sat in the car, smoking one cigarette after another, while Francesca went to visit him. Finally Francesca came out of the crooked single street of the village looking worried, a small figure in the distance, slowly coming closer. What was wrong? Julia got out of the car. Had something happened to Paolo?

"What?"

"He wants to see you."

"Francesca, why did you tell him I was here?"

"I don't know. I couldn't help myself. The question is, why did I have to meddle?"

"Where is he?"

"The third house on the left. Blue shutters." Francesca leaned back against the car.

Julia walked, unseeing, past the inevitable old men sitting in the sun in front of a café. Her heart was pounding. The door of the house with blue shutters stood open and she walked right in, knowing that if she hesitated, she would turn and flee. There was no chance to compose herself. He was standing before her in the simple whitewashed room, light and airy, windows open to the spring day and a view of peaceful farms in the valley below.

For a long time, it seemed, they just looked at each other. She soaked up the image of his suntanned face, the white teeth, the dark hair, still long. She would have liked to touch it. She had almost forgotten . . .

"You look just the same," Paolo said at last. He tried to smile.

No, no, not the same at all, a voice within her cried. If you only knew! But all she said was, and that almost inaudibly. "You haven't changed either."

"I'm glad you came."

"I am, too."

"The way we left each other that day . . . was terrible."

"Yes."

"Could you forgive me?"

"Of course. But what is there to forgive?"

"Everything. Francesca just told me that what I did was unforgivable, but I knew that even before I reached the Aquila bus station. I started to go back to you . . ."

Julia put her hand over her mouth to keep herself from crying out, why, why didn't you?

". . . but my pride wouldn't let me, even when I knew that I had spoiled things for good. Then I heard that you had married Angelo Morosini. . . ."

"Yes?" She felt a great rush of hope.

"I hope you're happy."

"Yes," she said, knowing that with the least encouragement she would have said "no" and run into his arms. Just as well, she thought bitterly; adultery was her husband's preserve. She loved Paolo too much to do what Angelo had done to her.

"I'm glad you're back in Italy, and safe," she said finally.

"Oh, I'm fine. Don't worry about me. Are you expecting?"

"A child? What makes you think that?"

"Your cheeks are so flushed."

"It's not that."

"You're not ill?"

"No."

"Then . . ." And she saw in his eyes that he had realized, that he understood everything, her marriage, what she had gone through, what she still felt, everything.

He stepped forward and put his hand on her arm. She recoiled as if from an electric shock.

"Don't," she whispered. "Don't touch me."

They stood facing each other, both breathing as if they had just finished running a race.

"I can't see you ever again . . ." she blurted out, "ever."

She turned and ran out of the house, down the street, past the old men sitting in front of the café. Francesca was standing white-faced beside the car, and took Julia into her arms.

"Julia, Julia, I'm sorry. I should never have . . ."

"It's all right. It's all right. It had to happen sooner or later. It's all over now."

She began to cry again. Would she never have any peace? Francesca's lip was trembling, there were tears in *her* eyes. She was even making her dearest friend miserable. They clung to each other.

"Julia, I'm so sorry."

"We'd better get out of here," Julia gasped. "We're making a spectacle of ourselves."

"Yes," said Francesca, wiping away her tears with a laugh. "They probably think we're a couple of lesbians, if they've ever heard of such a thing up here."

Chapter Seven

IT WAS LATE in the evening before Julia drove up in front of the apartment on the Via Giulia. Angelo was standing in the doorway looking distraught. Was he afraid that she'd been in an accident? Even his clothes were disheveled, which was quite unlike him.

"Where've you been? I've waited hours for you."

"Angelo, what's wrong?" He looked, to her amazement, as if he had been crying.

"My father died."

She put her arms around her husband and held him, wondering how many years it had been since *he* had last wept.

The next morning Julia and Angelo left Rome together for the first time since they had returned from their honeymoon. Her Fiat, the leather top down, seemed to skim over the roughly paved road that climbed up from Rome, through orchards pink and white with blossoms, into the Apennines, and down again into the lush fields of the Po Valley. Julia raced the sun across the plain, roaring down country roads lined with Lombardy poplars. Before they reached Verona, just as the foothills of the Alps were becoming visible, they turned off into a narrow country lane that led down to the banks of the Adige River where the Villa Serena stood, surrounded by ancient trees, its upper stories golden in the last rays of the setting sun. Julia braked the car and switched off the engine. There was no sound but the croaking of frogs. A mist was forming over the gray-green river that slid silently by.

"It is like a dream," she said. "Why didn't you tell me

it was so beautiful?" The white-pillared villa's central mass
rose solid and, yes, serene among the dark trees. Along the
edge of the red-tiled roof, marble statues stood, looking at
first glance like real people who might suddenly move and
walk away. The main floor opened out onto vine-covered
terraces above the wings of the house that reached out toward them with long arcaded arms as if to enclose them.

"I'm going to love it," she said.

"You won't be the first Morosini to fall in love with it.
My father said it is like a mistress, an expensive mistress.
The Villa Serena has eaten up several Morosini fortunes."

"She's worth it," Julia said, starting up the car.

"Never judge an old courtesan in romantic light. She
won't look the same in the morning."

Angelo was right. In the cold light of morning the disre-
pair of the Villa Serena was all too evident. No wonder he
had never brought her there. Pieces of plaster had fallen
from the ceiling, the murals in the ballroom were being
eaten away by dampness and mold. Rugs and upholstery
were threadbare. The smell of decay hung over everything.
But still she could see what it must have once been—and
what it could be again.

At eleven o'clock they buried Angelo's father among
three centuries of the Counts Morosini. The brief ceremony
took place on the grounds, in the family chapel, which had
been designed by the same late-Renaissance architect responsible for the main house. The chapel was in an even
greater state of ruin. The small dome looked as if it were
about to collapse on the funeral party of old friends and
colleagues of Angelo's father. There were no other relatives. Julia realized, looking into Angelo's tear-filled eyes,
why having a son was so important to him. The survival of
this ancient family depended on her. It was a funny feeling.
Yet, she also saw quite clearly that Angelo's tears were part
of the role he played. Tears were expected of an Italian man
when there was a death in the family, just as she was expected to provide an heir.

After they had lowered the casket into the open grave
and the priest had intoned the final prayers, the estate work-

ers threw shovelfuls of earth upon it, and the little party moved slowly back to the house. There, in a faded reception room, Julia, now truly Contessa Morosini, offered coffee and brandy to the few old guests, the priest, and the family lawyer. Her hostess duties over, Julia left Angelo and the lawyer to discuss family business, and for the rest of the afternoon wandered from one once beautiful room to another, an idea slowly forming in her mind. By the time she watched Angelo shaking hands with the lawyer on the front steps, she had made up her mind.

"I'm sorry, Angelo, I don't understand. If assets exceed liabilities, where's the problem?"

"You don't understand because you don't have the liabilities, only assets." He was really handsome by candlelight, in his dinner jacket and white winged collar. There were many women who would envy her.

"I have some money in a bank in Baltimore that Elmer Thornley takes care of for me, that's all."

"Exactly. And I have a large piece of land and a house on the Adige that nobody takes care of. Those are my assets, but I had no idea what debts Father left."

Julia helped herself from the silver serving dish, and the old servant disappeared into the gloom outside the circle of candlelight.

"My God, Angelo, breeches, white stockings, and everything. I didn't know such costumes existed anymore."

"Well, there won't be any more livery bought, that's for sure."

"Don't be so gloomy, old boy."

"Why shouldn't I be? Do you know that my family has owned the Villa Serena for three hundred years, and that I will be the one who has to sell it? That can't mean much to you on the other side of the Atlantic."

"I'm not on the other side of the Atlantic, actually. I'm right here."

"I wasn't talking about *you*. I meant that it's difficult for an American to understand."

"I'm not an American, as it happens, but your wife . . .

for better or worse, as they say. And you won't have to sell."

She awoke the next morning, alone in the damp, chilly bedroom, the house silent as a tomb. The wood fire of the night before was now cold white ash in the grate. Beyond the window, fog shrouded the trees along the banks of the Adige. Her green silk evening dress hung, inside out, from the back of a chair. It was the same one she had worn that night she had taken Angelo back to the Palazzo Rosalba and he had proposed. . . . And now? Julia got out of bed and went naked across the icy room to where a pack of cigarettes lay beside the dead fire. There was one cigarette left. She lit it and quickly got back under the covers. She puffed on the cigarette and flicked the ashes into the empty pack, and thought about the Villa Serena.

Julia went down to breakfast in her riding habit. There were horses on the place that hadn't been ridden in months; and she would start that morning getting them back into shape, as she would start so many other things.

"Good morning, *amore*," she said, bending over and kissing Angelo on the top of his head.

"You look radiant this morning."

Yes, she thought, you want to hear what a great lover you are. "That's from being properly laid," she said in the low husky voice she used for such remarks, and poured herself some coffee. Italian men were more easily shocked by what a woman said than what she did. They thought *they* were responsible for what she did, but for what she said, they couldn't take the credit.

"I can't complain, either," he said primly.

I should imagine not, she thought.

"Why did you sneak away this morning?" she said.

"Do you know what time it is?"

"No idea."

"Eleven o'clock. I've already been to see our lawyer."

So, her plan was already working.

"I've also called the ministry. I told them the estate is a

terrible mess . . . which is true enough . . . and that I simply have to have six weeks leave, and I got it."

"Marvelous."

"Want to hear the rest?"

"Please." Her irritable mood had vanished like the fog that had lifted from the lawn.

"There are two hundred hectares, producing nothing, that can be sold immediately. The Giustinians have wanted one plot for at least a hundred years, and we'll make them pay a pretty price." Angelo laughed.

"Angelo, look at this." She took a piece of paper out of the pocket of her riding coat.

TO ELMER J. THORNLEY, PRESIDENT, MERCHANTS AND FARMERS BANK, BALTIMORE, MARYLAND, USA. PLEASE TRANSFER FIFTY THOUSAND DOLLARS TO ACCOUNT OF CONTESSA GIULIA MOROSINI, BANCA DI SANTO SPIRITO, ROMA. REGARDS, JULIA.

Angelo reached into an inside pocket of his jacket and took out a fountain pen. He made several marks on the paper and handed it back to her. A straight black line ran through "Roma," which was replaced by "Geneva."

"Why?"

"Your money is safer there."

"You don't believe the Fascists will last, do you? You don't really believe in the regime?"

"I don't believe very much in anything."

Down below, a groom was bringing a steel-gray horse, which he could barely control, up to the stone staircase at the front entrance. Once again Angelo had said something that he really meant.

"All right," she said, "Geneva it is. Have someone take the telegram in to Verona and send it. I'm ready to get started."

He smiled. "How will you start?"

She hadn't thought of that. "Well . . ."

"You'll need help." He was smiling, indulgently now. After all, she was only a woman.

"I want to do it myself." She extinguished the spark of anger that he had lit in her.

"I'll get old Spagnoli, our estate agent, to come out. He can advise you."

"All right. But I'm in charge."

"Of course, darling."

And so she began. She was up at dawn for a ride before breakfast, or down on the lower lawn, where the fog from the Adige River still hung belly-high to her horse, taking the jumps. Then a shower and breakfast and she would put on an old pair of slacks and a sweater and go down to join the workmen. After working hard all morning, she would have a shower before joining Angelo for lunch on the terrace, when he was not in Verona attending to the financial side of the estate. Spring was late in coming, but by the end of May even northern Italy was warm and flowering, and she spent most of her afternoons outside working with the gardeners. In the evening she wandered through the empty rooms with a drink and a cigarette, admiring the work that had been done during the day. Gus would have understood, and—a lump rose in her throat—Paolo would have understood.

"Well, Carlo, what do you think?"

They stood in the center of the ballroom: Spagnoli, the estate agent, in his habitual black suit, and Julia in slacks and a workmen's paint-spattered smock.

"There is a certain result. Not entirely bad."

Julia smiled. Finally even old Spagnoli had had to admit that the American woman had known what she was doing when she turned the place upside down. The woodwork had been stripped of its layers of paint, revealing intricately carved walnut and teak that no Morosini in generations had seen. Eighteenth-century murals on walls and ceilings that had seemed faded and damaged beyond repair were glowing now with their original colors. The famous restorer that Julia had brought from Florence was perched on scaffolding high above their heads, finishing off the last section of the ceiling. She had spent hours sitting up there beside him

mixing solvents and paints and passing him brushes—
exactly as she had once done for Gus.

"Of course," Spagnoli said, "if you pour out money as if
it were water, I suppose you're bound to get *some* results."

"Thank you."

The estate agent turned and looked at her over his glasses,
suspecting that she was being sarcastic.

"Come on, then," she said, "let's see the rest."

They passed between the rows of furniture that lined the
ballroom floor, pieces that Julia had selected to be restored.
Workmen were sanding, gilding, upholstering in silk and
brocade. They all spoke to her. When they had started work
they would speak to her only when spoken to; they had
never, she imagined, seen a woman wearing slacks. But she
had worked as hard as any of them, polishing, stripping
paint, mixing plaster. She respected their craftsmanship, and
they knew it.

"*Buon giorno, signora.*"

"*Buon giorno, amici.*"

They did not call her "Contessa." She thought with distaste of the so-called friends in Rome with whom she
danced and drank, flirted and gossiped.

"There, for example," said Spagnoli, as they went up the
beautifully restored curved staircase, "is a quite unneces-
sary expenditure," pointing to where a workman was rip-
ping down old wiring.

"I am not having bare electric wires strung all over the
place like a tenement."

"It's your money."

"Yes, it is."

They passed through her suite into the bathroom, which
had just been finished in shell-pink mosaic tile, in which
was set a large mirror surrounded by lights in little Venetian
glass bowls.

"Isn't it lovely?"

Spagnoli said nothing.

She flushed the modern toilet imported from America.
"Wonderful."

Spagnoli snorted.

"And see," she said, turning a handle, "real hot water."

"Decadent. Fit for a pope."

"Oh, Carlo," she said, taking his arm, "don't be such an old sourpuss. Life is to be enjoyed."

"That's fine for the rich."

"And I'm rich."

On Julia and Angelo's first anniversary, Victoria and Bruno arrived unannounced from Milan in their yellow Bugatti to help them celebrate their first year together. Everyone played a role in Italy, and Victoria was playing the wife of a Milanese industrialist. The Bronzinis had brought them an antique silver bowl filled with yellow roses as an anniversary present, and several bottles of champagne.

Julia put on her new evening dress for dinner. The men wore dinner jackets. The bowl of yellow roses was placed in the center of the table, and the table was set in the small study. The walls were covered in raw silk—the study was the first room in the house to be completely finished—and by candlelight it was truly beautiful.

"Now I know why I never come to see you, Julia," Victoria said.

"Why's that?"

"Being around you gives me such feelings of inferiority. You pick out a dress and it's perfect. You have unexpected guests and . . . presto . . . there's a perfect dinner. When I do something it never comes out quite right." Julia smiled at Victoria across the table. It was true. The expensive red-and-green striped gown that Victoria wore didn't really go with her pink complexion; the diamond necklace was much too showy.

"To our Julia, who is perfection," said Bruno, lifting his champagne glass. He had put on weight, growing into his role as a leader of Italian industry.

"Hear, hear. To my perfect wife."

"Why, Julia. How sweet. There are tears in your eyes," Victoria said.

Julia got up from the table. "Excuse me. I'll have to leave for a minute."

In the next room Julia regained her composure, and by the time the others came in for coffee she was relaxed and smiling. The tears had come without warning. The others had no idea that her tears were not because she was touched by their compliments, but because she had suddenly realized how terribly unhappy she still was. Her restoration of the Villa Serena was just one more success that brought her no closer to what she really wanted ... and could never have.

"Coffee?" Julia said, "And thank you all. I was sort of overwhelmed by so much attention."

"Everyone should be so lucky as to shed tears of happiness after a year of marriage." Bruno smiled at her. She couldn't help but like him.

"Well, let's quit talking about me. What's with you, Bruno?"

"What's with me? The usual. It's like asking one of the machines in my factory what's new. The life of a businessman is very dull."

"But you like it."

"I love it."

"Why?"

"I love the problems. There's always a problem to be solved. That's where the fun is, not in making money. Although, God knows, that's a problem in itself when you have to work with this idiotic government we have."

"I thought the Fascists were pro–big business."

"All I want from the Fascists is for them to leave me alone. If they would stick to politics and let the industrialists run the economy, Italy would be a lot better off. Mussolini understands nothing about economics."

"Does he understand politics any better?"

Bruno paused, letting Angelo light his cigar. "I'll admit he has some rather childish ideas, but then the Italians can be a rather childish people. Nobody has been able to make parliamentary democracy work in Italy since Garibaldi's time. It's too sophisticated an idea for our people."

"It works well enough in America."

"Does it?" Angelo said. "The American economy is falling to pieces and your President and Congress are paralyzed. It's happening to every country in the West. I predict that if this man Roosevelt is elected he will take some of the same drastic measures as Mussolini."

"I hope that doesn't include dosing people with castor oil."

"Look, Julia," Bruno said, "there are worse things than that and breaking the heads of a few Communist agitators. You have to use a certain amount of force to keep Italians in line."

"I don't see the need for brutality."

"When we had a liberal democracy here in 1915, the politicians got us into a war that easily could have been avoided. And then they sent Italian peasant boys to the front without proper equipment to be slaughtered by the hundreds of thousands by the Austrians. I call *that* brutality."

"Yes, you're right of course. But what about the atrocities the Italian army is committing right now in Libya?"

Angelo gave her a quizzical look. "Where did you hear that?"

"One hears stories."

"Oh, for God's sake, let's not talk politics," Victoria said. "That's all we ever hear in Milano. It's such a bore."

In July 1932, Benito Mussolini dismissed Dino Grandi as foreign minister and assumed the portfolio himself. There was consternation in the Villa Chigi where the foreign ministry was located. Il Duce would arrive unexpectedly, dressed in riding boots, stride up and down the corridors, issue contradictory orders, dismiss an office director or two, and disappear. Please, the director general of the ministry begged, in a telephone call to Angelo, we need all the help we can get, and Il Duce knows you favorably through Ciano. So Julia and Angelo returned to Rome in August and reopened their apartment on Via Giulia. Everything was just the same, except that Julia was pregnant.

"Are you sure?"

"Given the importance of the event, Angelo, I wouldn't have told you unless I was sure."

"How marvelous."

"Dr. Saraceno wasn't all that impressed."

He got up and came across to her and took her in his arms.

Being pregnant was a lot more unpleasant than she had imagined it would be. Perhaps Angelo would have been able to show more interest in the child he had wanted so badly if the pressure on him at work hadn't been so great. No longer was he able to joke about the foreign ministry. He was thrust forward by his colleagues as a buffer between the ministry and Mussolini. Angelo was ambitious, but not that ambitious; and if he displeased Il Duce, his career would be at a dead end. Of course, Angelo charmed Mussolini as he charmed everyone, at the cost of frayed nerves, sleepless nights, and long hours of unrelenting work. All he asked of her was that she graciously entertain the people with whom he was now obliged to work. As he admitted with a bitter laugh, these were people of "shallow minds, bad manners, and doubtful morals." She did it out of pride, though the Fascist officials who came to their apartment were all of those things and worse.

Julia became more and more depressed. Her consolation that fall was knowing that she had left behind on the bank of the Adige something of beauty. She often thought of Gus and Claudia, and cried at the slightest provocation. There was another consolation: She had friends. Francesca seemed to have truly missed her, even though James had come back to Rome and was living at the studio again. Julia stopped by the studio several times a week and often stayed for hours. Paolo was still somewhere in Italy, but no one knew where.

Julia was so used to being careful of what she said that it was a novel experience to be able to talk without inhibition. James seemed to take nothing she said seriously, and that made her feel better than if he and Francesca had been overly sympathetic to her problems. He was the same way

about his reasons for risking opposition to the Fascists. All
he would answer, with a laugh, was that Italy wasn't big
enough for both him and Mussolini and *he* certainly wasn't
leaving.

"Oh, be serious, James."

"Why should I be serious? That's what's wrong with this
bloody country. Everything is serious. Mussolini says the
Italian army is the greatest war machine since the Roman
legions, and people take him seriously instead of rolling on
the floor with laughter. The Fascist state is the biggest joke
of the century, and you want me to be serious. Here, have
some more wine." There was the first chill of autumn in the
air, and they were sitting in one corner of the studio around
a small electric heater, drinking red wine and eating walnuts.

"The truth of the matter is James opposes Mussolini for
sport, and he's going to get killed if he isn't more careful."

"You take risks yourself, Francesca," Julia said. "I suppose that is part of the attraction. Maybe that's why I'm curious. I've never taken any risks at all. I've always played
it safe. Sometimes lately I've wished I could."

"Well then, don't take up resistance work, unless your
idea of thrills is waiting six hours on a street corner for a
contact that never happens."

"Or," added James, "staying up all night running off il-
legal pamphlets in the back of a print shop."

"Oh, I didn't mean that kind of excitement. I couldn't do
that unless I believed in the cause with all my heart. I don't
know enough to be able to do that. All I know is that I
think you are right, and Angelo and Bruno are wrong. But
I'm not that involved. Maybe both sides are wrong."

"That's at least more likely than that we're both right,"
James said.

"Also, I would be afraid. Still, I'm almost jealous of the
excitement of what you are doing."

Julia drove back across the Tiber with the top down. She
always felt good after being at the studio. At least she had
real friends. She liked James very much, and in Francesca's

eyes and voice she absorbed not only Francesca's presence but a ghost of Paolo's. It wasn't much, but it was enough to keep her going.

Behind the Pantheon she stopped for a traffic light, and while she was waiting Angelo and a woman came out of the door of a building farther up the street. Instead of driving on, as she had intended, she turned the corner and a few minutes later was in a bar on the Via Veneto frequented by foreign journalists. She had a couple of scotches and fended off several attempts to pick her up. She didn't want to be home waiting for Angelo.

When she got there, he was trying to start a fire in the fireplace—the first of the season.

"How domestic," Julia said, "but why don't you let the maid do that? She knows how."

Angelo turned from his kneeling position in front of the fireplace. It's a shame, she thought. He looks so content, handsome as ever, and his tailor-made shirt and jacket are so perfect on him.

"You'll get your clothes dirty."

"Where've you been?" he said, standing up.

She knelt down, quickly arranged the firewood, and lit a match to it.

"Seeing friends."

"Dressed like that?"

She stood up and looked down at her sweater and skirt. "Why not?"

"Which friends?"

"Well," she said, taking the still-flaming match and lighting a cigarette with it, "certainly not Fiammetta Gildo."

"What?" He looked as if she had struck him.

"It's a pity you're becoming deaf at such an early age."

"We just happened to run into each other and had a drink together."

She drew on the cigarette. There was a certain satisfaction in having him so entirely at her mercy.

"The Hotel Vecchia Toscana has a bar?"

"Yes, of course."

"Tell me something, Angelo." He was standing there,

with his beautiful English waistcoat hanging unbuttoned. "Did you fuck her before or after you bought her a drink?"

He flinched at her second strike.

"Or did *she* pay for the drinks?"

"I don't have to take this, Julia."

"No, you don't. But what are you going to do about it?"

"What you're saying is not true."

"I wish it weren't, Angelo. What grieves me most, I suppose, is your complete lack of taste. Is it true that *la* Gildo has a steady clientele because she will do certain things that even the most depraved of your friends' wives won't do for their lovers?"

"Very funny."

"I'm only telling you what I hear in the dressing room at the riding club."

"Anything else?"

"Yes. Which bedroom do you want from now on?"

The fire was burning nicely now.

Chapter Eight

ON THE FIRST Tuesday after the first Monday in November, Herbert Hoover was defeated for the presidency by Franklin Roosevelt, and Agnes's hopes for Charles to be named ambassador to the Court of St. James were dashed. Julia was at the Palazzo Rosalba for what was supposed to be a victory breakfast. A young man from the embassy appeared every few minutes with the latest returns taken from the Teletype until all interest in the election faded. Julia alone walked away in good spirits from the Maryland hunt breakfast growing cold on the refectory table.

She drove her Fiat back to Via Giulia at breakneck speed: Her pregnancy had entered a stage in which she felt good all the time. She would have to give Francesca a call and tell her how Aunt Agnes had been cast down, and she might even call Victoria in Milan. As she came in the door of the apartment the maid brought her an envelope on a silver tray. She took it with her to her new bedroom, with its single bed under an antique canopy she had bought in Sicily, and while she asked the operator for Francesca's number, opened it. As usual the operator made the wrong connection.

It was just another wire from Thornley, she saw. She kicked off her shoes and lay back on the bed. The Merchants and Farmers Bank of Baltimore had failed—had what? The court would, in due course, distribute any assets, etc., etc.

"Hello. No, operator, I did not want the Venetian Salon of Beauty. . . ."

She finally got Francesca's studio, but there was no answer. She put down the receiver and read the telegram more carefully, feeling numb all over. It simply couldn't be true that the same thing that had happened to so many others was happening to her. Her charmed life was over. There was no more money.

As she drove across the Tiber to Trastevere late that afternoon, Julia wondered what Francesca would have to say. What would Angelo say? If, as it seemed, she was once again a poor girl from Baltimore, what use would she be to him? She glanced in the rearview mirror. Even what beauty she had and her social graces would not be much use to him with his crude Fascist friends. They were impressed by power alone, and the power that she had had over Angelo, her money, was now gone. She ran the right wheels of the Fiat up on the curb, got out, and mounted the stairs to the studio. The door stood open, and the setting sun poured from the skylight onto a scene of incredible wreckage.

Julia walked slowly through the smashed sculptures and paintings torn to ribbons, trying to comprehend, yet not wanting to.

"Francesca," she said in a small voice, and then louder, "Francesca!" She sat down on the cloth-covered model's platform. Something terrible had happened and she couldn't make her mind focus on what it was. Amid the litter of plaster and shreds of canvas that had been works of art, only the bright red "war machine" that Francesca had been working on for so many months stood unharmed. Then she understood.

Julia was still sitting there in the growing dusk when she heard noises on the stairs outside. She went to the door and opened it. Francesca lay on the landing, half covered by a raincoat, and Julia heard someone running down the stairs. She lifted the raincoat. Francesca's naked body underneath was covered in fresh red paint, so fresh that it came off on Julia's sweater and hands as she held Francesca in her arms.

"Frància, what have they done to you?"

"I'm all right. It's James they were after."

"Where is he?"

But Francesca did not answer. She was unconscious.

* * *

Julia helped Dr. Saraceno remove the red paint from Francesca. They worked over her body, lying like a statue on the model's platform, with swabs of cotton dipped in alcohol; in the same way she and Gus had cleaned old paint off statues of the Virgin Mary or some saint. The little electric heater cast a warm glow over the three figures joined in a strange operation.

"That's enough, I think," the doctor said in his thick Sicilian accent. "The main thing is to keep the pores open." Francesca began to awaken. "Now you can go to bed, signora, without ruining the sheets. I will give you something to make you sleep."

"I don't want to sleep. I want to know what's happened to James," Francesca said, her speech slurred.

"I'll look after that."

The doctor expertly slid a needle under the skin of Francesca's forearm and pressed down the plunger with his thumb. Then he and Julia walked Francesca to the iron bed in the corner of the studio and put her between the sheets. By the time they had spread a blanket over her, she was asleep.

"A powerful sedative. Do you have a cigarette?"

Julia handed Dr. Saraceno the pack.

"American cigarettes."

She lit his cigarette with her platinum lighter.

"I'm American, as you must know."

"Do you have something to drink?"

Julia went to the closet-size kitchen and switched on the light bulb that hung by a wire. In the square of mirror nailed over the tiny sink she looked at herself, tense and pale, streaks of red paint drying on her black sweater, and over her shoulder she saw Dr. Saraceno, his brown eyes dark as chestnuts, watching her from behind thick spectacles. His brown skin was stretched over the bones of his head like old parchment. His gray-brown mustache, like a ragged toothbrush, was matched by two tufts of hair over his ears.

"There is only grappa," she said to his image in the mirror.

"So much the better."

She brought two glasses out into the studio. They sat on the platform.

"*Salute.*"

"*Salute, Dottore.*" She took a sip of the fiery liquid. "An unusual assignment for a gynecologist."

"I've done even more unusual things."

"Will she be all right?"

"She has not been physically molested, if that's what you mean. Tell me, Contessa, why did you bring me here?"

"You're the only doctor I know."

"And how are you feeling?"

"Tired."

"You know, of course, that it is not a good stage of your pregnancy for such excitement?"

"Yes."

He took off his glasses, breathed on them, and wiped them with a handkerchief. He often did that in his consultation room, but she had never seen him without his starched white jacket. This evening he looked more like a lawyer than a doctor.

"Do you want to tell me more?"

"She is my friend, my best friend . . . my only friend."

"You know who did this to her?"

"The Fascisti squads, obviously."

"You know why they would have done such a thing?"

"Yes. She had the effrontery to disagree with Il Duce."

"And why are you here, in such a neighborhood, with people like this?"

"People like this?"

"Well, you seemed so . . ."

"What?"

"Conventional, I suppose."

"Contessa Giulia Morosini, the society playgirl."

He smiled. "That was a conventional thing for me to say."

"You know why I first came to you?"

"You wanted to become pregnant."

"I don't mean that. I came to you because you were the conventional society doctor."

"Ah. Then perhaps we were both wrong."

Francesca was snoring evenly. The bare light overhead fell coldly on the wrecked studio. The panes of the windows and skylight had turned into black opaque squares.

"Why did you become a doctor?"

"To get out of Sicily."

"And why did you come here tonight?"

A row of white teeth showed in his brown parchment face. "You press too hard . . . I became a doctor because I saw my father stabbed in the streets of Messina by the Mafia, and he bled to death because no doctor would come to him."

"Ah. Can you find out what has happened to James?"

"I already have. The shopkeeper at the corner told me. Your friends were coming home. The men who did this," and Dr. Saraceno waved his hand around the studio, "were just coming out. They had expected to find your friends here, I suppose. They ran into them in the street and dragged them into an alleyway. They beat the man and painted the woman. It happens all the time."

"Where is James?"

"He's in the Ospedale Santa Cecilia."

"Seriously hurt?"

"I don't think too seriously. . . . Now, what are you going to do?"

"Stay here."

"Does your husband know?"

"My husband doesn't even know that I come here."

"He's in the foreign ministry, I believe."

"Yes."

"Go back to him."

Julia was silent.

"I will arrange for a nurse for your friend, and I will call you tomorrow."

"Why are you doing this?"

"Professional concern. If you want to have your baby, you

must go back to your own home and not worry about what's happening here. I will give you a call in the morning."

Julia sighed. "Yes, I will do that."

She was very tired. If she went back to the Via Giulia, she could be asleep long before Angelo came in from wherever it was he went at night.

But when Julia returned she found that Angelo had gone to Milan, leaving a note saying that Mussolini, who was touring northern Italy, had summoned him to discuss some foreign policy matters. It was a relief to have the apartment to herself, but during the night she began having cramps and hardly slept at all.

By morning she was bleeding. She called Dr. Saraceno who took her in his car to the hospital; and on the way she asked about James. He only told her to keep quiet and still. At the hospital they did what they could to prevent a miscarriage, without success. When it was over, they gave her a sedative, and she drifted in and out of sleep for the rest of the day. In the evening she woke to find Dr. Saraceno standing beside the bed holding her wrist, with his fingers on her pulse.

"How do you feel?"

"Not bad. Weak."

"You seem fine. I'm sorry we were not able to save the child."

"It's all right," she said grimly, "I've just got my figure back a bit early, that's all."

"You don't mean that."

"No, but . . ."

"There's no reason at all why you can't have another child."

"I don't want to become pregnant again. I want to be free. When can I leave?"

"We'll see tomorrow."

"Where am I?"

"The Ospedale Santa Cecilia."

"James is here?"

"James is dead."

Julia turned her face into the pillow.

"I'm sorry. He died last night. But as long as there was a chance to save the child, I thought it best not to tell you."

Dr. Saraceno sat down on the edge of the bed and took one of her pale hands in his brown ones. "They say that misfortunes always come in pairs."

Julia began to sob. "I'm so unhappy."

"It's natural to be depressed afterward."

"It's not that. It's my whole life. I wish I could just start all over again."

"We all wish that. You're young. You can."

"There's no divorce in Italy."

"You want a divorce?"

"I have never loved my husband. I love another man and always have . . . always will. But if I'm married 'till death do us part,' there's not any way I can start over, is there? Why am I talking so much?"

"The medication sometimes does that."

The doctor got up and took a pack of cigarettes out of his raincoat hanging on the back of the door.

"Would you like one?"

"I shouldn't, should I?"

He smiled. "Of course not."

She smiled back. "Yes, I'll have one."

He cranked up the hospital bed, sat back down on the edge, lit two cigarettes and put one between her lips.

"Thanks. Does Francesca know about James?"

"Yes. I've seen her."

"That was kind. All this has nothing to do with you."

"It should have very much to do with me. I was an idealist once and now I am a 'society doctor,' as you said last night."

"Was it only last night?"

"You described yourself as a 'society playgirl.' I think we're both ashamed of the roles we've played." He was silent for a few moments. "I'm going to do something that my head tells me I shouldn't do but my Italian heart . . . my Sicilian heart . . . tells me I should. Do you want some advice?"

"Very much."

"I knew you were an unhappy wife the first time you came to my office. I see the same thing several times a day in different forms. Most of these women will never escape from the roles they're trapped in. I think you can."

"How?"

"Forget yourself for a while. I told you I had seen your friend, Signora Danieli. She's very depressed, more depressed than is natural, even after what's happened. In my opinion, if she is left alone, she might try to take her own life."

"You don't have to say anything more, Doctor."

When Julia was discharged from the hospital she took a taxi to the Via Giulia, wrote a note to Angelo, who was still in Milan, packed a suitcase, put it in her Fiat, and drove to Trastevere. She wanted the break to be clean and final.

"Well, what do you think?" She held up the red dress that she had just bought off the rack at the Rinascente department store.

"Nice," Francesca said. "But you shouldn't be spending your money on clothes when you have closets full back at your place."

"I won't go back to the Via Giulia ever, even for those beautiful clothes. And besides, what would I do with such clothes here."

"I don't know why you want to go to Agnes's anyway."

"Well, she *did* invite me. Considering that I'm a penniless, estranged wife, that was pretty generous. And it's Christmas Eve. Spirit of the season, and all that."

"They're leaving soon?"

"I hear Aunt Agnes vows they'll never serve one day under Roosevelt. They plan to be back in Branwood before the inauguration. . . . Francesca, you've started to work again."

Julia walked across the studio to study the small clay model on a stand.

"Do you like it?"

"Yes. It's quieter than before."

"This afternoon for the first time I felt like working."

Julia took Francesca's narrow face between her hands. "I'm glad."

"I'm going to make it, Julia."

"I know. Now, I've got to get dressed. I won't stay long at the Palazzo Rosalba."

The December night was cold and clear; the sky above Rome, a mass of stars. She drove her car up on the sidewalk in front of the palazzo. She could hear a big, noisy crowd inside. Julia knew many of them, Americans from the embassy, Italian social climbers, and Fascist officials. A butler took her coat and handed her a cup of eggnog.

"Julia, I'm glad you could make it. We haven't seen you in ages. Where've you been keeping yourself?"

"Merry Christmas, Aunt Agnes. It's been a long time. I live over in Trastevere now, with a girlfriend."

"Then it's true that you and the count have separated?"

"I left him, yes."

"I'm not sure that was wise, Julia."

Julia sipped her eggnog. "Wise or not, that's what I've done."

"Well, it's your life, and you can do with it as you please, but you do have family obligations."

"I don't know what you are talking about," Julia said, and truly she did not.

"What I am talking about is that our family has a certain social standing, and your Uncle Charles holds a position of great trust and responsibility. He represents the United States government and our President in this country."

"I thought our ambassador did that."

Agnes's eyes narrowed. "You persist in pretending not to understand, Julia. What I'm talking about is that you did not even have the courtesy to tell me that you had just walked out on your husband. I had to hear it from Princess Colonna."

"The fact that I have left Angelo is hardly a scandal."

"It is the common way that you did it," Agnes snapped.

"If you mean by that that you don't like the people I associate with, that's too damned bad. They are my friends."

"You have turned out just like your mother."

"How proud I would be if that was true." She carefully put down her eggnog cup. "Well, Merry Christmas, Aunt Agnes."

Julia turned and went into the crowded reception room, and immediately ran into Victoria.

"Merry Christmas, Julie."

"Hi, Vicky. Merry Christmas. It's been a long time. Where's Bruno?"

"He's in Milan. . . . Julie, is something wrong? You look—"

"It's nothing. I just had a nasty run-in with your mother."

"What about?"

"Leaving Angelo and hanging around with artists and such. She finds my behavior common."

"She said that?"

"She did."

"She wouldn't have dared to say that before you lost your money. How hateful of her."

"She knows I've lost everything?"

"Of course. When one of the biggest banks in Baltimore collapses the news travels fast. You've lost literally everything?"

"Everything."

"You've had a hard year, Julie."

"Want to hear more? I've also had a miscarriage."

"Oh, my poor dear." Victoria put her arms around her and gave her a squeeze.

"In a way it's nice to be free again." Julia realized that what she had just said was true, and her spirits rose. "Tell me about Bruno."

"He's fine. We're happy. You know, Julie, we're suited to each other. At first I wasn't sure our marriage was going to work either. But it has."

"I'm glad."

"See what he gave me for Christmas." Victoria held out her hand, on which glittered a magnificent opal surrounded by diamonds.

"It's beautiful."

"I just wish I could look like you. Hard luck certainly hasn't affected your beauty. And that's a nice dress. . . ."

"You don't need to cheer me up *that* much Vicky. It's off the rack at Rinascente," she said, hugging Victoria and kissing her on the cheek. "Merry Christmas."

Julia took another cup of eggnog, left the crowded room, and wandered into the library. She would not give Agnes the satisfaction of driving her out with her rudeness. She stood alone in front of the fire.

"Julia, what are you doing in here all by yourself?"

"Merry Christmas, Uncle Charles."

"Beautiful as ever," he said, coming up to her. He had had too much to drink. "Where have you been keeping yourself?"

"Trastevere. I share a studio with a girlfriend."

"At least that's what you tell folks over on this side of the river," he said, winking at her. To her surprise he reached over and put his hand on her bottom. She stared coldly at him, not moving, until he withdrew it.

"If I were living with a man, Uncle Charles, I wouldn't be ashamed to say so."

She put down her empty cup and walked away, leaving Charles standing by the fire, befuddled. She found her coat and slipped quietly out the front door.

When she got back to the studio, Francesca was already in bed. She put on a nightgown and got in bed beside her.

"Well, how was it?"

"Dreadful. Charles made a pass at me."

Francesca laughed. "And Agnes?"

"My social standing with Aunt Agnes has come full circle. I'm right back to where I was when I was eleven years old and living with my mother and Gus Bramante."

Julia closed her eyes. She was going to have to buy a bed. Francesca was all right now, and she didn't really like sleeping with another woman.

On New Year's Eve, Julia and Francesca, with some of their artist friends, got terribly drunk. At midnight, along with everyone else in Rome, they threw the year's chipped and broken crockery out the window into the street. Julia woke the next morning with an awful hangover, but clear-headed, as if she had exorcised the old year and all that was in it. Francesca snored away in bed.

Julia put on a skirt and sweater and went down to the corner coffee bar. She ordered a *caffè latte* and looked at *Il Tempo*. It was the kind of day to go to a movie or a concert, but there was nothing worth seeing. What she really should do, she knew, was think about the future. Most of the money she had left was in Geneva, but that was in the Morosini Estate account and required Angelo's countersignature for withdrawals. She was down to twelve hundred dollars in her Rome account, and after that was gone she would have to sell the only material possession she really cared about, her midnight-blue Fiat.

In the end Julia decided to go to the one public place that seemed to be open on New Year's Day, the Colosseum. It was a fine warm day and Julia walked around in the great empty ruin where thousands had died, feeling not nearly, she realized, as unhappy as she might have been. Whatever else, she was free. She had not felt like this since she had played in the waterfront streets of Baltimore. She climbed higher and higher above the arena. A few old people were basking in the sun along with the usual cats, which seemed to inhabit the Colosseum by the hundreds. Reaching the top tier, she looked down through one of the giant arches onto the city of Rome, the city that she had once so confidently said she would make her own.

She almost laughed out loud at the thought and then realized with a start that a man was watching her from one of the archways. He came toward her, a tall, dark-haired man in a black raincoat. The Fascist secret police was her first thought; and then, as he came closer, she realized that no one with the Italian government would be working on a holiday, particularly in so unlikely a place as the Colosseum. He was only a few paces away. White pigeons on the dark stones fluttered up between them and rose against the blue sky.

"Paolo." Her voice was too weak to carry even the few feet that now separated them.

She moved forward, and they reached out to each other, as if across an abyss. Their fingers touched. He held her hands in his hands, large and warm and strong. Underneath the raincoat he wore the same kind of sweater he had worn that day in Aquila, when he had walked away from her; that day when, out of pride, they had conspired in the destruction of their happiness.

"You're very pale. Are you all right?"

"Yes, I'm all right," she said.

He took her by the shoulders with those hands, and he mustn't do that, she thought.

"You're trembling, Julia. Are you sure everything's okay?"

"Yes. You startled me, that's all." She tried to draw away, but he wouldn't let go of her.

"And Francesca, how is she?"

"She's much better now."

"You saved her life, I hear."

Don't look at me like that, she said to herself. It's all over between us. "In a way she saved my life."

"I've thought about you a lot."

She turned her head away.

"I was so wrong about you."

"No, Paolo, you weren't wrong. It's just that . . ." What?

"Things have changed?"

"Yes." Why was he walking her down the worn steps toward the arena? The roar of an ancient crowd seemed to rush up into her ears.

"You've changed."

His hand held her arm firmly just above the elbow.

"We should go see Francesca," she said.

"I don't dare. I'm sure the studio's being watched. I waited outside all morning hoping Francesca would come out. And then you came out, and I followed you here. I had given up hope, you know. . . ."

Hope?

"Julia, what *is* wrong?" he asked in a concerned voice as she staggered and held onto him for support.

They were in a dark passageway that led from the arena out into the street. She leaned against the cold stone, feeling dizzy again.

"I've been through a lot, I guess."

"I heard you left Morosini."

"More than that," and then she began to laugh. "Mainly it's just that I've the most beastly hangover. Francesca and I got drunk last night."

She seemed to hear the roar of the crowd again, the clashing of steel on steel. But she was safe. Paolo Danieli was holding her in his arms.

"You've lost a lot of weight." Then his arms must still remember the shape and feel of her body. "Let me buy you some lunch."

"All right," a voice that didn't belong to her said.

"*Aglio e olio*, the Roman cure for the morning after."

From then on what happened seemed unreal, a hallucination brought on by too much wine and too little food and sleep.

"Signora?" The waiter stood, pencil poised over his order pad.

"*Aglio e olio,*" Julia said.

The worst was over. And the spaghetti steeped in olive oil and garlic seemed the most comforting thing she had ever eaten. After a couple of glasses of red wine, the small cheap restaurant, the zinc tables, and the big pots of water on the wood-burning stove stopped spinning around. There had been more wrong with her than a hangover. Paolo had been talking for a long time, but she couldn't concentrate.

"You think Francesca will be all right now?"

"I think the worst is over for her . . . and for me."

"Then . . ."

"Could I have some coffee now?" she said.

"I suppose you'll be going back to America soon."

Julia studied the big potted fern in the steamed-up window of the restaurant. The fern was like a small jungle, and the room was like a small world that enveloped her in its warmth.

"No," she said, "my home is here now."

Julia ran up the steps to the studio two at a time. The room was filled with the warm glow of the setting sun, but—at that perfect moment—Francesca was not there. She had so much she wanted to tell her. There was a stirring behind the decorated screen that hid the bed.

"Francesca?"

"I'll be out in just a sec."

Julia stood, perplexed. What was going on? Then Francesca came out from behind the screen, wrapped tightly in Julia's bathrobe, her hair a mess, a dazed look on her face.

"Hi. Let's go to the kitchen and make some coffee, shall we?"

Standing over the two gas rings that brewed the coffee and heated the milk, Julia nearly laughed at how naive she had been, all absorbed in her own emotions. The sweet odor of sex enveloped Francesca's body.

"Hello, Julia." One of the young artists who had been at last night's party emerged, pulling on his sweater.

"You remember Arturo, of course," Francesca said in a husky voice, smiling down into the foaming milk.

"Yes, naturally." But she wouldn't have remembered his name. "Would you like some coffee?"

"No, thanks. I was just leaving," Arturo said, edging toward the door. "I'll call you tomorrow, Fran." Fran? The door closed behind the young man.

"Where've you been all day?"

"Obviously," Julia said, and smiled, "you managed without me. But where I've been, strangely enough, is the Colosseum."

"How odd. What were you doing there?"

"Having a big plate of *aglio e olio*. Did you know that's a marvelous cure for a hangover? The garlic clears your head."

"I have my own cure.... No, seriously, Julia. I can't

mourn James forever, and he wouldn't have wanted me to. I need to live again." Francesca leaned back against the wall and put her nose in the mug of steaming coffee.

"So do I. Francesca, Paolo's back."

"What?" Francesca's head snapped up, the look of sleepy satisfaction gone.

"He came looking for you. He followed me to the Colosseum. . . . Oh, Francesca!"

"He's all right?"

"He's fine."

"Julia, you ought to see your face. I haven't seen you look so happy for a long time."

"Not since . . . well, before I married." Julia looked up from her steaming cup. "Happy . . . and afraid."

"For Paolo?"

"For myself. . . . Francesca, what should I do? The second I saw him, it was like the last two years had never happened."

"Go to him, then."

"Suppose he doesn't want me? I'd . . . well I wouldn't kill myself. But I don't know how I'd bear it. Maybe it would be better just to leave things as they are."

"How was he toward you?"

"Kind. He said I'd changed."

"Then he sees what you've become."

"I have changed, Francesca, haven't I?"

"Julia, go to him. Don't you want to be happy?"

"Of course I do, but so much has passed between us. You know."

"Yes, I do. And that's why I'm telling you that you two must not spoil things again."

"You love him, don't you?"

Francesca closed her eyes and breathed out through flared nostrils. "I love you both."

"Francesca . . ."

"Go to him."

"If I could only go to him now. But he's leaving again today. He said he'll be back in a week, two weeks. He'll send a message to let us know exactly when. He wants to see you, but he doesn't dare come here. He's using another name now ... Paolo Rossi."

"Yes, I'd like to see him, and tell him to get out of the Resistance before the same thing happens to him that happened to James. ... Oh, I'm sorry, Julia. But it's true, you know."

"I know. I told him I was staying in Italy. Francesca, I've got to move out of here. You're okay now. And I've got to get a job or something. My money's running out, and I'm so afraid they'll make me leave. Angelo might see to that. And I just can't. Not now that there's a chance ..."

Julia stood up and began to pace the studio. "Francesca, what can I do?"

"Make Angelo release your money in Switzerland."

"He won't. He's already said so."

"Then make him get you a work permit. He can do that, and you can't work without one."

"He won't do it, I'm sure of that."

"You can make him. He's scared of you."

They met at the bar of the Excelsior Hotel, where Julia had so often swept in, in evening dress with a fur coat over her shoulders. Now she wore a plain tweed suit and no makeup. The last thing she wanted was for Angelo to get the idea that she was trying to look seductive, or that a reconciliation might be possible. It was four o'clock on a Sunday afternoon, and the bar was deserted except for Angelo seated by a window. He was staring out into the Via Veneto, as handsome as ever. He stood up when she approached, hesitated, and then kissed her hand.

"My, but aren't we formal," she said, sitting down opposite him.

"I'm just being proper. The bartender is watching us, and I'm sure you wouldn't have allowed anything more intimate."

He was right, of course. "I'll have a scotch and soda, Angelo."

"How've you been?"

She shrugged. "Not bad. I'm learning to live alone."

"You're not coming back to me, then."

"Never. Buy why? Would you have me back?"

"Of course."

"Even if there was nothing ... and I mean nothing ... between us?"

"Even then."

"Why?"

"I know what your American reaction is going to be, but there is a thing called appearances."

"I'm not a fool, Angelo. I've lived in Italy for nearly three years. I quite understand that appearances matter, but in a country that doesn't have divorce, living apart isn't exactly unheard of. I can think of a half-dozen cases in the foreign ministry alone."

"It's not that. You're making me look like a fool."

"You'll have to explain yourself."

"Contessa Morosini running around Rome trying to find a job. Didn't anyone ever tell you what that involves for a woman?"

"You mean sleeping with the boss?"

"Yes."

"I'm sorry that I am an embarrassment to you, but you should have thought of that before you started sleeping around yourself."

"Fiammetta Gildo means absolutely nothing to me."

"I'm sure she doesn't, nor any of the others that I've heard about since we separated. That's exactly the point, Angelo."

He sat silently, turning his glass on the table, the corners of his mouth turned down.

"You think I'm being unreasonable, don't you?" she said.

"Yes, I do."

"I never was able to get it through your thick Italian head that it was either me or the field. You chose the field, so you can't have me." The truth would have hurt him even more. For a moment she thought that he was going to slap her, but instead he said, "It's not too late."

"Oh, yes it is. And that, Angelo, is final."

"Then why did you want to see me?"

"I want you to help me get a work permit."

"That's impossible. You would be taking a job from an Italian."

"Angelo, let's be serious. You know very well that anything is possible with this Fascist government if you have influence, and you do."

"I don't look enough of a fool? Now you want me to beg someone to give you a job?"

"You won't do it?"

"No."

"All right. Then give me back my apartment and sign over the balance in my Geneva account, and I won't have to work."

"*Our* apartment and *our* Geneva account. The lawyer explained all that to you very carefully."

"Yes, I remember. It's all part of the marriage contract, and you broke that."

"If that's the way you feel, you should go back to America."

"You can't make me. I kept my part of the bargain."

"Either come back to me or go home to America."

"Angelo, I'm going to explain something to you very clearly. I will not go back to America, and I'm certainly not coming back to you. You can keep the apartment, but you're going to help me get a job so that I can support myself. That you owe me."

"And if I won't?"

"Then I will teach you what being made a fool of really means. I will make such a spectacle of myself, they will laugh you right out of the foreign ministry. I will drag the Morosini name through the gutters of Rome."

"You wouldn't dare."

"Try me."

Angelo was tapping his foot nervously. "All right, stay. You can get a work permit without my help."

"How?"

"A job with a foreign firm that requires English. Your embassy should be able to help you find something respectable. They give work permits for such jobs. I'll see there aren't any problems."

"Thanks, Angelo." She smiled coldly. "And I promise not to disgrace your name. I'll need to have my clothes sent over to my place."

"I sold them."

"You did *what*?"

"I needed the money. You know how hard up I am these days, and what with maintaining the apartment and Villa Serena . . ."

The bartender, who had been watching the tense, angry couple, was startled when Julia laughed out loud.

"Well, at least you didn't give them to one of your slutty girlfriends."

The next day Julia found an old typewriter with an English keyboard in the flea market, had it repaired, and began to teach herself typing. That same day a letter from a classmate at Goucher finally found its way to the studio in Trastevere. A clipping from *The Baltimore Sun*, months old, was enclosed. It was the obituary of Elmer J. Thornley, Jr. He had shot himself in his office on the eighteenth floor of the Merchants and Farmers Bank when it was discovered that he had diverted assets from a number of the trust funds he had managed in order to cover his own losses from 1929 on. Well, Julia thought, there are worse things than being broke.

When weeks had passed and still they had not heard from Paolo, Julia grew frantic with worry. Then one day in late February a telegram arrived: ROME TOMORROW STOP USUAL HOTEL STOP HOPE TO MEET YOU THERE 3PM—YOUR AFFECTIONATE COUSIN.

"Thank God! But tomorrow's today and . . . I don't have a thing to wear."

Francesca threw back her head and laughed. "How female."

"Well, I don't. I suppose *you* do?"

"No. But then I'm not going."

"What do you mean?"

"I've a date with Arturo."

"Francesca, Paolo's expecting you."

"I can see Paolo another time."

"What? Really, Francesca . . ."

"And as long as you're going to be out I think I'll have Arturo over here. . . . So don't come back too early."

They both laughed at that, and hugged each other.

When Julia got out of her little sports car, no longer new and shiny, in front of a small hotel on the Via Emilia, it was already a quarter past three. But she simply couldn't have let him see her the way she was. Now she was afraid she was overdressed, stockings and high heels and a dark suit, a cheap thing off the rack, but the best she could afford. What would she say to him?

There was no one in the dark lobby except for a concierge behind the desk.

"Signora?"

"I was supposed to meet . . ." And then she saw the back of a man's head at a table beyond the darkened bar.

"Paolo?"

He stood up and turned. "Ah, Cousin."

For a moment she couldn't speak. His presence overwhelmed her, as it had the first time she had seen him, standing over a table in a bar on the *Velonia*, unshaven, in old clothes, and needing a haircut.

"Francesca couldn't come."

"Oh?"

"She has a new boyfriend and . . ."

Paolo laughed. How good it was to hear his laugh again.

"What's he like?"

"He's *very* young."

He laughed again. "Francesca's incorrigible."

"I'm afraid so."

"Well, sit down. What would you like?" He slid the chair smoothly under her.

"Campari-soda, I guess."

He was so dark-eyed, dark-haired, thinner, different, all

of that diffuse power of his now focused into the fictional role of Paolo Rossi, commercial traveler, in a double-breasted gray flannel suit and plain blue tie. She had been too disoriented on New Year's Day even to see him clearly.

"Well."

"Well . . . Oh, Paolo, I don't want a drink and I don't want to be in this dreary bar. Can we go somewhere else?"

"How about a walk in the park?"

"Yes. That would be perfect."

They walked the two short blocks up to the old Roman wall and through the Pinciana gate into the Borghese Gardens. Julia looked across at the Palazzo Rosalba, the shutters all closed. By now Agnes and Charles would be back in their big house on Chesapeake Bay.

"It seems only yesterday that I arrived in Rome to visit Aunt Agnes, and now she's gone and I'm still here."

"It's nearly three years since you and Francesca and I came across on the *Velonia*. Do you remember how we met?"

How could he say that in such a casual way? She wanted to say I will never forget as long as I live, but instead she said, "Yes, I remember." And then, "In some ways it seems I've been here forever, so much has happened to me."

"I thought you were a rich young bitch."

She stole a glance at him. She couldn't make out what he was thinking. "Well, I'm certainly not rich anymore, and I hope I'm also not the other . . . anymore."

He said nothing, but took her arm in his. She could feel the warmth of his body through her sleeve.

"You're really going to stay in Italy?"

"I'm going to try to. I'm looking for a job."

"You understand now that things are going to be more and more difficult under the Fascists?"

"I don't care. This is where I want to be." She longed to tell him why, but she didn't even know how to talk to this strange man.

"Paolo, is what you're doing . . . and you don't have to tell me if you don't want to . . . very dangerous?"

"There's some risk, but I'm not actually *doing* anything.

We're making contacts, recruiting people, setting up a network throughout Italy for the day when it will be needed. It's much too early to try to move against Mussolini. He'd crush us right away."

Having him trust her enough to say that much made her spirits lift a little. She wished that he would keep talking in that warm deep voice that was a joy to listen to, and that they could just walk on together all afternoon, arm in arm. It was a gray February day, but not too cold. Rain the night before had brought down the last faded leaves, which were plastered on the broad asphalt walk between the umbrella pines. They had come to an old fountain with sea horses rearing out of its dark stagnant water. Paolo paused as if he were about to turn back. She took her arm from his and sat down on the edge of the fountain. She must hold him, must think of something to say. He sat down beside her.

"What kind of job are you looking for?"

He thinks I don't know how to do anything and he's right.

"Oh, nothing grand. I've taught myself to type, you know. I have an interview next week with an English news agency."

She picked up a dead twig and pushed a fallen leaf along the surface of the water.

"Well, good luck. I'm going to be in Rome from now on, I hope, if I can find a quiet, safe place to stay."

Her heart was beating fast. "You are?" She gave the leaf another push.

"Tell me, Julia, why do you want to stay in Italy?"

She had avoided his eyes up till then, but now she raised her head and looked at him. He was even handsomer than when they first met. A wave of desire flowed through her.

"Don't you know?"

He turned away and looked back along the deserted avenue. And then she was overcome by panic.

"Paolo, I've changed. I really have . . . You said so yourself."

Oh, God, she was going to lose him before she had even had a chance. He didn't want her. Why had she ever

thought they could start over? But she went on. "I understand now why you have to do what you're doing. I
wouldn't . . ." Her voice broke. What was the use?

He turned toward her, his dark eyes searching hers.
"Julia, what are you trying to say?"

"That I . . ." She sighed deeply. Why not? What difference did it make now? ". . . that I have always loved you
and always will."

"After the way I treated you?" he said very quietly.

"I know it's no use, Paolo. It was crazy of me to think . . .
But now, at least, you know." She turned her head to hide
the tears, the twig trembling in her hand plunged the floating
leaf down into the black water.

"You mean you would still have me?" he said.

She was so choked with emotion that she couldn't speak.
He took her by both arms and turned her around.

"Would you?"

She nodded her head, her eyes filled with tears so that
she could hardly see him.

"Of course," she gasped. "Didn't you know?"

"But when you married someone else . . ."

"In desperation . . . and to hurt you."

"Then there's nothing to keep us apart now."

"Oh, Paolo . . ."

"Don't you understand? I've never stopped loving you.
Why else do you think I went away? After you married, I
couldn't bear to be near where you were."

"Then why later . . ."

"I didn't know whether you would have me."

"Paolo, what a pair of bloody fools we've been."

He leaned over and kissed her gently on the lips. She put
her head on his shoulder, almost sick at the thought that
they could have lost each other again.

"Both of us had too much pride, Julia. This should have
happened a long time ago."

"I don't care. All I care about is that it's happened now."
His arms were around her. "I want to go away with you,"
she said, her face buried in the rough fabric of his jacket.

"Yes, and I'll never let you leave me."

"I hope not." She smiled, blinking away the tears.

They began walking back along the avenue of pines. Soon she would feel other things, but now, for a little while, she felt only the calm after the storm. They arrived back in front of Paolo's hotel without Julia having the slightest idea how they got there.

"I don't want to go there," she said.

"No?"

"What, then?"

He held out his hand. "Give me the car keys."

She opened her handbag and handed him the keys. He opened the door for her, went around the car, got into the driver's seat, and turned the ignition. They moved out from the curb and down the empty Via Emilia, the gray afternoon already turning into dusk. The lighted shops along the Via Veneto were so warm and cheerful, she thought. How quickly things happen, after wanting them for so long . . . and after having spoiled things so many times. She hugged her knees and closed her eyes. How perfect it was to be close to him and to be driving through the city with its lights coming on, not knowing or caring where they were going. How beautiful Rome was!

"Is Francesca expecting you to come back tonight?"

She put her hand on his thigh. "She'll know where I am if I don't come back, won't she?"

They turned down the Via Quirinale and sped through a maze of side streets, coming out beside the great dark mass of the Colosseum. And then they were racing down the Via Claudia, past rows of cypresses and fragments of Roman wall. Julia no longer knew where they were: in some far corner of Rome where city streets had given way to vegetable gardens and sinister ruins that loomed out of the dark. As they passed through a massive gate and away from the lighted streets of the city into the night of the countryside, smooth asphalt gave way to rough paving stones.

"Oh," she said, "we're on the Via Appia. Paolo, where are you taking me?" How delicious. They were driving along that most ancient of the Roman roads, in a starless night, leaving behind all the complications of the present.

The headlights of the car fell on ancient churches and farm-houses. There were no other cars, only a lighted country tavern here and there along the road. She could imagine the Roman legions marching along this road, and shivering, she moved closer to Paolo's warmth.

Paolo slowed the car and turned into an opening in an im-mense hedge of cypress. Inside, a courtyard of swept earth led to the front of a rambling stucco building. Oil lamps hung around the entrance and shone through the windows.

"Where are we?"

"It's a place I stay sometimes. It belongs to a couple who are active in the Resistance. It's just a simple country inn."

She could see only his dark shape next to her.

"You're making me part of your life, aren't you?"

"Yes." He opened the car door, and she could hear an owl calling in the night, but no other sound. She held him back by the arm.

"Wait." Her heart was pounding. "You remember that night on the Janiculum and what you told me?"

"I'll never forget," the dark shadow next to her said.

"You said that if we went on, there'd be no turning back . . . Well, I just want you to know that . . . I know . . . that's where we are now, and I understand . . . Paolo, this is the happiest moment of my life but . . . I know, too, that our life may not always be so happy."

A man, and a woman carrying an oil lamp, had come out of the doorway of the inn and were walking toward the car. Paolo got out and went to them.

"Giorgio! Anna!" He embraced each of them.

"You're in trouble, Paolo?" the woman said. Julia scram-bled out of the car.

"A kind of serious trouble. Julia!"

But she had already joined them, all of their faces dim masks in the lamplight.

"I want you to meet my good friends, the Velletris. Giorgio, Anna, my dearest friend, Julia . . . Morosini."

"I'm so very glad to meet friends of Paolo."

"You'll be wanting supper?"

"Julia?"

"Just something warm and a little wine."

"Quickly done," the woman said.

They ate in a darkened dining room, alone by the window, under a single oil lamp, served in turns silently by Giorgio and Anna; and then they were shown up the narrow stairs to a bedroom with glass doors opening onto an iron balcony, where a leafless gnarled grapevine twined. In the dim circle of light made by the single oil lamp, Julia sat down on the edge of the bed.

"Paolo Danieli?"

"Yes?" He stood half-hidden in the shadows, leaning against the closed door.

"What are you doing to me?"

"What you want, I hope."

"We could have done this all along, couldn't we?"

"Yes."

"Well, we were fools. But no longer."

"No."

"Come here, then."

When the blankets were pulled back, the bed smelled of the dried herbs Italians sprinkle in their linen chests; and while they fumbled to get each other's clothes off, the oil lamp went out, and their bare flesh came together before her underwear and stockings were half-off. Then, all at once, their bodies merged. She gasped and stroked the back of his neck while he made love to her. How gentle he was. For the first time in her life she let herself go completely in a man's arms, until suddenly all of her pent-up desire for him swept her into the last rhythmic movements of total release, which went on and on until she had nothing more to give. In the fierceness of their lovemaking they had uttered not a word, and afterward she burrowed up against his body under the covers, seeking only sleep, bruised, damp . . . and safe at last.

The gray cover of clouds had broken the next morning, and shafts of light moved across the fields of the Roman Campagna and played on the steel-gray sea. The room was cold and bare and Paolo was gone. It didn't matter. He would come back. She thought of the magnificent Villa Serena, her luxurious apartment on the Via Giulia, Palazzo Rosalba, Branwood. Then, looking up at the damp-stained ceiling and the cracked, whitewashed walls, she felt as if she had escaped from prison. The door flew open and Paolo came in carrying a tray of steaming pitchers of coffee and milk and a basket of hard rolls. He put the tray down beside the bed, pulled the blankets off of her, and stood looking down at her naked body stretched out on the sheet.

"It's the first time I've ever seen you, and you're even more beautiful than I imagined."

"Well, get used to it," she said with a smile, pulling the blankets up. "I'm yours now . . . for better or for worse."

Paolo sat down on the edge of the bed and poured streams of coffee and hot milk into the two mugs. She took a mug and tried to warm her hands on it. There was no heat in the inn, so she pulled the blankets close around her.

"Ah, *caffè latte* and Italian bread. That alone makes it worth staying in Italy. Oh, Paolo, what miracle has happened to us?"

"Maybe we've been punished enough."

"God, Paolo, you're beautiful to look at. Now I can tell you every day. . . ."

His smile faded, and then hers.

"You're leaving again, aren't you?"

He nodded.

"But you'll come back soon?"

"I've a few more things to do, rather important things for the organization. And then I'm coming back to Rome . . . for good."

"How long must I wait? I'll wait forever, you know." She put her cold hand on his cheek.

"A month. Two months. As quickly as I can."

"I'll be good, Paolo. I'll be a good wife . . . in all but name."

He laughed. "I don't use my real name anyway."

"Paolo, finish your coffee and come back to bed."

Chapter Nine

AT THE FOOT of the Via Veneto, in a narrow street off the Piazza Barberini, Julia found the address in the ad. She climbed the creaking wooden stairs with pounding heart. In her twenty-four years she had never had a job or been subject to anyone else's will. Now she must perform adequately or return to America—and that was impossible, could not even be contemplated. The week before, when she had had her passport renewed at the American Embassy, the young vice-consul had warned her that if she did not find a job with a foreign employer before her Italian visa expired, she would certainly have to return home. She tried not to think of those last hours with Paolo. To do that would be to admit that the paradise that she had just entered could be taken from her. She had made Rome hers once, she repeated to herself as she reached the fourth-floor landing, and she would do it again. She was angry, and proud—and scared.

On the frosted glass of the door the gold-leaf letters were precisely laid down, coldly edged in black: TRAFALGAR NEWS AGENCY, and in smaller letters beneath that, HOME OFFICE LONDON, ENGLAND—BUREAUS THROUGHOUT THE WORLD.

As she opened the door, a little bell rang overhead. A boy of about fourteen got up from the swivel chair to face her.

"Is Mr. Harrison in?"

"Not yet."

"Do you expect him?"

"Soon."

"I'm Julia Howard. I've come about the job."

"Armandi, Giovanni," the boy said.

"May I wait?"

"Sure." He opened the gate in the railing that separated the office from the entryway. She went in and sat down. Giovanni went back to the swivel chair and resumed slowly turning in circles. Julia took off her gloves. The office was more modest than she had imagined. Besides the chairs there were only a rolltop desk, an office typewriter on a wooden table, and, standing between the two tall windows, what she supposed was a Teletype machine: She had never seen one. That was it, except for a telephone, a wire waste-paper basket, an ancient pendulum clock and a wall calendar.

"You ought to get a job in the movies."

"What?"

"You look like Gina Franco."

"Why . . . thank you."

"What do you want to work in this place for?"

"Don't you like it?"

"It's all right. But we never had a woman here before. You speak good Italian for Englishwoman."

"Thank you. I'm American. You mean there hasn't been a secretary before?"

"No. Just me and Max."

"What do you do?"

"Answer the phone when he's out, get coffee, clean up." The boy grinned. "I run the office all by myself when he gets drunk."

Oh, dear, thought Julia, what am I getting into?

The Teletype started clattering. Giovanni went over and turned on a green-shaded bulb that hung over the machine. Julia stood beside him watching the purple letters appear mysteriously on the rough yellow paper: GOOD MORNING. TUESDAY, FEBRUARY 28, 1933. THERE FOLLOWS A RECAP OF PRINCIPAL OVERNIGHT ITEMS TO 0900 GMT. . . .

The German parliament building had been burnt down by an arsonist. A Communist plot, Chancellor Hitler said. Hitler? Julia remembered Francesca and her friends talking about him, but wasn't that old man Hindenburg still the leader in Germany?

The boy walked over to the wall calendar, pulled the "MONDAY 27" sheet off, rolled it into a ball, and tossed it across the room into the wastepaper basket.

Half an hour passed and there was still no sign of Mr. Harrison.

"You want me to go get some coffee?"

"That would be nice."

"Okay, but you have to answer the phone."

Some minutes passed before the little bell on the door rang, and then it was not Giovanni. A small man with a waxed red mustache came through the door. Julia was trying out the typewriter.

"Hullo. Who're you?"

"Julia Howard. I came about the job."

"Was that today? Dear me. And where's that wretched Johnny?"

"He went for coffee."

The man went over to where she was sitting. She stood.

"You type, I see."

"Yes."

"Well, if you don't mind, I'll take this out of the machine. I've just thought of a nice turn of phrase, and I'd best put it down before my poor brain loses it."

He took off his black bowler and sat down at the typewriter. He was wearing a navy blazer and a blue polka-dot bow tie. Julia would soon learn that it was the only costume Max Harrison ever wore, except that in summer a straw boater was substituted for the bowler. He typed out a couple of paragraphs on a sheet of yellow paper. Julia was dismayed to see that he typed much faster than she. He took the paper out of the machine and sat on the windowsill to read it. In the sunlight his thinning red hair was obviously dyed.

"You're American."

"Yes."

"What are you doing over here?"

"I'm married to an Italian. We're separated."

His eyes narrowed. "You speak Italian, then?"

"Yes."

"You live alone?"

"I live with a friend ... a female friend."

"Are you serious about wanting to work? You're an awfully pretty girl to be taking a job like this."

"It's the kind of job I want. One without complications."

He nodded his head. "Who're you married to, if you don't mind my asking?"

"Angelo Morosini. He's at the foreign ministry."

"Yes, I know. Count Morosini ... Look, Countess, I'm going to be honest with you. I don't want any trouble with the Italian government. ..."

"There won't be any trouble. We have an understanding."

"The pay's only four quid a week. It took me forever to get the home office to agree to even that."

Fourteen dollars. It wasn't much, but more than most of the jobs she had tried for, and with it they couldn't send her home.

"I'll take it."

"Well, I suppose you're hired then, since you're the only person who's applied for the job who's a native English speaker ... if you can say that of an American."

Max Harrison did drink. He was disorganized, lazy, foulmouthed, and impossible to keep track of: he was also a professional. When an important story broke he never missed it, but then he demanded a great deal of her. The first week of working for Max was absolute hell for Julia, who had never done a day's work before. She had, she realized, not even known anyone who worked for a salary. The second week Max made a halfhearted pass at her that she easily deflected. He seemed not to mind. The third week Julia began to relax. She was going to make it. And she was grateful that she had to work so hard, desperately trying to keep the job. For those hours at least there was no time to remember that Paolo was not with her, but following his own dangerous course somewhere in Italy. In the evening, she would talk to Francesca about Paolo. When she had told her that they were lovers, all Francesca had said was "I'm so glad for both of you," giving Julia a hug.

Soon Julia was confidently typing out copy, answering the phone, covering up for Max when London called and he was nowhere to be found, and generally taking charge of the office. From the day that she had left college until her marriage to Angelo had gone to pieces, Julia had thought hardly at all of what was going on in the world. That dreadful day when James had died and she had lost her baby had been the beginning of her awakening, yet for months she had thought of nothing but how to salvage something from her wrecked life. Now that she belonged to Paolo and was doing a job, and doing it well, her self-esteem began to return; and she wanted to do more and to learn about the larger world in which Paolo Danieli moved.

Julia had two teachers. One was Max, who, as an old newspaper man, believed nothing that he was told and suspected everyone's motives. He was, Julia noted, usually right. Angelo and his friends were equally cynical, but were smoothly hypocritical about it. Max was quite open about his mistrust of mankind in general, and of political figures in particular. He invariably referred to the leader of Italy as "that arse-hole Mussolini."

Julia's other teacher was the Trafalgar News Agency Teletype. The purple-lettered sheets that she tore off the machine told her more about what was going on in the world than she had ever known before. Soon she was talking back to it, sending Max's stories over the wire to London, and having the pleasure of seeing them repeated by London from Tokyo to New York:

ROME (TNA). THE ITALIAN GOVERNMENT TODAY AN-
NOUNCED THE APPOINTMENT OF AIR MARSHAL ITALO BALBO,
CHIEF OF THE ITALIAN AIR FORCE, AS GOVERNOR-GENERAL OF
LIBYA, THE ITALIAN NORTH AFRICAN COLONY WITH AN AREA
LARGER THAN THAT OF ITALY, FRANCE, AND GERMANY COM-
BINED. . . .

Max had a great laugh over that story. He had predicted that Balbo would regret having led a squadron of twenty-four Italian seaplanes across the Atlantic. The Italian community in America had gone wild, and Balbo and his aviators were given a ticker tape parade down Fifth Avenue. His return was not so grand, as Max had foretold. Max had not even bothered to cover the event, but had sent Julia instead on her first reporting assignment. Il Duce was insanely jealous of Balbo's exploit, and shortly thereafter relieved him of his position as head of the air force, making him instead, as Max said, "commander of Italy's sandpile," inhabited by the remains of the bedouin tribes Mussolini had bombed into submission.

None of Max's dispatches, Julia noted, reflected his amusement. They were, if anything, complimentary to Mussolini: It paid to be careful in Italy. Balbo had gained nothing from his triumph; but someone who did profit was Bruno Bronzini, whose company made the engines that powered the planes. He received a massive order for more engines from the Italian Air Force. Bruno was becoming a man of some importance in Italy, while Victoria had gone back to Baltimore to give birth to a child.

Julia ran her car up on the curb in front of the Stazione Termini and, as she got out, showed a lot of leg to the policeman who was coming toward her wagging a white-gloved finger. He gave her a conspiratorial smile and shrug that she knew well. It meant that beautiful women could park anywhere they wanted. How she hated Italian men! How she loved them! One month Paolo had said, or two at the most. It had been nearly three; and she went into the echoing vault of the train station fuming with indignation—and wild with desire. It was late May and the swallows were weaving in the sunset above the dark skyline of Rome; and all she had had were telegrams from her "affectionate cousin" saying that he would arrive on such and such a date and always, at the last moment, another telegram would arrive saying that there had been unexpected complications. These messages came from everywhere:

Venice, Palermo, Florence, Genoa, Turin. What kind of man had she given herself to? God, she thought, how happy I am.

As she stood there where Victoria had met her coming into Rome for the first time, she spotted Paolo immediately, and ran to throw herself into his arms. He kissed her on the neck and whispered into her ear, "Julia, Julia."

"Paolo, Paolo."

He held her so tightly around the waist that her feet left the platform and a shoe fell off. As he stooped to put it back on for her, his hand caressed her leg. Then he pulled his bag out of the compartment door with one hand and with the other grasped her again around the waist, leading her swiftly through the vaulted hall out to where the policeman stood beside her car. He tipped his cap in a way that said how much he wished he were in Paolo's shoes.

"You drive," she said, dangling the keys in front of him, "like the last time."

"Like the only time," he said, kissing her on the neck again. He pulled the little car, top down, out into the traffic flowing around the Piazza Esedra, the four monumental female nudes diving through the twilit spray of the fountain.

"Where?" he said.

She smiled and scrunched down in the white seat now worn in spots to the natural brown of the leather.

"The Pantheon."

"As you wish, signora," and he maneuvered the narrow sports car through back alleyways that she didn't know existed, until they drew up beside the fountain in front of the Pantheon's dark mass.

"The greatest surviving temple of the ancient world," Paolo said, switching off the engine, "surrounded by sidewalk cafés under strings of bare lightbulbs. Did you bring me here as an artist or ... "

"Both," she said. "You'd better put the top up. It might rain tonight."

She led him down the Via Minerva, past a statue of an elephant with an Egyptian obelisk planted on its back.

"Bernini did that," he said.

"Yes, I know. That's how I find our place."

"Our place?"

She opened her handbag and held out a large bronze key. "Welcome to Rome, Signor Danieli."

He looked at the key lying in his hand.

"What's this all about?"

"Don't ask questions."

She led him up flights of creaking wooden stairs until they stood before a massive door under the eaves.

"Go on, open it," she said, and he turned the key in the lock. Beyond was darkness and then a row of tall windows framing the great dome of the Pantheon, only a few feet across from them, dimly lighted from the square below. She turned a switch and lights went on all over the studio.

"Like it?"

He turned, shaking his head, and put his arms around her. It was the moment that she had waited for so impatiently.

"I love it. But you shouldn't have done it."

This is too perfect, she thought. It can't last. But while it does . . .

"There's a kitchen," she said. "Tiny, but supper's on the stove and . . ."

And then she sat down on the sofa that had cost her two week's salary and cried. Paolo turned the lights off and took her in his arms. In the dark, the columns and Corinthian capitals of the Pantheon, glowing like a stage set beyond the studio windows, made them feel more alone together than the blackest night could have.

"Let supper wait," he said, and there went all her long-thought-out plans for this evening. She hadn't meant to just come in and have her clothes taken off piece by piece until there was nothing left but her step-ins, and then they were down around her knees and the hand of the man she loved was there instead.

"Too long," she said.

"It won't happen again," he breathed into her ear.

Oh, yes, it will happen again, she thought, but it's worth it, and she drew him down on top of her.

* * *

"There's only this one room," she said. "It's all I could afford."

She walked around, putting her clothes on, in the early morning light, while he lay half-covered by a sheet on the convertible sofa that was their bed. How nice to have a whole wall of glass but complete privacy, high up next to the Pantheon's dome, ocher and russet and brick red against the blue sky.

"It belonged to Zanenga."

"The painter?"

"Yes," she said.

The Italian coffee pot, on one of the two gas rings that was her kitchen, whistled and spewed steam. She took it off and poured it, with hot milk from the other gas ring, into a pitcher.

"I got it for you." She turned and stood there holding the pitcher. "Artists need light to work in, don't they?"

He got out of bed, quite naked, and taking her in his arms, kissed her. She was dressed for work in a suit and stockings.

"Whatever else, Paolo, you must keep painting. I'm willing to live through what you must do, but you must do this for me."

He kissed her again, but she pulled away. She would be late for work.

"Just give me some hope that one day we can have a normal life." She touched his face. "That's all I ask."

Chapter Ten

ON THE LAST day of May, Julia collected her salary and, after setting aside the rent money, decided she had enough left over to buy a dress. She had so few clothes, and since Max was talking about letting her cover some routine stories for him soon, she had to look presentable. After work, she went to the big Rinascente department store on the Corso, where she ran into Francesca in a dressing room trying on a blouse. They approved each other's choices and, in fact, liked them so much that they wore them out of the store, drawing male glances all the way to the Pantheon like, Francesca said, "two high-class tarts." There, at a sidewalk café beside the fountain, they treated themselves to dishes of fresh strawberry *gelato*.

"It's been ages."

Francesca shook her red curls, laughing. "I do miss you, Julia, but Arturo keeps me awfully busy. I hope you won't be offended if I say it's nice to be sleeping with a man again, even if he's years younger than me and, well, you know, they're insatiable at that age."

"And you haven't even the modesty to blush."

"No, never could. . . . But seriously, I will never forget your staying with me. You saved my life."

Yes, Julia thought, perhaps I did, but I also saved my own. She had held Francesca in her arms when she had awakened sobbing, as she had once held Gus after Claudia died. She felt it was the first unselfish thing she had done in all those years. And by bringing Francesca back from the edge of black despair, she had restored some sense of her own worth. But those were things she could not express in words.

"You helped me, too," was all she said.

"And how is it now?"

Julia paused, a spoonful of *gelato* halfway to her mouth.

"An awkward question, since I'm sleeping with your brother."

"Almost incestuous, isn't it?" Francesca laughed again. How nice it was to be sitting here in the deep shadow of the Pantheon's dome with her, eating ice cream.

"Yes, almost. But what am I to do with him?"

"It's serious, then?"

"Like you and James."

Francesca reached across the table and grasped Julia's hand, for only an instant, but her grip was like steel.

"Oh, God, Francesca, where will it all lead? I don't know anything about politics, but I do know that the world is turning toward night."

"What does Paolo say?"

"He says we were born at the wrong time."

"Ah, well . . . *carpe diem.*"

"What?"

"Pluck each day like a fresh flower, my dear. That's all one can do. . . . Coffee?"

"Yes."

Francesca snapped her fingers at the waiter. "But you're happy?"

"Wildly, even knowing that it can't last."

"And you'll go on like this?"

"Even if I knew for sure that it'll all end tragically, I have no choice."

"Lucky you, then . . . lucky Paolo."

And they were. Whatever problems Julia faced at the office, whatever frustrations Paolo was obliged to live with, they had found on the Via Minerva the calm at the eye of the storm. They explored each other in every conceivable way, often lying in bed for hours after making love, discussing their different pasts, compensating for all the years that they should have had together. It was a happy time. Julia was now making twenty-four dollars a week, and Paolo maintained his end of things by doing stage designs and movie sets, for which others got the credit. Now that Paolo's Resistance network was set up throughout Italy, all he had to do—to Julia's great relief—was wait until the time was ripe. He could resume his own identity again. But Paolo Danieli's art remained confined to the walls of the little studio across from the Pantheon's dome. Some of the leading artists and critics came to see it, and shook their heads in sorrow, knowing that so long as the views on what was good "Fascist" art prevailed, Paolo's work would never be shown in Italy. Julia also saw that these men were ashamed, having compromised so that they would not be banned.

The summer wore on, and the leaves of the plane trees along the Tiber grew tattered and dusty. Julia and Paolo escaped the heat on weekends by driving in her open car up into the Alban Hills to drink the cold, fresh white wine of Frascati in the shade of arbors, where the grapes were already beginning to turn purple. Below, the Roman Campagna shimmered in the heat. For all of July not a breeze stirred. The world, too, seemed to be in a state of suspended animation, while Europe went on vacation and forgot its troubles for a few weeks.

Then Max took his vacation and left Julia in charge of the office. Even during that sleepy August there were a few queries from London, and Julia filed her first stories on her own. They were nothing more than reports of statements by some government spokesman or an account of a train wreck, but she found that she was a natural-born writer—a point confirmed by a terse "well done" over the Teletype from London. She almost forgot that it was Max and not she who was bureau chief in Rome.

My God! She looked at her watch. Five past nine. Monday morning. Max would be coming back from vacation. Johnny would be switching on the light over the Teletype, which five minutes before had sputtered out GOOD

MORNING . . . The phone was probably already ringing. She had to be there to cover for Max, to protect her job. If she lost that job she would lose their apartment. She leaped out of bed and kissed Paolo on the neck.

When Julia got to the office, with no makeup on and the seams of her stockings crooked, Max was already there. She couldn't believe it. He'd never arrived before ten since she had been working for him—and there he was on the Monday morning after his annual vacation.

"Max!"

"Surprised, ducks?"

"Well, yes. Welcome back."

"Thought I'd turn over a new leaf. New year and all that."

"You needn't frighten a poor working girl by coming in at nine-thirty."

"Somebody has to cover the office."

"Very funny, Max."

"And what should I find upon my return but this." He handed her a strip of paper torn from the Teletype: FOR ROME BUREAU ONLY. RUMOUR HAS IT THAT MUSSOLINI MEETING WITH HITLER SOON. ARE YOU AWAKE DOWN THERE? THIS IS YOUR CHANCE, JULIA. TED.

"Has this been going on for long?"

"Has what been going on for long, Max?"

"You and Ted."

"Oh, for Christ's sake. I've never even met Ted. He's your boss, not mine. I'm just a secretary, remember?"

"Sorry, Julia. Ted doesn't like me, you know." Max sat down on the windowsill. His blue polka-dot tie was worn and greasy. The white at the roots of his red-dyed hair had begun to show, and he was having difficulty holding a match to the end of his cigarette.

"Max, why don't we go down to Pastore's and have a coffee and brandy, and to hell with the office."

"Bless you, girl. Where's that wretched Johnny?"

"At Pastore's, I imagine. We'll send him back to hold the fort. I've got news for you, Max."

In the cool depths of Pastore's, and after a coffee and two brandies, Max calmed down.

"Now tell me what's the matter," she said.

"Nothing. But it's always a shock having the harness put back on."

"There's more to it than that."

"Well, it also doesn't help to come back and find that your boss has lost confidence in you. Julia, I can't afford to lose my job. You read what he said—'Are you awake down there? This is your chance, Julia.' They'd like me out, that's what."

"Max, Max. It isn't so. You write like an angel."

"What other messages did Ted send you while I was away?"

"Nothing," she lied. "My big story was a train wreck at Cortina d'Ampezzo. I got it all over the phone from the stationmaster. Trafalgar cut it down to exactly twelve lines." Actually there had been several messages from London questioning Max's stories, and her replies. She couldn't afford to lose her job, either. She had to keep Max *and* London happy.

"Enough of that," he said, downing a third brandy. "What's this big news of yours?"

"There's a man in my life."

"Julia, you're not going to leave me?" he said in genuine alarm. So, he did realize how much he needed her.

"No. Don't worry. It's just that I wanted you to know that now things are different, have been, actually, since May."

"I knew when you got your own flat something was fishy. I was much happier when you were living with Francesca Danieli."

"Now I'm living with Paolo Danieli."

"So that's it."

"We would get married if it weren't for the laws in this bloody country. No divorce."

"He's a pretty radical fellow, you know."

"He's out of politics now," Julia said firmly.

"For your sake, I hope so . . . You're sure now you aren't quitting on me?"

"I need the job, Max. Paolo can't work until things change. Just consider me a happily married woman in all but name. I love him, Max."

"Then I'm happy for you. Now let's get back to work. You gave me quite a scare there."

"But what I wanted to ask . . . was may I have the first week in October off?"

"Well, I don't know . . ."

"*Max*, it's my honeymoon."

She slipped quietly out of bed at dawn and went onto the little balcony in her nightgown. Lake Nemi was a dull silver coin at the bottom of the deeply wooded crater. How could such peace exist less than twenty-five miles from Rome? The only sound was a lone bird singing since long before dawn in the top of one of the pines that almost enclosed the inn. They had found the place one weekend in August and decided they would come back to be alone one day when it was possible. She would never have dared ask for a week off then. But in only a few months she had made herself indispensable to the TNA Rome bureau. She shivered with pleasure at the cold air after a long hot summer in Rome, and looked down at her car, all alone outside the inn, the white seats dotted with the first fallen leaves of autumn. Then she got back into bed and snuggled up against Paolo for warmth. Nightgown and pajamas! Like an old married couple. His arm went out and around her. Their last day.

"Paolo, get up."

"What?"

"Get up. The honeymoon's over, or almost. I want to go down to the lake. We haven't been anywhere or done anything."

"Isn't that what honeymoons are for?"

"Never mind that. Get up." How happy she was.

They drove as far as the little town of Nemi and left the car in a narrow back street. Passing a restaurant where a man was stoking a grill with charcoal, Julia called, "What's for lunch?"

"*Guarda*, signora." The man held up a wild mushroom the size of a saucer in each hand. "Grilled, with a little garlic, perfection."

Julia laughed. "Shall we?"

"Why not?" Paolo said.

"We start serving at noon," the man called back. "And the mushrooms go fast. Don't be late."

Beyond the restaurant a path led down into the woods and toward the lake. She took Paolo's hand in hers.

"It's been a good time."

"Yes."

"Almost as though everything were normal."

"It almost is."

"But what do we do, Paolo? Do I just live in sin with you from now on?"

"Things will change one day."

"I wonder."

They walked on in silence down through the dappled shade of beeches. The lake shone like a polished mirror, and when they reached it the surface was as still and calm as it had seemed from far above. They followed the path that wound through deep forest close to the lake's edge and paused beneath a giant beech.

"There used to be a sacred grove somewhere around here in ancient times."

"With wood nymphs and all, I suppose," Julia said.

"Oh, I'm sure."

Paolo walked away, leaving her standing by the beech, and sat down on a flat rock at the edge of the lake. Her heart ached for him: a decent man, a man of courage, her lover, in an indecent time.

"*Guarda*," she said. "Look." He turned. She was standing with her back against the trunk of the beech tree, her clothes lying around her on the ground. He ran quickly to her.

"Julia! You're a vision, but you'll catch cold."

"Wood nymphs aren't mortal. They don't catch cold."

"I'm mortal."

"Too bad," she said, pulling his sweater over his head, laughing. They slid down onto the grass together, and made love fiercely.

"You're late," the trattoria owner said. "Nevertheless, I have saved some mushrooms for you." He put two steaming plates in front of them and a boy brought a pitcher of red wine. Beyond the open doors the lake sparkled through the trees.

"And as a second course, signori?"

"Something else grilled," Julia said. "Liver or steak. I'm starving."

"The liver's excellent. . . . Oh, your friends were here."

"Friends?" Paolo said.

"Yes. They were asking for the couple who were staying at the inn. . . . You are the Rossis?"

"Rossis?" She looked at Paolo. Why had he registered them under that name?

"Yes," Paolo said. "What did they look like? I'm not sure which friends these are."

"Two men. Nothing special about them."

"Where did they go?"

"They haven't gone. They're waiting for you in the bar. Ah, there they are now."

Two men, one with sandy-colored hair, balding, the other dark and heavyset, probably a Sicilian, stood in the arch that separated the bright dining room from the dark bar. The radio in the bar was tuned to *Madame Butterfly*, which was being broadcast live from La Scala in Milan.

"The OVRA," Paolo said under his breath.

"What?"

"The secret police."

She tried to grasp his hand under the table, but he pulled it away from her. He was as tense as a coiled spring.

"We're leaving by the terrace door," he said lightly, turning and smiling at her.

"Paolo?"

"Run when I do."

The two men were moving shoulder to shoulder across the room toward them. A waiter came out of the swinging kitchen doors and crossed the two men's path, balancing a tray piled high with plates of food under warmers, glasses, and bottles of wine. Paolo stood up, put both his hands on the waiter's shoulder and hurled him into the two approaching policemen. The three bodies went down across the next table, taking the couple seated there with them to the floor in a cascade of shattering china and glass. The Sicilian rebounded to one knee and had a pistol halfway out of his coat when Paolo's foot caught him in the mouth. The man slid across the floor in a pool of wine. A woman screamed.

As Julia rose from her chair in fright and disbelief, Paolo seized her wrist and dragged her out the open doors, across the terrace, and into the dark labyrinth of alleyways where they had left her car. Not thirty seconds had passed since she had been happily ordering grilled liver for lunch.

She sat tensely silent beside him until they were all the way out of the Alban Hills and on an obscure back road to Rome.

"Why Rossi?" she finally said.

"Paolo Danieli never leaves Rome. That's part of the fiction I live."

"I thought Paolo Rossi was finished. You said—"

"He is now. Obviously they've found out something." Paolo reached into a pocket and handed her an Italian identity card. "Tear it up. He's dead."

She tore up the card, held her arm up in the open car, and released the pieces. Paolo Rossi's identity was swept away.

"That must be the end. I told you that I would share your life . . ."

"Yes, yes you did. . . ." His jaw was set, and his long black hair rippled in the wind of the speeding car.

"But you told me that it was all over. . . ."

"All right, it's over. It's over."

* * *

In December, 1933, Prohibition ended in America, and Victoria Bronzini gave birth to twins in a private suite in a hospital in Baltimore. First there was a telegram and then a letter, in which Victoria said that she had done her duty by Bruno all in one stroke—two boys—and she was going to have something done to herself so there wouldn't be any more kids. She also had news about Aunt Agnes and Charles. It seemed that Roosevelt had swept Maryland so completely in '32 that Charles didn't have a chance of being elected to the Senate from Maryland for years. Still, Agnes was down but not out. A senator Charles might not be, but that Italian son-in-law was more of an asset than Agnes had imagined. Baltimore had a large Italian population—and an even larger German population. Agnes and Charles had moved into town, and with the new year Charles would begin his campaign to become congressman from Baltimore, on an anti-Bolshevik platform. Winning the Italian vote would be no problem: Bruno would see to that. Julia tore up Victoria's letter and did not mention it to Paolo.

Julia stirred in her sleep. Time to get up, make coffee, go to work. She opened her eyes to early morning light. Why was it so quiet? Across the way a male pigeon, puffed up, pursued a female along a ledge beneath the dome of the Pantheon, where tufts of weeds sprouted among the ancient bricks. There was no sound. New Year's Day. One year ago on this day she had wandered aimlessly into the Colosseum and come face to face with Paolo, and her life had begun. She rolled over in the bed. Yes, he was there, the blanket rising and falling with his breathing. She pulled the blanket away. His body was still marked by the tan of two summers before, when he had worked on a farm in order—he told her afterward—to try to forget her. She walked her fingers up his spine, awakening him.

"Happy New Year."

He rolled over into her arms.

"Julia."

"And happy anniversary, Paolo."

She fought him off for a while, just for the fun of it, and then let him have her, her body arched up against his, her head buried in the pillows. When it was over, she found she was grasping something metallic and rough that had been beneath the pillows. She opened her eyes and looked at a rusty iron key dangling from a pink ribbon entwined around her fingers. It swung back and forth from her upraised hand.

"What's this?"

"Happy anniversary, Julia."

She turned her head on the pillow, and her eyes were close to his dark smiling eyes.

"But what is it?" she asked again, sitting up in bed, a last little shiver of pleasure running through her body.

"Get on some clothes."

She smiled quizzically. "What *is* this all about?" But she didn't argue. He led her out onto the landing at the top of the stairwell.

"There," he said, motioning to the door under the eaves where the owners of the building stored trunks and unwanted chairs and broken tables.

"Curiouser and curiouser," she said, turning the rusty key in the lock and ducking through the low door into the storage room. It was empty and swept clean. Pale bars of light fell through the shutters of the doors onto the bare floor. Paolo threw open the doors and led her out onto a tiled balcony. A whole new view of Rome opened up all around them.

"How beautiful!" she exclaimed.

"Happy anniversary."

"What are you talking about?" She looked up into his smiling face, the tiles cold, on New Year's morning, beneath her bare feet.

"I've bought it."

"Paolo," she said, shaking her head, "you haven't a lira."

"No? Then what is this?" He reached under his sweater and brought out a thick folded document. It was a deed to the top floor of their building on the Via Minerva.

"But it's in my name."

"How does it feel to be a kept woman?"

"I've always wanted that."

"Happy New Year, darling."

While Julia made breakfast, Paolo took tools, which he had found somewhere, and cut a door through the light board wall that separated their studio from the storage room. By the time they were having toast and eggs and coffee, the sun was shining in to their new apartment from two directions.

"A balcony," she said, marveling. "I can't believe it. We can have pots of geraniums and an arbor of vines and . . . oh, Paolo, how did you do it?"

"It's a secret."

"You robbed a bank."

"No."

"You . . ." A shadow passed before her eyes. "This doesn't have anything to do with the Resistance? Because you promised."

"No." His hand reached across the table and covered hers.

"It has nothing to do with the Resistance. Do you really want to know?"

"Well, yes, I do."

"You won't believe it."

"I want to hear anyway." She was apprehensive now. How little she really knew about this man.

"In 1918—we were just kids—mother took Francesca and me to a charity show at Madison Square Garden. It was organized to sell Liberty bonds for the war effort. She bought a large-denomination bond for each of us. Francesca cashed hers a long time ago. Mine stayed in a safe-deposit box in New York until last summer. It's taken me months to get the proceeds here without going through the Fascist banking system."

"But why?"

"I can't live off you forever."

"Oh, yes you can."

They looked at each other, both surprised at what they had said.

* * *

Julia went around the studio lighting candles, while across the way, the Pantheon dome faded mellow gold into the April night. Had she really recreated a world, there on the Via Minerva, as elegant in its own way as that apartment on Via Giulia where she, Contessa Morosini, had entertained cardinals and ambassadors and cabinet ministers? Or had Paolo created it? In the glow of candlelight the large green and purple and deep blue semiabstract canvases depicted variously a female form. Her presence was everywhere in this glassed-in room. Beyond, in their bedroom, once the attic storeroom, there were drawings of her nude: standing, lying, draped across chair or bed. The nudes were for their eyes only. Visitors would catch only a glimpse of her in the large, strongly colored canvases in the main room. The door that Paolo had put in the wall opened and he came through wearing tight dark pants, a white long-sleeved shirt open at the neck, and a square of bright paisley scarf tucked in the collar. She wrinkled her nose at him, smiled nervously. He was doing this for her—and she for him. The doorbell, an ancient rusted thing that you turned with your hand, rang.

"Herr Reiner."

Ernst Reiner had really come! It was as if the Pope had dropped in at Julia's old apartment on the Via Giulia.

"Mr. Reiner these day, signora." The small man with wisps of silver hair brushed over his ears, lenses in a silver frame perched on the bridge of his nose, walked right past her, his eyes on a painting.

"Extraordinary," was all he said, standing in front of the largest painting. Paolo stood beside Ernst Reiner, his hands behind his back, looking not in the least concerned that his paintings were being scrutinized by probably the most influential art dealer in the world.

"I hadn't realized," Reiner said with a heavy German accent, taking off his pince-nez and rubbing them with a silk handkerchief, "that any real painters survived under Mussolini."

"There are others," Paolo said in his deep melodious

voice. A thrill ran through Julia's body. How like Paolo to immediately try to help his friends who were struggling to keep painting alive under this oppressive regime. How proud she was of him.

"You must give me their names," Reiner replied, turning to the other paintings that crowded the walls.

Other guests were coming through the door, the rich and titled of Italy, or at least those who were so secure they didn't need to be afraid of Mussolini, and who were fit enough to walk up four flights of stairs. The lights on the dome of the Pantheon came on, right on cue. Two uniformed waitresses, hired on a gamble and costing Julia a week's salary, walked through the opposite door with trays of canapés, and a striped-trousered waiter carried in a tray of drinks.

"Julia."

A thin, freckled hand, taut as a bowstring, clasped her. She looked into Francesca Danieli's china-blue eyes, sparkling with happiness, Julia knew, for her and Paolo.

"You've done it again."

"Yes, I guess I have," Julia admitted.

"But why?"

"A throw of the dice. Why not?"

"More than that."

"Yes, of course."

"Happy?"

"Delirious."

"I'm so glad." Her hand squeezed Julia's.

Julia kissed her on the cheek, and young Arturo, too, whose arm Francesca held tightly, as if he might run away.

"That's Ernst Reiner, isn't it?"

"How'd you know?" Julia asked casually.

"Picasso's drawings of him. He's very important," Arturo said, in awe.

"I know," Julia said, and lit a cigarette. She also knew that, once again, all eyes were on her. The long velvet skirt, the color of dark tobacco, the gold lamé blouse that clung to her figure, had cost her not a week's but a month's salary. She smiled. All eyes were on her, except Ernst

Reiner's. He hadn't even glanced at her. He had eyes only
for Paolo's paintings—at last, the possibility of recognition.
Whatever success there would be this evening would be
Paolo's, not hers. She glanced at Francesca, who she could
see had read her mind.

"Julie! You look marvelous. And this place. How *do* you
do it?" A blond presence stood in the doorway.

"Vicky! What are you doing here?"

"Quick in and quick out. I couldn't resist the temptation
to see what you were up to."

Victoria's nostrils flared like a high-strung mare's; her
face was flushed. She was excited, Julia guessed, by having
ventured for the first time into the anti-Fascist world.

"You remember Francesca Danieli."

"Yes, of course. We met once—at Julia's wedding."

Francesca nodded, looking amused.

"I still see Angelo," Victoria added, hesitating, ". . . from
time to time."

"How is he?" Julia asked coolly.

"Oh, the same old Angelo. And that must be Paolo over
there. Golly!"

Julia laughed. That was what Victoria had always said
when they were teenagers together on Aunt Agnes's Eastern Shore estate, when she saw a male who really took her
fancy.

Victoria flushed even more and laughed herself. "And
isn't that little man . . ."

"Ernst Reiner. Would you like to meet him?"

"I'd better not. And I'd better not stay long, either. If I'm
seen here, the secret police will be around to see Bruno.
But I couldn't resist."

"Well, you *are* going to meet Paolo."

When the guests were all gone, Julia, Paolo, Francesca,
Arturo, and Ernst Reiner sat down with leftover canapés
and wine, while Reiner wrote out a contract on a sheet of
Paolo's drawing paper. The document guaranteed the pur-
chase of a minimum of five of Paolo's paintings each
year—at a substantial price—over a period of three years.

"This is very generous," Paolo said as he signed his name.

"Not at all," Reiner replied, scratching his signature below Paolo's. "I expect to make a profit."

"But you are also a patriot."

"Patriot?" The small man turned intense gray eyes toward Paolo. "I have left my country, perhaps forever."

"It won't be forever. I've heard what you have done to help artists leave Hitler's Germany for America."

"I could help you, too."

"No, I must stay in Italy." Paolo's eyes and Julia's met for an instant. "But I'm grateful for your support."

"It's not support. As I said, I expect to turn a tidy profit on your paintings. But you really should get out of Italy." And Reiner put away his large fountain pen.

"I couldn't, but thanks all the same," Paolo said, looking all the while at Julia.

Paolo and Julia walked along the beach at Ostia, their bare feet washed by the foam that slid across the shining wet sand, a pearly pink in the first light of day. Little shorebirds raced ahead of them, dodging along the water's edge. Julia looked back at their footprints down the beach, being eaten away by the incoming tide. They had gone a long way without saying a word.

"Well . . ." She sighed.

"What?"

"We've done it . . . you've done it." But she really meant "we." The art was his, but behind last night were four months of hard work to bring everything together for that moment when Ernst Reiner had stood before Paolo's painting of her and said, "Extraordinary." She had scrimped and saved from her small salary to make their apartment attractive; had come home tired from work yet had sanded and painted far into the night; had used all her old connections to ensure that the right people were there; had even gone into debt to be able to look again, for one night, the way she had when she had been at the pinnacle of Roman society. Yes, they had done it, but Paolo, who had finally achieved success, seemed to care less than she.

"Is it really important to you?"

"What?" She was startled to have him read her mind. "Yes, it is. You deserve success."

"My paintings were just as good before last night as they are this morning."

That hurt. She had worked hard to bring him success and now he didn't even care. No, that wasn't fair. He was just being honest. She squeezed his arm and put her head on his shoulder.

"I still say you deserve success."

"I can't afford too much success."

"What do you mean?"

"Mussolini will remember that I'm still around."

"So what? You haven't done anything."

"The Fascists are vindictive. They'll make life difficult for us—for you, too."

"We could go to America. Reiner offered to help."

She felt his body stiffen.

"I couldn't leave Italy. You know that."

"Well, since you've stopped working for the Resistance what difference . . . Oh, let's not talk about it. We're together. We have our own place. I've got a job. You *are* a success, whether you like it or not."

"I do know what you've done for me, Julia." He put his arms around her and kissed her on the mouth. "And I know what you have sacrificed. I love you."

"I love you, Paolo." He knew he had hurt her, and that was his way of apologizing. He seemed to know her so much better than she knew him.

"Well, enough seriousness." She looked around. They had passed the last small hotels, and behind the beach there were only rows of dark umbrella pines. "Let's go swimming."

"In what?"

"In our skins, silly. There's no one around."

"It's April. The water will be freezing."

"It'll wake us up. We haven't been to bed at all, you know."

They had driven down to Ostia on impulse to see the dawn, after celebrating with Francesca and Arturo at a nightclub on the Via Appia. Julia was dead on her feet and had been running on adrenaline for three days.

Before he could protest anymore she had slipped out of her clothes.

"Come on," and she turned and ran into the surf. Seconds later they were both floating on the surface of the sea.

"You see, it's not so cold."

"You're crazy, Julia."

"No, just happy. Very, very, happy."

And they kissed, treading water.

They walked back to the seaside resort of Ostia, salty and covered with sand from rolling naked on the beach, exhausted, and as she had said, very happy.

"You know, that's the first time I've been in the sea since my mother drowned when I was eleven years old. I wasn't even sure I'd have the nerve to do it."

"You are crazy."

"No," she said, taking his hand in hers, "It's just that I realized standing there on the beach with you that I've escaped the past. You've made a new woman of me, Signor Danieli."

"I'm not sure anyone ever escapes from the past. But what counts is now, and I never thought I could have what I have with you on the Via Minerva. Not in my wildest dreams."

They had stopped walking. His dark hair, matted by sea salt, was beginning to dry in the morning sun. A streak of sand crossed his cheek where her hand had been.

"It's paradise. Tell me it can go on forever, that things won't change."

"I don't know." He looked away from her. "The world is moving somewhere."

"Too fast. Oh, Paolo, I want to make love, desperately."

He put his arms around her. She was trembling.

"Desperately?"

She nodded her head. "And right now."

"Well, we should be able to find one of those cheap hotels where they take naughty couples like us with no bags."

When she awakened it was midafternoon. Paolo was still asleep on their hard bed in a little hotel by the sea. Light seeped into the drab interior through a torn shade. The only furnishings in the room were the bed and a pitcher and washbasin on a small table. Just the kind of place for couples whose urgent desire blinded them to everything but the need to make love. Julia was glad to be among that number. Quietly she got up and put on her clothes. She didn't want to bathe yet. She wanted to leave the feel and scent of their lovemaking on her body for a while. What she really wanted, she realized, was food. She was faint from hunger. She tiptoed down the narrow wooden stairs.

The beach was almost deserted; it was too early in the season for the Romans. But she found a restaurant open with two tables outside in the sun, where she ate alone, ravenously consuming a huge platter of spaghetti with clam sauce. Then she ordered a coffee, lit a cigarette, leaned back in the chair, and closed her eyes. She supposed it couldn't last. No one could continue to be as happy as she was at this moment. She opened her eyes. Across the road a traveling circus was setting up on the edge of the beach; a yellow-and-red–striped circus tent was being raised. A white-haired woman, trim in leather coat and slacks, crossed over, looked in the restaurant door at the empty table in the sun, then sat down at the table opposite Julia and ordered a cup of coffee. There was something vaguely familiar about her. Her short, fashionably cut hair seemed unusual for an old woman with a traveling circus, as if she had once known much better times. An actress? Of course. It was the owner of the little circus she and Paolo had gone to on their first evening together in Rome.

"Signora Oteo?"

"Yes?" the woman said suspiciously.

"Do you remember me?"

"In fact, I was sitting here thinking you looked familiar.

But one doesn't expect to meet anyone at Ostia in April. God knows why I'm here."

"I'm Paolo Danieli's friend."

"Ah, yes, that's it. I congratulated him on having found you. Where was that?"

"Your circus was set up near the Piazza Navona."

"Yes. That was quite some time ago."

"April 29, 1930. Nearly four years to the day."

The old woman's shrewd brown eyes studied Julia. "You have quite a memory for dates."

"That date means something to me ... Won't you join me?" Julia moved her chair to make room.

"And where is Paolo now?" the woman asked, sitting down beside her.

"He's here with me in Ostia. We live in Rome ... together." Her voice trailed away. Why was she saying these things to a woman she barely knew? Because, she realized, she needed to talk with someone.

"You've been living together all this time?"

"No. Well, I married someone else but—"

"And it didn't work?"

"No, it never could have."

"It should have been Paolo?"

"Yes. How did you know?" Julia asked, surprised.

"I've been reading palms at my circus for years," Signora Orteo said, turning Julia's hand over on the table.

"Do you believe you can?"

"Of course not. But you do learn how to guess what's going on from just a few words that are dropped."

"And in my case?"

"You're afraid it won't last."

Julia smiled weakly. "Right again. If we could only be married. . . . Paolo said you were a friend of his father's."

The woman sniffed. "I'm sure he didn't. I'm sure he said I was his father's mistress, which I was," she said, a smile flitting across her face, "for two glorious years."

"And then?" Julia was in suspense, as if her own future hung on the answer.

Signora Orteo shrugged. "He was no older than Paolo is now. I was nearly forty. And we were *both* married."

"But still . . ."

The old woman cast an appraising eye at the circus tent rising up across the road, the sea beyond now as still as a sheet of glass.

"Love conquers all? Well, who knows, it might have, if there hadn't been other women."

"Oh."

"You needn't worry about Paolo, if that's what that look on your face means. I think he has reacted against his father's way of life. I watched Paolo grow up from a distance. He was always true to whatever or whomever he believed in. He was, well, serious."

"Too serious, sometimes, I think. Yes, and he's very honest."

"You love him?"

"With all my heart. I . . . I don't know why I'm telling you these things."

"Why not? Every woman needs another woman to talk to from time to time."

"You know about his politics?"

"I've heard things."

"What should I do?"

"Live for the present. What else can one do?"

"That's what Francesca says. She's Paolo's sister."

"I know. I remember her as a child, redheaded and skinny."

"She still is. And I *do* live for the present. But still . . ."

"Things may change?"

"Oh, things will change. There's no question about that. There are dark clouds building up over Italy, over all of Europe. It's just a matter of time. That's not what bothers me."

"What then?"

"We could escape."

"But Paolo won't leave?"

Their eyes met, and she sensed that this old woman, with the figure of a girl, her white hair swept back in a fashionable cut, knew very well that Julia's rival for Paolo was more to be feared than another woman. Signora Orteo was an oracle, asking questions that answered questions. What would she say next?

"Why don't you come see our little circus? The tent's almost up, and I must get back to work."

"Well, I . . ."

"Do you remember my granddaughter? The little girl on the trapeze?"

"Yes. Yes, I do."

"Well, come then. She's sixteen now."

Under the striped tent, still being pulled together, and leaking bright strips of spring sky and sea into the darkening interior, two tough, hairy men, Sicilians judging from their accent, were stringing the high wires and hanging trapezes. A slim form leaped out of the dark into the center ring, bowed deeply to an imaginary audience, and ran toward them on her toes, like a ballerina.

"Antonia. Come here. I want you to meet a friend of mine."

The girl curtsied, tossed back a mop of dark curls, laughed.

"Signora."

"I saw you once, on a trapeze," Julia said, "when this same tent was set up near the Piazza Navona." The memories came flooding back.

"I'm on the high wire now. No net." The girl threw a defiant glance at her grandmother, who shrugged.

"You've grown up."

"One does," the slim, dark-eyed girl tossed back. "Watch me," she called as she ran toward the trapeze.

"You said Paolo's here in Ostia?" Signora Orteo asked.

"Yes."

"Bring him tonight to the performance."

"I wish we could, but we must go back to Rome. I have to be at work quite early in the morning."

"Do remember me to him."

"Of course. . . . Before I go, would you tell me my fortune?"

Signora Orteo took one of Julia's hands in hers, turning the palm up. She was silent, frowning.

"What do you see?"

"I think . . . and I'm not reading your palm . . . that you've chosen a path that is going to take a lot of courage to stay on to the end."

The late spring of 1934 brought the most glorious weather that anyone in Rome could remember for a generation. In New York one of Paolo's paintings had been sold by Ernst Reiner for much more than the price guaranteed under the contract. Julia had progressed from Max Harrison's secretary to his equal. In fact, Julia knew that those faceless deskmen at the other end of the Teletype line now depended more on her than on Max, whose spells of drinking and black depression were growing ever more frequent. The more Max ridiculed the Fascist regime in private, the more obsequious he was toward Mussolini in his dispatches home. Julia found herself rewriting his copy and hiding from him the sarcastic comments from the London desk. She couldn't afford to let the Rome bureau fall to pieces. She did some well-received pieces on how Mussolini was extending his influence in Austria at Germany's expense, and predicted, correctly, that Austrian Prime Minister Dollfuss would become Mussolini's puppet, and that Hitler would be obliged in the end to meet Mussolini on Il Duce's terms. So when finally the first meeting between the two dictators was arranged, it was she, not Max, who was asked to cover the event. It was just as well. Max had disappeared again.

Chapter Eleven

"I DIDN'T ORDER all these flowers," Julia said over the telephone to the receptionist, "and you've put me in a suite. I asked for a single room at the minimum rate."

"But, signora, the bill has already been paid."

"Well, I didn't pay it. There must be a mistake." She was sure that the Trafalgar News Agency didn't pay it. Her expenses were supposed to be covered by her per diem of one pound sterling. That hadn't changed, Max had told her, since 1928.

"The press office has paid all of the correspondents' bills, Signora Howard."

"Oh." How naive of her. Of course. The Italian government would take care of such things—particularly since Count Galeazzo Ciano had returned from China to become propaganda chief. She put down the phone. As usual, Galeazzo had overdone it. There were vases of cut flowers everywhere, even in the marble bathroom. He was also, no doubt, responsible for the limousine that had brought her and two French correspondents from the Padua railway station to the hotel.

The next morning she attended a briefing in the hotel ballroom. The first meeting between Hitler and Mussolini would take place the next day at the grandiose Villa Pisani, in the little town of Stra on the Brenta Canal. As she and a hundred other correspondents were filing out of the ballroom, a man from the Italian government press office appeared at her side and asked if the signora from the most respected English news agency would be interested in an exclusive interview with some of Chancellor Hitler's chief aides? Indeed, she would. Then a car would call that evening to take her to a villa on the Verona road where members of the German party were staying.

Later, Julia asked herself why she had not realized until the last turning in the road that she was being taken to the Villa Serena; and why she had felt, first of all, a shiver of excitement as, at twilight, the big Fiat rolled up the long drive between the cypresses.

Angelo Morosini, in perfectly cut evening wear, came slowly down the great sweep of stone stairs, his eyes never leaving her. She thought about getting back into the car but her feet wouldn't seem to move. In the background the frogs were croaking, as always on summer evenings, from the misty banks of the Adige.

"Julia."

Angelo stood above her on the first step. There was regret in his eyes, but she knew that it was only regret that he had not been able to hold on to the most important ornament of his social life and career: his wife. But she had too much pride not to answer in a civilized manner.

"Hello, Angelo. How've you been?"

"The press office sent us their best, I see."

"Angelo, spare me the pretense. And someone might have told me that we were dressing for dinner."

Angelo relaxed. She wasn't going to leave, after all. "It never occurred to me that whatever ace correspondent they were sending wouldn't assume evening dress."

"As I said, Angelo, you aren't fooling me. And besides, I'm TNA's second-string."

"That's not what I hear. Julia, we're both adults and we can handle these things as professionals. You and I . . ."

"There's no more you and I, Angelo."

"Right you are. But then it's to your advantage to be here, now isn't it?"

They dined by candlelight, with painted nymphs and shepherds looking down on them from the ceiling she had had so lovingly restored. Julia could not help but feel a pang of regret at having lost this world of grace and beauty. The antique silver bowl Bruno and Victoria had given them for their first anniversary stood in the center of the table. No yellow roses in it now. Instead there were stiff spikes of red gladioli thrusting up from it. And her own husband sat across the table addressing her as "Miss Howard," coolly polite, with a slightly crooked smile, as if they shared some naughty secret. She tried to remember what evening dress she had worn for their first anniversary, but couldn't. That evening they had talked about fascism, which for her had been abstract and far away. Now Italian Fascists sat around the table with their women and really quite presentable German Nazis.

After dinner, Julia retired with the two most presentable of these Nazis to the library, which she had also had restored, for "a quiet talk." A box of Havana cigars sat on the eighteenth-century table that she had brought from Florence next to glasses and a bottle of brandy. Julia slipped into a velvet armchair and lit a cigarette.

"Brandy, Miss Howard?"

"Yes, please."

"There you are. A bit of a relief to get away from all of that Mediterranean intenseness, isn't it?" The blond German was as slim as a girl, his blue eyes as pale as Charles Pemberton's.

"I live in Italy, you know."

"Then by now you must be used to all of that garlic in things," said the other German, who was equally blond and slim. They were not high-ranking Nazi officials, as she had been led to believe, but trained animals of the party propaganda apparatus. She had met their kind in Rome. The two men were also, Julia decided, lovers.

"I don't mind it. I like the Italians."

"Please don't misunderstand, Miss Howard, so do we. They are a people with great potential. All they need is firm leadership, and Il Duce will provide that . . . Nevertheless, it is a relief to be amongst one's own kind for a while. I was educated in England, you know."

"I supposed so," Julia said. "Oxford or Cambridge?"

"Oxford, actually. I believe Count Morosini was also there for a while. It shows, doesn't it?"

"Does it?" Julia said. She could not decide whether the Germans knew she was Angelo's wife or not. Probably not. He would be too vain to admit his wife had left him and was working for a living; yet he was willing to use her for his purposes. What kind of judgment of her did that imply?

"Of course. Educated people are a kind of international fraternity. Men of action need us to explain what they are too inarticulate to express. We—you and we—must interpret for these men of action who are trying to pull us back from the edge of the abyss."

"That is why," said the other German, "it is so important that the world understand that the civilized nations must restore order to society, and that this is the only aim of Chancellor Hitler and—although I cannot speak for him—Signor Mussolini. It is the weak nations that go to war. The strong can afford peace."

Julia opened her notebook and wrote something down.

"You might also add that this meeting between the two leaders is a concrete expression of their desire to avoid the kind of misunderstanding over national aims that so tragically led to the Great War."

Julia looked up from her notebook where she had written "rubbish."

"What about Austria?" she abruptly asked.

"What exactly about Austria?"

"Is it, in your opinion, in the German or the Italian sphere of influence?"

From that point on the two Germans never regained control of the conversation. Julia filled pages of her notebook with their comments. She didn't believe a word that they said, but she made them talk. It was good copy.

When she came out of the library it was past midnight, and she accepted Angelo's invitation to "sleep over," as he put it. She could be just as cold-blooded as he. She was given the Tiepolo room, where she stayed up until three o'clock getting her notes in order. She meant to stay one jump ahead of the competition.

The meeting between Mussolini and Hitler at Stra was poorly managed. The press arrangements were chaotic, and

Julia found herself just one of a crowd of noisy, shoving journalists. She never even got a good look at Hitler. She didn't file a story at all, despite two urgent telegraphic pleas from London. She wanted her first dispatch to be one that would wake them up. Angelo, and behind him—she guessed—Ciano, were trying to use her. They underestimated Julia Howard.

The next day the Italian and German delegations were forced to move to Venice, driven from Stra by swarms of mosquitoes that came off the canal. The press corps was thrown into confusion and frantically began scrambling to book rooms in Venice. Julia took her time packing in her flower-laden hotel suite. An official Fiat awaited her to take her from Padua to the little port of Mestre on the Venetian lagoon. There she hired a speedboat that skimmed past Venice and the other islands floating like ancient galleys on the water, to the outer bank of the Lido, where a suite had been reserved for her at the Hôtel des Bains. She had an early supper, took a sedative, and set her travel alarm for five a.m.

By six o'clock the next morning, Julia was sitting on a bench at the first tee of the Alberoni Golf Club. Venice and the Lido were still asleep. The sun in the transparent early morning sky was like a giant orange egg yolk hanging over the gray-green Adriatic, which was as calm as the lagoon on the other side of the undulating emerald-green fairway.

Although she had been to the Lido a number of times, mainly to gamble with Angelo at the casino, she had not known until the day before that there was a golf club at the very tip of the narrow strip of sand separating the Venetian lagoon from the sea. When she heard that the meetings between Hitler and Mussolini were being moved to the clubhouse and that Count Ciano was flying up from Rome to try to straighten out the muddled press arrangements, Julia had had a sudden inspiration. She hoped her hunch was right. She poured some coffee from the thermos the hotel had lent her, and lit a cigarette. If she was wrong, nothing would have been lost but a couple of hours of sleep.

At seven o'clock the police began to arrive, and one of them came down to where she was sitting to check her identity. She showed her press card, and the policeman said the two leaders would not arrive for several hours. Julia said yes, she knew that. The policeman shrugged and went away. A little later workmen arrived and began hanging Italian flags and red-and-white banners with a black swastika in the middle on the old fort, which had once guarded the sea channel and was now the Alberoni Golf Club. Finally at a quarter past eight, a group came out of the clubhouse: four men in plus fours and four caddies with their clubs. The course would, naturally, be closed for the day. So, she had been right.

"Why, Contessa Morosini, I didn't know you were a golfer."

"I'm not, Count Ciano, but I know you never miss a chance for a game. I'm here as Julia Howard of Trafalgar News Agency, and I wonder if you could spare me a few moments before you begin your round?"

Ciano scowled. Someone had once, quite accurately, described him as "brutally handsome." He was wearing argyle socks that matched a sleeveless sweater and a gray golf cap that matched his plus fours. Just a bit too much.

"I've been waiting since six o'clock."

"Well, in that case . . . But only five minutes."

Ciano watched while the others teed off and then came over and sat down beside her.

"Julia, how nice to see you after such a long time." He smiled in his most ingratiating way. His reluctance to grant an interview had, of course, been nothing but an act.

"You know that Angelo and I have separated?"

"Yes. Edda and I were most distressed to hear that when we returned from China. . . ."

I'll bet, thought Julia. Now you think you'll have more success in getting me into bed.

"Well, Angelo's loss is our gain. We need good people in the foreign press corps here. Unfortunately, many of your colleagues are no more competent than the staff I have inherited at the press office." He crushed his cigarette under a two-tone golf shoe. "But I'll soon have that straightened out. Italy has a story to tell, and I am determined to see that it's told well. Now, Miss Howard, I am at your disposal."

Julia was taken aback. This was not at all what she had expected from Galeazzo Ciano. She opened her notebook to the questions she had jotted down.

"Well, I suppose first of all, how are the talks going?"

"The talks are going quite well. Il Duce and Herr Hitler had more than an hour alone together yesterday—though God knows how Il Duce managed it. He *thinks* he speaks German. . . ." Ciano stabbed at her notebook with his finger. "Don't write that down. That remark is strictly off-the-record. I'm willing to help you get a start, Julia, but if I ever see anything like that in print, you'll lose your work permit within the hour."

"I understand you, Galeazzo. I'm not all that green."

"Right. Then for the record, the talks are going extremely well. There has been an identity of views on all issues."

"Even on Austria?"

"Even on Austria. However, you may attribute to 'circles close to the Italian side' the view that Italy must retain its present degree of influence in Vienna. There is no possibility of recognizing German territorial claims to any part of Austria, although we accept that the German government cannot publicly renounce such claims."

"And off-the-record?"

"Off-the-record, we will move militarily to meet any German intrusion into Austria. England and France have an equal interest in containing German expansionism."

"Others see it differently. England and France are democracies. Italy and Germany are Fascist."

"I'm interested to hear you say that. Herr Hitler does not admit to being Fascist . . . a purely Italian term."

"But there are similar ideas in both Italy and Germany."

"Hitler apes Il Duce, if that's what you mean. But so will France and England, one day. For once, Italy points the way to the future."

"Not Germany?"

"Hitler trots at Il Duce's heels like a trained dog."

"Off-the-record, I presume."

Ciano threw back his head and laughed. "Bravo, Julia. We will work well together."

The interview lasted more than half an hour. By then Ciano's golf partners were too far ahead for him to catch up, and Mussolini's son-in-law, who was reputed to take his golf clubs on every trip, played nine holes alone. Julia might have asked herself why she was shown such deference, if she had not been caught up in the arrival of the official parties, the honor guards, the bands. She stayed only long enough for a look at Hitler, an insignificant man in a dirty raincoat and crumpled felt hat, and Mussolini, resplendent in his black uniform, strutting in riding boots at the club entrance. Then she slipped away, while all the Italian and foreign journalists crowded around the two men, asking questions. She had already been told that nothing of substance could be expected from the two dictators. She walked across the golf course to where her hired boat was waiting at a jetty beside the ninth tee.

Julia was only vaguely aware of the islands of the lagoon as the boat sped across its glassy surface. She was already composing her dispatch, and when she stepped off the boat at the Piazza San Marco she walked past the Doges' Palace without even seeing it. She took a table at Florian's and, over several glasses of wine, wrote out a telegram to London, while an orchestra behind her played waltzes and the rival orchestra at Quadri's across the piazza answered with medleys from Italian operas. In an hour's time she had written the inside story of the first meeting between Mussolini and Hitler and its implications for Europe and world peace. Before the two dictators' meeting was even over, Julia's dispatch was on the wires to London. Then she treated herself to a gondola ride to the railway station, where she booked a seat on the evening train for Rome. When she returned to the telegraph office just before train time, what she found, instead of confirmation that her dispatch had been received in London, was a message far more satisfying to her than that long-ago telegram from Elmer J. Thornley telling her she had just come into her large inheritance: SPLENDID STUFF STOP BONUS POUNDS 100 WIRED ROME STOP KEEP UP THE GOOD WORK—ABP.

"ABP." That was Arthur Burns-Peckham, the legendary figure who had founded and still owned Trafalgar News Agency. Max, she knew, had never received a personal message from "the boss."

The sun was low over the lagoon when Julia slung her bag into a first-class compartment of the *rapido* for Rome. They had pasted a "Hôtel des Bains (Lido) Venezia" label on the virgin leather. She leaned back on the cut-velvet banquette and lit a cigarette. Her success was like alcohol or drugs in her veins: Everything was now possible. Beside the single label on the bag in the overhead rack she imagined others: Munich, Paris, Le Havre, London, Southampton, New York, Chicago, San Francisco, Tokyo, Shanghai, Calcutta . . .

There was a slight movement, and the cast-iron columns, the clock with Roman numerals, the porters in blue overalls leaning against their baggage trolleys, slid away, slowly at first, then faster and faster. A blue-uniformed man at the end of the platform waved them on with a red wooden paddle, and then they were out in the golden sunlight, the tracks beneath them twisting and splitting and doubling like strands of spaghetti. An incoming train passed in a blur, faces like frames of film flicking by. With a touch of sadness, Julia realized that she was alone in the compartment, alone with her triumph. It seemed a shame that there was no one to witness what she had done. The train hurtled out of the pink crumbling brick backside of Venice and onto the causeway. The water of the lagoon was like molten gold. Dark seabirds winged alongside; fishing skiffs moved away by oar toward Venice. The long wail of the train's whistle sent pleasant shivers up her arms. What couldn't Julia Howard do?

"Which sitting, signora?" the dining car attendant asked, in starched white jacket and black bow tie.

Julia hesitated. "Second."

The waiter gave her a slip of paper with a printed "2" on it. The train left the lagoon behind and entered the green, leafy corridor that ran from Venice to Verona. She closed her eyes and dozed. They were long past Verona when the dining car attendant touched her shoulder and said, "Second sitting, signora. The dining car is almost full. If you wish to wait until after Bologna . . ."

"No, no. I'm coming."

The dining car was packed. She had the choice of a seat opposite a priest with a missal in one hand and pasta expertly wound around a fork in the other, and someone hidden behind the *Corriere della Sera*. Julia chose the man behind the newspaper. A silver basket of hard rolls, a half bottle of red wine, napkin wrapped around cutlery, plate, and menu, arrived all at once, while a boy with a miniature broom and silver shovel whisked away the crumbs from the first sitting. A face appeared over the newspaper. She had seen it somewhere before: not that face exactly, but one very much like it.

"Good evening," the man said, taking off his reading glasses and putting them into the breast pocket of his jacket. "You are American, I believe."

How often she had heard that.

"How did you know?" It was the expected thing to say.

"Howard is hardly an Italian name." He was speaking English. The accent was part British and part New York. Julia looked casually at the menu.

"Howard?"

"Signora, it is written." The man tapped her water glass that had just been filled. There was a slip of water-stained paper under the foot of the stemmed glass, the other half of the piece of paper with a "2" on it that had been handed to her outside of Venice: "Howard" was written across it.

"Ah. I thought . . ."

"You thought I was a magician, a sorcerer."

Julia studied the menu again. Yes, he was right about that. What was her memory searching for?

"*Julia* Howard, I believe."

Their eyes met, then. He was a man of indeterminate age, anywhere from fifty to sixty-five. There was something not quite right about him: a three-piece suit in a large check, white piping along the edge of the vest; several rings on his hands; his curly dark-red hair streaked with gray and far too long. He looked like a traveling salesman who had something expensive but rather disreputable to sell. No, not quite that . . .

"Julia?"

"You are Julia Howard, Contessa Morosini, I believe."

What a theatrical way to put it. Of course. Theatrical. *That was it.*

"And you are . . ."

At that instant the soft Italian landscape, caught between the fading dusk and moonrise, disappeared with a snap: it was black outside and coldly lighted in the dining car. The train hurtled into that first tunnel between Verona and Rome that always surprised her.

"I know who you are now, but I don't even know your first name."

"Francesco."

"What an odd place to meet, Signor Danieli."

"As good as any other, Miss Howard. How is Paolo?"

"Not the same since *My Soul Is Not For Sale.*"

The big man's laugh boomed out, and heads turned all over the dining car. The priest lowered his missal to look over his glasses at them.

"Even I am ashamed of that film, but given Italian taste, it made more money than any of my others. Paolo said he was ashamed for it to be known that he was my son. I paid him back by making sure his name was in the credits." Danieli laughed again.

The train sped out of the tunnel and into the summer evening.

"Tell me, truly, how is Paolo? I never hear from him."

"Oh, he's fine," Julia said, "considering."

"Still fighting the Fascists?"

"Paolo is no longer active in the Resistance."

"Really? That very much surprises me."

"Well, he isn't."

"You obviously have more influence on him than I ever did," Danieli said, looking skeptical. "Then you should persuade him to go back to America. He could make a fortune there. He's a genius."

"Yes, I know."

"He won the gold medal of the Academy of Fine Arts when he was only eighteen."

Julia hadn't known that, and she felt resentment that there were things Paolo hadn't told her. But then what did she really know about the man with whom she lived, except that he was kind and tender and stubborn and had come to her when she had most needed love? She had barely thought of Paolo during the trip, so absorbed was she in getting her first big scoop. She could at least have sent him a telegram, so that he could have shared in her triumph. Her resentment faded into a vague feeling of guilt.

"And now he will hardly speak to me," Danieli continued. "He says I have no principles because I work with the Fascisti. I asked him what I was supposed to do, not work at all like he does? He became very angry. 'Principles.' A very un-Italian idea. He gets such nonsense from his mother. Francesca is the same. It's all right to have such ideas in America where they don't make you drink castor oil."

"Perhaps Paolo is right," Julia said. "He says that if everyone who was really against Mussolini spoke out, Il Duce would fall from power tomorrow."

"Nobody is going to speak out. The Fascisti chose a very good symbol—the old Roman *fasces*, an axe tied in a bundle of sticks. You can break the sticks one at a time, but you can't break them when they are all tied together. The Fascists know that. The Resistance won't learn. They are Communists, Socialists, Paolo's group, which is not even a stick—it is a twig—a few hundred romantics like my children. Mussolini will break these sticks, these twigs, one by one, and throw them into the fire."

Julia shuddered. He was right, and she had been right to

make Paolo stay out of Resistance activities. They would have killed him, just as surely as they had killed James.

"It's frightening."

"Why don't you take him to America?"

"He won't go."

"Then I'm afraid he'll have to sit out the rest of this piece of theater. That's all it is, you know. Theater. You know why I was in Venice? They wanted me to help stage-manage the musical evening they put on for Hitler at St. Mark's; to make sure the lighting just happened to fall on Il Duce and that the cheers sounded spontaneous. I don't normally do that kind of thing."

"But you did."

"I was having a problem with a censor over this new play of mine in Bologna. Now I won't have a problem. . . ."

Francesco Danieli got off at Bologna. As the train slid away from the station, Julia saw a young woman with exaggerated makeup run across the platform and throw her arms around the big man with red ringlets curling over his collar. Danieli wore a black homburg set at an angle on his head, and carried an ivory-headed cane. She decided not to tell Paolo that she had met his father; but the meeting had thrown a shadow over the first triumph of her life.

It was nearly one in the morning when she let herself into the apartment, on a hot, steamy Roman night. The lights that played on the Pantheon had been turned off, and the dark shape of the dome was like some enormous black zeppelin nosing at the studio window. She undressed quietly and went naked into their bedroom, closing the door behind her. There was no sound, no light. Pulling back the sheet, she slipped quietly into her side of the bed. She lay there for a long time, hardly breathing. Tears that she did not understand ran down her face. She reached across the bed for Paolo, irrationally feeling he would not be there. Her hand touched Paolo's bare back and he started with surprise. Before she knew what was happening they were making love.

* * *

"Max has flown the coop," Paolo said.

"Oh, he'll turn up in a few days." Julia sat at the dressing table, brushing out her hair, feeling worn out and bruised, but luxuriating in having had every ounce of pleasure wrung from her body.

"I don't think so. His apartment's closed. Your London office called. That's what they said they were told."

"My London office called? Oh, Paolo, I haven't even told you. Look." She held out to him the telegram from Arthur Burns-Peckham.

"A hundred pounds. Good for you, Julia." Paolo took her in his arms. "You're going to do great things."

"Paolo, I'm so happy. Everything seems to be going right. Do you think Max has really gone, though? I'd better get back to the office." She pulled away from his embrace. "I don't believe it. He can't leave me all alone."

"You'd love it."

"Well, I could do it," she said, and finished putting on lipstick in the mirror. She turned. "You wouldn't be jealous of me if I became famous?"

"I could never be jealous of you."

"What a stupid thing for me to say. It's just that I don't want anything to change, and last night coming home on the train I was afraid things might."

"I won't change."

Max had, in fact, disappeared. His apartment was vacated and his mistress, Rosanna, who shared it with him, had vanished, too. Julia assumed that they had gone off on a spree together until she received a message over the Teletype saying that Max had surfaced in London and his association with Trafalgar News Agency had been terminated: no other explanation. Julia was put in charge of the Rome bureau until a successor could be named.

As Julia had predicted, the feared alliance between Mussolini and Hitler did not materialize. In late July, Nazi thugs murdered Dollfuss, and Il Duce went into a terrible rage. Hitler had promised to leave Austria alone! Four Italian divisions were moved to the Brenner Pass. The Nazi takeover attempt in Vienna failed, but relations between the two dictators were now soured. A few days later, Julia received a call from the government press office. It was to inform her that Il Duce had read her articles and he congratulated her on having been one of the few foreign journalists to have understood that Fascist Italy would stand up to that madman in Berlin. The doors of official Rome were now open to her. When Hindenburg died in early August, and Hitler became reichsführer, Julia was the first to report the Italian reaction from the "informed sources" now available to her.

The following week the mystery of Max was cleared up. Julia's London editor passed through Rome on the way to Egypt, and Julia drove out to Ciampino airport, where they had half an hour together. Julia learned what she had preferred not to think about. Max had for some time been taking bribes from the Italian government to write favorably of Mussolini. Julia might be in charge of the office for some time, since the Italians were so annoyed at being found out that they were refusing to grant a visa for Max's replacement. Actually, the Trafalgar man said, Julia was just as good as any man they could send out and—ha, ha—a damned sight prettier; but the board of directors were a stuffy lot, and no one dared suggest that a woman be put in charge of a bureau. Julia was furious; but she quietly accepted the small raise that was the sop thrown to her, vowing that one day she would make them beg her to take the job.

In early September, Julia received an invitation from the Bronzinis, who had been spending the summer at their villa in Tivoli, and a car was sent for her. The lawn of the big house was strung with Japanese lanterns. A jazz band played on the terrace. The party was not nearly as wild as the other one that Julia had been to there, but the crowd was, if anything, more vulgar. Julia recognized leading Fascists and their mistresses, as well as Bruno's old nightclub set, and his fellow industrialists, all growing ever richer from their association with Mussolini's corporate state. Julia

went up to the nursery with Victoria, who was tan and fit—
and had had a little too much to drink—to see the twins,
who had been brought back to Italy in the spring and were
beginning to walk. Then Victoria insisted they have a drink
together in the library, away from the noise and confusion.

"Cheers."

"Cheers, Vicky." The glasses they held were heavy
pieces of cut crystal, each worth a week of Julia's salary.

"Julie, you're more beautiful than ever, radiantly beautiful I believe it's called." Victoria kicked off her finely made
lavender pumps that, as usual, did not go at all with the
equally expensive dress she was wearing. "I've always en-
vied you."

"I'm just a poor working girl now."

"Bruno says you're getting quite a reputation as a foreign
correspondent."

"I'm trying hard."

"Yes, you always did. Do you remember the day you
came into Rome? You said you were going to make the city
yours."

Julia smiled and shook her head and turned the heavy
glass in her hands. "It seems ages ago."

"Four years, actually. And you did, too. The toast of
Rome in 1932, as I remember."

"It seemed important, then."

"It doesn't now?"

"Vicky, I feel as if it happened to another person. I don't
even understand what it was I wanted."

"That's why I envy you."

"You envy me? You have a rich and handsome husband,
two beautiful boys, a full life, everything. I've lost my husband, my baby, my money. I'm working for a pittance and
living with an unemployed artist."

Victoria poured herself another drink from the crystal de-
canter and lit a cigarette.

"I still envy you. You love him, don't you?"

"Yes."

"Perhaps that's why you're so radiant . . . Can I be frank
with you, Julie?"

"Have you ever been anything else?"

"I had to bite my tongue when you decided to marry Angelo. I knew that you loved Paolo, but perhaps you didn't know it yourself. I could have married Angelo and been, well, more or less happy, I suppose. I was born to this kind of life. I know I'm not very intelligent. . . ."

There were tears in Victoria's pale-blue eyes. Julia had never seen Victoria cry before.

"Vicky, what is it?"

"Make Paolo stop before it's too late. They'll do the same thing to him that they did to your friend James."

So that was it, she thought, and she saw her whole world speed away from her, shrinking like a gaudy balloon from which the air had been released.

"Tell me."

"They were going to arrest him. Last week. Bruno stopped them."

"Go on."

Victoria's voice came from a great distance. "Someone in the police knew that you and I are cousins, and they sure don't want to embarrass Bruno. They showed him Paolo's dossier. You know Paolo's one of the chief Resistance leaders in Italy? Only Bruno's influence saved him."

"I didn't know."

"I thought not. Anyway, Paolo's dossier has been 'lost' . . ."

"He swore to me that he had quit Resistance work. . . ."

" . . . on the condition that he never again have contact with the Resistance movement. The next time even Bruno won't be able to help."

"He promised me. . . . Am I not going to be allowed even this happiness that I fought so hard for?" Now Julia was crying.

"It's the times we live in."

"But all this doesn't have to bother you, in your position."

"No?" Tears were running down Victoria's cheeks, which were splotched with red. "Why do you think I had myself fixed so that we can't have any more children?"

* * *

The next morning, open warfare began in the room across from the Pantheon's dome.

"Why, why, why?"

"Because there is no other way."

"What do you mean, no other way?"

"Because I had to protect you."

"How gallant."

"Julia, stop it!"

She had opened her mouth to say "Stop what?" but she knew. She knew very well. The fear and tension that was just over the horizon of their world of passion and happiness was rising like a dark moon.

"Paolo. Paolo, darling. Please."

He stood there facing her; he who had been her lover for a year now seemed almost a stranger to her. He had betrayed her.

"I love you, Julia."

"Then show me. Give it up."

"I can't. I told you. If I give up what I believe in, it's as bad as giving you up."

"There's no room for such lofty sentiments in Mussolini's Italy."

"I'm sorry you feel that way. Perhaps I'm a romantic."

"That's what Signora Orteo says. That's what your father says. . . . "

"What do you know about my father?"

Julia sat down on the edge of the bed.

"I met him on a train."

"You didn't tell me," Paolo said, sitting down beside her.

"And neither did you tell me that you were still up to your neck in the Resistance. I believed you when you said you were no longer involved."

"I had to say that."

"Oh, really? Why?"

"Now even foreigners are not safe. Suppose they had arrested and tortured you, to learn the truth about me. I can't make you a part of what I'm doing. I love you too much."

"Thanks so much, Paolo. You thought I wasn't up to it, I suppose."

Why was she saying these things? Pride? Her pride matching his pride? She didn't know. Perhaps the more two people loved each other, the easier it was to misunderstand one another, their emotions too strong for reason to find its way. Certainly their love had been stormy from the first moment they met.

In October 1934 a Croat fanatic fired on the King of Yugoslavia, who was riding in an open car in Marseilles with the French foreign minister. The king died instantly, Foreign Minister Barthou a few hours later; Pierre Laval was named minister in his place, and Julia Howard was awakened by a telephone call from London. There were reports that the assassin had been living in Italy and receiving money from the Italian government. What were the facts?

Julia hurried down the Via Veneto the next morning, eager to get to work. There was a big story brewing again and she needed the challenge and distraction. She and Paolo had had another fight over coffee that morning. He had announced without warning that he was taking the morning train to Switzerland. Why? He wasn't able to tell her. I will tell you, Julia had said: to meet Carlo Rosselli, the Resistance leader living in exile in Paris. She knew that much from Victoria, and that Rosselli met secretly abroad from time to time with his chief lieutenant in Italy. And how did Paolo propose to travel to Switzerland, since he was forbidden to leave the country? Paolo only shrugged. A false passport, no doubt. She left, without kissing him good-bye. Even though she knew he was probably risking his life. Exactly the point. He had no right to. She loved him too much.

Julia marched into the office, setting the bell on the door to ringing violently. Giovanni leaped out of the swivel chair in which he had been lounging.

"What's wrong?"

"Nothing's wrong," she snapped.

"You look beautiful this morning."

"Oh, shut your mouth." That sounded good in Italian. She had sworn, after Max had left, that she was going to fire Gianni. What she needed was a secretary, not a lazy, insolent office boy. Somehow she had not been able to do it.

"What's on the ticker?"

"Somebody shot the King of Yugoslavia."

"Oh, really? And what else?"

"Nothing much. You had a phone call from your husband."

"What do you mean, my husband?" she said, glowering at Gianni, who was now trying to grow a mustache.

"Morosini, Angelo. Ministry of Foreign Affairs. He's your husband, isn't he?"

"What do you know about that?"

"I know."

"Give me that." She snatched the piece of paper with a telephone number on it from Gianni's hand. "You mind your own damned business."

Julia picked up the phone and gave the operator the number. While she waited, she sat on the edge of the desk and lit a cigarette.

"Pronto."

"Angelo?"

"Julia?"

"What do you want?"

"Are you interested in a story?"

"Meaning what?"

"The assassination in Marseilles. I thought you might like to hear the Italian side of the story."

"Of course I do. Just leave your government's handout in my box at the press club."

"Julia, I'm serious."

"I'm sure you are, but I'll write my own stories."

Gianni was grinning, and she made an obscene gesture at him.

At the other end of the line there was irritation in the voice she knew so well. "I'm only calling you because you're the best foreign correspondent in Rome . . ."

"Ha!"

" . . . with the exception of the AP, and Reuters men, and they're out of town."

Julia had to laugh at that.

"Could you meet me for lunch?"

"No, indeed."

"Listen, Julia, I'm calling you on instruction . . . from quite high up . . . about a professional matter. Surely you and I can act like grownups."

"I've heard that one before."

Passetto's was crowded, but Angelo was waiting at the best corner table, set with an exquisite bouquet of fall wildflowers. She slipped in beside him.

"How lovely," she said, touching the flowers with her fingertips. "Fall's in the air." Her thoughts were far from Angelo, though; in her mind she was back in the Abruzzi mountains on an autumn afternoon.

"And on the menu," Angelo said, looking over reading glasses perched on the end of his nose. She was surprised, imagining him too vain to admit to needing glasses.

"Wild boar, partridge, pheasant, quail roasted on a spit. Would you like some game?"

"Why not? The quail sounds nice, provided the foreign ministry pays, and not you."

"Of course."

Angelo took off his reading glasses and put them in the breast pocket of his Irish tweed jacket. His mannerisms had changed: He was growing into his role as an up-and-coming foreign ministry official. "Let's have a bottle of Barolo to go with the quail."

They chatted amiably enough through an excellent lunch, switching back and forth between English and Italian. If she was going to make it as a journalist, there could be no more adolescent outbursts like that morning's. With the second cup of coffee, Angelo finally came to the point, and then abruptly. He took a folded paper out of the inside pocket of his jacket and handed it to her. It was a foreign ministry document marked "Secret." Julia read it through.

"So what's this supposed to mean?"

"Just what it says. That the ministry strongly advised the security services against giving any assistance to the Croat group to which the assassin belonged. It's quite authentic . . . if that's what you are thinking."

"Even if it is, that doesn't mean that the services followed your advice."

"They did."

Julia looked into the soft brown eyes of the man who had once been her husband. No point in looking for the truth there.

"There's no reason why you should believe me, Julia, but if you like I can make a senior security official available to answer your questions."

"No, Angelo, I'm not getting myself into the kind of compromising position that Max did."

She thought he would pretend not to understand; but he only said, "I see. You're probably right."

After two days of chasing down rumors, and worrying about Paolo, Julia sat down at her desk and typed out a piece on possible Italian involvement in the assassination, weighing the pros and cons but coming to no conclusion. In the end she had not had much more to go on than what Angelo had told her at Passetto's. She wondered if he remembered—or had ever known—that it was the same restaurant that had catered all their dinner parties when they lived on the Via Giulia.

That evening Paolo came home from Switzerland. He found Julia sitting in her robe on a rug in front of the wall of glass that faced the Pantheon, her chin resting on her knees. The last light was fading behind the dome, turning her skin a pearly pink and casting blue shadows in her long dark hair.

"Paolo. You're back."

He put down his battered valise and knelt beside her.

"Julia, what's wrong?"

"Nothing. I took a shower when I came home from work, and when I came out there was this magnificent sunset, and I've been sitting here ever since."

He took the back of her neck in one hand and kissed her mouth, while running his other hand along her leg.

"You've just shaved your legs."

"Yes," she said, lying back on the rug, opening her bathrobe, and closing her eyes. Her body in the dusk seemed like a long rose-colored lake with one dark island. Paolo knelt silently gazing at her.

"Poor working girl waits expectantly to be violated by the savage Resistance leader."

He smiled hesitantly. "So that's what you want?"

"That's what I want."

"Let's go to bed, then."

"No. I want it here and now."

"It's cold here on the floor."

"I don't care about that. I want it now." She raised her knees higher up and then let them fall apart.

The whole time they made love, Julia lay quietly, the soles of her feet lying lightly on the back of his calves, her fingertips planted gently on the small of his back. When he came it was with such relief that he cried out. And then they moved apart for a while, to lie on their sides, looking at each other.

"That's better," she said, "much better. You needed that."

"You were different."

"I told you. I wanted to be violated."

"Why?" he said.

"Ask Dr. Freud. I haven't the slightest idea."

"Now do you want to tell me what's wrong?"

"What's wrong is that I don't have a cigarette." She rolled over on her stomach.

Paolo got up and brought back two lighted cigarettes and pulled her bathrobe over her bare behind.

"There."

"Grazie."

Lying there propped on their elbows, smoking, an ashtray between them, they stared out at the ancient masonry. Paolo pulled part of her bathrobe over him.

"Well?"

She looked at him. "I can't take it, Paolo. I know it's selfish, but I don't see how this is going to work."

"I thought about it a lot on the train coming back. You're right, of course . . ."

"I am?"

" . . . but I'm right, too. If one of us were wrong, we could do something about it."

"And as it is?"

"As it is . . . I don't know. I've always been very sure of myself, but now I don't know."

"The truth is that two people in our situations should never have fallen in love."

"You know how hard I tried to avoid it."

She ran a hand through his hair. "Well, that's the way things are, *amore*." She rolled over on her back. "Oh, how much easier it was when I was dumb. Now I know the world is going to hell and that you and I are going with it." She sighed. "Did you see Rosselli?"

Paolo got up and put on his pants and sweater. "Yes, I saw Rosselli. We met in Montreux."

"What does he say?"

"He says Mussolini is going to attack Ethiopia."

"How does he know that?"

"We have sources, even in the foreign ministry."

Julia glanced at him quickly. "Why are you telling me this?"

"I don't know. Let's talk about something else. How's the job?"

"There was a big story. Someone killed the King of Yugoslavia and the French foreign minister. But you know that. You probably also know they suspect the Italians."

"You have another big scoop, I hope."

"I did a rotten job. Maybe that's why I've been such a bitch tonight."

The home office didn't think so. The next morning, as she came in the door, Gianni handed her a piece of yellow paper torn from the Teletype: YOUR SOUND, BALANCED PIECE KNOCKED COMPETITION'S FAIRY TALES RIGHT OFF FRONT PAGES

ALL LONDON DAILIES. KEEP IT UP. Julia's spirits soared. There was nothing like a good night's sleep to put things back into perspective. Before she had a chance to lose her nerve, she shot back a message suggesting a whole series of features she wanted to do, slanted particularly to the American market where Trafalgar was running a poor fifth to AP, UP, INS, and Reuters.

A few days later she had another call from Angelo. He thought she would like to know that he had been promoted, named director of African affairs at the ministry, and that he was available to talk to her "on background" about any of the matters within his new "parish," as he called it. By the way, he said, good piece of work on the assassination, even though you were rather harsh on the Italian regime.

The next day there was a reply from London: CAN USE THREE OF PROPOSED PIECES IN FOLLOWING ORDER OF INTEREST: MUSSOLINI VS. THE MAFIA; SCIENTISTS PREDICT MAJOR ERUPTION OF MOUNT AETNA; ETHIOPIA: THE COMING CONFLICT. Damn! In her enthusiasm she had proposed topics that she wasn't ready to handle; and out of the whole list they had chosen two that would require a visit to Sicily, whenever she could get away from her desk for that. As for the third, well, there was one way to get a story. She called Angelo.

They met in the Excelsior bar, where Julia had once negotiated her freedom from Angelo. What a long way she had come in eighteen months. Already a seasoned journalist, she was able to treat her estranged husband as nothing more than what he was, a professional contact. Angelo had once again adjusted his appearance to his station in life. He wore a three-piece pin-striped suit that made him look like a young foreign minister, and he spoke with a crisp authority to match the material.

"Well then, Angelo," she said, closing her notebook, "What more can I ask? I really don't understand how you could have made yourself such an expert on Africa in just a few days." A little flattery never hurt with Angelo.

"Anything else I can do?"

"No, I think not, unless you can lead me to someone

who can give me some quotable quotes. I can't work on background alone."

"Would Mussolini do?"

"Serious?"

"Of course I'm serious."

They walked out of the Excelsior together and nearly ran into Paolo Danieli who, turning his head, disappeared into the crowd.

Chapter Twelve

As soon as she opened the door to the apartment Julia knew something was wrong: It no longer felt like home. Perhaps it was only her feelings of guilt, she told herself, putting her keys down on the table and closing the door behind her. When she had left Angelo, after having caught a glimpse of Paolo, she walked toward her office remembering the day that she had seen Angelo and Fiammetta Gildo coming out of a hotel together. Why hadn't she told Paolo that she had been seeing Angelo, explained the professional reasons making it necessary? With a sinking heart she realized what had changed in the apartment. All of Paolo's drawings and paintings had been taken down from the walls, leaving the room, despite the furniture, as bare and vacant as if someone had just moved out. And then she saw his clothes laid out on their bed. At the foot of the bed stood two suitcases. Paolo came out of the bathroom.

"Why?" she said.

"It was your choice, Julia, not mine."

She looked at her wristwatch. Anything to take her eyes away from his: half past nine. Why had she stayed on and on at the office, finding things to do, when she should have come straight home and told him everything? Now it looked as if . . .

"Paolo, there's nothing between Angelo and me. You can't possibly believe that."

"I'm not accusing you of anything." He looked sad, not angry. She had once used those same words with Angelo. But *she*, she had been faithful.

"It was only about a story."

225

"Three times?"

"Three times *what*?"

"You've been with Angelo Morosini three times."

"You've been spying on me," she said in a shrill voice.

"As you wish," he said, opening one of the suitcases and laying it out on the bed. "I kept hoping you would tell me. I kept hoping it wasn't true. But the last time we made love I knew. There was no hiding it then."

"So that's it. The second I don't perform to your entire satisfaction you assume I've just come from another man's bed. And Angelo's, at that. How could you think such a thing? That makes me sick. Don't you understand? It was only because . . ."

It was only because she had been so afraid for him, so thankful that he had come back safely to her, that she had lain passively beneath him, wanting him to use her body to release the fears and frustrations that he could not share with her in words. But the ringing of the telephone cut between them like a scream.

"Well, answer it. It's always for you."

She lifted the receiver from the hook.

"Pronto."

"Julia?" The voice crackled into the room.

"Yes."

"Angelo here. Are you alone?"

"More or less."

"It's all arranged. Two o'clock tomorrow afternoon."

The hand holding the receiver to her ear trembled.

"Julia?"

"Yes."

"You won't fail to be there? It would be very embarrassing if you didn't show up."

"No. I won't fail to be there."

"Good. You won't be sorry."

Julia hung the receiver, damp from her hand, back on the hook.

"I have an appointment tomorrow . . . with Mussolini."

"Congratulations."

"Somebody around here has to make a living," she said.

Paolo closed the suitcase. "I'll help you cut down on expenses. I'm going north for a while."

"Running away again, Paolo?"

"I seem to be getting in the way of your career."

"So you *are* jealous. What else do you think of me? That I'm being paid by the Fascisti?"

"There are other bribes than money. For you it's . . ."

He never finished the sentence. She hit him across the mouth as hard as she could and ran into the bathroom. When she came out he was gone.

The door closed behind her. It was a vast room, perhaps sixty feet long, with no furniture except a desk at the far end, where a man sat reading a newspaper, his polished boots crossed on the desktop. Julia began the long journey toward him, her high heels clicking on the marble floor. When she got halfway down the room, the newspaper was lowered; the man got up hastily, as if he had just become aware of her presence, and came forward to meet her. Above the boots and riding breeches he was wearing a black tailcoat and a bow tie fastened to a winged collar. "Signor Mussolini came forward to meet me," she said to herself, composing her lead, "dressed like the lion tamer in a circus, a role that he obviously relishes. His lion is Europe."

"Miss Howard," the man with the shaved head and piercing black eyes said in resonant English, "you are so kind to give me of your time. I am a great admirer of you."

Julia immediately said in Italian, "Excellency, it is I who am honored. I only hope that I am not keeping you from more urgent tasks."

A scowl passed across the dictator's face, followed by a smile that faded just as quickly. It was common gossip that nearly every day at two o'clock—which it now was—following his lunch, Mussolini had ushered into his office in the Palazzo Venezia the most attractive female petitioner from the waiting room below. Naturally, after a brief engagement on the marble floor, the petition was granted. Julia walked straight to the chair in front of the desk and

snapped open her stenographer's notebook. Il Duce meekly
sat down behind the desk and folded his hands in front of
him.

"I am at your complete disposal," he said. "I believe you
wished to ask me some questions about Abyssinia."

"Actually, Mr. Prime Minister, I would like to ask you
about yourself."

. Mussolini glared at her. She knew she was running the
risk that he would terminate the interview, which had been
granted her on the strict understanding that only the Ethiopian question would be discussed; but there was no story in
that. He would only tell her what he had already told a
dozen other journalists—the official line.

"Myself?" The thrusting jaw relaxed. "What is there to
say, Signora Howard? My people allow me no private ex-
istence. My life is an open book."

"Not entirely, Excellency. For example, I would be interested in knowing, as a journalist, whether it is true that
every morning you call the editors of the major Italian papers and tell them how to present the news . . ."

The jaw thrust out again and the dictator almost rose out
of his chair. "That is an impertinent question."

". . . and even where to place stories on the front page."

Mussolini's rocklike face split open into a wide grin.
"You are a most audacious young woman. . . . Of course I
guide the press daily. Why else do you think Italian journal-
ism is admired and respected throughout the world? Certainly not because of those imbeciles and pumpkin-heads
who call themselves editors. As in everything else, I must
personally show the way."

He grasped the edge of the desk with his stubby hands
and thrust out his jaw as he did when making speeches
from the balcony of this same room.

"I am aware, of course, that you began your own career
as a journalist. . . ."

"Signora, the press is a sword, with which one cuts down
his enemies. He who ignores the press is a fool. Not a day
passes without my having perused the major newspapers of
the civilized world."

"That must be quite time-consuming."

"Not at all. I read with lightning speed and in six languages. And I remember everything." Mussolini stole a glance at a folder lying open in front of him on the desk. "For example, last year the *London Times* carried a story you wrote on my decision that the Roman salute would replace the handshake as the proper Italian greeting. Is that not true?"

"Quite true." But he obviously hadn't read the article, since Julia had reported that Italians ridiculed the order in private and went right on shaking hands when they met.

"And may I say that you write quite well."

"Thank you, Excellency. But why are there almost no female journalists in Italy? Is it because, as you said recently, you believe that a woman's life should be totally dedicated to her role as wife and mother?"

Mussolini was flustered, and annoyed. "Italy has its own social and moral climate. I do not expect other nations to be governed by . . ." He had lost the thread of what he was trying to say.

"I have some Italian blood myself."

Il Duce slapped the desk with an open palm. "I thought so. Such beauty could not have come into being without at least some seasoning from our noble Roman race."

Julia's twenty-minute interview went on for an hour and a half, and by the time it was over Mussolini had totally forgotten that they were supposed to have discussed Ethiopia. Julia had had the most personal interview with Mussolini of any foreign journalist in years.

Instead of returning to the office and the telephone, Julia went back to her apartment to compose her story. Before getting out her portable typewriter, she sat for a while, taking stock of her new situation. The interview with Mussolini would be the making of her reputation, of that she had no doubt.

At least she was able to stand on her own feet now, no longer quite so vulnerable to being hurt—as Paolo had once again so deeply hurt her. The last time she had vowed never to see him again; this time she could make no such promise. She knew her heart better now, and knew she could not commit it to some future course. She had control only over the present, and she must close her mind completely to Paolo, drive out his image, not let it cause her sleepless nights in this tiny empty apartment in the Pantheon's shadow. That she must do, and work, most of all work.

In November Charles Pemberton was defeated for Congress in the Baltimore district, in a one-sided race that prompted *The New York Times* to describe his campaign as lacking in any ideas except that Italy had found the key to stable government. Julia was able to sleep nights, but only because of the pace at which she drove herself at work. The Mussolini interview was given wide play in the American and British press, and to her annoyance some chose to see in it that Italy's dictator was a human being, after all. Angelo continued to call her from time to time with inside information on Italian policy and plans, and her career prospered. There was no more talk of sending out a replacement for Max.

The Baltimore Sun ran a feature on the local girl who was reporting so brilliantly on the ominous events in Europe. She correctly predicted the Italian-French accord of January 1935; and when Hitler denounced the Versailles Treaty, reintroduced conscription, and occupied the Saar, Julia wrote a well-received piece on the Italian reaction to German rearmament. It was widely used by papers in both England and America. There were editorials calling for an alliance of France, Italy, and Great Britain. Perhaps, she told herself, she had had a bit to do with that. What a long way she had come since she had given herself fully to her job. She still couldn't keep Paolo out of her dreams, but she managed to convince herself that Paolo had been jealous of her success. And she still got angry every time she recalled that Paolo thought that she had been unfaithful to him with Angelo.

In April an alliance against Germany seemed about to come out of the Stresa Conference, and for the first time since that fateful day six months before when they had met at the Excelsior bar, Julia accepted an invitation from Angelo. He had just returned from Stresa, where he had been sitting all day right behind Mussolini, in the discussions with the British and French. It was an opportunity she couldn't afford to miss.

"Well," she said, closing the stenographer's notebook that lay on the checked tablecloth between them. "It's a failure, then."

"Yes, but you mustn't file your story until tomorrow. I'm sticking my neck out by telling you as much as I have."

"Why are you doing it?"

"I know you'll get the facts right. My only interest is in seeing that the Italian point of view gets across." He grinned. "That's my price for giving you the inside story. Tell our side, too."

She smiled back at him. "Fair enough."

"More wine?"

"No, thanks. I've already had too much." She could feel her face flushed with not only the wine but the excitement of the story. She looked around the brick-vaulted cellar where they had dined. Steaks and chickens sizzled over charcoal: a trio composed of piano, bass, and clarinet played seductively in the shadowed alcove.

"Nice place. I've never been here."

"I picked it because it hasn't been discovered yet. It wouldn't be a good idea for us to be seen together on the last night of the Stresa Conference."

"Even though we're married?" She noticed a slight change in his eyes. She shouldn't have said that.

"It's Julia Howard of TNA that I'm out with, not Contessa Morosini," he replied quietly.

A boy in a motorcycle cap with goggles made his way through the crowded tables toward them.

"Signora Howard?"

"Yes."

"International telegram. Sign here."

Angelo looked annoyed. "How did he find you here?"

"My office knew where I was." She blushed. "I told them to stay open, that I might have a story tonight."

Angelo just laughed. "Well, you've got it. But remember, nothing on the wires before ten o'clock tomorrow morning. You'll still beat the competition by miles."

"Your office wants to know if there's a reply." The boy had pulled off his leather cap and his tousled hair stood up all over his head.

She tore open the envelope.

"Well?"

"It's from *Harper's* magazine. They want me to do the lead article for the June issue, with the title, '1935: The Year in Which Peace Was Saved?' . . . for seven hundred dollars."

"Congratulations. You've made the big time."

"Yes, I guess I have. I can't believe it." She opened her notebook and wrote across a page, "Offer accepted. What is deadline?" She tore out the page and handed it to the messenger boy.

"This calls for champagne," said Angelo, looking for a waiter.

"I don't think . . ."

"The foreign ministry pays. Besides, it's a double celebration."

She looked at him blankly. "What do you mean?"

"It's also your birthday."

"Oh, my goodness, I'd completely forgotten. I've been so busy. But you remembered."

"I'm not totally insensitive."

"Sorry . . ."

"Not many women make it professionally by their twenty-seventh birthday."

"No." She felt her eyes grow moist. Angelo, always discreet, turned his head to summon the waiter.

"I remember . . . I remember getting up that morning the ship arrived and looking out the porthole and seeing the Bay of Naples and Vesuvius. I've been in Italy five years tomorrow morning."

"Would you like to dance?"

Angelo held her close, but not too close. How smooth he is, she thought.

"You're really looking good, Julia."

"I have to. Attractive women journalists get the best stories. Haven't you noticed?"

Angelo chuckled. When they returned to their table the champagne was being poured.

The next morning Julia woke up in Angelo's bed—their bed—in the apartment on the Via Giulia. He had left discreetly while she was still asleep, after picking up her clothes from around the bedroom, and hanging them neatly over the back of a chair. What had she done? She searched with her toes at the bottom of the bed and found her step-ins and stockings rolled together. She sat up naked in the bed, her head throbbing. She had to get out of the apartment before the maid arrived.

The following evening Julia, still shaken by what she had done, sat down at her typewriter and began an outline of the article. By midmorning on Friday the only question was whether she should come down for or against peace being saved in 1935. She lit a cigarette and looked out the window. Which would it be? The phone rang. Who? A friend of Max's? Could she meet her at the bar where they used to go at noon? A matter of life and death. Aren't you— Julia began to say, but the phone clicked off. Damn. Whether it would be war or peace would have to wait a few minutes. She took some bills out of her handbag and put them in the pocket of her jacket. She was prepared to make a small "loan," but that was all.

Rosanna was at the back of the bar off the Piazza Barberini where the three of them sometimes had gone for a drink before lunch. Julia had heard that Max's mistress was back in Rome and out of work. She looked awful, as if she had been sick. She sat down across the table from Rosanna and ordered two pink gins, which had been Rosanna and Max's usual.

"*Salute.*"

Rosanna did not raise her glass or change her expression. Something was very wrong.

"Rosanna, what is it?"

"I should have come to see you a long time ago."

"Yes, actually, you should have. You and Max skipped out on me without even a word."

"Julia," she said in her heavy Neapolitan accent, "listen to me. I'm not going to stay here but two minutes." She picked up the pink gin and downed it in one gulp. "If they know that I have been talking to you . . . I will be in big trouble."

"Well, then, tell me quickly. . . ."

"Tonight they arrest your friends."

"What friends?"

"The Danielis."

"How do you know? You'd think you worked for the secret police."

"That's very funny. For four years I have been working for the OVRA."

"Then why have you come to me?"

"I do not wish it to happen again. I did it to Max."

Light played over the dark recesses of the bar, flashing off mirrors, from the opening and closing of the swinging doors with frosted glass panels. "He never knew, I think. I hope not. They did not even pay him much money."

"What are you talking about?"

"He overdid it. The OVRA read all of the messages on the Trafalgar wire. They knew that London thought he was too pro-Italian. So they made sure the British Embassy found out. The secret police thought you would do a better job for them."

There was no need to hear the rest. Everything that she had accomplished, every triumph, every move up the ladder of the career in which she took so much pride, had been steps down a path that had been carefully, cynically prepared for her. Julia could hear the laughter in OVRA headquarters as they prepared yet another trap for that foolish American woman.

"Go on," Julia said.

"Max had orders to hire you. At first, I think, it was just to keep you from causing trouble. But then they discovered

you could write and that you believed the things you were
told. . . ."

"Oh, God, no."

"I'm sorry, Julia. . . ."

"What will they do to Paolo and Francesca?"

Rosanna turned away. "I don't know. One never knows.
But this time I think they will disappear. . . . I could not do
it. I'm going home to Naples on the evening train. My life
is over. . . ."

Julia took both of Rosanna's hands in hers. "Life is not
over. I will never tell. . . ."

"My brother is a priest, in Caserta. . . ."

"Who did it, Rosanna?"

"I must make confession. . . ."

"Who?" She squeezed Rosanna's hands hard.

"Your husband . . . Morosini."

Julia took the crumpled bank notes from the pocket of
her jacket and thrust them into Rosanna's hand.

"You don't need to make any more confessions. Now get
out of here fast. And don't ever try to get in touch with me
again."

Rosanna got up and walked straight through the swinging
doors at the front of the bar. Julia never saw her again.

She sat alone in the back of the darkened-bar and sipped
the pink gin, feeling strangely calm. Perhaps that was what
happened when your last illusions—God, that these were
the last!—were swept away. Now it was a matter of moving in the most effective way to assure that Paolo and
Francesca were not arrested in the night. Julia Howard had
just joined the Resistance to Benito Mussolini.

She walked out of the bar and into the busy street. A
streetcar was passing by and she jumped aboard. At the
next stop she got off and into a cab that she had drop her
several streets from Sabatini's. It was too much to expect
that she would find Francesca there, and she certainly did
not dare approach her studio. She ordered some pasta and
then gave a large tip to the busboy to take a note to
Francesca.

Julia was just finishing her pasta when she saw Francesca approaching across the piazza, a frown on her face.

"*Ciao*, Francesca. Let's have a coffee inside."

"What's going on?"

She took Francesca's arm and guided her through the bar, past the ladies' room, straight through the kitchen, and out the back door and into an alley.

"Julia, what is this all about?"

"The OVRA are coming for you tonight, and Paolo. Can you get a message to him?"

"The OVRA? What do you know about such things? Paolo hasn't gotten you involved, has he? Because if he has, I'll break his neck!"

Francesca's face was flushed and she held Julia's wrist in that steel grip of hers.

"I only wish that he had. How different things would be now. No, what's happened is that I've just found out that the OVRA had been using Max, and now me. I've been a total fool. But someone with a guilty conscience—don't ask me who—came to me this morning and spilled the whole story, and told me that you and Paolo are to be arrested tonight."

"You're not the first to be entrapped."

"Can you get a message to Paolo?"

"I don't know where he is, but there is someone I can phone. We have a code for different situations."

"If I hadn't been such a fool—again—*I* would know where Paolo is."

"Yes, I heard what happened. You two. . . ." Francesca shook her head. "But the OVRA, it's really serious?"

"Very, and this time . . . Well, I don't know what they intend. You mustn't go back to your studio, and we mustn't hang around here any longer. Can we meet somewhere in an hour? I'll have money and some clothes."

"Just like that? What about work? What about Arturo, for God's sake?"

"Francesca, they mean to kill you." For the first time, Julia saw the world they lived in from Paolo's perspective. And she understood why he had had to act as he did. "Well, where can we meet?"

"The classic place to stay out of sight is in a dark movie theater. As it happens, Father's new film, *The Girl From Sorrento*, is playing at the Alhambra in the Corso."

"I'll pick you up there in my car at exactly two-thirty. You have some place outside of Rome to hide, I'm sure."

"Yes, at Rieti."

"Good. We can be there before dark."

"Julia, I'll do what you say, you seem so sure. But what's come over you?"

"I've finally gotten serious, Francesca, that's all."

All Saturday morning Julia sat, numb, beside the telephone in her apartment, waiting for a call confirming that Francesca had reached Paolo, wherever he was, and warned him. Nothing mattered but that. Her life had been smashed like a vase thrown in rage against a wall. The pieces of it lay all around her in the studio. The phone rang.

"Pronto." Her heart was racing.

"Julia." It was Angelo.

"Yes?"

"About the other night. I'm sorry if . . ."

"Nothing to be sorry about. I rather enjoyed myself."

His voice changed. "Oh, I'm glad. I wonder if . . ."

"But it was a onetime thing, I hope you understand."

"How can you say that? You were . . ."

"I was drunk, plus the excitement. I would have probably gone to bed with any man that night."

"I see." His voice was cold now.

"That need not change our professional relationship."

"Really, Julia!"

"Sorry, Angelo."

He tried to say more, but she wasn't listening. Cold perspiration beaded her forehead. How had she managed to keep her voice from shaking? When he had finished talking she put down the phone. She sat there in a daze, remembering in detail what had happened that night. Not only had Angelo, in the vilest way, made her the instrument of Italian policy, he had manipulated her as if she were a child. He had even had the sweet revenge of having sex with her in their bed in the Via Giulia. But her complete humiliation didn't matter. Nothing mattered except that two people, the only man who had ever loved her and the only real friend she had ever had, escaped from this monstrous government and people like Angelo who worked for it. Francesca she had driven to Rieta herself, but Paolo . . .

The phone rang again, and a cryptic message from an unknown voice confirmed Paolo was safe. Only then did she fall sobbing upon the bed. That evening she typed out a cable to *Harper's* saying that, after all, she did not feel competent to undertake the article they proposed.

That was the longest summer of Julia's life. She had desperately wanted to be with Paolo, to explain, to be forgiven. But even if she had felt it was safe to go to him, she would not have done so. She felt unclean. She was obliged to resume her professional relationship with Angelo, once he became convinced she would not go to bed with him again, so that his suspicions would not be aroused. She showed no concern that an order had been issued for Paolo's and Francesca's arrest. She did it all, apparently believably enough, but she moved automatically in her daily chores, like a zombie, neither knowing or caring what was going on about her. And she filed copy. Anthony Eden came to Rome for a meeting with Mussolini; there was an Anglo-German naval limitation treaty, to which Italy adhered; the Teletype reported that Will Rogers and Wiley Post had disappeared in a plane over Alaska, that Huey Long had been assassinated; in Germany the Nuremberg laws against the Jews came into force.

In October Mussolini announced to a huge crowd beneath the balcony of the Palazzo Venezia that Italy had gone to war with Ethiopia. The long summer was over.

Julia came back to life. She saw an opportunity to make up in some small way for what she had done. She would pull every string to be invited to Ethiopia along with the Italian stable of kept journalists. There were promises from

Angelo, but December came and nothing happened. The
Prince of Wales was crowned as King Edward VIII, and for
a while the world lost interest in Italy's aggression and
whether the League of Nations' sanctions would bring
Mussolini to his knees. Now that Julia's eyes were wide
open, it was obvious to her that sanctions would not work.
Winter turned into spring, and the hundreds of thousands of
Italian troops sent to Ethiopia were finally making their
way up through the Abyssinian highlands toward the capital
of Addis Ababa. Julia was afraid the war would be over before she got there.

But at last the summons came. In three day's time a seaplane would take off from Ostia and fly via Brindisi and
Alexandria to the Ethiopian front. Julia was invited to join
the press party. Only then did she communicate through a
mysterious intermediary of Francesca's with Paolo. Could
she come to see him? Whatever answer came back she
would accept.

The answer was yes.

The next day she drove to Aquila, left her car there, and
hired another to take her to the foot of the Gran Sasso,
where melting snow was interlaced beneath the fragrant
pines with spring wildflowers. She saw him from far below
as she trudged up the path toward the pine forest. He
looked like any other shepherd or woodsman, standing
where the path disappeared into the trees. He did not look
haggard or downcast, as she thought he might, but fit and
confident. When they came together, they behaved like two
strangers, not even shaking hands. An enameled teakettle
hung over a fire of twigs; on the ground were two enameled cups. Paolo poured the tea, the two of them sitting on
flat boulders, as if she were paying a formal call.

"Paolo." His name almost stuck in her throat.

"Julia."

"May I say something first?"

He sat silently, looking into his cup.

"I'm going to Ethiopia tomorrow. It has taken me six
months to get invited. Is there anything that I can do for the

Resistance while I am there? I will, of course, tell the truth, and I suppose that's the most important thing. But is there anything else?"

Paolo, a dark stubble of beard on his chin, his clothes worn and dirty, sipped his tea.

"Haven't you done enough?"

Well, she deserved that. All she wanted now was to do something to help the cause, whatever it cost her. But why should he care? Why should he trust her ever again?

"Can you forgive me?" she whispered.

"For saving my life?"

Had she misunderstood?

"Julia, can *you* forgive me for spoiling everything with my 'principles'?"

"Paolo . . ." She was so surprised, she couldn't say more.

The sun was setting behind the great stone mass of the Gran Sasso. A lone shepherd and two dogs, whose yipping carried up from far below, descended to the village with their flock of sheep, looking like golden grains of wheat in the last rays of the sun.

"It's nearly night," he said. "You know what we do up here? There are more fugitives on the mountain than you imagine. When the sun goes down we bury our fires. You can see even a little fire like this at night all the way from Aquila. The next morning the police come up here asking questions. So we cover our fires." Paolo pushed dirt on the fire with his heavy boot. "Then the next morning we build a new fire."

"I must go. I have a driver waiting at the village."

"I know him. He's quite safe."

"Even so . . ."

She stood up and brushed the pine needles off her skirt, turning from him.

"Will you forgive me, Julia?"

She walked a few steps away and then leaned against a pine tree and wept. He came up behind her, still not touching her.

"Well, will you at least sleep with me? Have pity on a man who hasn't even seen a woman in six months."

Paolo couldn't have said anything better calculated to break down the wall of pride they had built between themselves.

"Of course I will."

His hand, smelling of wood smoke, took hers and led her inside the rough stone hut. There was a straw mattress on the dirt floor, a cane-bottomed chair, and on a stone that jutted from the wall, a candle. He lit the candle and closed the door behind them. Lying on the stone shelf beside the candle was a school notebook and a pen.

She picked up the notebook and turned page after page of beautiful drawings of trees and rocks and wildflowers. Even here on the mountain his talent had not been wasted.

"So beautiful," she said. Their life together, his triumph in having his painting recognized internationally, and much more, was summed up in those two softly spoken words.

Slowly she took off her clothes and hung them on the peasant chair, remembering all too clearly waking up on the Via Giulia and finding herself in Angelo's bed, her clothes neatly hung over a chair back. She faced Paolo in the candlelight, naked and open to him, without shame and without guilt.

"It's you who are beautiful," he said, looming over her in the flickering light.

"If I please you, I'm glad."

They came together then, almost reluctantly, knowing that their time together would be measured out in hours.

She was awake as the first rays of light slid under the rough door of the shepherd's hut, but felt as though she had passed a week, a year, a century in this alpine hideout with her lover. To be restored to him for hours, with all forgiven, with all misunderstandings, the folly of pride, willfulness burned away like the mist in the sun, turned that brief time into forever. Scary, that. To know that, if they never saw each other again, their love would last forever, was too much to even think about. She crawled out from under the rough army blanket, her teeth chattering with the cold, and got into her clothes. She slipped quietly out the door and stood in the little clearing high on the mountain and breathed in the cold clean air. She wandered along a forest path and gathered twigs, and filled the teapot from a mountain stream. She remade the fire and put on the pot to boil, watched the sky lighten, pink and then gold, and stood quite calmly while Paolo came up behind her and folded her in his arms.

"Good morning."

"Good morning, my love."

"You should be going soon."

"I'm not leaving you."

"What?"

He turned her around to him and looked into her face.

"I'll always be with you now."

His face relaxed. He understood. He held her close.

"Six years we've fought each other." She laughed, a bit hysterically, into his chest. "It's all over. We've won."

"Yes, we've won. This one night together was our eternity."

She pressed her face closer against his chest. He understood.

Anthony Pierce, the man from Trafalgar, was waiting for her when she came through the gate at Ciampino. While they had coffee she slipped him a bulky envelope.

"What was it really like?" he asked.

She didn't want to talk about it, particularly to this fop in striped shirt and starched white collar.

"Read it on the plane to London," she said.

"Of course, old girl. But the reality? I was in the trenches in the Great War, you know."

"Oh."

"Was it bad?"

"It was awful."

"Not like the Iteys tell it, then?"

"No."

"You look rather shaken up, Miss Howard."

"Yes."

"Why don't you tell me about it?"

* * *

The seaplane had taken off from the same pier at Ostia where she and Angelo had left on their honeymoon. It was the same type of plane, powered, too, by Bronzini engines. Now, however, the whole plane was marked with the Bronzini emblem. Bruno had taken over the company that built the seaplanes, in one of a series of moves that was making him one of the most important industrialists in Italy. Victoria had sealed her fate, too, Julia realized. She had tied her little pleasure-craft to Bruno's yacht and found that it had turned into a warship headed toward dark seas.

The interior of the seaplane was a reminder of where they were headed. The split-bamboo easy chairs and soft red carpet had been replaced by rows of metal seats. Julia went up the aisle greeting the newsmen she knew, and she knew most of them: the incompetents, the drunks, those on Mussolini's payroll. It was not a group she would normally have traveled with, but she had a job to do. She was even indulgent toward her companions. After all, she had so much to be happy about, and most of them had so little. She had just come from Paolo's arms and was safe in the new and precious knowledge that love was more than sexuality, more than tenderness; it was sharing the same fate.

Then they were off, circling over Rome and heading south. In a few minutes they passed over the Bronzini villa at Tivoli, with its long reflecting pool beneath the trees, in an hour over the wild lower reaches of the Abruzzi mountains where Paolo was safely hidden, in two hours over the gray-green Adriatic. They came down in the harbor of the old port of Brindisi, and that night Julia lay awake in a waterfront hotel thinking about her lover. She had so much to consider now that Paolo was back in the center of her thoughts.

The takeoff was to be early the next morning, and Julia arrived first at the dock to make sure she got the one single seat at the back of the plane. She was the only woman in the party and had no interest in talking with any of the unshaven, bleary-eyed journalists who straggled aboard, cursing and joking. Because it was her first journey beyond Italy, she had no idea what to expect. The light on the mountains of Greece and the islands in the blue Aegean was as beautiful as her guidebook promised, and not unlike Italy.

But a feeling of estrangement began at Alexandria, a low, dusty, ragged city alone on the flat empty coast of Egypt. She took a horse-drawn carriage from the dock with a young man from the *Chicago Tribune* who was on his first foreign assignment and had not yet picked up the tiresome mannerisms and smart-aleck talk of the others. Their hotel, the Regina Palace, was on the sea front. Under the striped awnings that shaded the hotel terrace, fat Egyptian men in Western clothes, with waxed mustaches and upturned red flowerpots on their heads, smoked scented cigarettes and fingered strings of amber beads, while fat Egyptian women with kohl-blackened eyes devoured large dishes of ice cream. Below the hotel terrace in the fierce heat a mass of Egyptian humanity flowed in a dusty stream, all robes and turbans. A man passed carrying the whole carcass of a skinned sheep over his shoulder; its eye looked up balefully at Julia standing at the balustrade.

Her room was large and cool and dark. A wooden fan turned lazily on the high ceiling. The chambermaid, who was Italian, mentioned that the staff were all Europeans.

"All?"

"The bootblacks are Egyptian. That much they have learned, signora. To shine shoes."

"And the rest?"

"Italians, Greeks, some Maltese, not much better than Arabs, the Maltese. Without us Europeans this country would not run at all. And the Jews, of course, and the Armenians."

"Someday they must run their own country." It was more a question than a statement.

"Never. Lazy, stupid people. They will never learn. All the Egyptian wants is his bowl of beans and his little Fatima between the sheets."

"Isn't that what we all want?"

The maid looked surprised and shocked.

"That's not the same. Would you like to bathe now?"

"Yes," Julia said, looking down at her dust-covered shoes. "And have these cleaned, please."

She floated in the six-foot long tub set on iron lion's paws, feeling like Cleopatra. To her surprise, the maid had watched her undress and step in. Then she had taken a long-handled brush, lathered it on a bar of brown soap, and scrubbed Julia's back.

"What happens if the Egyptians can't run their own country?"

"Every day there are more and more of us. I read in the *Sphinx* that there will soon be one hundred thousand Italians in Egypt. Imagine that. When we have our African empire we will march on Cairo. Chambermaid no more!"

"What African empire?"

"Ethiopia. Soon it will be over."

"Yes, I suppose so. But why are we doing it?"

"To make Christians of them."

"They're already Christians."

"Oh, that," the maid said, pouring a wooden bucket full of water over Julia's head, "I mean real Christians."

The flight from Alexandria across the lush Nile delta followed the green thread of the river down to the sprawling mass of Cairo with its domes and minarets, and then crossed the desert to the Gulf of Suez. From there they flew along the coast of the Red Sea, which was in fact a brilliant emerald green. The only sign of life was an occasional line of camels winding along the barren shore. They landed once on the emerald sea, at a place called Foul Bay, at a crude dock. The plane tied up there to take on fuel from a drum equipped with a hand pump, while its passengers stood on the dock, gulping air so hot it seemed to sear the lungs, and looked up at hills as barren as the moon. The dock had a signpost with two arrows, one pointing north to Egypt, the other south to the Anglo-Egyptian Sudan.

In the late afternoon they came down in the harbor of Massawa. After the shore of the Red Sea, the town looked almost like civilization. Julia was taken in a sand-colored army staff car to the best of the two hotels, leaving the tired, sweaty men standing on the dock. The port area was utter chaos. Thousands of tons of military equipment stood rusting on the docks. No transport, the press-office man said, but it will come. Italian youths in ill-fitting uniforms were being herded into formation as they came off the gangplank of a transport ship, and they couldn't even form straight lines. That was what Mussolini had described as the greatest army since Caesar's legions.

There were flowers in Julia's hotel room. Now it was her turn to enjoy what she was going to do to Galeazzo Ciano and Angelo Morosini. This time they had, truly, underestimated Julia Howard.

What she was not prepared for was the reality of war. The journey up-country was sheer torture. Her khaki clothes stuck to her body, her hair was a wet mass under her sun helmet. She was doubled up with the pains of diarrhea, in a staff car that seemed to have no springs. In two days they climbed up a rocky path that was called a highway to an elevation of four thousand feet, where they caught up with the Italian army. Their numbers were staggering. How could they not defeat the Ethiopians? The only Ethiopians she saw were porters, tall and black, moving with an aristocratic gait.

As they went higher the foliage grew more lush, with masses of ferns, creepers and vines, and the signs of war grew more frequent. In burned-down villages jackals and wild dogs scavenged in the debris, disputing with the vultures that came flapping down from the trees where they perched in the hundreds. Higher still there were abandoned coffee plantations, clouds drifting through passes, monkeys screaming down from the trees, and endless lines of marching men. Finally they came to a complete halt behind a great jam of military vehicles. Julia's driver, a boy from Agrigento, turned off on a side road in an attempt to bypass the congestion, and promptly got lost.

What she saw after that was all down on paper, as she said to the silent news-agency man curiously watching her across the table in the Ciampino airport bar. She had closed her mind to it all. There was, however, one image she could not get rid of. Lost in the forest, they had come out on a small clearing where a refuse heap smoldered under the low-hanging clouds, a refuse heap out of which stuck a black human foot. There was a young recruit standing guard, a simple peasant boy from Sicily. He and Julia's driver conversed in whispers in their own dialect. The guard, her driver said, had explained that they had rounded up a hundred or so Ethiopian "rebels," ringed them around with barbed wire, poured gasoline over them, and burned them alive. Julia walked away from the stench, to a grove of frangipani trees. There, holding onto a branch, she vomited all over the exquisite ivory blossoms.

Two days after Julia had passed her dispatches to Anthony Pierce, the Trafalgar man, headlines in New York and London read: "Addis Ababa Falls to Mussolini's Forces"; "Abyssinian War Over," but also, "American Correspondent Documents Italian Atrocities." Strangely enough, nothing happened to Julia for a month. She began to think that perhaps her international reputation had saved her from retaliation.

On June 9, 1936, Mussolini, swollen with triumph, turned over the foreign ministry to his son-in-law, Galeazzo Ciano, age thirty-four. The next day Julia was called in by the new foreign minister.

The room was not as vast as Mussolini's office in the Palazzo Venezia, but the setting was the same: a single, ornate desk at the end of the room, where the new minister pretended to be absorbed in reading some document. As she drew closer, Julia saw a pair of spiked golf shoes beneath the desk, next to the polished black ones that Ciano wore.

"I hope I'm not keeping you from more urgent duties, Excellency."

Ciano looked up, rose to his feet, and came forward to shake her hand. In his black cutaway he was sleek as a seal.

"Ah, Julia. How nice to see you again. Cigarette?"

"No, thanks." Julia sat down in the single straight-backed

chair in front of Ciano's desk. She let him have the pleasure of playing games with her for a few minutes. She was, after all, the first victim of his new power.

"Well, Galeazzo, what do you really want?"

"Unpleasant," he said, "to do this."

"I'm sure."

"Still such a beautiful woman."

She said nothing.

"I am obliged to expel you from Italy." He looked at the document on his desk. "It says here that you have 'told monstrous lies and slandered the honor of the Italian army.' That's a quaint way of putting it."

"How long do I have?"

"Twenty-four hours. Longer if you want, of course."

"No, thanks. Twenty-four hours will do just fine."

"I'm sorry." He was enjoying what he was doing.

"That's all right. May I go now?"

"Really, Julia, I hoped we would part friends."

She stood up and started to turn.

"Oh, by the way, have you heard that they finally arrested your old friend Danieli?"

"Well," she said, carefully, "I warned him to stay out of politics."

Ciano's eyes narrowed. "Don't worry. He will only be sent away to a 'resort island' for an extended vacation. There he can meditate on his antisocial behavior."

"If you are trying to hurt me, you're wasting your time, Galeazzo. There hasn't been anything between Paolo Danieli and me for ages."

Ciano dismissed her with a nod of his head, picked up another document and began reading it as if it were of the greatest interest. Julia walked out of his office and slowly down the marble stairs of the Villa Chigi. At the landing a marble statue of a nymph that during the Renaissance had held aloft a candle or torch now held a burned-out light bulb in outstretched hand. It was a perfect image of what the Fascists had done to Italy.

Chapter Thirteen

DAWN WAS A streak of pink-gold between dark sea and gray sky, small clouds were floating like white roses on the surface of the water. The ship's engines had gone dead, but the rhythm of the sea still moved through her body. The white roses were not clouds but white roses on delft-blue wallpaper. She turned over on a bed, surprised it was not the bunk of a ship's cabin: no porthole, only a narrow strip of gold between windowsill and drawn shade. The golden light was water, and someone stirred it with oars—an oysterman on the still surface of the Chesapeake Bay. Julia was back in her own room in Branwood after six years in an enchanted land. Her two suitcases lay open on the floor. She got out of bed and raised the shade by its crocheted ring. It was such a lovely place. Too bad that she wouldn't be coming back to Branwood again; she loved the house and grounds.

She descended the dark curving stairs with her two bags. The smell of tomatoes frying met her at the landing. She put her bags at the foot of the stairs and went down the darkened hall that smelled of furniture polish, and through the swinging doors, the squeak of the hinges like the voice of a long-lost friend. A large black woman stood in front of the wood-burning stove as if she were a figure in Madame Tussaud's waxworks who had not moved in six years.

"Good morning, Maude."

"Morning, Julia."

"I'm hungry, Maude."

The woman turned her head. "You always was, Julia." That was all she said.

"You don't seem very happy to see me."

"I already heard about last night. I'm sorry. You going to leave?"

"Yes."

"I hoped you would come back to stay. We read about you in the newspapers."

"I'm going to Baltimore. Can Wiley take me?"

"After you've had some breakfast. Where're your manners, girl."

Julia laughed. "I'm sorry."

"That's all right." Maude took a plate from a stack on the warmer above the stove and filled it with grits, scrambled eggs, fried ham, and tomatoes. Julia sat down at the kitchen table and ate greedily. Soon there would be silver-covered breakfast dishes on the eighteenth-century sideboard in the dining room for Agnes and Charles.

Maude sat down heavily in the chair opposite her.

"You're better looking than ever, Julia."

"I look awful."

"No. You was pretty before, but you didn't have no character in your face. Now you got character."

"I got it the hard way."

"We all get it the hard way. There ain't no other way. You in love?"

Julia looked up. She had not expected that.

"Yes."

"I hear he's in jail, or something like. At least that's what Victoria says."

"It's true."

"My first husband got sent to jail. It's not easy."

"For how long?"

"Seven years."

"Oh, Maude, I hope it won't be."

"I hope not, too. I was sorry about Mister Gus dying, and while you was away."

"He was my father."

"I know that."

"How did you know?"

"He told me."

"He never told me."

"No need to. He wanted to be sure you'd get some of the Howard money."

The Dusenberg had been replaced by a new Packard, and Wiley was rinsing off the white sidewall tires with a garden hose. A scrub brush and a bar of Octagon soap lay in the grass.

"That's a pretty fine car, Wiley."

"Not so nice as the Dusenberg, Miss Julia. They don't make them like that anymore. Sold it to a Jewish man who runs a junkyard in Baltimore. If it was for me to say, I would swap back even today."

Wiley moved the lever of the ancient pump back and forth, raising pink-tinted gasoline in the glass cylinder. Then he filled the tank of the Packard, put Julia's bags into the trunk, and they drove away. She did not look back: Europe is not a dream, she told herself, it is the only reality. She repeated again what she had said over and over to herself before she had finally drifted off to sleep in her old room in Branwood. She would do anything, descend to any depth, commit any crime, to see Paolo free. She put a handkerchief to her eyes to hold back the tears. Wiley looked quickly at her in the rearview mirror and then turned his eyes back to the road. She put her handkerchief back into her handbag. There would be no more tears. She had work to do.

"How've you been, Wiley?"

"Can't complain, Miss Julia. Aged a bit, that's all."

"We all have. Do you realize that I've been away for six years?"

"We missed you."

"I missed you and Maude."

Wiley delivered her at the front entrance of the Lord Baltimore hotel. She had decided to establish a good address for as long as she could afford—which wouldn't be long. The hotel was not nearly as elegant as she remembered it, and her room was plain and drab. She could have stayed as long as she liked at Branwood, but with her usual willfulness she had ruined any chance of that or of financial help from the Pembertons. She had gone straight from the dock in New York to Branwood, where she had planned to mend fences with Aunt Agnes and Charles, who was running again for Congress, this time as the candidate of a small isolationist party. She figured that with his outspoken defense of Mussolini, Charles must have accumulated a few IOUs with the Italian government. Let them pay off by releasing Paolo. She had had visions of Paolo coming to America and of them having a new, secure life together, but she had deluded herself. Charles's praise of Mussolini was not just to win Italian-American votes. In the library before dinner Charles had spewed out hatred against everything that she believed in. She had quickly realized that it would be unwise to say anything about Paolo. As it was, she hoped Ciano and the Italian government thought she no longer cared for Paolo. Better to leave it that way, better to hide her true feelings.

At dinner there had been a number of Charles's like-minded friends who asked her about life in Italy, and she had told them the truth. Charles had gone red in the face, but she hadn't been able to stop herself. The words "Fascist" and "Communist" were thrown across the table, and Julia had stormed out of the room in the middle of dinner.

She took her shoes off, stretched out on the bed, and looked at the ceiling. What did she do now?

The first thing she did was to pay a call on the head of the trust department of the Merchants and Farmers Bank, which had reopened its doors. She took the elevator to the eighteenth floor and was shown into a mahogany-paneled office. A small man in a dark suit with slicked-down black hair and a pencil-line mustache, and thick gold-rimmed glasses that made his dark eyes seem much too large for his face, came round from behind a large desk.

"Mr. Parsons?"

"Mrs. Morosini. Please sit down. I certainly am glad to see you."

"You are? I mean, you wanted to see me?"

"I should say so. We've written you a number of letters over the last year but have had no reply at all." Mr. Parsons looked at her in a reproachful way. Then he seated himself behind his desk, and opened a folder. "Yours is one of the last of our old accounts yet to be settled. We tried both addresses we have for you . . . in Rome and Verona, Italy . . . several times. Via Giulia . . . is that how you pronounce it?"

"Yes. Just like my name. I haven't lived there for years."

"You should have let us know."

"For what reason? Merchants and Farmers went bust. I had no idea you would reopen."

"Well, for quite a while it looked that way. In fact, we were the last bank in Baltimore to get back on our feet. On top of everything else one of our officers had been playing the stock market with large amounts of our customers' money . . . including yours."

"Elmer J. Thornley, Jr. This used to be his office. The last time I was here was in 1930 to get an advance against my inheritance. He wrote out a check at this same desk. He didn't seem the sort . . ."

"They never do. It's taken us years to regain our reputation. Well, he paid for his crimes."

She wondered if the tight-lipped little man across the desk, so self-righteous now, would be capable of doing what Thornley had done. If he were caught embezzling, would he put a gun to his head, too? What things people did for money. She had always taken money for granted, but then look where that had gotten her.

"Now, let's see. The last major transaction was a transfer of fifty thousand dollars to a Swiss bank. But that still leaves over three hundred thousand as a claim against the bank. What we have been trying to reach you about is that we are now in a position to offer you a settlement—"

"What?"

". . . at ten cents on the dollar, the same amount we offered to our other old customers. That's about thirty thousand dollars. You are free to decline the offer, of course. It's not much."

"Mr. Parsons, thirty thousand dollars to an unemployed journalist is a fortune. I'll take it."

"Very well. There will be some papers to sign. Now, about your properties . . ."

"What properties?"

"Mrs. Morosini, you haven't paid much attention to your business affairs, have you?" He looked at her over his glasses. "You're aware of the waterfront properties that your father owned?"

"No."

"Well, they were part of your inheritance. There was no way Thornley could touch those."

"You mean I could have had the money from them all along?"

"After the bottom dropped out of the real estate market in '30, they were virtually unsellable. However, Baltimore is beginning to recover now. Real estate prices in the port area are rising fast. I would recommend that you hold on to those properties for a few years. The port is growing, and if . . . as some people are already prepared to say . . . there is another war in Europe, well then, there could be the kind of boom there was in Baltimore in 1915."

Julia lit a cigarette. "How much could you get for these properties now?"

"Oh, forty or fifty thousand, I suppose. But I would strongly recommend against putting them on the market at this time."

"Forty or fifty thousand. My God. I'm rich again." She laughed out loud.

"I would not use the term 'rich.' It's a comfortable nest egg, perhaps. However, if you hold on, you might well become rich."

"Sell everything, Mr. Parsons. As soon as you can."

He shook his head. "As you wish, Mrs. Morosini. I'm just trying to give you some good advice. I think you have shown that you need it."

"It's your bank that lost my money in the first place, Mr. Parsons. This time I'm taking it with me." She decided that she disliked the man intensely. "I have a lot of things to do, and they can't wait for a war to come."

"Of course, there may not be a war. . . ."

Julia stood up. "Mr. Parsons, I may not know much about money . . . and I'm sorry if I don't show proper respect for it . . . but I do know what's going on in the world. I'll give you a good tip. There *is* going to be a war, and this time it won't just be in Europe."

Julia took a taxi from the bank to the waterfront, not to look at the properties left her by the man who was supposed to be her father, but to visit Gus's studio. It had been so many years since she had last been there. She wanted only to look at it from the outside. When she reached the place where the studio had been, however, there was nothing but a steam shovel excavating. As Mr. Parsons had said, real estate was booming on the waterfront. According to the sign, a modern office building was soon to be erected on the site. All that remained of Gus's studio was a painted plaster triangle against the brick wall of the next building, once the end wall of the old sail loft where she and Gus and Claudia had lived. How quickly the lives of a generation were erased. When she was gone, who would remember this place where there had been love and happiness? What would happen to the apartment in Rome where she and Paolo had known happiness? Would it disappear in a rain of bombs when the war came?

In a drugstore, Julia called the number on the business card that Gus had given her at lunch at the Lord Baltimore before she sailed for Europe. She still carried it in her handbag, but the penciled address of Gus's mother written on the back was now almost illegible.

"Hello." A woman's voice.

"Mrs. Bramante?"

"No. You got the wrong number. This is the Cohen residence."

"Excuse me, but did some people named Bramante live there before you?"

"Oh, yeah, you're right. Bramante, the Italian couple. He died."

"Do you know where I could find Mrs. Bramante?"

"She went back to the old country."

"Oh. Thank you very much."

"Not at all."

Poor Maria. She had picked a bad time to go back to Italy.

Three days later Julia signed a one-year lease on a small apartment in downtown Baltimore. She gave herself a year to work out some way of getting Paolo out of Italy. Then they would need a larger place. Maybe he would want to live in New York; it wouldn't matter to her as long as they were together. Until some way could be found to get Paolo out, she would keep herself busy with work. She knew she could get a routine newspaper job, but she wanted a position that would give her a chance to help wake people up to what was happening in Europe.

The Baltimore Sun was interested. With the growing threat of war in Europe, they were expanding their international coverage. Perhaps they would have a job for her in the new year. In the meantime they agreed to take a series of articles on the threat of fascism: Many people were ready to listen. Emperor Haile Selassie of Ethiopia, driven from his country, made one last desperate appeal in a speech to the League of Nations in Geneva; but Italian journalists in the gallery had drowned out his words with jeers and whistles. In July the Spanish civil war began, and Mussolini and Ciano quickly sent troops to Spain to fight for Franco. Julia's articles for *The Sun* brought an angry phone call from Charles. *The Sun* had made no secret of the fact that Julia was Agnes Pemberton's niece.

Charles was defeated for Congress a second time that fall. A few days later the Germans and the Japanese signed an "anti-Comintern" pact and *The Sun* offered Julia a job in its newly created European bureau. She took the job because there was the eventual possibility of an opening, they said, in their London or Paris offices. Rome was, of course, closed to her.

The *Sun* building on the corner of Charles and Baltimore streets was quite different from the one room that had housed the Trafalgar News Agency bureau in Rome. But she found herself in a room half the size of her Rome office, where she assembled stories on events in Europe from wire service Teletype items and dispatches from *The Sun*'s own correspondents. She was nothing more than a glorified copy editor at first, but she loved it. She had her fingers on the pulse of the world. She cared not at all that she had no role to play in *The Sun*'s massive coverage of the marriage of a Baltimore woman to the once King of England. She was probably one of the very few people in Baltimore who had no interest in Wallis Warfield Simpson's wedding to Edward VIII. Her interest was in the well-documented and accurate stories that she saw to press every night on the approach of war in Europe and writing an occasional feature on Italian politics.

In December Victoria came home on the pride of the Italian maritime fleet, the liner *Rex*, bringing the three-year-old twins with her. A few days later, she and Julia had lunch together in the tearoom of the Hub department store across the street from the *Sun* building. Above seven floors of merchandise and Christmas decorations they were served chicken salad and potato chips and tea by a white-aproned black waitress, while Julia listened to Victoria's accounts of the latest twists to scandals that had been going on even in Julia's time in Italy. Victoria laughed, rosy-cheeked, switching now and then into Italian. Over chocolate éclairs she asked suddenly, "Do you still love Paolo?"

"You know I always will."

"I suppose so. Julie, Ciano knows."

"What do you mean?"

"He knows how you feel about Paolo."

"How?"

Victoria shrugged. "Who can say? But he called Bruno. He heard I was coming home. He passed me a message for you."

"Yes?"

"He said that you must stop writing against Mussolini."

"I won't."

"Julie, you know me. I don't care a damn about politics, neither does Bruno, for that matter. But we want to help you."

Victoria took a bite of éclair. Her pinkish blond hair was beautifully cut, her rose-pink suit chic, her jewels real.

"I'm doing okay," Julia said defensively.

"Ciano said if you don't stop, he will see that Paolo is taken from his 'resort vacation' and given the kind of treatment a 'traitor' deserves."

"They could have done that in the beginning. I half expected it."

"If Paolo was a nobody, they might have. But if you've got family connections or a known name they're more careful. Who knows? One day the Fascists may be out, and then the shoe could be on the other foot. They all hedge their bets. But if you really provoke Mussolini . . ."

"Where is Paolo, Vicky? Do you know?"

"Bruno says he is being kept on a little island off the coast of Sicily. He lives with a family. Really, he's all right."

"But if I don't stop?"

"You know them, Julia. You know Ciano."

"Yes." She put her head in her hands. She was beaten. She had only been kidding herself.

"What about Francesca?" How she would have liked to see her, talk to her.

"Nobody knows. I've heard different stories—that she is still hiding somewhere in the Abruzzi, that she is in jail . . . or dead. I'm sorry, Julie, but you'd better know the truth."

"You'll be writing Bruno?"

"Of course."

"Tell him . . . in some kind of double-talk . . . that I've gotten the message. He can tell Ciano I won't cause any more trouble. He can tell Ciano that I will never write another word . . . as long as they don't touch Paolo."

"You know, Julie, what that would lead to is working for them. Bruno says the best thing is just tell them you've taken another job, that you're out of politics, that you don't care a damn about Paolo. Don't let them get their hooks into you. Bruno can help."

By January 1937 there were forty thousand Italian troops in Spain, but Julia wrote nothing about that. Much to the puzzlement of her editor, she asked to be transferred to the city desk. For the next two years, as Europe moved ever closer to war, Julia wrote on women's affairs in Baltimore. The closest she came to the world scene was a feature on Amelia Earhart, after the aviatrix's plane disappeared over the Pacific.

But she read every word that was written about Europe. Her spirits rose when a small group of Italian exiles soundly defeated Mussolini's Spanish expeditionary force at Guadalajara, and sank again when she learned that the exiles were led by Carlo Rosselli, the head of Paolo's organization. Her fears for Paolo grew even more when Rosselli was murdered near Paris, it was said by assassins sent by Ciano. But Victoria, who had gone back to Bruno in the spring, got word to Julia that Paolo was alive and still on his island. There was no chance that he would ever be released now.

She could do nothing but hope. Julia worked hard, not because she liked what she was doing, but to keep herself occupied. A newspaper was a good place to spend long hours, leaving time for little but sleep. Her waterfront properties were sold for more than had been expected, and if she wasn't rich by Mr. Parsons's standards, she was once again quite well-off. The Germans occupied Czechoslovakia. Mussolini and Hitler met for the second time, and this time the meeting was ominously cordial. Italy joined the anti-Comintern pact two months later, and in December 1937 Nanking fell to the Japanese and Italy finally left the League of Nations. Victoria did not come home that year, and there was no further word of Paolo.

Shortly after her thirtieth birthday, Julia was eating alone one day in a cafeteria near the *Sun* building, where she often went for lunch. While she ate she read, as she usually did, about world politics, about Europe in particular, and especially Italy. As she skimmed through the pile of British, French, and Italian papers to which the European desk of *The Sun* subscribed, she had an odd feeling that she was being watched. She looked up and into a mirror across the room and into the eyes of a woman who looked vaguely familiar; an older, rather dowdy woman, with her hair pinned up in an untidy bun. She continued staring at the woman, who did not move, until she realized that she was that woman.

Chapter Fourteen

THE PHONE WAS ringing. Julia went through the routine familiar to anyone who has worked on a news desk: light on, pencil out, receiver up. You don't have to be awake to do it.

"Hello."

"Is Miss Howard there?"

"Yes."

"New York calling, person-to-person. Are you Miss Howard?"

"Yes, yes."

"Hold on, please. Go ahead. Your party is on the line."

"Julia?"

"Yes?"

"This is Francesca."

"What?"

"Francesca Danieli."

"Francesca?"

"Did I wake you?"

"Francesca!" At last the message had gotten through to Julia's brain. "You're alive!"

"Alive and in New York. I bring greetings from Il Duce."

The receiver was moist in Julia's hand. "You're alive . . . and safe."

"Safe and at my parents' apartment. I must see you right away."

"Yes, yes."

"Can you come up this weekend?"

Could she come up? Could anything stop her?

* * *

Pennsylvania Station seemed to know that hope was born again. There was hope in the air of that vast space, hope on the faces of travelers arriving and leaving. Julia even had a cheerful taxi driver, who took her to the address on upper Fifth Avenue.

The black woman operating the elevator wore a uniform of the same blue with gold piping as the beefy, red-faced doorman. An enormous starched lace handkerchief sprouted from her breast pocket. The Danieli apartment was on the twenty-sixth and -seventh floors of a building thrown up with great exuberance just before the crash of '29. Beyond the ceiling-high casement windows, soot-stained gargoyles stuck their tongues out at Central Park far below, where the first breath of autumn had tipped a few leaves with red and yellow.

They were all there, except Paolo: the mother, recipient of incomes she had never clearly understood and now understood not at all; Francesca, looking younger than when Julia had last seen her on that wild ride of escape to Rieti, vibrantly alive, with clear blue eyes and a head of red curls; and the father, the producer of bad films and notorious womanizer. He had been felled by a stroke and was confined to a wheelchair. So, here was the couple who had conceived the man who was the source of all the joy and pain in her life, the old roué now taken in by his estranged wife. Julia felt both tenderness and perplexity. What strange, unknowable courses lives took.

The mother said little, wandered restlessly about the apartment in several layers of pink satin, playing with the several arrangements of fresh flowers, lighting cigarettes that she would put out after a few puffs. Julia longed to be alone with Francesca, to hold her in her arms, as if she could feel Paolo through her. As Francesca grew older she looked more and more like her brother. The two younger women sat together on the sofa, talking about everything except what Julia wanted to hear. Francesca was obviously keeping most of what had happened from her parents, who knew only that Paolo was under some kind of travel restriction. Such restrictions were a common thing in Italy these days; and they believed he would soon be coming to America.

"And then, maybe," the father said, "he can do an honest day's work." He shook his head. "All these years he has wasted when he could have been here making a name for himself . . . and a fortune. He's a fine artist. He won the gold medal at age eighteen. But, no, he has to fight Mussolini all by himself. You thought you could change him, but I knew better. He has a head like Carrara marble."

Julia laughed. "Yes, on that we can agree. Then you do remember me and our conversation on the train."

"Oh, I never forget a beautiful woman. At least my son has taste, I told myself. And I told you to get him out of Italy."

"He wouldn't go."

"Of course not." Danieli tapped his head with his knuckles. "Marble." He was silent then, thinking about something in the past, his hands folded on his lap robe. He still wore his hair long; but the thick mane had now turned completely white, making him look like an old lion.

"This one, too," he said nodding toward Francesca, "she believes in principle. She would be there still if it weren't for me. Even after my stroke, I was the one who had to arrange for the false passport and other documents. Where were her Resistance friends then? They could do nothing. I, being a man of no principle, knew how to do such things."

"Papa, you were the one who had to leave. I would have stayed on. Somebody had to come with you. You were sick."

"My friends would have taken care of me," he said stubbornly.

"What would you have done? Even if you'd been well, there is no more work for you in Italy."

"It was my life, the theater. So my mother was Jewish. Who cares? I was raised a good Catholic, and my father fought with Garibaldi. Does that count for nothing?" He looked at Julia, trying to remember her name. "You know Italians."

"I'm half-Italian myself," Julia said.

"There, you see! And what difference does it make? Who knows? Who cares?" And then, contradicting himself, "If you have Italian blood, you know even better that Italians care nothing about race. Nothing. How many times did Mussolini himself laugh at Hitler, make fun of him for his stupid racial ideas. And now this *Manifesto on Race*. It is absurd. And only fifty thousand Jews in Italy when they got around to counting them. And what trouble have they ever given? From Mama's family there came lawyers and doctors, even army officers. One was on the municipal council of Perugia, another was a deputy."

"Hitler made him do it," Francesca said. "As Mussolini grows weaker Hitler gets stronger. Now they do the goose step at parades in Rome. They call it, of course, the *passo romano*."

"Do you remember the Rite of the Wedding Rings?" Danieli asked, ignoring his daughter. "I was there. There was a big caldron over a fire to melt them down in. Victor Emmanuel, the midget king, came first with his cretinous wife. They threw their gold wedding rings into the pot, and two hundred thousand Romans followed them. It took all day. And the rabbi threw into the caldron the gold key to the tabernacle of the chief synagogue of Rome. A synagogue the king himself had dedicated. This, if you please, to help finance Mussolini's war in Ethiopia."

A maid brought Danieli's pills and a glass of water, a butler wheeled in a drinks cart, and Mrs. Danieli finally sat down. They talked of the New York theater, sitting in the growing dusk, while the ponds below in Central Park turned to mirrors the color of silver ash. Julia was invited to spend the night.

As she walked down the hall with Francesca to their bedroom, Julia said, "I never realized that you and Paolo had a Jewish grandmother."

"I guess nobody ever bothered to tell you. As Papa says, who cares?"

"Hitler does, and now it seems Mussolini. . . . When I found out that my real father was not Tim Howard but an Italian immigrant, I still felt I was the same person."

"Well, aren't you, and who cares?"

"My Aunt Agnes would care."

"Your Aunt Agnes and Hitler have a few things in common."

They went into the bedroom, and Francesca shut the door.

"Oh, Francesca, I'm so relieved you're here. Victoria said . . . you might even be dead."

"I nearly was a couple of times. I've been one jump ahead of the OVRA for the last two years."

"I've missed you so." She held Francesca tight and kissed her face and eyes and lips, unembarrassed by the sensuality of their embrace.

"Let's get ready for bed, and I'll ring for some sandwiches and drinks. I've got lots to tell you."

"I won't have much to tell you. All I do is work and hope."

"You really love him, don't you?"

"I don't know what will become of me if I lose him . . . but I'm helpless."

"You won't lose him. We'll find a way."

Julia awoke the next morning saying to herself, "We'll find a way." To think that she had almost given up after Ciano's warning. Francesca was sitting at the dressing table in her slip, applying makeup. Julia sat up in bed. "Good morning."

"How do you feel?" Francesca asked.

"Fine. A slight hangover."

"Didn't we talk the night away, though?"

"We haven't had such a session since we lived together in your studio in Trastevere."

Francesca's face in the mirror was as fresh as a newly opened flower. Her image smiled at Julia.

"Do you often think of James?" Julia asked.

"I'll always miss James. But James is dead and I'm alive, and I mean to live."

"You look great."

Francesca put down the makeup brush and swung around on the stool.

"But what about you?"

"What do you mean?"

"You know damn well what I mean. Do you remember when you were considered the most beautiful woman in Rome. Well, look at yourself now. Look at your hair. Look at your clothes. I was shocked at what you were wearing yesterday. You, of all people. Christ, Julia, with your beauty how could you let yourself go like that?"

"I don't know what to say. After what you've been through, you look so good, and I . . ."

Francesca went over, sat on the bed, and held Julia's hand. "I know what you have been through, too, but it's no excuse."

"I'm so glad you're here, Francesca. This morning everything looks different."

"Everything will be different."

"I said when they arrested Paolo and expelled me, that nothing could keep us apart, that I would find a way. And then, somehow, I lost heart. Never again, Francesca, I promise you. Never again."

The next day Julia had her hair cut short. She bought a complete wardrobe, some new makeup, and several pairs of shoes. Then she dropped everything that she had brought with her to New York down the incinerator shaft outside the Danieli apartment. What had she sworn? That she would do anything, descend to any depth, commit any crime, to see Paolo free. She had forgotten one thing—that she must also live for Paolo. She knew that her new vow to live for Paolo did not free her from her earlier oath. She might still have to descend to any depth, commit any crime. . . .

The same weekend that Julia awoke from her long sleep, there was a meeting in Munich of the leaders of a very frightened Europe: Hitler, Mussolini, Deladier, and Chamberlain. The meeting was a success, a success for which Mussolini took the credit. Peace was saved.

In January, Barcelona fell to Franco's forces. The Spanish civil war was as good as over, and America turned to preparations for the World's Fair. Julia went up to New York to do a feature for *The Sun*, taking a staff photographer out to Flushing Meadows with her to record the completion of the pylon and sphere that were to be the symbol of this international exhibition, with its plaintive theme of world peace. Julia nearly wept over the Italian pavilion, but in her article she refrained from describing it. The *New York Times* called it "one of the low points in the history of Italian architecture." Poor Paolo. At least, on his island of exile, he was spared this humiliation to Italy.

The New York World's Fair opened on April 30, 1939. Foreign Minister Ciano was scheduled to come for the inauguration of the Italian pavilion, but he was otherwise occupied—observing from a plane the Italian invasion of defenseless Albania. Instead, a boorish Fascist hack, styled minister of culture, cut the ribbon in the red, white and green colors of Italy. At his side, in the *Times* photograph, was the director general of the Italian Ministry of Foreign Affairs, a handsome man in his mid-thirties, with slightly graying temples. Count Angelo Morosini, the caption read.

The next day Julia received a call from Angelo. He had seen her name on the article in *The Sun*. He would like to see her. After their brief conversation she had put down the receiver in confusion, saying to herself in a whisper, "I'll find a way." She went to the mirror. After months of grooming she looked as good as she had ever looked in her life. Scrutinizing herself in the mirror, she also had to admit, to her annoyance, that Maude had been right. Suffering had lent character to her face. She picked up the phone again and called *The Sun*. She needed a few days off.

When she spotted Angelo in the Palm Court of the Plaza, Julia thought he looked like a youngish Ronald Coleman; in any case, as if he had wandered in from a nearby movie set. Had he always had that air of playing a role on stage?

"Julia!"

"Hello, Angelo."

"My God, I didn't think you could get more beautiful, but you have."

On your toes, Julia, she said to herself. "You're not looking bad yourself. Prosperous."

"I've put on weight, you mean." He looked at his waist.

"A bit. It suits you."

He gave her an appraising glance. His eyes asked, "What are you up to?" But all he said was, "Buy you a drink?"

"Why not?"

They took a table in a corner of the crowded bar.

"The usual," she said. He looked confused, and she laughed. "Was there a usual? I've forgotten. In any case, I'll have a scotch and soda."

His eyes narrowed. He wasn't so sure of himself now, but he was getting his script in order. She could see that. A saucer of potato chips and another of olives were put down on the round oak table, and two scotches.

"Cheers," he said. "It's been a long time." His eyes were the same soft brown.

"Yes, it has been."

"No hard feelings, I hope."

"I thought we parted friends," she said, stirring her drink with the little wooden stick.

"Well, all that unpleasantness."

She shrugged. "That was Ciano . . . unless you put him up to it. Did you, Angelo?"

He put his hand on his heart. "Why would I have?"

"In any case, I knew what I was doing. When I wrote that story about Italian atrocities in Ethiopia, I knew what to expect."

"Why did you do it?"

"It was true."

It was his time to shrug. "War is war. Your story doesn't change that."

Good old Angelo, she thought, still unable to understand the simplest moral judgment. And this man was the director general of the Italian Ministry of Foreign Affairs. He was also her lawful husband. She saw people at other tables looking at them. She knew what they were thinking: what a handsome couple.

"I want you back," he said.

She stared at him, stunned.

"Why, if I may ask?" She was trying to control her voice.

"You're still my wife."

"In name only."

"It could be different."

"You're crazy, Angelo."

"No, I'm not crazy. You know better than that."

She couldn't argue with him. He was certainly not crazy, just cold and calculating and pleasure loving. What should she say next?

All that she could think of was, "I'll find a way." She couldn't afford to close any doors now.

"We've burned our bridges, Angelo. At least I've burned mine. I couldn't go back to Italy, even if I wanted to" ... not too fast ... "and I don't want to." Keep the door open just a crack, that's it. What advantage could she take of this unexpected development?

"But, actually, you could ... if you wanted to." Very slow drawl, lowered eyelids of the director general.

"Don't be silly. I'm prohibited from entering Italy, on the personal order of Foreign Minister Ciano. Nothing can change that."

"Ciano could."

She started to laugh. But Angelo knew what Ciano would or would not do. She looked away; watched as two well-dressed couples entered the bar. Things were moving too fast for her to think them through.

"What makes you think he would?"

"He got your message. There were no more attacks on Il Duce, you've stayed out of politics for two years now, and you're my wife. If I asked him, I think he would let you come back."

His eyes gave away nothing, but she figured he'd already asked Ciano and knew that it was possible. She lowered her eyes.

"I was just curious. I'm not coming back to Italy, and I'm certainly not coming back to you."

"Why not?" He feigned surprise.

"Oh, don't be ridiculous. Because we haven't been in love for years ... if we ever were. I'm being honest. And because of all that's happened between us."

"I still care for you."

"I don't believe you."

Still his eyes did not waver. "Well, think about it."

"There's nothing to think about."

"There is. You're my wife. I can never have another. I am growing old without children ..."

Aha. There was the answer.

"... and I've changed. There'll be no other women. Only you. I'm a lonely man and," his voice broke, "... I love you. You don't know how I've suffered, unable even to see you. You gave me everything, and I threw it away with my foolish behavior. I've learned my lesson."

He looked as if he was about to cry. But she knew Italian men. They start off trying to persuade you of something and get so carried away they convince themselves.

"Sorry, Angelo. I'm sorry there's no divorce in Italy, and I'm sorry you don't have children." She reached across the table and put a hand on his arm. "I'm not trying to hurt you. I wish you no ill, believe me. But we can't start over again. The spark died a long time ago."

"Do you remember that night you came home with me to Via Giulia ... long after we separated? The spark wasn't dead then, Julia."

"That was purely sexual. I told you then it could have been any man."

"Thanks so much."

"Sorry. I didn't mean it that way. I can't pretend to you that there was anything wrong with that side of our marriage."

"No, you can't," he said. "Well, I didn't come here to fight with you. Let's talk about other things. That is a beautiful dress you have on, silk shantung, the color of your eyes."

"How long will you stay in New York, Angelo?"

"I'm not sure. It depends. A week or two. Perhaps we could have lunch one day."

"I'm afraid . . ."

"I promise not to raise the subject again . . ."

The next day Julia met Francesca for lunch at Schrafft's and related, almost word for word, her meeting with Angelo.

"It sounds to me as if you left the door open more than a crack."

They were eating club sandwiches on the mezzanine, looking down through the big oval window onto the crowded Fifth Avenue sidewalks. People walked so much faster in New York than they did in Baltimore.

"I suppose I did, but I wanted to keep him talking. I was interested."

"Careful, Julia."

"Oh, heavens, Francesca, I don't mean interested in him, but interested that Ciano might let me go back to Italy. If I could get back . . ."

"What would you do?"

"I would get Paolo off that island."

"How?"

"I don't know, but there must be a way. I have quite a bit of money again. I've changed, Francesca. I would do anything, absolutely *anything*. And I'm not afraid."

Francesca took a long time to say, "I could help."

"Then you don't think I'm crazy."

"Maybe we're both crazy. But he's my brother, and I love the stubborn fool."

"The stubborn, wonderful fool. War is coming, Francesca, and then it will be too late."

"War is coming and when it does people like Paolo won't be left on islands. It will be prison . . . or worse. You're right. It will be too late to help him then. There are people in the Resistance who could help. I could give you names. . . ."

"But first I have to get to Italy."

"Yes, first you have to get to Italy."

That evening Julia stayed awake for hours, seeking a solution, any solution but the obvious one. Then she slept for a couple of hours, and when she awoke she had half thought, half dreamed exactly how it might be done. She picked up the bedside phone and called Francesca.

"I've got to see you."

"What time is it?"

"Well, quite a bit past midnight."

"Can't it wait till morning?"

"No."

"All right, but where are you staying?"

"The Bristol. I'll tell the desk to let you up."

When Francesca came in the hotel room Julia was sitting by the window in her nightgown, smoking a cigarette. There were several other cigarettes stubbed out in the ashtray.

"I had to see you before I changed my mind. I'm going back to Angelo."

"I thought you would."

"You did?"

"You said you would do anything, and I believed you."

"It's the only way, until Paolo's free."

"Can you do it?"

"That's what I'm afraid of. Would you do it?"

"Yes."

"But I'll have to let Angelo make love to me. That's obscene!"

"Millions of women despise their husbands, but they have to do it for thirty years." Francesca laughed. "God, what a thought."

"Even if I didn't loathe him, I couldn't forget that he used me to spread Fascist propaganda. And I'm convinced he's the one who was responsible for Paolo's arrest."

"All the more reason for you to use him now. If you go back to Angelo, who could suspect that you have any feeling for Paolo?"

Francesca sat on the chair arm and put her hand on Julia's shoulder. "These are cruel times. I was a decade with the Resistance movement, the last two in hiding. I've seen many of my friends killed—not just James—tortured, hunted down like animals—some of the best, most decent people in Italy. You do what you have to do to fight that, and to fight for what you love."

"I guess that's what I wanted to hear," Julia said with resignation. "But I can't believe I'm doing such a thing. I feel like I'm playing Tosca and about to give myself to Scarpia to save my lover."

"Well, Italy under Mussolini is certainly opera . . . *opera buffa.*"

"I forgot," said Julia with a wan smile, "they shot Cavaradossi anyway, didn't they?"

"You'll have to be careful. I can teach you some things. Oh, I'm a real professional at conspiracy."

"I already have a plan. There is this cottage in Sicily, near Agrigento, where Angelo and I spent . . . our honeymoon."

The next day, when Julia had lunch with Angelo, her plan was easily accomplished. He thought he was gradually entrapping her. She resisted just enough to maintain the illusion that he was still a skillful manipulator of women. Angelo was as vain and shallow as he had ever been; he had not matured emotionally at all. In the week that followed they saw each other nearly every day. She gradually let him understand that she was lonely and unhappy in America. She left the impression that she missed the glamorous life of Roman society—none of it in so many words, but he followed her cues. He reopened the subject of her coming back to him. Perhaps love was not there, but with time, who knew? They both needed stability, a place in society. There need be no hurry about having children, still plenty of time. It was a sophisticated line and she let herself be carried along, ever so slowly. They even walked arm in arm one evening. Everything was going well.

Then it happened. Angelo called to say that Ciano had

summoned him back to Italy: no delay, no excuses. There
was a ship in three days' time. He needed to see her urgently.

They met again at the Plaza, where Angelo was staying,
for a drink. He was wearing one of the best-looking tweed
suits she had ever seen. She knew that she looked her best,
too, in a light wool dress, very understated, from the spring
showings in Paris, a misty blue-lavender. Angelo came right
to the point.

"I've come to propose to my wife."

She smiled. "Why, Count Morosini, how unexpected."

He was trying on his most serious look. "Don't joke,
Julia. I mean it. I'm proposing that we start all over
again, wipe the slate clean, start over as if we were newlyweds. It's not too late." Nervously, he turned the gold wedding ring that he had put back on since their last meeting.

"Even if it weren't too late, Angelo, it's not something I
could decide that quickly."

"Oh, damn Ciano! But you know how he is. I have to do
what he says. I must go. I wanted more time, too. I wanted
you to get to know me again, to see how I've changed."

"You've behaved fairly well so far."

"Won't you take me seriously?"

"I take you seriously." She gave him a steady look, not
smiling now.

"I don't want any more arguments. It has to be now. I
have no idea when I can get back to America. Won't you
come with me?"

"I can't come with you, Angelo."

His face fell. He tapped his fingers impatiently on the table. This was not how it was supposed to go.

"I would have to put my affairs in order. That would
take several weeks."

"Do I understand what you are saying?"

"If you simply *have* to have an answer today, I guess the
answer is, well, in principle . . . yes."

"Oh, Julia, how wonderful! You won't regret it."

I hope not, she thought.

"Now we must celebrate. I'll have some champagne sent up to my room."

The moment that she had dreaded so much was, without warning, upon her. And there was no way she could refuse.

He kissed her for the first time in the elevator and told her that she was ten times as beautiful as when they married. Then they were in his room together, the champagne had already arrived and a silver vase of roses. This was it: Tosca and Scarpia. She ducked into the bathroom and locked the door. What did she do now? Submit to his embraces, in the language of opera? Yes, that. She could say her period had just started, but that would hardly do. She turned on the cold water tap and filled a toothbrush glass with water and drank it down, and then went back into the sitting room of Angelo's suite without any idea what she would do next. He had closed the venetian blinds, the champagne was open, the odor of roses cloying.

"Cheers," he said.

She touched her glass to his, saying nothing. They drank, his arm around her waist. He still wore the same cologne. Italian men were creatures of habit. They sat and talked, but she wasn't concentrating. It was like being back in Roman society, speaking in clichés. What repelled her most was that nothing had changed. It really could have been Rome in the first year of their marriage. He saw nothing, understood nothing. He thought he had won and had her again. As he drew her to him and kissed her, she felt like a whore that some man had paid to come up to his hotel room. His tongue was in her mouth. Why not look at it that way? Nothing but a cold-blooded transaction. It would be easier.

"Excuse me," Angelo said, letting her go. He went into the bathroom, and she quickly got up and pulled her dress over her head. She didn't want him undressing her. Standing in the middle of the room, she looked at her image in the mirror on the back of the open closet door, naked in black pumps, except for stockings and garter belt and a string of pearls: white body, dark eyes, dark hair on her head and between her legs. Julia Howard, who had brought Angelo to her room of mirrors on the Via Pinciana, was no longer there. In her place was another woman, reflected in one narrow mirror, but in an icy way more sexual. She wasn't afraid anymore. She was moving already toward her goal—saving Paolo.

"You were never so beautiful, never," Angelo said, looking at her in the mirror. She kicked off the shoes and stretched out across the bed while he undressed. She kept her eyes closed while he fondled her, and she said as he entered her, "Easy, I haven't in a very long time." That excited him. At first she lay quietly under his moving body, then moved with him. "Just a little more," she whispered in his ear, "and I'll come." He could have been anybody—that was the secret. She moved faster. She had never faked it, the one thing she wouldn't do. And didn't. "I'm coming," she gasped, and she was, in waves and waves. The more she fought it the more intense it became. When she cried out it was from the frustration of not being able to stop herself. That night she told Francesca, to exorcise the shame of it. Francesca gave her a look that could have had a dozen meanings, but all she said was, "So much the better for your purposes."

The next day, as agreed, Julia renounced her American citizenship before the Italian consul general in New York and received her Italian passport, and the following day Angelo sailed for Genoa. She would follow in a few weeks. Both of them, and Galeazzo Ciano, knew that from the moment she set foot on Italian soil she would be defenseless. No longer would there be an American consul to appeal to, to protect her from the savagery of Fascist "justice." Julia went back to Baltimore, quit her job, and put her affairs in order. Then she booked passage on the next ship to Italy. This time when she sailed on the *Velonia*, there was a large picture of her in the Sunday rotogravure section leaning on the rail. Julia Howard, former women's editor of *The Sun*, had been transformed once again into Contessa Giulia Morosini, the very image of the cold, classical beauty that was in vogue in that last summer before the war.

Chapter Fifteen

MORE THAN EIGHT years had passed since Julia and Angelo had honeymooned on the ridge, high above the Mediterranean, overlooking the ancient town of Agrigento. Nothing had changed. It was still dry, hot, and silent except for the hum of cicadas in the olive trees around the little guest house beneath the crumbling palazzo. When they had arrived Angelo was eager, boyish, as if he'd opened a sealed tomb where the golden days of their honeymoon lay before him, newly minted, untouched by all of the ugly things that had passed between them. How egotistical, Julia thought, of Angelo to imagine that he could repeat the youthful coming together that two people can never repeat—least of all they.

They were sitting in canvas chairs beside the garden reservoir, a bottle of Sicilian wine in an ice bucket between them. In the late morning the cicadas sang all along the ridge that ran between the purple plain of Sicily and the sea. Angelo had been talking for a long time but she was not listening: He simply did not exist for her. She had learned to be as cruel as the times in which they lived. She was half-asleep, and only after a long time realized that buried deep in the cicada's song was the sound of a phone ringing. She opened her eyes. Angelo's chair was empty and the ringing of the phone had stopped.

When he came back down the path from the house his mouth was set in a tight line.

"What is it?"

"Ciano. Damn him!"

"You have to go back to Rome?"

"Yes. Not even two weeks can I have alone with my wife, after all these years."

"But if it weren't for Ciano, I wouldn't be here at all."

She could hardly contain her joy that he was leaving. Everything was working out. For nearly two months she had endured being his wife, living with him in *her* apartment on the Via Guilia, having her body violated by him night after night, playing hostess again to his Fascist colleagues, all for the purpose of leading him here. The world was on the verge of war, yet she had wheedled, pled, done everything she could think of to entice him into going back to where they had spent their honeymoon. All right, Angelo had finally said, Ciano agrees—always Ciano—on the understanding that he could be called back to Rome on a minute's notice. She had said she would wait patiently in such a case.

"He's sending a seaplane to pick me up. It's already left Rome. It'll be here in about an hour."

"Enough time to make love," she said, getting up and walking toward the house, chilled by what she was doing to assure that he would have not the slightest suspicion about her faithfulness.

She lay across the bed for a long time after he had withdrawn from her, showered, kissed her, and gone away. In these times one did what one must to survive: faked orgasms—no longer a problem there—took precautions not to get pregnant, and showed not the slightest trace of emotion. But then she thought of Paolo, and a flood of tears came. After the emotional storm was over she got up and soaped and showered away the smell and feel of Angelo's body. A half hour had passed; and by now he would be down at the port. She pulled out of the closet the antique brass telescope and its wooden tripod that had been a toy to play with on their honeymoon. After setting it up on the terrace, she watched Angelo being hoisted from a motorboat into the cabin of the seaplane. Then the plane lifted off from the water and headed out to sea.

* * *

Her new sports car was parked in the shade of an olive tree, its gleaming metallic surface lightly powdered with road dust. It had been waiting for her outside the apartment on the Via Guilia in Rome, a gift from Angelo. He said that he had tried to find one in the same shade of midnight blue, but Fiat no longer made that color. The new car was a gunmetal blue, but in every other way as elegant as her old one. She opened the car door, paused, and took the keys out of her handbag, and also the square gold compact, a gift from Angelo. Her eyes looked back from the mirrored lid, serious and perhaps a little frightened.

She ran a finger over the silk mesh that held in the loose face powder. Beneath the powder was a sheet of tissue paper folded into a square the exact size of the interior of the compact. The hiding place was Francesca's suggestion. The sheet of paper was covered with notes in tiny block letters: all of the names, addresses, and odd facts that Francesca had been able to dredge up from her years in the Resistance movement, facts that might conceivably be of use to Julia.

She dropped the compact back into the handbag and felt, sewn inside the leather lining, a brand-new American passport that she had applied for in New York without revealing that the day before she had renounced her American citizenship.

She was both Guilia Morosini, contessa, and Julia Howard, *Baltimore Sun*. She started the car, turned it in a cloud of dust, and headed down the winding track to Agrigento. She wondered where Angelo had gotten the money for the car, and suspected he had found a way, without her countersignature, of drawing on what was left in their Swiss bank account. After all, she had deserted hearth and home and Italy. Had he found out that she had money again? She wouldn't be surprised. That would explain a lot.

The road that led to the westernmost tip of Sicily hugged the shore. It was narrow and in incredibly bad repair. There were a few trucks, but almost no cars, only donkeys ridden by peasants with huge mustaches and old women in black. For God's sake, there were even camels! The modern world had barely touched Sicily. She was unsure what she was doing in such a place; but whatever it was had started. She drove past the ruins of ancient Greek temples, marshes on one side, bare mountains on the other. For half an hour her open car was stalled, caught behind a thousand sheep and goats being driven along the road to Marsala, until she was covered with powdery dust. She arrived at Trapani in the late afternoon, and drove right down to the ferryboat landing. The last boat was heading out to the small islands, three lavender triangles on the horizon: Favignana to the south, Marettimo in the center, and Levanzo to the north.

Paolo was on Levanzo. She took a room there, in a small family pensione as far away as possible from the dock—the kind of place where a single woman might hope to stay without being reported to the police.

The next morning she mingled with the crowd of holiday-makers from Rome who poured off the first ferry, men in funny straw hats and women in bare-backed dresses, their flesh already turning pink. She was swirled along with them into the center of the little town. Before the morning was over she had made friends with a shoe salesman and his girlfriend. They ate lunch together under the grape vines in a little square that opened onto the sea: grilled sardines and the sour white wine that the island produced. As they ate watermelon and drank more wine, the shoe salesman flirted with Julia. Village boys in dirty white jackets brought coffee to the tables scattered about in the speckled vine-shade. The streets leading into the little piazza began to fill with shadow; the shutters were closed; the afternoon siesta was settling in.

The shoe salesman and his girlfriend drifted off, probably to make love in some rented room. Now what? What was she supposed to look for? How to begin to find Paolo? And what then? She had been so confident when she had been conspiring with Francesca in New York. Tears of frustration came to her eyes.

"Signora. May I see your identity papers, please?"

She looked up into the face of a young *carabiniere*, no more than nineteen, just out of police school, proud of his stylish uniform and tricornered hat.

"Of course."

She took the elegant leather-bound foreign ministry identification papers out of her handbag and then, too late, realized in a cold panic that a single telegraphed message to Rome would be the end of both her and Paolo. Fool! In desperation she turned over her glass of wine and it ran off the glass-topped table and onto the policeman's razor-creased trousers.

"*O, scuzi.*"

She was up on her feet, handing the *carabiniere*, all flustered, white napkins, slipping the identity papers into her blouse, talking very fast, watching him backing away, regaining his only newly acquired dignity, adjusting his sword.

"You should be on the stage," a gravelly voice said from the shadows. A tiny, one-legged man in cloth cap, sitting on the pavement, his crutch propped against the wall of the church, a wooden tray of cigarettes spread out on the cobblestones before him, held her gaze.

"Don't worry, Your Excellency, I won't tell," the one-legged little man said to Julia.

Julia sighed with relief. She had lived long enough in Italy to know that there were underworld people you could trust, people who were with you simply because you were in trouble with the authorities. She was inspired now. She took a very large bill out of her handbag, folded it into a neat square and passed it down to the little man in the shadows.

"A pack of Turkish, please."

"And what else?"

"Have you heard of a Paolo Danieli?"

"Danieli? No."

Her heart sank.

"But I could ask around if . . ."

She took another large bill out and passed it to the one-legged seller of cigarettes.

"I'm usually along the seaside in the evening, in the park. There're benches there. It's a nice spot, sea breezes. The moon's full tonight. Comes up about nine."

* * *

The moon came up in splendor over the Mediterranean just after nine. Julia strolled back and forth in the little park built up over the rocks on which the sea broke with a sound like deep whispers. She had been there for half an hour, trying to look like a woman who was impatiently waiting for a friend; but her act was wearing thin. The benches were filling up with the dark shapes of couples out to watch the moonrise and embrace with more or less innocence, but there was no sign of the seller of cigarettes. Finally she decided that she would have to get out of the public eye. She slipped into the inky shadow of a clump of fragrant jasmine and sat down on a dew-wet bench. What if she was wrong and the one-legged man was a police agent? In any case, time was running out and she had no other . . .

"Julia."

She leapt up in panic, her heart racing as it never had in her life, her mind tumbling ahead with every kind of wild surmise. A hand seemed to be holding her arm tightly. Her legs gave way and she sat back down on the bench. The moon was going around and around, as it once had long ago.

"Paolo."

"There was another night, on the Janiculum."

There are moments in your life, she thought, that no one would believe, that you wouldn't dare tell anyone about. She turned, and in the dark put her head on the shoulder of the man that she had come four thousand miles to free. There were no tears; there wasn't even very much to say. What was needed was to be practical.

"Are we being watched?"

"No. My keeper is across the way in the wine bar."

"Listen then. I'm getting you out of here. I don't know how yet, but be ready. I'll send a message. I'm here in Sicily and I'll . . ."

No point in trying to be practical when a man was kissing you on the back of the neck and his hands were on your breasts. She gasped for air in his embrace.

"Paolo, don't. We can't take any risks. Not now, not

when . . ." But his mouth was on hers, and who was she to talk to him about risks? The moon was blazing over the water and illuminating the other kissing couples on benches. But they were still safe in the deep tangled shadow of the perfumed jasmine.

"You came," he whispered. "If I live to be a hundred, this is the one moment in my life . . ."

"Paolo."

"What you are asking is quite improper, criminal even," the colonel of *carabinieri* said. "I could call the guard now and have you arrested."

"I know," Julia said humbly, "but I am only a woman, and all that I ask is mercy for someone who has done no wrong. You must know how miscarriages of justice happen so easily the way things . . . well, the way things are in Italy these days."

The colonel's eyes narrowed. "And even supposing that what you say is true, what makes you think that I could or would help you?"

"A friend told me that you were generous and had helped others in similar trouble." What the woman in the slums of Palermo, whose name Francesca had written on the sheet of tissue in Julia's handbag, had really said was that Colonel Buoncampagna was totally corrupt—but expensive.

"Hmm," the colonel said. He got up from behind his desk and walked across the room. He was wearing military riding breeches with a wide red stripe down the sides, and the spurs of his polished boots clanked on the floor as he walked. Julia was scared out of her wits. He walked toward the door. Was he going to call the guard? She had risked everything on one turn of the wheel. Light coming through the shutters, closed against the Sicilian sun, threw dark bars across her body, rigid on the edge of the chair. The colonel locked the office door.

"For privacy." His smile lifted the corners of his gray waxed mustache that seemed pasted on his dissipated face. Knowing how often sex was in Italy part of the price of granting a favor, Julia's heart sank. Could she do that if she must? Yes, better the colonel, impersonal, on his worn leather sofa, than Angelo. But the colonel walked past her and leaned against the edge of the desk.

"What you ask would require complicated arrangements involving a number of people."

"I'm prepared to pay."

"How much?"

"How much does such a thing cost?"

He looked her over carefully from head to foot. Foolish to dress up for the occasion, she thought. Any Italian could calculate your worth accurately just from your clothes. The colonel moved a paperweight around on the desktop, studying it.

"Perhaps . . . twenty thousand dollars."

"Twenty thousand *dollars*!"

"Signora, I don't know who you are and I don't care, but you are certainly not an authentic Italian, and you absolutely reek of money. Twenty thousand deposited in a certain Swiss account, if you want your friend off the island."

"Very well. I can do that."

"He must be a *very* close friend."

"He is."

"Lucky man. How soon can you get the money together?"

"When you have done your part, the money will be transferred."

"Ten thousand now and ten when he's released."

Julia sighed. She had no choice.

"All right."

"Released here, you understand. Under no circumstances will I help in getting him out of Italy."

"I didn't ask that. I want him brought to Agrigento no later than August thirtieth."

"That would present certain problems . . ."

"Colonel, twenty thousand American dollars deposited wherever you say."

"It's risky, but . . . *fatto*." He slapped the desk. It was done.

"Now," Buoncampagna said, taking a pen from the holder on the desk, "what was his name again?"

The remaining days passed uneventfully, and Julia, alone in the cottage above Agrigento, began to fear that Colonel Buoncampagna had simply taken her money. By noon on the thirtieth she was sure that he had. Ten thousand dollars wasted, Paolo still a prisoner, and Angelo returning tomorrow. Mustn't give up, though. She would pay any price, do anything . . . The phone rang. She ran across the room and grabbed up the receiver.

"Pronto!"

"Contessa Morosini?"

"Yes, yes."

"Don't you recognize your cousin's voice?"

Julia's knees gave way and she sat down hard on the floor, still holding the phone.

"Julia, are you there?"

"Yes, I'm here," she said weakly, "but where are you?"

"A bar and grill, Tonio's, on the waterfront in Agrigento."

"Oh, thank God . . . just stay there . . . don't move . . . I'll be there as soon as I can . . . Oh, my God . . . don't go away. . . ."

She heard Paolo's deep laugh on the other end of the line. "I can't leave. I don't have the money to pay for this phone call."

A dull silver light seeped into the blackness around them. Soon it would be dawn. Julia could barely make out Paolo's sleeping form in the dim light from the open doors. The muslin curtains moved like ghosts in the first stirring of the morning breeze. There were only a few hours left. Had he really said that he must go into hiding again? Had she really agreed? They had talked so much, amazed that the passage of time made no difference between them. It seemed only yesterday that they were living on the Via Minerva. The last time they had had a few hours in a shepherd's hut in the Abruzzi mountains, this time they had had a few hours in the bed where she and Angelo had spent their honeymoon. She was glad for that. What she had done in that bed in the last two weeks had now been washed away.

"Julia, are you awake?"

"Yes."

His hand reached out and took hers.

"I love you."

"I love you, Paolo."

"Few women could have done what you have done."

"To have you I could do anything."

"Have me? We met more than nine years ago. Nine years out of your life, and in the last five we have been together twice. And now I'm a fugitive."

"When you're in the grip of a grand passion, as the Italians say, you don't calculate profit and loss. I consider myself the luckiest woman on earth."

"We'll be together again, and for good."

"I'll wait, however long it takes."

"Julia, on that island I almost gave up hope. Finally, when I tried to think of you I couldn't even remember what you looked like." He was trembling in her arms.

"I almost gave up hope once, too . . . but in the end we didn't, did we?"

She was running her hands over his naked body, *his* body, actually there, not just dreamed of. And then she was laughing.

"What is it?"

"To think that I paid twenty thousand dollars for one night with a man. That must be the most expensive lay a girl ever had."

"Was it worth it?"

"All I know is that I'm lying here at this moment absolutely sizzling with desire and nobody is doing anything. Oh, Paolo!"

Julia and Paolo had breakfast together on the terrace above the blue Mediterranean, once again like man and wife. She couldn't take her eyes off him—he was even better-looking than before, darkened by the island sun, lean, even more intense. She picked up the only thing he had brought with him from Levanzo. It was another of the school notebooks he used, filled with page after page of his superb drawings.

"Poor darling, you never give up, do you?"

"You keep it," he said.

"No, you take it with you. It's only half-filled. Keep working . . . and don't take risks."

"You did."

"Yes, I did." For the first time she felt his equal. They had been like two swimmers in turbulent water, finding and losing each other, able only to exchange desperate glances; but now they were together, and she knew that even when they had to part, still they would move steadily side by side.

"And I want you to know that I'll never lose hope again. I'll put you on that nine-thirty train with a smile, because now it's you and me forever, Paolo Danieli, no matter what."

"No matter what."

"It was nice of Colonel Buoncampagna to provide false papers at no extra charge."

"He has very good reasons of his own for not wanting me to get caught."

"And to finish answering your question, yes, last night was worth it. Sex was always good with you, and now it's even better. I've never been made love to like that."

"I wanted the impossible . . . to possess all of you," Paolo said, and kissed her.

"Well, I don't know about that, darling. But I feel like there's not very much of me you haven't had."

Chapter Sixteen

JULIA TURNED THE key in the lock, opened the front door of the cottage, and stood hesitantly in the doorway. To go inside was to face the fact that she was alone again. For a few hours these rooms, her bed, had known Paolo Danieli. This place could not now be the same. Up beyond the olive trees, the palace stood as it had for years, shuttered and decaying, sleeping in the straight-down light of noon. The song of the cicadas rose and fell in the olive grove. How perfect it could have been if life had been different; if she had married Paolo and they had come to live in this place. A fairy tale, and no less a fairy tale for the fact that she could have, in fact, married Paolo rather than Angelo Morosini. She dropped the keys in her handbag, and walked into the house. The French doors stood open and the white muslin curtains fluttered in the sea breeze, now blowing strongly and wrinkling the blue surface of the Mediterranean far below. There was a clarity to the light, a fresh salty smell to the air, that hinted of autumn. The last day of August.

She picked up the antique brass telescope on its tripod, carried it to the balcony, and focused on the dock that thrust out from the gray-green carpet of olive trees below. A *carabiniere* paced back and forth on the dock; she could make out the sergeant's stripes on his sleeve. Angelo's plane would be landing soon. How would she act? Would he suspect? Would he feel the ghost of Paolo's presence in the house, as she did? He would want to go to bed with her, if not immediately, when night came. She could not let him inside her again, where Paolo had been, where only Paolo belonged. It would be so much worse now that she and Paolo had finally come together again. For a few days she could claim it was that time of the month, but after that . . . Her eyes filled with tears. She wiped them away.

All Paolo had said was, "I understand what you had to do." But the way he had said it was like an absolution. More than that, he had taken the guilt on himself, letting her know that the courage it had taken to do what she had done was the important thing. The shame of it—for both of them—was made to seem of no consequence. Paolo had said, "I feel sorry for all of us, even Angelo." Just the right thing to say. What a wonderful man. She put her face in her hands, and the tears ran through her fingers. That wouldn't do at all.

After she had held a cold wet cloth to her eyes, she went into the kitchen. She was hungry and didn't want to face lunch with Angelo. She opened the door of the refrigerator, a white cube on crooked legs with a cylinder of coils on top that made it look like a fat bowlegged woman with an elaborate hairdo. The refrigerator was new, as was the telephone that Ciano had insisted be installed so that he could summon Angelo to Rome when he needed him. She cut a slice from a piece of cold veal roast and made a sandwich. Somehow she would face what had to come.

One o'clock passed and two and three. The sergeant on the dock below was napping in the shadow of the overhanging pine that lengthened beneath the sinking sun. The phone rang. That must mean that Angelo was delayed and the ordeal was, at least, postponed. She picked up the receiver.

"*Pronto!*"

"Contessa Morosini?"

"Yes."

"The Ministry of Foreign Affairs calling. Please hold on."

"Yes?"

Silence. Buzzing. More silence.

"Contessa Morosini?"

"Yes?"

"Please hold on for the chief of protocol."

"Contessa Morosini?"

"Yes? Yes?" How annoying.

Silence.

"This is the chief of protocol."

"Yes?"

Silence. And then, "I have the most painful duty of informing you that Count Morosini has met with an accident." Pause. "A fatal accident." The antique clock on the wall showed three minutes past four. A small second hand ticked away like a heartbeat. A smiling moon was rising in the circle that showed the phases of the moon. Beneath the clock's face the brass pendulum swung back and forth.

"Fatal accident?"

"Plane lost at sea . . . valiant Fascist to the end . . . foreign minister sends . . . sends a car for you . . . brave . . . hero . . . profoundest regrets."

The next morning Julia began the long drive back to Rome. She had had enough wit to stop them from sending a car for her. She could drive herself—needed to be alone. She had told them that she would take the train, knowing that they would not be able to imagine an Italian woman who had just lost her husband driving the thousand kilometers from Agrigento to Rome.

The first of September was a perfect day, the sky a blue bowl over the sunburnt mountains of Sicily. Julia wore slacks, a knit shirt that left her arms bare, sunglasses, and a scarf tied over her hair. When the sea came into view, she stopped the car and got out. She could see the palace on the ridge far below, and half-hidden in the olive trees, the cottage where she and Angelo had spent their honeymoon, which she would never see again. She felt no more a widow than she looked. She lit a cigarette, pulled on her leather driving gloves, and pushed back the roof of the car. She could not help it if she felt so little over Angelo's death. Sighing, she started the engine and drove off at high speed around the hairpin curves.

By noon she had come down from the mountains into

Palermo. If she kept driving, she might be able to make Messina before the last ferry left for the mainland, but she was ravenously hungry. She stopped at a country tavern and sat down at a table under the trees. It was almost shameful to feel such exhilaration, but nothing could diminish the sense of freedom that had come back to her after so many years. She stretched luxuriously in the chair, and then her eye caught the headline of a newspaper left lying on the next table: "War Again in Europe: Germany Invades Poland."

So that was why Angelo had been called back so urgently to Rome. Suddenly she felt the first pang of sorrow for the man in whose arms she had slept. Angelo's death was the beginning; there would be so many more. Without conscience, Angelo had served Mussolini; but was he any worse than the rest of them who had let this terrible thing happen again to the world? Julia was able to see Angelo as a human being born into a tragic generation, and tears came to her eyes. She knew, too, she would not see Paolo again soon.

The following day she drove from early morning until dusk and reached Naples exhausted. The next day was a Sunday, and she hoped to slip quietly into Rome. On the outskirts of the city she stopped for something to eat. The bar was crowded with working-class men in their Sunday shirts, buttoned at the neck with no tie. A radio was blaring from behind the bar. The British Parliament had just voted a declaration of war against Germany; France had, too, it seemed. A man with his sleeve pinned up where he had lost an arm said, "Poor Italy. It starts again after only twenty years."

"No," someone else said, "we'll stay out this time. You can be sure of that."

But the man with one arm just kept shaking his head and saying, "Poor Italy." He was crying, the tears running down his cheeks.

"What can I say, Julia, at such a moment, but that you have our profound sympathy." Ciano held her hands in his, and Julia stared at the pearl stickpin in his black tie, not wanting to look into his face. Edda stood beside him, her face obscured by a black veil.

"He was a fine man, a patriot, and our good friend." Angelo had been none of those things, but she supposed that Ciano imagined that for Angelo to be considered a "good friend" of his, and of Mussolini's daughter, would be a source of pride for her. How she detested him.

She insisted on having only Bruno and Victoria accompany her to the Via Giulia, and Ciano protested only mildly. He had to get back to the foreign ministry: It was the first working day since the declaration of war. Few of Angelo's colleagues were at the church, and she had no real friends. She looked back from the limousine to the little church of San Carlino. She and Angelo had been married there, and she had known on that day that she was making a mistake. But she could never have suspected that it would all end at the same church with a mass for one lost at sea. He had been returning to her, and she had dreaded his return; and then suddenly it was all over. Engine failure, they said. The plane had been powered by Bronzini engines. She had heard stories about shoddy equipment supplied to the Italian Air Force by the man sitting next to her in black morning coat and striped pants. But she also knew that Bruno was no more guilty than many other Italian industrialists. The limousine turned into the Via Giulia. Someone had hung a piece of black crepe over the entrance to their apartment— her apartment now.

The next morning Julia packed a bag and drove north from Rome. She could send for her other possessions later. Now the important thing was to disappear, to make herself invisible. Not everyone had forgotten the anti-Fascist articles she had written. As long as Angelo was alive he could hold Ciano to his word. But she knew that she was an embarrassment to the foreign minister, and that he would like to see her return to America. Suppose Italy—or America— entered the war? She drove fast, wanting to make Verona in one day if possible.

She had called ahead, and when she arrived in Verona that evening, she was met by the estate agent, old Spagnoli. He was truly ancient now. It had been seven years since she and Angelo had closed the newly renovated house and gone back to Rome so that Angelo could help the foreign ministry to cope with Benito Mussolini's interference. What would the Villa Serena be like? She knew that Angelo had rarely gone back after they separated.

"You should have stayed in Rome," Spagnoli said after a long silence, punctuated by the clicking of his false teeth.

"Why, Carlo?"

"Can't get servants anymore."

"What about Giuseppe and Franco?"

"Dead. Didn't you know?"

"No." She barely remembered the two old men, whom she had first seen wearing eighteenth-century livery. Did anyone still have servants in livery?

"Well, they're dead all right. I tried to hire some young men, but they've all been conscripted. Besides, no one wants to go into service anymore. It's all over."

She supposed he meant the old way of life was all over.

"There's a girl. It's the best I could do. You can't even hire farmhands these days. You'll see. The Fascists said they would change everything." The old man snorted. "Well, they did."

They turned into the long drive to the house, and the Villa Serena stood before them, just as beautiful as ever.

Italy did not go to war, and Julia's fears for Paolo were eased. Yet she did not know where he was. She had promised him that she would make no attempt to get in touch, no matter how long the wait. He would get in touch with her when he could, he had said. She told herself that she would have to be "brave," a dramatic, banal word having nothing to do with her and Paolo. She loved him so much that she could do anything that was required. She didn't need to be brave.

* * *

Autumn passed and December came, and there was still no word from Paolo. If he had been killed or captured, she thought it would have been in the papers, but she wasn't sure. Nothing had appeared in the papers about his escape—that was an embarrassment to the government. Julia filled her days at first with estate matters. She was able to draw on the bank account in Switzerland and, with her funds in Baltimore, she had no money worries. She read a lot and listened to classical music on the phonograph, living as quietly as possible, with only her maid for company. It was important to stay out of the public eye.

As Christmas approached, Julia became depressed. Her resolve not to try to get in touch with Paolo was weakening. Even if she did give in, how would she find him? It was extremely difficult to make contact with anyone in the Resistance movement. She dreaded spending the holidays alone, but her resolve held, and she spent Christmas by herself. That evening, for the first time, she broke down and wept. Life was passing her by, her best years were fleeting.

New Year's Day she was awakened by the doorbell ringing. The maid had three days off, Julia remembered as she put on a robe and went downstairs. It was only the postman with a telegram for the contessa. She signed for it and exchanged the envelope for one from a stack on the hall table that contained holiday gratuities for all the people who would ring the bell during the day. Profuse thanks from the postman. She closed the door and tore open the envelope: PROSEPERITY TO YOU AND YOURS STOP WE RECALL WITH JOY THE NEW YEARS DAY WE VISITED THE COLOSSEUM—YOUR AFFECTIONATE COUSIN. Paolo was still safe.

Toward the end of February Victoria drove over from Milan for a visit. Julia had prepared lunch in the big barrel-vaulted brick kitchen, where they sat for warmth on kitchen stools around the wood stove, drinking red wine, while a stew of veal and olives and orange peel slowly cooked.

"You really should think about central heating," Victoria said, crossing legs stockinged in smoky silk. Her uniformed chauffeur sat with Julia's maid at a table at the other end of the kitchen, another bottle of red wine between them.

"I've sunk enough money into this place already. I've got to think about the future."

"There'll be war, of course," Victoria said, as if she were discussing tomorrow's weather.

"Mussolini's stayed out so far."

"He's just waiting for Hitler to attack France. He'll be there for the kill, you can be sure of that."

"Is that what Bruno thinks?"

"That's what I think. Bruno . . . well, he's like an amateur on skis going down the big run at Cortina. He knows it may end in disaster, but it's all so much fun. The faster he goes, the harder it is to stop. Now, it's almost too late. I'm thinking of sending the twins back to America before it *is* too late."

"You'll stay?"

"As it happens, I'm in love with Bruno. I hadn't counted on that in the beginning." She laughed. "And I'm behind him on the skis, holding on for dear life. Then one day . . . zoom . . . we'll be over the edge of the cliff."

"Where will you send the twins?"

"Not sure. Mother's not at home much anymore. She and Charles are always away making speeches."

"Surely Charles isn't running for Congress again?"

"No. They belong to something called 'The American Way.' It's supposed to keep us out of the war. The Germans and the Italians must be happy about that. I imagine Mussolini is giving them financial support. Charles even has a weekly radio program in Baltimore. It's all sour grapes, of course. They're terribly bitter that Roosevelt spoiled Charles's chances for the Senate."

Julia tasted the stew. "Ready, I think. Let's go upstairs to eat."

They went through the cold dark house together, their arms locked. The furniture was draped in white cloths, ghostlike in the gloom. One o'clock in the afternoon and still the fog hung all around the house. It was a cold, damp winter. Julia's apartment, though, was warm and dry. A fire burned in the grate, and a big wicker basket piled high with split logs stood beside the fireplace.

Julia walked over to the dumbwaiter to take out the tray with covered dishes that held their lunch. She had most of her meals in this three-room apartment, an island of warmth in the cold empty house.

"There. Isn't this cozy?"

"Fantastic. And when did you become such a cook? I can remember when you had all your dinners catered."

"Oh, I have plenty of time for self-improvement now. I do a lot of cooking."

"Your figure doesn't show it."

"I ride for an hour every morning, and when the weather's good I work outside."

"In fact, you look terrific, Julie."

"I try to keep up my appearance." Her lip trembled. "Oh, God . . . Vicky, how lonely I am. . . ."

"You haven't heard from Paolo, then?"

Julia froze.

"I know he escaped from Levanzo, Julie. Bruno told me. And you don't have to tell me anything more if you don't want to."

Julia felt mean-spirited for not having trusted Victoria. "I've heard from him once since the war started, but I have no idea where he is."

"You haven't had an easy time, old girl. But all I can do now is keep my fingers crossed for you."

At eight o'clock every morning the maid, Cecilia, brought Julia's breakfast tray to her bedroom—coffee, a soft-boiled egg, toast, and the morning paper. On Monday, Wednesdays, and Fridays, the mail was added, though often there was none. One morning there was a telegram. She slit open the envelope with a butter knife: PASSING THROUGH VERONA ON BUSINESS THE EIGHTEENTH STOP ON TWELVE FORTY NINE TRAIN FROM ROME STOP HAVE ONLY A FEW HOURS BUT HOPE WE CAN MEET—YOUR AFFECTIONATE COUSIN.

The eighteenth? She opened the paper: Monday, March 18, 1940. She leaped out of bed and then realized that it was nearly five hours before the train arrived. She would have liked at least a day or two to savor the knowledge that she was going to be with Paolo again. She felt slightly cheated. But at least there was time to take a leisurely bath, to pick out just the right clothes. Despite all her careful preparations, and driving slowly into Verona, she was at the station half an hour early. She lit a cigarette and walked the length of the platform, turned and walked back again; and then saw scrawled in chalk on the notice board that all trains would be delayed up to one hour. No one could say why. At one o'clock a train with only three cars, the shades drawn, pulled into the station, and out of nowhere a military band and hundreds of Black Shirts materialized. Mussolini and Ciano, wearing military uniforms, appeared on the rear platform. Ciano looked as sleek and satisfied as ever, but Il Duce looked old and tired. The two men took the Fascist salute, and before the band could get through its off-key rendition of the Fascist anthem "Giovanizza," the train pulled away.

She had to wait till nearly three o'clock before Paolo's train arrived. He was wearing a raincoat and a black felt hat and was indistinguishable from the other commercial travelers with their briefcases and newspapers—except to Julia.

"Hello, Cousin," she said quietly. They embraced briefly, as cousins might.

"I think we'd better go quickly," she said, taking his arm. "Someone may recognize me."

"Where can we go?"

"A hotel."

"They'll ask for your identity paper, Contessa."

"I know a few tricks, Cousin, from my days as the toast of Rome. You must go to the most expensive hotel in town—that's the Due Torri—and take a room. Wait a quarter of an hour, and then call the bar and ask for Signora Bianco. When she answers give her the room number. There won't be any problem."

"You sound as if you've had practice."

"Maybe," she said smiling up at him. "There's a taxi. I'll see you later." She walked quickly away from him, not looking back.

* * *

The bar was dark and warm and there was a piano player. She ordered a gin fizz, sitting at the bar and feeling properly sinful.

"I'm expecting a phone call—Signora Bianco."

The bartender gave her a look which was both knowing and respectful, a combination only Italian bartenders seemed to know how to manage. *"Bene, signora."*

By the time she had finished the gin fizz, Paolo had called to tell her that he was in a room five floors above. She paid the bill and left the bar, walking across the huge dimly lit marble lobby, as if she were preoccupied with private thoughts, and casually entering the elevator. When she got out on the fifth floor she fumbled in her handbag as if looking for her room key, until the elevator door closed behind her. She wasn't sure where the room was. After several wrong turns, she found it and knocked gently. The door opened instantly. She slipped inside and closed the door with her back.

"How long do we have?"

"Only two hours now. Mussolini always seems to be getting in the way."

"What was that all about?"

"He's going to meet Hitler at the Brenner Pass. Maybe Italy will enter the war."

"Damn him. It's not fair. Only two hours."

Paolo had taken off his coat and tie, and his collar was open at the neck. He looked less like a commercial traveler and more like himself. She wanted him to be only himself and always with her. With a rotten mess the world was. Two hours!

He took her hands and pulled her toward him. "Did you really used to do this in hotel rooms?"

"No. But it's not too late to start."

"Show me."

"Well, when you only have two hours . . ." She began fumbling with the catch on the skirt of her blue suit. She had dressed so carefully: the white silk blouse with blue polka dots, the blue leather pumps, even a hat. She tossed her hat across the room and the skirt fell to the floor, then the lace silk underwear. She went straight to the bed.

"Just like that?"

"Come to me, Paolo."

Their lovemaking was quick and delicious and when she came she gave a little cry of delight. Then, lying quietly, she let him take off the rest of her clothes. After that they made love properly and for a long time.

She looked at her watch. Twenty minutes left. "How long until the next time, Paolo? We've hardly even talked."

"I kept trying," he said, running his hand through her damp hair. "Julia, I think I have good news. I'm going to be traveling to Switzerland on a regular basis."

"For how long?"

"Who can say how long anything will last these days. But I can come to you perhaps . . . even several times a month. There's a risk, of course."

"I'll take any risk." She raised herself on one elbow and smiled down at him. "The next time we may even talk."

"Talk," she said.

He was silent, but she knew he was awake. The moon was setting, and it was somewhere between midnight and dawn. The air was so full of the scent of flowers, the songs of tiny insects, the chorus of frogs on the bank of the Adige—sopranos, tenors, baritones, and basses, like an Italian opera—that she was almost drunk with the romance of it. Was it possible to be happier than she was at this moment? She had given a different kind of loving care to making perfect the room where she and Paolo slept when he came to her, different from the desperate fury she had put into making the Villa Serena the symbol of her success in marriage. The room she chose as theirs was as far as possible from where she and Angelo had had their rooms. It was at ground level, overhung with trees, close to nature.

"This is where we were meant to be."

"What?" She was startled by his voice, having almost forgotten that she had spoken to him.

"Star-crossed lovers. Verona was where it happened, after all, Giulietta . . . my little Giulia."

"Say more."

"I suppose everyone grows into what they are meant to be, or at best they do. The times we live in, I think, have done us more good than harm."

"How?" She put her head on his bare chest.

"A long time ago, when the world was young, we were two shallow people. No offense, but it's true."

"I was. You were always serious."

"Julia, I want you to understand me. My posturing was of a different kind—the artist who refused to work unless he could have everything his own way. Well, I've learned."

She turned over on her back and crossed her arms behind her head. "Suffering is ennobling, is that it? I don't believe it. We could have been happy without all this."

"Maybe. But I love you much more than I could have before."

"Sorry, Paolo. I do understand. I just wish things weren't this way."

"But they are."

"And you have to change them."

"I have to try."

"You still believe that one person could change everything?"

"If you don't believe that's possible, then why did you risk everything to free me from Levanzo?"

"Paolo, please. Serious is okay, but maybe we'd better not get too serious. Perhaps we are star-crossed lovers."

Spring imperceptibly turned into early summer and Julia worked the estate with whatever help she could get, driving the horse-drawn mower and hayrack herself, and turning as brown as she had been that first summer of her marriage to Angelo. She tried to pretend that the pastoral life she was leading would go on forever, but she knew that the long pause in the war would soon end. It was just a question of when. The answer came quickly and brutally: The German armies struck at France through Belgium and Holland and

met little resistancē. By early June the British army was being evacuated across the Channel. Paolo was on one of his
brief visits to her when it happened. They heard the news
on the radio at breakfast, listening silently. When the news
was over, she turned off the radio and carefully buttered a
piece of toast. She tried to swallow the toast but it stuck in
her throat, and she put her head down on the table and
cried. She felt Paolo's hand on her shoulder, trembling; and
she knew he was afraid not for himself, but for her.

"Oh, Paolo, what's going to happen now?"

"It's too early to say. If the Germans invade England, it
may be the end. All Europe will be Hitler's. Mussolini may
declare war, now that France is already beaten. But if Britain can hold, it may not be the end."

"Is there any chance?"

"I don't know. Would you like me to stay on here for another few days?"

She nodded, wiping her eyes with the sleeve of her
dressing gown. Whatever happened, she would lose him
now. They had come too far for her to ask him to stay or
to run away with her. Soon, it would be too late to run. . . .

"Paolo, I think I'll send Cecilia away. We can be alone.
I'll fix a picnic lunch, and we'll take it down to the dock.
It's warm enough to swim now." She had made up her
mind what she would do.

That afternoon they were lying on the dock, watching the
river flow by and dropping pieces of bread to the ducks.

"Do you remember that first night on the Janiculum? I
didn't know it was possible to fall so deeply in love, and
so suddenly. Also, I didn't know . . . oh, I thought I knew,
but I didn't really . . . that there could be such passion."

"That hasn't changed."

"It just gets better." Lying on her back with her hand in
his, she watched the soft white clouds float across the sky.
"If we're going to go on like this, don't you think you
should make an honest woman of me?"

"What do you mean?"

"You know what I mean. Will you marry me?"

"Do you want that?"

"Yes, I think I do. Nothing could bring us any closer than we are now, and you know that I don't give a damn about appearances. But I want to be yours in every way. I want to do something that's irreversible, something that flies in the face of this madness that is about to swallow us. Do you understand what I mean?"

"I understand."

"Well?"

"The most important thing is to protect you. At a moment like this, marriage may not be the best way."

"I see. You've toyed with me all these years only to abandon me when I've become old and unattractive."

"What?" Paolo raised himself on one elbow, long and beautiful in black bathing trunks.

"You heard me."

She began to laugh, on the edge of hysteria. France had fallen. If England went, Europe would belong to Hitler, and what would happen then to people like Paolo?

"Be serious."

She slipped her hand into his bathing trunks. "How's that?"

"You started this." They rolled over together on the dock. He pulled the straps of her tank suit off her shoulders. She gasped with laughter.

"No. You shan't have my fair white body unless . . ."

"Unless I marry you?" He pinned her shoulders to the wooden boards.

"I'd settle for a honeymoon."

"What do you mean by that?"

"We could be at Lake Garda in an hour."

"It's three o'clock already. Besides, we can't get there in an hour."

"You want to bet? In my little car, with the top down, we'll fly like the wind."

"You're crazy. On those mountain roads! We'd be killed."

Quickly she put a knee against his stomach and rolled him over on his back. She leaped to her feet.

"Suit yourself. But tonight I'm going to be in bed with

a man in a little hotel in an olive grove on a mountainside. . . ."

Rising swiftly to one knee, he reached for her legs, but
she jumped from the dock to the shore, shrieking with
laughter. While all of Europe crowded around radios, learning about the collapse of their world even as it happened,
a figure in black bathing trunks chased another who held up
her bathing suit with one hand across a wide green lawn toward a great house that had survived three centuries of
wars.

On the third day of their "honeymoon," Julia and Paolo
walked through the olive grove that surrounded the small
hotel above the lake. The dappled light fell on masses of
wildflowers under the ancient trees. Birds sang everywhere.
She put her hand shyly in his.

"Thank you for these days."

"You were right to insist. It was a honeymoon."

"It's what we should have had way back when. . . ."

"But in the end . . ."

"No regrets. Who knows? If the path of true love had
been smooth we might have ended up hating each other, or
as a boring old couple. As it is . . ."

"You have given me days that will last me for all the bad
times. . . ."

"They may not come, Paolo. We may be lucky yet."

"You were wild. . . ."

"My driving?"

"No." He put his arms around her in a cloud of light and
shade, blossom and bird song.

"Once, a long time ago, I was in love," he said unexpectedly. "I thought that nothing could ever measure up to a
love like that. Now I've known a love far deeper. I'll always remember, though. She died. Her name was . . ."

"Bianca."

"You remember?"

"Oh, yes."

She took his hand again and they walked on, nearing the

dining room doors of the hotel open onto the tree-shaded terrace.

"If only . . ."

"If only everything would work out." She smiled. "Just say, just suppose, they can patch peace back together again? What would you do then?"

"Paint."

"I keep hearing that Ernst Reiner would give a fortune for some new Danielis."

"I have something far better now. I'm past that flashy stuff. When I was in hiding on the mountain, and in exile on the island, I began working out some new ideas. There was plenty of time. Those sketches you saw . . ."

"Signor! Signora! Come quick!"

The waiter was waving a napkin at them from the hotel dining room, the only waiter, for them, the only guests in these days when everyone stayed close to home, waiting. . . .

"Citizens of Italy. Il Duce speaks!"

In the hotel kitchen the chef, the busboy, and the two kitchen helpers stood around a radio as if at attention, frozen in anticipation. It only took a few minutes of Mussolini's bellowing and the hysterical cheering of the mob, with cries of "Duce! Duce!" to know that Italy was at war.

Julia and Paolo packed their bags. Everything had already been said, and they had as happy memories as two human beings could have of three days together, Julia thought. She drove Paolo to the little railway station and waved good-bye as he disappeared on the back platform of a train headed for Verona, where he would change to the express for Rome.

How long would it be this time? All she knew was that the time had come for Paolo to activate the Resistance network that he had so painstakingly set up over the years, with all of the increased danger that it would bring. There would be closer checks now, and he would have to assume yet another identity. He didn't know when he would be able to visit her again. The only link she had with him was a phone number in Rome, to be used only in an extreme emergency.

Julia drove back to the Villa Serena and for a whole long summer afternoon listened to Beethoven quartets on the phonograph. That evening she began, once again, to put her affairs in order. As she undressed for bed she looked at herself in the full-length mirror in the bathroom: a woman of thirty-two years, with short-cut dark hair, bronzed arms and legs, and a bronze *V* ending between her breasts; a woman, she decided, who had indeed known more happiness than pain. She was proud of the way she had behaved these last few days with Paolo, but would she be able to keep her courage up when things got worse, as they must?

The Battle of Britain, as it came to be known, raged over England throughout that summer, and Britain held. In August, Italy invaded British Somaliland, and in September the Italian army crossed from Libya into Egypt. By then Julia, with help from a few old men and women and some children, was gathering in the grapes. After they had turned the winepress in the cool, dark winery, Julia went back to the house, her hands stained purple, to find a police official waiting for her. He asked about the status of her American citizenship, wanted to see her papers, inquired about her activities. He left with a polite bow, but took her Italian passport with him, for "safekeeping." Julia was surprised that it had taken so long for her file with the secret police to reach Verona.

As luck would have it, Paolo arrived unexpectedly the next afternoon at the Villa Serena, after nearly four months without a word. He had taken a taxi from the Verona station, and after finding out from the maid where Julia was, crept up behind her as she sat reading. It was a perfect, warm late-September day, and Julia was curled up with a book on a rustic bench under the old willow tree at the end of the great sweep of lawn, above the banks of the Adige.

"Julia."

She leapt up, turned, dropped the book, and threw her arms around him in one fluid motion.

"Paolo. Darling. But why didn't you send a wire?"

"It's getting too risky. I didn't dare."

"Yes." The joy of being with him drained away. "You should have, though. I would have told you not to come. I'm being watched by the police."

"How do you know?"

She sat back down on the bench, pulling him down close beside her. A flock of white pigeons soared up into the blue sky above the magnificent sunlit facade of the house. She picked up her book from the grass.

"You made me lose my place," she said, and kissed him on the neck and cheek and eyes. "You always do. And, well . . . I know because a nasty little man from the police called on me yesterday and took my Italian passport away."

He half rose. "Then I can't stay."

"Wait," she said, grasping his wrist. "He hinted that he wants money, like our good friend Colonel Buoncampagna."

"Are you sure?"

"Sure enough to risk having you spend the night with me. . . . Will you?"

"Yes, but it will be the last time."

"What do you mean?" She drew away from him.

"In a few days Mussolini will be fighting on another front . . . right here in Italy."

"And what does 'the last time' mean?"

"I can't say for sure, but for the next twenty-four hours we won't think of that."

That winter Mussolini's luck ran out. The British drove the Italian army back into Libya, the Greeks annihilated another Italian army in the frozen mountains of Epirus, and active resistance to Fascist rule began in Italy itself. Julia had several visits from the plainclothes policeman. In January, just after Roosevelt was inaugurated for a third term, she turned over the first of the money to him. He had looked at the amount of money in the brown envelope and told her that an investigation was under way. He would not be able to have it stopped by himself. There would have to be something for the others, perhaps a great deal more. After all, the matter under investigation was extremely serious. Paolo Danieli was one of the most wanted men in Italy.

The next morning Julia got on the train for Bologna; there she changed trains for Florence. In Florence she changed again. It was dark before she reached Rome, but she was certain that she had left no trail. She called from the train station and, thank God, her "cousin" answered instantly. She had to see him. All right, he said, at the "usual" place.

The restaurant across from the Colosseum hadn't changed in all those years, and Paolo was there waiting for her at the same zinc-topped table where they had sat on that long ago New Year's Day. He took her coat.

"Do you remember? It's the same table."

"How could I forget that day?"

"I certainly won't." She laughed, trying to appear calm. "I had the worst hangover I've ever had."

"Shall we have *aglio e olio* again?"

"Let's. With plenty of garlic."

When they had ordered Julia began speaking in a low voice.

"The police officer came again. I gave him the money. He wants more."

"They always want more."

"He thinks it's worth a great deal more. They know about you."

"He said that?"

"The secret police don't talk to the regular police, as you must know. For a long time they didn't know about us in Verona. They're very slow and inefficient, but now they know you have been visiting me. They've discovered that I was with a man once at a hotel in Verona, and they have your identity card number. You may not have much time."

"Your blackmailing police friend must have been watching your movements."

"Paolo, I haven't betrayed you again, have I?" She was on the verge of tears.

"Julia, you mustn't." He reached across the table and grasped her hands. "You mustn't ever doubt yourself again. Not after what we've been through. There's no room for doubt anymore."

"No, there isn't. I'd do anything for you."

"And I for you."

She smiled and withdrew her hands from his. "Then you'll have to let me spend the night with you."

"That would be impossibly dangerous."

"I thought you would do anything for me."

He shook his head. "You're fearless, aren't you?"

"Yes, I am. Anything that I have now and in the future is part of the continuing miracle that began on this very spot, at a time when I thought my life was over. How can I lose?"

"I love you, Julia." And he got garlicky oil all over his cheek when he kissed her across the table.

"There's a place near here where we would probably be safe for one night."

She laughed. "Where will this flaming affair lead next, Cousin?"

All through the spring Julia kept buying time. The police officer who she paid claimed he had convinced his superiors that the best way to apprehend Paolo was to wait until he visited the Villa Serena again. But they were under pressure to make an arrest. Eventually they would decide that he wasn't coming, and they would want to interrogate her. How long would they wait? He couldn't say. She held out the prospect of a much larger sum of money in Switzerland. She needed time. There was so much to be done.

Time, however, was running out. The Germans had had to go to Mussolini's rescue in Greece. Fascism was turning sour. Now when internal foes of Il Duce were caught, they were subjected to torture—or death. Soon even bribes wouldn't save them.

But then something happened, as Paolo had predicted it

would. The police officer who stood between them and Fascist "justice" was becoming nervous. He had received ten thousand American dollars by June, the equivalent of four or five years' salary for him. He was in over his head. An ordinary bribe was all that he knew how to handle. If Julia was arrested and interrogated, she might be forced to tell the truth, and he was part of that truth. He now faced the same justice that awaited the enemies of fascism. Why, he suggested, didn't Julia leave Italy? He could help. How? Passports, papers. No. That was being handled more professionally by Paolo. She showed only mild interest. Could he, for example, cover her absence from the Villa Serena for three days? Perhaps. But what guarantee did he have that the rest of his money would be deposited in a Swiss bank? That, said Julia, looking him in the eye, is a chance you're going to have to take. They had changed roles completely. Paolo had told her how to handle such things, but it saddened her. That was what his life in the Resistance had taught him.

In late September Paolo and Julia crossed the border into Switzerland. Their papers were very closely inspected by the Italian customs. By the fall of 1941 any family leaving Italy was suspect. But everything was in order: passports, military exemption certificate, a letter from the chief surgeon at a famous hospital attesting to Julia's rare—and possibly fatal—disease, a letter from the head of a renowned clinic in Switzerland accepting her for treatment, a police certificate, etc. At the Swiss border there was an equally close examination, and then they were on a train moving slowly away from the border post. At the Lugano station they were met by a young couple, the man Mediterranean, dark-eyed and intense, a smaller version of her lover, almost. The woman was pale and auburn-haired, with large eyes that held Julia's, asking if she, too, lived in constant dread.

"Julia, this is the real Paolo Rossi, whose identity I so often took, and his wife Sophia. They will be our witnesses."

It was the first time she had been inside the world in which Paolo had lived for so long.

"Certificates," Paolo Rossi said, handing over two pieces of paper, "attesting that you have resided in the Ticino canton for the required time."

"Forged?"

"Of course. Even priests must be protected."

Julia opened her handbag and held out another folded square of paper. "The death certificate of Angelo Morosini. Quite authentic."

The two women exchanged anguished glances again. A cold breeze was blowing off the lake across the deserted platform, and the sky above had turned a leaden gray.

"The car's over there."

The hired car was a limousine with seats facing each other behind a glass partition that closed them off from the driver: meant for funerals and weddings. Julia and Sophia chatted as though they were old friends, as two people do who find that they have the same secret. Like two jailbirds, Julia thought, the women of those two dark men in the jump seats across from us, talking in calm voices of the destruction of fascism. How proud she was of *her* Paolo. They drove out of Lugano and along the lakeshore, past rich villas half-hidden in pines, down to the suburb of Paradiso. The chapel at the water's edge would have been a most romantic spot in other times. Now it was bare and cold, and even the sympathetic priest in plain black vestments seemed subdued by the state of the world in the autumn of 1941.

"I do," Julia said, in response to a question that involved sickness and health, for better or worse, and . . . till death do us part.

When she signed the marriage register, Julia wrote in the space for "father's name" in a clear, firm hand, "Agostino Bramante." There, beside Lake Lugano, Julia Howard made peace with her past.

The Rossis left in a taxi that had been waiting outside the church, and Julia and Paolo drove back to the Lugano station in the hired car.

"Would you wear this?" Paolo asked, taking a plain silver band out of a vest pocket.

"Of course," she said.

Paolo slipped the ring on her finger and folded her in his arms.

"Pledging troths and all that . . . I never did know what that meant . . ."

"Neither did I," she said, burying her face in his warm embrace.

". . . but if we come through what is about to begin, the rest of my life is yours."

"Fine talk, Paolo Danieli," she said, rising up, "but now you listen to *me*. You are a strong, beautiful, impossible man, and I love you to distraction. But I, Julia Howard Bramante Morosini, tell you that I am now Julia Danieli, your wife, and that I will come back to you no matter what, no matter how dangerous, no matter how foolish. . . . No, Paolo, don't try to argue with me. Ten years we have fought and loved and . . . Oh, Christ, just stay alive. . . . That's all I ask. . . ."

Then for a few seconds his warm mouth covered hers and his arms were around her. She inhaled the smell of him. How long, she wondered, can my senses keep sharp and clear the memory of my lover, my . . . husband.

The rain began to fall, and she watched from the car as Paolo's train moved away toward Italy. Then she told the chauffeur, to his great surprise, to drive her the hundred and fifty miles to Zurich. This time there were no tears.

The next morning Julia boarded a Ford trimotor for the long flight to Marseilles, Madrid, and then Lisbon, where there would be a week's wait. The American consul flatly refused to accept her American passport or consider granting a visa to the widow of a Fascist official who had renounced her American citizenship. Julia composed a long and eloquent cable to the congressman who had twice defeated Uncle Charles and who knew something of her story. Two days later she was on a flying boat to the Azores and New York.

Chapter Seventeen

JULIA SWIRLED THE few dishes in the pan of hot soapy water, stood them in the wooden rack, poured steaming water from the teakettle over them, picked up the Atlantic Ale bottle from the windowsill, drank the last inch of warm foam in a swallow, and tossed the empty bottle into the brown paper sack that stood beside the sink. Then she wiped the fogged window over the sink with the dishcloth. The surface of Chesapeake Bay was gray and feathered by the wind as softly as the breasts of the pair of doves that lay on the kitchen counter, drops of blood coagulating where the bird shot had struck. Who needed friends who brought you game to clean on Sunday morning? She dried her hands, rubbed some Jergens lotion into them and, irritably, reached for the knob of the little brown plastic radio to turn off the singing and clapping sounds of the African Methodist Episcopal church of Sumnersville.

"We interrupt this regularly scheduled program," the brown box said, "to bring you a special news bulletin from the network. . . . The American naval base at Pearl Harbor, Hawaii, has just been attacked by the Japanese Air Force. According to the first reports . . ."

Julia went to the refrigerator and took out another bottle of ale. She opened it, went into the living room, and turned up the kerosene heater. The radio was still blaring from the kitchen. What had happened at Pearl Harbor was still being reported with confusion, but whatever it was was enough to have the whole government headed back to Washington on a Sunday afternoon. She went into the bedroom of her tiny house, where in the back of the closet she had stowed her

Underwood portable. She pulled it out from under a pile of
shoes and carried it into the living room, opened the case
and lifted the typewriter out onto the card table. She felt as
if she had drawn a sword from its scabbard. Before there
were any declarations of war she would make her own declaration. She put a sheet of paper into the machine and began:

DECEMBER 7, 1941

THE EDITOR
THE BALTIMORE SUN.

DEAR SIR:

A FEW MINUTES AGO WE LEARNED THAT THE WAR IN EU-
ROPE HAD, AFTER ONLY ONE GENERATION, BECOME A WORLD
WAR AGAIN. AMERICA MUST NOW ENTER THIS WAR AND, BY
THE TIME THAT YOU RECEIVE THIS LETTER, MAY ALREADY BE
A BELLIGERENT. I WOULD LIKE TO SAY, AS ONE WHO IS A CIT-
IZEN OF BOTH COUNTRIES, THAT THE PEOPLE OF ITALY DO NOT
SHARE THE AIMS OF THEIR LEADERS. . . .

From where she sat, in the living room of a little
asbestos-shingled house, she could see the dark-red brick
and white columns of Branwood across the bay. The
shadow of a cloud passed over the brilliant green of the
lawn, seeded in winter rye, that ran down to the shore. At
that hour, if they were at home, Agnes and Charles would
be seated at the oval mahogany table, being served from
silver dishes by Wiley in white jacket and Maude in
starched apron: quail and wild rice, creamed chestnuts,
frosted silver goblets of bourbon over ice, in a world that
had not changed much in two hundred years. Now what
would happen to them? Had they already heard? Probably
not. But there would soon be phone calls from Baltimore.
Would Agnes's thoughts fly immediately to Victoria in Italy, to her only child? Julia thought not. Agnes's first
thoughts would be about what this meant for Agnes and her
plans for Charles's fading political future.
What Pearl Harbor meant for Agnes and Charles was so-

cial ostracism. Their pro-Fascist friends quickly rallied to the colors and put behind them, the best they could, their connections with "The American Way." By February Agnes and Charles, under investigation by the Justice Department, were holed up for the duration of the war in Branwood, old and broken.

For Julia, Pearl Harbor meant vindication. Carried away by emotion, she had hired a taxi from Sumnersville to deliver her letter to the *Sun* offices in Baltimore. Hers was the only letter that reached the paper in time for its early morning edition. The paper lay before her on the card table at noon as she listened to Roosevelt speak of that "date that will live in infamy." Her relief that America had entered the war was tempered, however, by the knowledge that it meant even greater danger to Paolo.

Winter passed like a gray cloud over Chesapeake Bay and spring came. Even Jimmy Doolittle's raid on Tokyo did not move Julia. She was waiting for something else: some sign that the Allies would turn their force against Mussolini. She kept a map of the Mediterranean region pinned to her bedroom wall, with colored pins stuck in it, always hoping. But in May 1942, she had to move black German pins back into Egypt, from which the Italians had been driven, as Rommel raced the Afrika Korps toward Alexandria.

Julia went back to work for *The Baltimore Sun*. At age thirty-four, she was treated with awe by cub reporters. She overheard them saying that she had seen and fought against the rise of fascism. More than that, they said, she had an Italian lover who was leading the Resistance to Mussolini. She discovered that Julia Howard, Contessa Morosini, had become something of a legend. And she could write, oh yes, they all had to admit that. She would have liked to write under the byline that she had never used: Julia Danieli. But it was not possible, not only because of Paolo, but because Francesca had disappeared. Julia knew, despite the elder Danielis' protestations of ignorance, that Francesca was back in Italy in the underground. What Julia could do was tell the simple truth. The editors and publishers knew something of Julia's story and they were afraid that she would try to use her position as a propaganda platform. She would not. The truth was sufficient.

All fall Julia moved the black pins back into Libya. Soon there was red and blue American and British pins stuck into Algeria and Tunisia. The tide had turned. What that meant for Paolo, Julia knew, might not be good. The Resistance in Italy was on the offensive; and the danger was all the greater, particularly since the Germans had begun taking a hand in suppressing Italian opposition to the Axis.

By May 1943, the war in North Africa was over. At that point, Julia, as she had long planned, proposed herself to the board of the *Baltimore Sun* as a foreign correspondent. Julia had a meeting with the *Sun* board and persuaded them that her knowledge of Italian and her connections in Italy would be a considerable advantage. By that time the Allies had landed in Sicily, and Mussolini had been ousted by the Fascist Grand Council and put under arrest.

"Next? Yes, ma'am?"

"A half-dozen bluepoints and a half-dozen cherrystones."

The wet towel made a half circle on the pink marble counter, sweeping bits of oyster cracker onto her new khaki slacks.

"I'll bet you're from Baltimore."

She looked into the face of the barman. "And a dry martini."

"Yes, ma'am."

Why had she cut him off so sharply? She had placed him on the Eastern Shore in the first three words he had spoken. It was not his fault that she wanted to leave all that behind.

"There you are, ma'am." She lifted the frosted glass, leaving a wet ring on the marble. A platter of six oysters and six clams on the half-shell appeared beside the ring made by the glass, a cup of seafood sauce, horseradish, a silver-plated fork stuck in half a lemon. The barman's face was closed now. She was just another customer. What did

it matter? She was content to be on her way, breaking with
the past. That was it. She wanted no more reminders.

The barman slapped down the penciled bill on the rings
made by the martini glass. Cathedral-like streams of light
fell into the long, narrow passageway of the Oyster Bar.
The loudspeaker announced trains to Westchester and Con-
necticut, to the West Coast and Florida. Everyone was moving. There was a war on. Behind the bar a giant finger was
held in front of closed lips: "LOOSE TALK COSTS LIVES."

Something, something, and Bangor, the speaker blared.
That was her train. She looked at her shiny new military
wristwatch with the khaki canvas band. Twelve forty-eight.
Twenty minutes. There was too much cigarette smoke and
loud talking. A captain sat on one side of her, a major on
the other. It was time to leave.

The great olive-green plane sped down the concrete strip
between the masses of dark firs as if it had no intention of
leaving the ground. Out front was solid fog. The runway
ended, the dark tips of the firs fell beneath them and disappeared; everything was white outside. The metal frame of
the plane creaked and groaned as it struggled up into the
light of early morning over fog-covered Maine.

Wearing sheepskin-lined flying jacket and boots, Julia
was curled up in the nose of the B-17 rising steadily into
the sky. She was cradled in a cocoon of duffel bag, parachute, and sleeping roll, in a greenhouse of Plexiglas plow-
ing through the sky. Only the twin barrels of the .50 caliber
machine gun that rode at anchor out front spoke of war.
Above her was the shallow dome where the navigator fixed
their position on the stars, beneath her was an empty space
where the Norden bombsight would be fitted in, once they
had arrived in England. The navigator was from Kansas,
the pilot and copilot from Oklahoma and Nebraska. Only
an hour before, they had taken over command of the huge
aircraft from three young women who had flown it all the
way from an assembly line in California.

Julia noted in her spiral stenographer's notebook something that she, a female journalist, had taunted Mussolini

with in that famous interview she had had with him: "A woman's life should be totally dedicated to her role as wife and mother." What would Il Duce have to say now about those soft, degenerate Americans, whose men were even now moving up the Italian Peninsula, who had so completely mobilized themselves that the ferrying of the bombers needed to bring Italy and Germany to their knees was in the capable hands of a corps of American women pilots? She wished there was time to write a story about it.

Already they were over the Atlantic, the ferry crew, pilot, copilot, engineer, navigator, talking quietly to each other over the intercom. She made her way back from the sunny forward area across the catwalk over the bomb bay to the radio shack, beyond which was another small greenhouse where the tail-gunner's weapon was strapped in place. Light came from a turret above and one below, unmanned. The radio operator let her listen over his headphones to the crackling weather advisories and warnings of when they would enter the zone where encounters with German aircraft were possible. These men would take this fortress of metal and glass across the Atlantic, and then join thousands of others flying over Germany and dropping death down from the sky, or meeting it coming up from below.

Julia, who had never seen war, filled her notebook with such thoughts, as she sped finally toward Paolo, while the sun sank behind the pink marble surface of the Atlantic. The navigator from Kansas covered her with an army blanket. She awoke to a cup of coffee and a pale-green line on the horizon that was Ireland.

They came down on a runway of perforated metal strips laid out on an English meadow. There was an orange wind sock, a row of corrugated iron huts, a glass-and-sheet-metal control tower on spindly iron legs, British and American flags transparent in the September light, and, beyond, black-and-white cows set like toys in the green landscape. A young man in a gray-blue uniform, with strange insignia on his shoulders, lifted her down from the plane's ladder. He held her up beneath her arms for a second or two, her toes reaching for the ground. She looked down into his gray-blue eyes and saw there that male longing that had always followed her. Then her feet sank into the deep grass that pushed up through the rusty metal grid. The ferry pilots in their olive-drab overalls were moving off together, waving good-bye, like America leaving, and the young English "lef-tenant" was saying something about how the nine-hundred-and-thirty-second something or other welcomed her. She was not listening. She was on her way home. There was a captain on her other side. Great opportunity, he was saying, she could move right out. A few hours later and it would be too late. A whole armada sailing for the Med. Of course, she didn't have to, but . . .

Within two hours she was on a troop train from Wolver-hampton to Bristol. At Bristol there was a staff car to take her to a drab red-brick hotel near the harbor. Evening was coming on, and Julia went to her room and fell across the bed. She was immediately asleep.

The phone rang. No lights outside. That would be due to the blackout. She reached for the phone. It fell to the floor. Groping, she found the receiver and brought it up.

"Hello."

"Julia?"

"Yes."

"Max Harrison. How are you, love?"

"Max? Where are you?"

"Downstairs. In the bar. Shall I come up, or will you join me?"

"I'll be down. Give me ten minutes."

"Spiffy getup you have there, Julia."

"Well thanks, Max. It should be. Mainbocher."

"What?"

"An American designer. I'm test pilot for a female war correspondent's uniform."

"Now imagine that. Not like the old days, is it? What'll you have, by the way?"

"Gin and bitters."

"The same, twice," Max said to the barman. Julia looked

around the dreary place. Even in the semidark she could make out the streamers and tinsel hanging like cobwebs from the ceiling, left over from the past Christmas. Men and women were crowded around the bar. A couple sat kissing at a corner table. Everyone was in uniform, everyone but Max.

"How on earth did you know I was here? For that matter, what are you doing here?"

"Working for the local rag again. Bristol's where I come from, you know. Born not half a mile from this very spot."

"I always thought you were from London."

"That's what I used to say. It sounded grander. A lie. Told lots of lies in those days. That was a long time ago."

Max no longer bothered to dye his hair, which was completely gray. His face was puffy and his hand shook, but he still wore the jaunty little waxed mustache, and it was still red.

"It seems a million years, Max. Do you remember Johnny?"

"I hope you sacked the little bugger."

Julia laughed. "I swore I would every week, but I never did. I wonder what ever happened to him. Probably in the Italian army now. Maybe dead."

"It's bloody awful, isn't it? What's happened to the world. I always took Mussolini for a fool. If I had known where all this was leading, I'd never have taken money from Il Duce's press boys. To think that I helped glorify that arse-hole."

"Oh, come on, Max. You're still working for a newspaper, and that's all you've ever wanted."

"And in the same job I had when I was nineteen. I had to go back to the same job. Can you imagine that? It's all I could find. I was blackballed by the London papers once the word got out. I was happy in Rome. I wonder who it was that ratted on me?"

"My husband, Angelo Morosini. Didn't you know?" What Julia didn't say was that Rosanna, too, had betrayed him.

Max looked at her, incredulous. "I don't believe that. Why should the Iteys turn me in? I was working for them."

"They figured they had gotten as much as they could out of you. Angelo wanted me to have your job. They thought they could get even more out of me. They almost did, but then I went to Ethiopia and gave them something they didn't expect."

"But I heard you went back to Morosini."

"I did, but that's a long story, and it certainly wasn't for love. Anyway, he's dead now. But you haven't answered my question. How did you know I was in Bristol?"

"The army press boys let me know when correspondents pass through. It's nice to have a chat about old times. Quite a few I know have shipped out from here. Wish I were going to do a real job again, but they won't have me, not with my record. You're on your way back to Italy, aren't you?"

"At dawn tomorrow."

"I've seen your name from time to time. Now, tell me what you've been doing all these years. . . ."

They drank a lot of gin and bitters, and before the evening was over Julia had told Max what she had told no one else. She was going back to Italy for only one reason: to search for Paolo. She also told him that they were all equally guilty, or innocent, of what had happened to the world. Max didn't understand, but by then both of them were rather drunk.

The alarm rang at four A.M., and Julia woke with the worst hangover she could remember having since that New Year's when her path had again crossed that of Paolo Danieli. There was no coffee, and hot tea didn't help. Bristol was cold and dark and wrapped in fog. The streets were empty except for a few cars with blue-painted headlights speeding toward the docks with other last-minute passengers. She stood in a long line at the gate, the huge black outline of the ship towering above her in the first light, while British and American MPs checked identity papers and orders. She felt ill and very depressed at the thought of being jammed into a troopship with thousands of men for many days. But she was lucky. At a desk at the top of the gangplank her papers were checked and she was assigned a cabin to herself, a large one on the top deck. A sergeant carried up her duffel bag and canvas suitcases, while she carried a cup of black coffee and a doughnut. After drinking the coffee, she crawled into the bunk and turned out the light.

She was awakened by the wail of a siren and the sound of hundreds of boots. Men were running in the passageway and on the deck outside. A dim light came through the curtained portholes. She jumped out of the bunk, ran to the porthole, and pulled back the curtain to brilliant sunlight and a calm blue sea. Soldiers in life jackets were lining up. Her heart stopped pounding—it was only a boat drill. She looked at her watch. Noon. Her headache was gone, she was hungry, and she was on her way back to Italy. After a shower she put on a pair of slacks and a sweater. She wasn't required to wear a uniform, she had been told, except in combat zones. As she put away her clothes in the quite luxurious cabin, she came across a sheet of stationery that had caught in the back of the drawer: "SS Velonia, Southampton."

That first day she ventured rather timidly out of the cabin, expecting to be the only woman on the ship and to be greeted by hundreds of stares and whistles. Her first lesson in military life was that officers and men were segregated, with the first-class section of the ship just as strictly off-limits for the other passengers as when the *Velonia* had been a luxury liner. There were a dozen other women, Wac lieutenants, four to a cabin like the male officers. Captains and majors were three to a cabin, colonels doubled up, and she, four brigadiers, and a major general had private quarters. Rank had replaced wealth as the criterion, but otherwise the system was the same as when she had first sailed on the *Velonia* in 1930.

Out on the deck the illusion that nothing had changed quickly vanished. The ship had been painted a uniform gray and the barrels of guns poked out from the deck below. On the promenade deck, where the senior officers had their cabins, a double-barreled anti-aircraft gun, manned by British sailors, pointed toward the sky, like some medieval machine of war, bolted into the teak planks beside the blue-tiled swimming pool.

She walked unerringly to the first-class dining room. A steward stood at the top of the steps beside a penciled chart tacked to a wallboard, making the last table arrangements. The dining room was full of uniformed men, cigarette smoke, and noise.

"General Vernon has kept a place for you, ma'am, at his table."

Julia's eyes scanned the high-ceilinged room, from which all decoration had been stripped. She realized that she was probably the only person in the vast room who had ever seen it before. Later she would go down to the first-class bar, but she already knew that Paolo's gold and glass mural of her as a mermaid would be gone.

The young Filipino steward pointed with his pencil to her place on a seating chart. A table of serious-looking men, gray mustaches, paunches, bald heads. They would know something about how the war was going; they had made special arrangements for their special passenger. But the sea and the sun were already speaking to her of Italy, and she was back on the *Velonia* at age twenty-two. . . .

"Isn't there any other place to sit?"

The steward ran his finger over the chart. "No, ma'am."

"Why not there?" She pointed to a round table directly below them where three young second lieutenants sat at what the chart showed to be a table for four. They would all be about . . . twenty-two. Their names were penciled in: Bauman, French, Stone.

The three men stood up when a fourth chair was brought to the table and Julia asked with a smile if she might join them. Maybe the generals would kick her out of her private room for snubbing them.

"Julia Howard, *Baltimore Sun*."

"Lieutenant Bauman."

"Lieutenant French."

"Lieutenant Stone."

Black, blond, and red hair. French was taller than the

others, but with their identical haircuts and uniforms and second lieutenant's bars, they could have been brothers.

"Bauman, French, and Stone. You sound like a law firm."

"We're sort of a team. We all went to Rutgers, belonged to the same fraternity, and got our commissions from the same ROTC unit."

"And every time one of us gets orders the other two get the same orders."

"Now they're sending us to Italy to die together." They all grinned but looked at her as if they hoped she would tell them it wasn't so.

"I wouldn't be so sure," Julia said, cutting into a sizzling steak. They were still using the *Velonia's* first-class china. Somehow she had expected they would be eating off tin mess trays. "Actually, the casualty rate is higher for war correspondents than for troops."

"Not higher than it is for second lieutenants in an infantry regiment," the one named French said. The three lieutenants weren't smiling anymore.

"I've heard of you, Miss ... uh ... Mrs. Howard," Stone said. They were all looking at the band on her left hand.

"Now hear this," the ship's loudspeaker bellowed. "This is a special announcement. Supreme Allied Headquarters has announced that the Fifth Army, under General Mark Clark, has just entered Naples, Italy."

There were cheers, and Julia suddenly remembered the cheers when it was announced that the *Velonia* had broken the transatlantic record from New York to Naples. Bauman, French, and Stone would have been in knee pants then.

"Oh, boy, that does it. The major said if we took Naples, it would all be over in Italy by Christmas."

"Maybe they'll be in Rome by the time we get there."

"Maybe we won't have to fight at all. Somebody's got to be lucky. Why not us?"

Julia wondered what made the major think it was all going to be over by Christmas, but she said nothing.

"Rome. Wouldn't that be great? I'd rather be fraternizing with some Italian chick than shooting at her brother."

"You'd better worry about the Germans. You'll never get a shot at an Italian. They run too fast." Stone was grinning again.

"Is something wrong?" French asked.

"No, nothing. . . ." Quite unexpectedly, Julia's eyes had filled with tears; and now they were streaming down her face.

"Did I say . . ."

"It doesn't matter. I don't know what came over me. It's just that my husband is Italian . . . and in Italy."

"You dope." Bauman was glaring at Stone. "The last time you put your foot in your mouth it was Jews."

"It's all right. Besides he's half-Italian and half-American." Julia smiled and wiped her eyes. "And he's on your side . . . our side. He's a leader of the partisans . . . if he's still alive."

"Mrs. Howard, I feel awful."

"And I'm half-Italian myself."

"Oh, gee."

Julia laughed. "Now that we've broken the ice, my name is Julia."

"John."

"Paul."

"Frank."

"Well, John, Paul, and Frank, I'll make a deal with you. No more jokes about Italians and no more talk about death. Do you play bridge?"

"We're the greatest."

"Well, I'm a little rusty, but if you'll bear with me."

"That would be swell."

For the rest of the voyage it was Bauman, French, Stone, and Howard at meals and at the bridge table, and walking the decks. When she analyzed her motives for becoming the three lieutenants' constant companion, Julia realized that she had wanted and needed intimacy with someone. She had also wanted to take their minds off what they would soon face, and it helped her to avoid the advances of the older officers. She was wrong, of course, to think that the fact that they were so much younger would make any difference. They all devoured her with their eyes and sought every opportunity just to touch her. Dancing was a strain on them, and on her. She knew perfectly well that if it were not for Paolo, she would have taken one of these young men into her bed.

She was also wrong that death could be banished for a few days. One fine morning, as she was leaning on the rail watching the convoy that stretched from horizon to horizon move silently along, there was a tremendous explosion. She turned to see the small freighter to their stern disappear in flame and black smoke. Pieces of the ship rained down from the sky. Sirens screamed and men ran to battle stations. Destroyers circled where the ship had been hit like terriers around a rat hole, dropping depth charges; but the U-boat got away. The ship that was hit had been carrying munitions, and there were no survivors. Her three young lieutenants stood silently on the deck below, watching like everyone else and, like everyone else, saying nothing.

The next day they passed Gibraltar and entered the Mediterranean, and from then on there were always Allied planes overhead. No more ships were sunk. A British naval officer told her that before the air cover, sent out from North Africa, it was not unusual to lose six or seven ships out of a convoy. Julia wrote a story on life aboard a troopship and took it to the radio room to be sent. When she checked the news ticker, she read that Mussolini—who had escaped from detention and had been set up by Hitler as head of a puppet state in northern Italy—had had his son-in-law, Galeazzo Ciano, arrested for having participated in Il Duce's ouster from power. Ciano, the man who always landed on his feet, had finally stumbled.

As the ship drew closer to Italy, Julia's spirits rose for no definable reason. The calm blue Mediterranean seemed to promise that all would turn out well. It obviously did not have that message for her three young lieutenants, who were growing ever more tense. The last night out they had a kind of party, and afterward she went out on deck with each of them in turn and let them hold her in their arms and kiss her. Then she walked the deck alone, thinking of that first voyage when she had let Angelo Morosini kiss her for the first time on that same piece of deck. Poor Angelo. Poor all of them.

The smoke still drifted up from Vesuvius into the clear Italian sky, and the great sweep of the bay still took your breath away. The men all crowded to the rail, and there were bad jokes such as "See Naples and die." When they finally came alongside the docks, however, the good humor ceased. Much of the waterfront had been bombed into rubble. A vast area had been bulldozed flat to make room for the thousands of tons of war material that were piled up in mountains. Uniforms were everywhere, and Julia had no idea how to go about finding the press officer, a Major Green, who was supposed to look after her.

"Julia!"

"Why . . . Chester, what are you doing here?"

"What are *you* doing here is the question. We've been through this routine before, haven't we?"

"Yes." She looked at the name tag over his breast pocket, and broke out into laughter. "Major Green!"

"What's so funny?"

"Chester, what's so funny is that I never could remember your last name. How was Iceland?"

"Cold."

"And how did you get here?"

"There's a war on, lady, haven't you heard?"

She took him by the arm and they walked out of the port area to a waiting car.

Julia was assigned an apartment in a once grand palazzo in its final stages of decay. The Germans had destroyed the best hotels before pulling out, which was "not sporting at all," as a British colonel said. All the furniture in the apartment Julia was given had apparently been stolen, and it had been replaced by an army cot, a rickety table and chair, one olive-drab towel, and a bar of GI soap. There was no heat for the first weeks and no water except in the middle of the day. She didn't mind at all. She hung her canvas clothes-bag from the one wall sconce that had not been stolen and put her Underwood portable out on the table. She was back in Italy.

The war did not end by Christmas. The Allied offensive was stalled a few miles north of Naples, and the rumble of artillery never ceased, day or night. The city was blacked out by the simple expedient of shutting off the electricity, which by Christmas was on only four hours a day. Cold, rainy weather had set in in late November, and Julia worked on her stories in her room, her breath billowing in front of the typed page. Rolled in the four army blankets she had managed to acquire, she would lie awake, teeth chattering, on the canvas cot until fatigue brought sleep.

But Christmas Day was warm and sunny; and if the war hadn't ended by Christmas, at least everyone felt it wouldn't be much longer before the Germans would be forced to retreat. Julia didn't let herself think much about Paolo or where he might be. She knew that he might be dead; but she had awakened that morning, with the sun pouring through the tall windows of her room, sure that he was alive and that they would be together again soon. She got up and quickly dressed in the freezing room, putting two sweaters over her uniform and a khaki field jacket on top of that. She walked the half mile to the officers' mess where most of the correspondents ate, her hands in the pockets of the field jacket and a cigarette in her lips. The smoke helped disguise the stench of the city. Someone had already been along on Christmas morning scattering lime in the streets as a disinfectant. She had taken to wearing infan-tryman's boots because of the filth, but this morning the terrible poverty and the bombed-out buildings did not depress her as much as usual. She had a feeling that her long ordeal was nearly over.

The officers' mess was warm, and fresh eggs and ham were being served for Christmas breakfast. She took her tray to the long table where the correspondents usually gathered to swap information. Men turned to look at her. The cold had brought color to her cheeks and the expensive

Scottish sweater that she wore matched her gray-green
eyes. The heavy army clothes only emphasized her femi-
nine features. The men watched her pass silently, longingly.

"Merry Christmas, everyone," she said sitting down next
to Carter, the Hearst correspondent.

"We were just talking about you, Julia." It was the AP
man. "We're having a Christmas raffle, for the benefit of
the Naples Correspondents' Benevolent Fund."

"What's the prize?"

"Turkey and trimmings, all the Itey wine you can drink.
Chester has commandeered a captured German staff car,
which belonged to General von Vietinghoff himself. Christmas dinner will be served on the slopes of Mount Vesuvius
to the lucky winner. Only two dollars a chance."

"I'll take one," Julia said.

"Well, actually, that's what we want to talk to you about.
I'm afraid we can't do that."

"Why not?"

"Because you're part of the prize. The chances weren't
going very well until we told them you would be the winner's date."

"What?"

"Now don't get excited. You've got to do it."

"I don't have to do anything."

"Julia, listen, we've sold a hundred and forty tickets.
They'll kill us if you don't go."

"Good." She looked around the mess. All of the officers
at the other tables were looking at her.

"You're blushing, Julia."

"Okay, okay, I'll go. But I'm going to get back at you
guys."

Actually she was pleased, glad to be the companion of
one of these men for Christmas Day, happy that they
thought her desirable. Chester himself won the draw and
there were cries of fraud. But Julia got up and announced,
to cheers, that she was willing to squeeze in tight to make
room for one more. A lieutenant just back from the front
won the second drawing.

Christmas dinner was spread out on the hood of General

Vietinghoff's Mercedes: canned turkey, canned sweet potatoes, even—with olive trees right below them on the
plain—a can of California olives. The young lieutenant who
had won the second drawing brought a fruitcake sent by his
mother in Ohio, and Chester had found several bottles of
1934 Barolo to bring. They sat on the running board of the
Mercedes and ate from the tin plates and drank from the
passed-around bottle. Chester had forgotten the glasses. Below them Naples and the bay basked in the winter sunlight.
Above them the plume of smoke from Vesuvius's crater
rose straight into the blue sky. The sergeant who was driving them had pulled the big car off the road into a meadow
close to the summit of the volcano. They were all alone.

"It looks so peaceful," Julia said.

"And clean," Chester added. "You wouldn't know from
here that in Naples people are dropping like flies from ty-
phus and cholera."

"They're getting it under control," the lieutenant said. "I
just wish they were getting the war under control."

"They will," Chester said.

"I'm *they*, and we aren't."

"What's it like?" Julia took a swig of wine from the bottle and passed it to the sergeant.

"What's it like? You mean you haven't been up there?"
The lieutenant was even younger than her companions on
shipboard.

"I've been to the front several times."

"Then you tell me what it's like." He looked as if he was
about to cry.

"Well," she said, stretching out her legs and looking at
the toes of her army boots, "I guess the main thing I felt
was that one day of war is very much like another. . . ."

The lieutenant was disappointed. He wanted sympathy.
He had won her as a prize and he wanted her to be warm
and reassuring, to tell him everything was going well, that
it would all be over soon. But all Julia could think of was
the long lines of trucks in the mud heading north with fresh
troops and ammunition and supplies, and heading south
with the exhausted, the wounded, and the dead. When you

reached the front there was nothing to be seen but the barren, rain-soaked mountains where the continuous artillery barrages seemed to do nothing but raise puffs of smoke on distant mountainsides. What could one say after having written about it so much?

"You're right," the lieutenant said. "Just boredom, day after day, my men dug in like animals all up and down the mountain. Week after week. The Germans up on top dropping stuff down on us. The generals don't know what they're doing. They just keep doing the same thing over and over again. They keep sending replacements. That's all they know. We've had more casualties in my company," he said, his voice rising, "than the number of men we started with."

"You shouldn't be telling me such things," she said. She saw Chester's nervous looks. "I might write them up."

"I don't care."

"I'm very sorry," she said softly, putting her hand on his shoulder, feeling the cold metal of his lieutenant's bar against her palm. And then he did begin to cry.

Tactfully, Julia walked away from the German staff car and the Christmas dinner that was supposed to have been a celebration. Chester followed her. They strolled together through the upland meadow of winter-bleached grass that looked like white hair against a skull of black volcanic rock. Above them were the barren slopes of Vesuvius, the column of smoke rising as it had forever. A ship was coming into Naples Bay, a big gray troopship.

Julia pulled a stalk of grass out of the ground and flicked it as they walked along. "This was supposed to be fun."

"It'll do him good, actually," Chester said. "How are you?"

"Me?" she said, looking at him, surprised.

"I think the war is getting to us all. Why are you here, anyway?"

"I don't know what you mean."

"When you were expelled from Italy in '36 I heard about it. But you came back to Italy in '39. I was surprised."

"You seem to know a lot about me."

"You made a big impression on me."

She looked at him again and smiled. "You were at an impressionable age."

He took her by the arm. "You're still beautiful."

"Thanks," she said. They had come to a little promontory of rocks and twisted pines. "I came back to try to find my husband."

Chester's arm released hers. "I thought he died."

The whole Bay of Naples was spread out beneath them, a sheet of glass on which dozens of ships sat like tiny toys.

"I married again. He's in the Italian Resistance . . . if he's still alive."

"You married Paolo Danieli?"

"Yes. But I've told hardly anyone."

"Why did you tell me?"

She didn't answer his question but asked, "How do I find him?"

"Go to the villages. There're plenty of Italian deserters sneaking home now through the German lines, from Rome and further north. Keep asking. Someone will have heard something."

"I'm not so sure I want to hear." She linked her arm again with his, and they turned back.

They returned to the press office in General von Vietinghoff's car at dusk. Before going back to her cold room, Julia checked the releases. She ran her eyes, as usual, over the casualty list. Lieutenants Bauman and French had been killed in action.

Chapter Eighteen

IN EARLY JANUARY Galeazzo Ciano was put on trial in Verona, on the orders of his father-in-law, Benito Mussolini, and was found guilty of treason. The next day Ciano and the other defendants were taken to an open field, tied to chairs, and shot in the back. Good riddance, the correspondents said. Julia said nothing, but she did not feel the slightest pity for the man she had once known so well.

Two weeks later there was a landing of Allied troops behind the German lines at Anzio. But once again the Allies were checked. Though they managed to hold their beachhead, they could not break out of it. All that winter and into the spring the Allied armies pounded the German lines without success. The Germans were still dug in around Monte Cassino, and the numbers of casualties on both sides were appalling. Each day of war was like the one before. There was nothing new.

Nevertheless, Julia filed a great deal of copy. She had taken Chester's advice and gone to the villages in search of Paolo. Out of her search came a series of stories on the effects of war on the civilian population. They were the best pieces she had ever written, and there was talk in Baltimore of nominating her for a Pulitzer prize. She traveled all over southern Italy, writing about how fascism had reaped its final harvest, bringing death and destruction to every village and town, to every family. She saw so much suffering that she finally became numb to it. And everywhere she asked released Italian prisoners of war and deserters if they had been in Rome, if they had heard of a Resistance leader, Paolo Danieli, or of Francesca. A few had heard of Paolo.

There had been a large reward offered for his capture. But no one knew what had happened to him.

Finally at the end of May, the great Allied breakthrough came. The Germans were driven back, and began retreating north to re-form for another stand. The Allied armies began moving, slowly at first, then faster. The road to Rome was open, and Julia used all of her influence to get herself assigned to a forward unit.

On June 4, 1944, Julia entered Rome again, this time with the American Army, dreading what she might find. At least the city was intact. The two sides had been able to agree on declaring Rome an "open city." But while there was no destruction, the disease and poverty were the same as they were everywhere else in Italy. For three frustrating days Julia could find no one in Rome she knew, no one who might have word of Paolo.

The fourth day she went in an army jeep across the Tiber to Trastevere. She was driven to the street where Francesca's studio had been. Lines of washing could be seen through the studio windows. Probably three families lived there now. She asked around the neighborhood, but everything had changed. Years had passed; no one even remembered Francesca.

As she was about to get back into the jeep, Julia saw an old woman in black coming out of an alleyway. The woman, if she was not mistaken, used to do Francesca's washing. Yes, the woman admitted, she had. Where was Francesca? No idea, the woman said, trying to move away. Julia took a handful of American military scrip out of her handbag. Already, after four days, they understood that in Rome. She held half of it out to the old woman, who took it.

"Where is she?"

The woman lowered her eyes.

"I don't know. I have only heard things."

The soldier who was driving Julia leaned against the jeep, looking bored.

"What have you heard?"

"Signorina Francesca was with her brother, they say, and their friends. You remember them?"

"Yes."

"They were all foolish. They were all in the Resistance, since . . ." The old woman waved her hand in the air ". . . since many years. They were all together . . . they say . . . when the Germans found them."

"When?"

"One, maybe two months ago."

"Her brother?"

"He, too."

"What happened?"

"They say . . . that's all I know . . . that Signorina Francesca was taken by the Germans to prison. They say she was tortured."

Julia was holding the woman by both wrists, looking down at her. She was very small and white-haired, and had something wrong with one of her eyes. The jeep driver was combing his hair in a metal pocket mirror.

"What else?"

The washerwoman pulled loose from Julia's grip.

"The rest I know. Everybody knows. When the Germans left they took all of the partisans from the prisons . . . in trucks . . . they took them outside the city, to an old quarry. They made them line up on the edge." The old woman clucked her tongue. "They made the Italian soldiers do the killing. They're all dead. Signorina Francesca's dead."

"Her brother?"

"Only Signorina Francesca was taken by the Germans. Here, all the rest were killed when the Germans came for them." The old woman shook her head. "It's terrible."

"The brother and all the others?"

"Morti, tutti morti."

Julia thrust the rest of the scrip into the old woman's hand and turned to go. The jeep driver was coming toward her.

"Is something wrong, ma'am?"

"My husband . . ."

"You want to look for him some more?"

"No. It's too late. . . ."

The driver reached out to catch her as she fainted. She remembered nothing after that.

It had been a long, dark night, like all the others. But this time when the angel came, the pink oval of her face and her dark curls were framed by a cap of starched white linen all pleated in knife-edges, and there was a man with her. His face loomed into the circle of warm light around the gooseneck lamp, dark skin stretched tight over his skull, horn-rimmed glasses, eyebrows that turned up at the ends. Smoke swirled around him. The angel had been joined by a devil, a familiar devil.

"Dr. Saraceno?"

"Well, well. You've decided to recognize me."

"I've lost my baby, haven't I?"

"That was a long time ago, contessa."

"It was only yesterday."

"In a manner of speaking, yes. But by the calendar, twelve years."

"Twelve?"

"I last saw you in 1932. Don't you remember?"

"Oh, yes. So . . . it's . . . it's 1944."

"That's right."

"You're crazy."

"Probably. As far as I can tell, we're all crazy."

"Lost my baby."

"No, Contessa. If you had, you would be feeling the shock of it, pains. Do you?"

Julia moved her hands down over the sheet. Her stomach was flat, too flat. There was no pain. That was twelve years ago. What was wrong was that Paolo was dead. She began to sob.

Dr. Saraceno lit another cigarette. "Give her the sedative, Sister."

Arm brought out from under the covers, dab of alcohol, the needle, all quiet.

* * *

It was late June, and it was 1944, and Paolo was dead. Those things were sure. Julia was lying in the sun on a long cushion of flowered fabric attached to a bamboo chaise-longue.

"Pineapple juice?" the angel said. Her name was Angelica and she was twenty-two years old. The man to whom she was engaged was a captain in the Italian Army, and he had been sent to the Russian front. She estimated the chance of his return at one out of ten, at best. Still that was better than zero. Yes, it was better than zero.

"Where did you get pineapple juice from?"

"American Army."

"Ah."

"You look much better. Soon you can go home."

Home. Where was that? What was there to go home to? The small balcony on the roof of the Santa Cecilia Hospital with an orange tree in a wooden tub was as much home as anywhere else.

"Light me a cigarette."

"The doctor says no."

"Screw the doctor."

"Signora!"

They both laughed, and the nurse lit two cigarettes.

"How long have I been here?"

"Seventeen days."

"Did I behave badly?" She thought she had.

"Look at yourself."

Julia looked. There were dark streaks from both wrists halfway up her arms.

"What did I do?"

"You said, signora, that you were going to kill yourself, but in my experience that is not possible with a fingernail file."

"You're looking great, sweetheart."

Yes, she was looking great. She could see that in the mirror. There was something obscene about the fact that her body—by some chance combination of genes—had always been considered beautiful and was still considered beautiful when her life was over. Why had it not withered and grown ugly, too?

"Chester, what happened to me?"

"You had a nervous breakdown. That's why I had them bring you here. If the army doctors had found out, they would have shipped you home."

"I wouldn't have cared."

"I would have. There are few enough good journalists left on this front without losing you." He reached over and put his hand on her arm. She smiled wanly.

"I guess they should have shipped me home. I went all to pieces."

"There's nothing wrong with you that time won't cure. Say, how do you like my new uniform? There's a guy in the Piazza Barberini who can turn these out in forty-eight hours. Beautiful material. God knows where they steal it from."

"I used to work in the Piazza Barberini. Trafalgar News Agency."

"Never heard of it."

"Reuters bought them out when Burns-Peckham died."

"Never heard of him, either."

"It was a long time ago, Chester. Tell me, why are you being so nice to me?"

"I don't want them shipping you home with the crazies. There's a plane twice a week. Mondays and Thursdays. They have the MPs there to help the orderlies get the worst cases on board. That's no way to go home."

"Why do you care?"

"Maybe I'm in love with you."

"Why don't you tell me the real reason."

"That Italian doctor says what you need is to get back to work. He's reporting he treated you for fatigue. You have been working too hard, you know. Well, I've got to go. I'll send over some more goodies from the PX, but you'll probably be out of here in a couple of days."

Chester stood up, bent over, and kissed her on the cheek. "And I would be in love with you, if I thought there was any possibility."

Later that afternoon she left her hospital room and went out on the balcony again. Rome was sunk in a heat fog, the domes of its churches like a chain of mountains rising above clouds. Somewhere beneath the clouds was the apartment where she and Paolo had lived, and that other apartment where she and Angelo had lived. . . .

"So there you are. We were beginning to think you had run away."

Dr. Saraceno was standing over her. His body was in the late afternoon shadow but the sun fell on his bald head and glittered on his glasses. Julia's mind was clear now, as clear as it had ever been in her life. She observed everything around her with the detachment of a scientist looking through a microscope. What went on in the world didn't involve her anymore. Before, she might not have noticed that Dr. Saraceno's suit was threadbare around the cuffs, and that the collar of his shirt was frayed, his tie grease-stained. His expensive clothes had gone with his position as gynecologist to Roman society. Now even the white smock he wore over his suit was rumpled and soiled. But then there was a war on, as they said.

"I was suffocating in my room. When can I leave?"

"Anytime you wish. I think we will have a thunderstorm tonight. That will clear the air."

"Sit down, Doctor. I want to talk to you."

Saraceno sat down as though he had expected to be asked.

"What are you and Major Green up to?"

He lifted his eyebrows quizzically. "Up to?"

"You conspired to keep me from being sent home. Why?"

"Because I think the best road to recovery for you is to go back to work and work hard. And Major Green . . ."

"Suppose I don't care whether I recover."

"You will one day, but you can't if you let yourself get sick again."

"And Major Green?"

"He thinks you can help his cause, your cause, by staying."

Saraceno lit a cigarette, an American cigarette from the PX, Julia noted.

"How many of those do you smoke a day?"

"About sixty."

"Do you think that's good for you?"

"At this point maybe I don't care," he said.

"Tell me what it was like for you."

"Do you remember what I told you about how I became a doctor?"

"When was that?"

"After your miscarriage."

"No, I'm afraid I don't." Julia was ashamed. He must have, for whatever reason, revealed something very private to her, which he expected her to remember after all these years.

"I didn't have much time for other people's problems then. I was very selfish."

"It doesn't matter. In any case, I went on being a society doctor until one night in '38 when a man with a gunshot wound came to my door. I started to turn him away. I knew that if I did, he would die within a few hours, but the regime was very tough by then, not like earlier when they beat your friend. You remember?"

"James. Oh, I remember. He died anyway."

"Yes. But the point of my story is that I realized that what I was about to do was what the doctors in my town in Sicily did when my father was stabbed in the street. They closed their doors and shut the blinds."

"I remember now. That's why you became a doctor."

"Yes. So I let this man in and treated him. He lived, and I was drawn into the Resistance."

"You finally did what you started out to do."

"Yes. The Allies even gave me a medal."

"For what?"

The parchment skin around Dr. Saraceno's eyes crinkled when he smiled.

"For all the information I obtained from the wives and mistresses of top Fascist officials for whom I performed abortions."

* * *

Julia left the hospital the next morning. Chester Green came for her in a jeep driven by a private who appeared to be all of eighteen. He eyed her as if he could overlook the fact that she was twice his age. On the way to her new quarters, Julia read through a pile of cables from her editor. What the paper wanted was more human interest stories on what life was like in liberated Rome. There was no human interest for her, but she could do it. Dr. Saraceno had given her just one piece of advice: Work. She had told him about Paolo, and he had pointed out that there were several million other women who had had the same thing happen to them. That was meaningless to her, but she had listened when he said that she might find some purpose in life, with time, and that the best way not to think about what had happened was to work.

Her new quarters were in a requisitioned apartment building overlooking the Borghese Gardens. A few doors away a British general was lodged in the Palazzo Rosalba where she had first stayed with Aunt Agnes. But she tried not to think about the past. Instead she organized her room, a large one with a balcony, into an office with a bed in one corner. She even had a telephone that worked. She clipped all of the news items that she had missed while in the hospital, typed out a work schedule, made herself a kind of kitchen with a hot plate, tacked a large map of Italy on the wall, washed her underclothes and hung them out on a line she had strung up on her balcony. What would they have said in the old days if someone had put out washing on the Via Pinciana!

She came home late most nights after dining with fellow correspondents, generals, Italians who were certified anti-Fascists. Anything to fill up the evening until she was so tired she could sleep. But she learned things. All of this activity produced information and impressions that went into dispatches that were well received back home. She knew Rome like none of the other correspondents, and she turned out some of the best copy she had ever filed on what Rome had been like under the Germans and how the people of

Rome had reacted to the Allied advance and liberation. But she felt as if it were all being done by another person.

The old foreign correspondents' club off the Via Veneto had been reopened by the Allied command. Now Julia's mailbox was filled with US Army handouts, just as badly mimeographed as those that the Italian press office had sent over in the old days, and just as badly written. She told Chester that, but he didn't seem to mind. He invited her out to dinner. There were five other correspondents at their table at the officers' club, on the roof of a hotel where Julia had often gone dancing with Angelo. She wished the past would quit rising out of the grave everywhere she turned. But then in Rome how could Julia Howard Morosini Danieli avoid the past?

"Well, once again, Julia. Same place, you know. Same rooftop garden, same . . ."

". . . stepping on my feet." She laughed and, hugging Chester, led him around the dance floor as she had done many years before. Chester had had a lot to drink. She pointed him to the men's room and went back to the correspondents' table, laughing to herself. Yes, life did go on. Dr. Saraceno was right.

"Where do you suppose Colonel Bailey picked up that old whore?"

The question came from Carter, the Hearst man, who had pulled his chair up beside her. Carter had tried for several weeks to get her into bed; and when he had failed at that, he tried to get on a friendly basis with her for her inside knowledge of Italy. She didn't like Carter. Julia looked out at the dance floor. The tall, angular woman dancing with Colonel Bailey had dyed blond hair with dark showing at the roots. Her face was that of a woman of fifty.

"That 'old whore' used to be considered one of the most beautiful women in Rome, and she's no more than forty."

"You know her?"

"Her name is Fiammetta Gildo. Yes, I know her."

Carter was right, of course. The woman who had broken up her marriage now looked like an old whore.

"Has Chester boy made his pitch to you yet?"

"What do you mean by that?"

"He will."

"He'd better make it soon or he'll have to make it from under the table. What pitch?"

"He has an 'interesting assignment' he's talking up. That's why he's buying us all dinner tonight."

"What kind of assignment?"

"Very mysterious. He won't say, except that it might be 'a tiny bit dangerous.' Maybe females don't qualify, so he hasn't said anything to you."

If Carter hadn't said that, she might never have become interested. "I'm just along for my decorative qualities, then?"

"Which are considerable, my dear."

Julia made Chester take her back to her quarters in his jeep. He wasn't drunk enough to be incoherent, but he was drunk enough to say more than he had meant to. Carter had been right. No females. Why? Behind enemy lines. Shouldn't have said that . . . Told the general . . . you're best correspondent in Italy . . . Speak Italian. Hate the Fascists . . . Going to talk to him about you again.

By the time word reached Julia that General Squires would see her, the general had been called to a meeting in Naples; but the Wac captain in charge of his office said he had left word that she could go to a certain address for more information.

The address turned out to be on the broad avenue leading from the Tiber to St. Peter's. Julia climbed the stairs to the top floor, thinking there must have been a mistake. The only door on the dark landing was to the office of an Italian freight-forwarding firm. She opened the door and a little bell rang, like the bell that had been attached to the door of the old Trafalgar office. Three young Italians in shirtsleeves were working at desks. One of them got up.

"Sì, signora?"

"Is there an American Army office in this building?"

"No, signora. This building is in Vatican City. No American Army here . . ."

"Oh." Julia took the piece of paper from her handbag.
"But it says here . . ."

The Italian took the paper from her. *"Un momento."* He
disappeared down a corridor and returned immediately.

"This way, please." She followed the man down the corridor to a frosted glass door. He tapped on the glass and
opened the door. The door closed behind her. A man in
shirtsleeves and suspenders rose from behind the desk. He
was short and stocky, with pale blue eyes and prematurely
gray hair parted down the middle. He held out his hand.

"Arthur Perkins."

"Julia Howard, *Baltimore Sun*."

"Please sit down, Miss Howard. I was afraid you might
not show up."

"You don't make it very easy for visitors."

"No."

"But you wanted to see me."

"You wanted to see General Squires, and he referred you
to me."

"Do you mind if I smoke?"

"Not at all. I should let in some air, anyway." Perkins got
up and took a long wooden rod leaning in the corner and
pushed open a pane in the skylight. There were no windows.

"You aren't with the army, then?"

"No."

"OSS?"

"I would rather not go into that at this point. But we can
work on that assumption, if you like."

"Look, Mr. Perkins, I am only here because I wanted to
clear up a couple of professional matters. Number one, I
don't like being excluded from an assignment because of
my sex, and number two, I don't like—and my paper
doesn't like—attempts to use me for propaganda purposes."

"Number two would seem to cancel out number one. In
any case, this has nothing to do with propaganda. This is a
straight reporting assignment. Perhaps the best assignment
you'll ever have."

"I'm a woman. Remember?"

"That makes no difference to me. It may to the army, but they have no jurisdiction over me. That's why I set up in Vatican City—to keep them out of my hair, although I'm not always successful. By the way, the three correspondents they interviewed for this assignment turned them down when they found out it was behind German lines. Not that they could have done it, anyway. Not a word of Italian spoken among the three of them."

"Was Carter one of them?"

"Yes. We're putting out the word that the whole thing is off. Washington has told the army to stay out of it. Your Major Green wasn't very helpful."

"He isn't my Major Green."

"Miss Howard, are you interested in hearing what we have in mind? If not, I would prefer not to say any more."

"I'll listen."

"All right, then. If I were a colonel, I would now pull down a wall map and get out my pointer. But I won't insult your intelligence with a lot of hot air about strategy. Actually, the situation is fairly simple. The Normandy landing was predicated on a pincer movement, with the Allied forces in Italy driving across the Alps into Germany. But as you know, the Germans have held at the Gothic Line just south of Florence. We'll have to break that line, whatever the cost. The number of casualties could make those in Anzio and Cassino look small by comparison. But if we can tie down enough German divisions elsewhere, we might just be able to break through quickly, and save thousands of lives. We are counting on the Italian partisans for that. They've become a real fighting force, and the more success they have the more Italians will join them. With fifty thousand men they could stage a regular uprising at the moment the Allied offensive begins. If they had fifty thousand men . . . but they don't. The picture is as simple as that."

"And?"

"And I have been instructed to attempt to recruit a foreign correspondent of known reputation to join the partisans and send out firsthand reports on what they're doing to the Germans and to what's left of Mussolini's forces. We figure nothing could be more helpful to the partisan cause . . . and ultimately to ours."

"You make it sound very grand."

"I'm not trying to make it sound grand, Miss Howard. I'm simply stating the facts."

"All right, I've listened. Now I have a few questions."

"Go ahead."

"What makes you think my paper would agree to such an idea?"

"We're assuming that they wouldn't, particularly since you are a woman. The chances of capture, torture, and death are quite considerable. The American public wouldn't understand how we could do such a thing."

"No, but I understand."

"We would have to say you went off on your own. We would have to lie to your paper."

"You're not doing a very good selling job."

"I'm not trying to do a selling job. I'm offering you an opportunity to help conclude what Paolo Danieli began so well and to avenge his death. You have Italian blood yourself, I believe."

"Mr. Perkins, you are touching on very private matters that you know nothing about! Vengeance is the last thing I would offer to my husband's memory."

"Forgive me, Mrs. Danieli. You are quite right. I have lost nothing in this war, a childless college professor whose wife is safe at home." He passed his hand over his eyes. "It would be quite understandable if you walked out. In any case, no decision is necessary right away. And I do have some knowledge of what you have been through, what you have done. In fact, I have something of yours."

Perkins came around the desk and handed her a brown envelope. It held a child's school notebook, the notebook that was filled with the sketches Paolo had made on Levanzo.

"How did . . ."

Perkins took her elbow and helped her into the chair.

"Where did you get this?"

"You asked Dr. Saraceno to see if he could find some document in lieu of a death certificate?"

"Yes."

"Saraceno asked us to help. We have access to captured German records. They were very methodical. The Germans kept a record of everything right up until the day they evacuated Rome. This was turned in by the man who . . . killed your husband . . . as proof. He claimed a rather large reward from the Fascists."

"Give it to me."

"Of course."

"About what you want me to do . . . I wouldn't be prepared to give you an answer right away."

"There's no need. We aren't ready yet. We'll get in touch with you when we are."

Her room on the Via Pinciana, which she had arranged so well to drive out the past in order to concentrate on the present and her work, was powerless against the child's notebook that she clutched in her hand as she came through the door. Julia sat down on the narrow cot and turned the pages: Levanzo, place of exile. There were earlier sketches from Gran Sasso, where he had been in hiding. These sketches were all that had been possible for the man that Ernst Reiner had called one of the most promising artistic talents of his generation. Paolo had seen the work as a gift, a breakthrough born of suffering to an even higher art. But in the end, all this notebook had meant was that someone had claimed a reward from the Nazis for murdering Paolo Danieli. She closed the notebook quickly to keep her tears from flooding it.

Perkins, or whatever his real name was, had not called. In mid-September the German line broke, and by the end of October it looked as if the Allied armies would sweep through northern Italy. Either Perkins or his employers—or the whole Allied command—had misjudged the situation, or they had deliberately been using her in some game that she didn't understand and that had come to nothing. In any case, they had wrung out of her the last emotional reserve that remained. She had made the decision to accept their offer when it came, as a gesture to Paolo, not believing that it would succeed. The whole thing would be botched. She had seen it happen so many times. Truckloads of bodies of privates coming back from the front as a result of an operation agreed to over brandy and cigars by colonels and one-stars looking for promotions. She would do it because it would be at least a gesture. She wasn't, she told herself, afraid to die ... The phone was ringing.

"Mrs. Danieli?"

"Yes."

"Perkins here."

"Yes?"

"Are you free for dinner this evening?"

"Yes."

Chapter Nineteen

SHE FELL OUT into the blackness and dropped like a stone. In the seconds before her parachute opened she realized that she very much didn't want to die. And then the familiar snap of the silk and the wrench of the harness told her that she wasn't going to die, at least not at that moment. She was dropping more slowly. A big slice of moon shone over her shoulder, a few stars and, down below, a broken piece of mirror lying on a cushion of black velvet. Lake Garda. She closed her eyes against the icy, stinging air. Her face was protected by a layer of Vaseline, her hands by aviator's gloves. Against one side she felt the hard shape of the pistol they had tried to teach her how to use, against the other, Paolo's sketchbook. She had slipped that into her jacket after the final checkout. They had even made her leave behind her wedding ring because of the initials engraved inside it.

The drop was perfect. They wanted to put her as close to the lake as possible, and she was coming down in the inky darkness just beyond its silver rim. The earth rose to meet her, and the grassy slope of the mountain looked like silver cat's fur in the moonlight, soft and welcoming. She bent her knees and grasped her sides, ready for the impact of the earth slamming up against her. In the last second she saw the dark shape of a boulder in the tall grass, but it was too late. She hit it with one foot and flew wildly through the air. The chute dragged her briefly through the grass and then became entangled in brambles that ripped across her face. Thank God there was no wind, or she would have been dragged down the mountainside on her back. She lay

looking up at the moon through a lacework of grass stems
stiff with frost. The first thing was to hide the chute. They
had had to risk dropping her on a night with a new moon,
and she could have been seen. They might already be looking for her. She unsnapped the harness and leapt to her feet
only to fall to her knees again. Her left ankle wouldn't
work. If it was broken, she was finished, finished before
she had even begun. Think about that later. She began to
crawl through the grass, gathering up the nylon lines of the
chute. All at once the shock wore off and the pain shot
through her ankle like a red-hot ice pick. The moon made
crazy loops in the sky, and she blacked out.

When she came to, the sky above her was pink. The sun
would soon be up. Tears of anger and frustration filled her
eyes. They had allowed an hour of darkness for her to hide
her chute and make it to the high forest, and she had spent
most of it lying unconscious on the ground. She turned her
head. The green-and-brown–patterned chute was draped
over a bramble bush for all the world to see. She turned her
head the other way. There was a farmhouse not two hundred yards from where she lay. Well, that did it. In those
war movies they were always showing at the officers' club,
the patriotic peasants hid the downed aviator in the hayloft.
They must never have met an Italian peasant. The only way
he had ever survived was by staying out of the path of
whoever was in power. They would turn her in as soon as
they found her. What should she do? She knew what the
Germans would do to her, and the dregs of the Fascist party
that had retreated north to join Mussolini were, if anything,
worse. She tried not to think of the horrible stories she had
heard but began to cry again, this time from pain. She sat
up and unlaced her heavy paratrooper's boot, and the pain
flowed away. No wonder—her ankle in the tightly laced
boot had swollen to twice its normal size.

There was still no sign of life from the farmhouse, a
rough stone building of two stories with a roof of stone
slabs, the poorest kind of peasant house. Rays from the rising sun spread out behind the mountain. She should at least
be able to hear some sound of farm animals unless . . . Of

course. The farm was abandoned, like so many others had been during the war. There was no sign of cultivation. How stupid of her not to have noticed. There was no sign of life anywhere on the mountainside. Only dark, silent fir forests above, the empty meadow, Lake Garda far below. She must not panic again.

She couldn't find even a fallen limb to use as a crutch, and she had to crawl all the way to the farmhouse. It had been abandoned long ago. The kitchen garden was a tangle of dead weeds, and the shutters were falling off their hinges. She pulled herself over a windowsill and dropped to the dirt floor inside. She knew she couldn't make it to the forest, and if her chute hadn't been seen, she was probably as safe in the farmhouse as anywhere else. She ate a chocolate bar and then remembered the packet of strong painkiller they had given her. She really must start using her head. What was the next logical thing to do? But the drug was already taking effect.

The sun was overhead when she awoke. It was a cold, clear day, not a cloud in the sky and not a sound to be heard, not even a bird's song. She felt as if she were alone in the world. She got up and, supporting herself on the wall, hobbled to the far window. The world was not entirely deserted. On the far shore of the lake, clusters of red-tiled roofs indicated several small towns. That would be useful in getting her bearings. She had only one more chance. The rendezvous was supposed to have been for dawn. If she was not there, they would return at dawn on the second day. They would not return a third time. Then what? She could hide in the forest until she ran out of chocolate bars.

Why had she done this? When she had leaped from the C-47 into the night, she had realized with great clarity that life was still precious to her. By then it was too late. And now her chances for life were narrowing with each hour that slipped by.

Julia thought about what she might have to do if her ankle was in fact broken, but she did not panic. If capture became inevitable, she would have to take her own life. There was no other choice. She would not let them do to her what they had done to Francesca. Julia reached inside her field jacket and took out the small, flat Italian pistol and held it in the palm of her hand. "A lady's pistol," the instructor had called it. After her last lesson, when he considered her to be minimally proficient with it, the instructor, a tough old noncom from the Appalachian Mountains, had taken her aside and told her, "sort of off the record," that if worst came to worst, and she ever had to use it on herself, the only sure way was to put the barrel in her mouth. She would be surprised how many people missed their own heads. He felt awful about having to bring the subject up, but he would have felt even worse if he hadn't and . . . Julia put the pistol back and took out Paolo's notebook. Tears fell on the pages as she turned them. At least she wouldn't have to go through the rest of her life without him.

Far below, a bell in a clock tower chimed twelve. Funny she had not heard it before. In five hours it would be dark. She must pull herself together. She must.

She did not need to be reminded again of the time. She had laid out the topographical map in the square of light on the dirt floor. She couldn't believe how swiftly the shadow moved across the paper as she tried desperately to remember how she had been taught to orient the map to the compass and the landscape beyond the window from which the light fell. Finally, she was sure she had it right. The five towns on the far shore of the lake were from north to south: Gargnano, Toscolano, Maderno, Gardone, and Salò. With a thrill she realized that the farmhouse that she was in was the tiny brown square all by itself below the trail marked on a worn pre-war chart of the Italian Alpine Club. She was less than a mile from an "X" that marked where two trails crossed up the mountain. The clock below struck one. She was dying of thirst. It must have been the medicine she had taken. They had assumed she would be able to drink from mountain springs. She couldn't make it up the mountain without water, a crutch. Could she even make it then?

Her watch said three by the time that she had fashioned

a crutch from part of a broken high-backed chair. She made her way back to the parachute, cut off a cord, went back to the well, and let down a wine bottle, which maddeningly wouldn't tip over to fill with water until she tied a rock to it. She drank the bottle of water, refilled it, and then started up through the field to the forest above, her silk scarf tucked under her armpit to cushion the stick she was using as a crutch. The shoe that she could not get on was tied by the laces to a belt loop. She would have to take the chance of being seen. She knew that with all the instruction in the world she would never be able to find that trail in the dark. And in her condition she would be lucky to go one mile in the two hours of light that remained. Already the shadow of the mountain was moving down out of the forest across the empty field.

She had not calculated badly. It took exactly two hours to make her way up to the forest edge and into the trees. From there on, the path was too steep to attempt to use the crutch. She drank some water, left bottle and crutch behind, put on her aviator's gloves, and crawled up over the rocks on hands and knees. A glossy black crow eyed her from the top of a boulder, cawed, and flapped away. The trail to the summit of Monte Baldo ran parallel to the shore of the lake. She was bound to cross it if she kept going up—if she could keep going up—but would it be visible after years of disuse during the war? The chill of the night was coming on, and her woolen underwear was soaked with sweat. The effect of the painkiller had worn off. Her ankle throbbed terribly. If she was going to make it, she would have to rest a few minutes. She pulled herself onto a rock and sat panting. The dark shape of the farmhouse in the empty meadow was far below. Had she already crossed the trail without knowing it? She wouldn't think about that. She got down on her hands and knees and began pulling herself up the rocks again. In half an hour it would be dark and the moon wouldn't be up until after midnight.

She couldn't have missed the trail if she had tried. Deep in leaves, it was broad and level and even had a rough stone retaining wall. She found herself a branch to use as a crutch in the woods and began to hobble along the trail in the direction of the summit of the mountain. Almost immediately she heard the sound of water. A hundred yards farther on was a small waterfall and, beyond it, just as on the map, another trail ran off down the mountain. No one had even bothered to take down the weathered board on a tree. There was just enough light left to make out "Lake Garda" and an arrow, and "Summit" and another arrow pointing in the opposite direction, and "CAI," Club Alpino d'Italia. In the war movies the enemy always took down the road signs. But this was Italy.

Julia went back to the waterfall, drank, took another painkiller, and ate half a chocolate bar. Then she crawled under some bushes near where the two trails crossed and covered herself with leaves. She had done all she could. What happened next was up to fate, and she was too exhausted to care. She woke up once. The moon was already high in the sky and something was howling, but it wasn't a dog. The wolves must have come down from the mountains during the war.

A sound awakened her again. Or perhaps she dreamed it. She felt warm and safe curled up in her many layers of clothing beneath the leaves, now etched with frost. Beyond the first circle of bare black trees there was only blank whiteness. A dense fog enveloped the forest. She heard real sounds now, perhaps animals moving through the underbrush, the sounds coming from all directions. Feet were moving; and then a dark form passed by where she was lying, not ten feet away. She fumbled for her gun but there were four layers of clothing buttoned over it. She could make out three dark forms standing together, just visible through the fog.

"Signora Howard?"

She opened her mouth to call back, but the sound stuck in her throat. Suppose they were from a German or Italian Fascist troop? Suppose it was all a trick? She had heard a story whispered about how the British had sent one of their own women into France and deliberately betrayed her to the Germans. The information that she was carrying, and which was extracted from her by torture, was false, and the Germans had moved several divisions to the wrong place. They hadn't doubted the information because it never occurred to them that British gentlemen would do such a thing. She hadn't believed the story, but now all she could remember was the cold look in Perkins's eyes. They would commit any crime to win the war, she was sure. She had the pistol free now and pushed the safety catch forward with her thumbnail.

"I'm over here," she called out in Italian.

The three forms dropped from sight.

"Stand up."

"I can't. I've hurt my foot."

"If you don't stand up, we will shoot."

She felt around her for her crutch, and as she pulled herself up on it, she dropped her pistol in the leaves.

"Come forward."

She didn't dare drop back down to retrieve the pistol. She hobbled forward on the crutch. Out of the corners of her eyes, she saw other forms in the trees to each side of her. One of the men came forward to meet her. They stood looking at each other, not a yard apart. A field jacket, a knit cap pulled down to the eyes, breath steaming out through a black beard, a submachine gun pointed at her stomach.

"Signora Howard?"

"Yes."

"Show me the cross you are wearing."

She pulled out the gold cross that hung from a chain around her neck. The man squinted at it in the dim light. He was trying to make out, she thought, the date engraved on the back: 15 May, 1920. He looked up at her and said, "Okay."

They had given her the cross as part of her manufactured Italian identity. They hadn't told her that the First Communion date engraved on the back would mean something to this man, who like all Italians said "okay" when he found out you were an American.

"Why didn't you come yesterday?"

"I told you. I hurt my foot."

"Did anyone see you?"

"I don't think so."

"You don't *think* so?"

"I'm sure not, unless they saw the chute come down."

"Is your foot broken?"

"I don't know."

"Sit down there." He motioned to a boulder. He knelt in front of her and pulled the three layers of socks off and felt her bare foot with his hands.

"Please! That hurts."

"Move your toes. Now turn your foot."

"Is it broken?"

"No. You can't walk on it?"

"No."

"Okay. We'll have to carry you."

He whistled and a dozen men emerged from the trees.

"Luigi, Carlo, make a sling. We'll have to carry her. She's sprained an ankle. I want to be back at camp before this fog lifts."

The man put his hands under her armpits and lifted her from the ground. White teeth appeared in the beard. "She's light as a feather."

She began crying.

"What's wrong?"

"I'm sorry. I thought you might be Germans."

"Signora, the only Germans up here are dead Germans. This is the Republic of Monte Baldo."

"I dropped my pistol over there."

"You must never lose your weapon."

"I know."

The next hours were almost pleasant. She floated through the misty forest in a sling made from field jackets, tied to a long tree limb, carried on the shoulders of two strong men. She had made it.

"Signora Giulia, wake up. It's Christmas Day."

She knew it was no use. She would have to get up. More and more, the space between the straw mattress and the eiderdown quilt, which was her special privilege, had become her refuge. She would often stay in bed until mid-morning. Outside was the cold and damp and boredom, and her dreams were the best part of the day. She put her feet out on the rough wooden floor.

"Coming, Flavio." She pulled on her socks and went to the door in long woolen underwear that had once belonged to a German lieutenant. The name "Krebs" was inked on the neck band. Two bullet holes decorated the chest, but she had darned them neatly.

"*Buon Natale.*"

"*Buon Natale*, Flavio."

The boy held the charcoal burner full of glowing coals that he brought her every morning for her tea. His other hand was behind his back.

"I brought you a present." He held out an egg.

"Where did you get that?"

"I stole it. I had to go halfway down the mountain before I found a farm with chickens. The Capo wants to see you."

"All right. Tell him I'm coming."

"Okay. *Ciao*, Signora Giulia."

"*Ciao*, Flavio . . . No, wait. I have a present for you, too."

She lifted a stone from the hearth of the fireplace she was not allowed to use and took out a coin from the small sack of British sovereigns that she had signed for along with the pistol and the gold cross.

"Signora Giulia, it's real gold."

"Yes. Hide it well. You can spend it after the war is over."

After Flavio left, she put the can of water on the coals and waited for it to come to a boil. Flavio was not yet sixteen and, for a few months more, still too young to fight. They had assigned him to her as an orderly. Julia put the egg into the water, looked at her wristwatch, and walked over to the window. There was no sign of life. All of the other houses had their windows shuttered. A sign on the house opposite said, "Piazza Garibaldi." She smiled. Even the smallest village had to have its "piazza." This one was no more than an open space around which a dozen houses of rough stone were clustered. She lived alone in the deserted village except for a sentry, which was changed every twelve hours, and Flavio, who came and went. The Capo wouldn't let her live close to the men. He had been very blunt about that the first day. No sex. If that started, with everyone armed to the teeth, they would be fighting over her rather than fighting the Germans.

She took the egg out of the boiling water and put in a handful of the dried mountain herbs that Flavio had picked for her "tea." It really wasn't bad tea at all. They took very good care of her, but she was a prisoner all the same. The soft-boiled egg was perfect. She dipped small pieces of the hard dark bread in it. It was the first egg she had had since she had come to the Republic of Monte Baldo, as the Capo liked to call it. That was more than a month ago, and she had yet to send her first dispatch. They claimed their radio was broken, but she didn't believe them.

After she had eaten she climbed down the ladder from the loft where she lived and walked through the village. The fog was lifting, and it was going to be a beautiful day. Along the path men nodded at her from the windows of abandoned farmhouses. The path ran along the edge of a ridge, with terraces of fruit trees and vines above and below it. The grapes, unpicked, had withered on the vines, but strings of dried tomatoes and ears of corn hung from the farmhouse walls. The partisan camps were strung out all along the ridge, in the deserted villages and farmhouses joined by the path. That way the men could reinforce any point quickly but the entire force would not be trapped by a surprise German raid. The Germans came only in large contingents, and since August they hadn't come at all. What was left of Mussolini's army never set foot on the mountain. She had no idea how many men the Capo had under him. Hundreds at least. They were organized into small squads that lived together and went out on missions together. Sometimes an entire squad would not come back.

She climbed the stairs to the Capo's headquarters in a large farmhouse. A balcony hung out over the edge of a high cliff. A guard opened the door at the top of the stairs.

The Capo was alone, standing at the door to the balcony, binoculars to his eyes. The room was bare except for some chairs and a table with a pile of papers on it weighted down with a hand grenade. A submachine gun hung on the wall. A map of the Lake Garda area and pictures torn from magazines of Lenin, Stalin, and Roosevelt were tacked up around the room. She suspected that the picture of Roosevelt had been put up just before she came.

"Buon Natale, Comandante."

He turned. *"Buon giorno*, Signora Howard. What did you say?"

"I said Merry Christmas."

"Is it?" He looked embarrassed. "I hadn't noticed. Here. Take a look." He handed her the glasses.

The day was the clearest one they had had for weeks. She could make out every detail on the far shore of the lake.

"Do you see Salò?"

She turned the glasses south, passing briefly over the little town of Garda where she and Paolo had stayed for some of the last happy days they had known.

"Yes, I see it."

"Up at the top of the town there is a big villa."

"There are several big villas."

"The one with the anti-aircraft gun on the roof."

"Yes."

"That is the capitol of the Republic of Salò. I was thinking of sending a note asking if they would care to open diplomatic relations with the Republic of Monte Baldo." White teeth showed in the black beard, as they rarely did.

"That's Mussolini's headquarters?"

"That's where the swine lives with his wife. He keeps his mistress in the villa above them." Julia raised the glasses to where a red-tiled roof showed through the trees.

"While we freeze our balls off up here on the mountain, he is down there among the palm trees filling his belly with pasta. Since it's Christmas, though, he's probably having goose, stuffed with sausages and chestnuts."

The villa was surrounded by palm trees and magnolias and even banana plants.

"Those anti-aircraft guns won't do him any good. We'll get him. We'll cut the swine's throat and Clara Petacci's, too. If Badoglio had had the guts to do it when they arrested him in Rome, we would have been saved the comedy of the Republic of Salò. The next time there won't be any Duce for the Germans to rescue."

She lowered the glasses. "You wanted to see me?"

"Yes, signora. I need to talk to you." He began pacing the room as he always did when he had something to say. She remained standing in the doorway, feeling the warmth of the December sun through her field jacket.

"We have finally had an answer from Milano."

"Yes?"

"You must remain here for yet some time."

"You still don't trust me."

"It is not that . . ."

"Yes, it is. One of your men told me, and you won't find out from me which one. Your superiors in Milano learned that I was once married to a Fascist, Count Angelo Morosini, that my cousin is the wife of Bruno Bronzini. You think I'm a spy."

The creaking of the floorboards under the Capo's boots ceased.

"If I thought that, Signora Howard, you would be dead by now."

"Then let me do my job. I didn't risk my life coming here to sit idly. I came to help you, but you won't give me a chance." If only she could explain, tell them about Paolo. But Perkins had said no. The Capo was a Communist, and Paolo had been a leader of a non-Communist resistance group. There were spies and spies.

"I have known about your past all along, before you ever came to us."

"Then why did you let me come?"

"I know I can trust you."

"*Comandante*, why don't you explain yourself and quit being mysterious."

"I'll have to, I suppose. We need your help, very badly."
He came out on the balcony with her and shut the door behind them.

"It's better to talk out here. You see, Signora Howard,
there are spies, and I am responsible for the lives of my
men. There are traitors on my side, there are traitors among
the Italians who work for Perkins. Sometimes the people
sent to us are spies. Perkins knows, but he can't tell me
without revealing to others that we know. I have a private
channel. A trusted man of mine meets with a trusted man
of his. He assured me you were okay."

"I see. Suppose your trusted man or his trusted man is a
spy?"

Again the white teeth showed in the black beard. The
Capo was a very handsome man, she thought.

"That is, of course, always a possibility."

He reached out and put his hand against her throat. She
started. Had he read in her eyes what she had been thinking? But then he pulled on the fine gold chain, and the
cross fell out of her shirt. He held it in his hand.

"The date—Perkins and I have a private code. That
number says you're okay. Another number would have
said, 'Pay no attention to any other message. She is a
spy.'"

"And then what would you have done?"

"You would have met with an accident." He let the gold
cross slide out of his hand.

"You would have killed me?"

"As I said, there would have been an accident. So, you
see, I am telling you everything. I started the story that my
superiors in Milano were checking out your background to
explain why we were not letting you send out your stories.
The real reason is that some big policy decisions had to be
made, including how to handle propaganda."

"I'm not here to do propaganda."

The white teeth showed again. "No, of course not. Why
don't you give me one of those German cigarettes my men
smuggle to you?"

She smiled back at him. She liked the Capo ... when she didn't hate him. She lit the cigarette for him.

"I received my instructions yesterday. With the new year a big campaign will begin in the cities—sabotage, strikes, assassinations. Here in the mountains we stay still, recruit, train. Our forces will grow with the help of the reports you will send on what we are doing. In the spring there will be a big Allied offensive. At the same time we will attack the enemy from behind, everywhere at once. But for now we stay still so that they do not realize how large are the forces we are building up. I am telling all this to no one but you."

"How do you know you can trust me with secrets?"

"If I weren't a good judge of character, I would be dead by now. You have some strong reason for coming here to help."

"Yes."

"What is it?"

"It isn't ideology."

"Ah. Yes, I'm a Communist. My wife was head of a Communist cell in Bologna. The Fascists tortured her to death ... Anyway ... now, you are free to write. Your dispatches will be taken by courier to where we have our radio transmitter. A squad came back from an operation last night. I have told them they are to tell you anything you want to know. I will not interfere with what you write except to protect the location of our bases."

The Capo opened the door, went to his desk, and turned the crank on a German field telephone. The interview was over.

That afternoon when Julia got back to her quarters there was an antique typewriter on the table in the loft and a stack of paper. She sat down, put a sheet of paper in the machine, and flexed her fingers. She began, typing hesitantly:

DECEMBER 25, 1944. FROM JULIA HOWARD, SOMEWHERE NORTH OF VERONA. I AM WRITING MY FIRST DISPATCH FROM THE HEADQUARTERS OF THE NINTH BRIGADE OF THE PARTISAN

ARMY OF NORTHERN ITALY. I WAS AWAKENED THIS MORNING WITH CHRISTMAS GREETINGS AND A PRESENT—A FRESH EGG. THIS AFTERNOON I ATTENDED A SIMPLE GRAVE-SIDE CEREMONY FOR ANTONIO PALLAVICINO. MORE THAN THREE HUNDRED ARMED MEN STOOD IN AN OPEN FIELD WITH HEADS BARED FOR A MINUTE OF SILENCE WHILE HIS BODY WAS LOWERED INTO THE GRAVE. ANTONIO WAS WOUNDED ON CHRISTMAS EVE, THE ONLY CASUALTY OF AN OPERATION THAT DESTROYED AN ENTIRE TRAINLOAD OF AMMUNITION COMING FROM GERMANY. HIS COMRADES CARRIED HIM FROM WHERE HE WAS HIT, ON THE MAIN RAILROAD LINE BETWEEN TRENT AND VERONA, TO THE PARTISAN CAMP WHERE I AM WRITING THIS DISPATCH. HE DIED EARLY THIS MORNING. AFTER THE CEREMONY THE PARTISANS DISPERSED IN SMALL GROUPS. THEY CARRY THEIR WEAPONS AT ALL TIMES, BUT IT HAS BEEN MONTHS SINCE THE GERMANS AND MUSSOLINI'S SO-CALLED REPUBLICAN ARMY HAVE DARED TO VENTURE INTO THIS MOUNTAINOUS AREA CONTROLLED BY THE PARTISANS. . . .

The fine days of December were followed by weeks of rain and fog, days when she typed out her dispatches by the light of a kerosene lamp at midday. When there was a sunny day the Allied bombers came in waves. Even from the mountain she could hear the dull thud of the bombs falling on Verona, reducing a city she loved to rubble. After a day of blue skies and bombing, the warm air would precipitate the fog, and she would again awake to blank whiteness outside the window of the loft. The tedium was relieved by her interviews with the tired, often wounded, men who had returned from missions. The Capo kept his word. He did not interfere with her dispatches, and she soon learned that the men told her the truth. They did not exaggerate their successes or try to hide their failures. The war had brought out a better, deeper side of the Italian character than she had known before.

But often days would pass when she had nothing to do. Then she would go visiting. The Capo had eased up on the restrictions he had placed on her. She was free to go where she wished along the "Via Veneto," the name given to the path that connected the scattered outposts of the Ninth Brigade. She would often start out with no object in mind, after a breakfast of herb tea and brown bread, along the path that led from the deserted village. She would return in the evening, shake the water from her field jacket, fatigues and stocking cap, take off her muddy boots, and go straight to bed. Hours were spent playing cards and drinking grappa with the squad lodged in one farmhouse, or arguing with the "intellectuals" lodged in a stone barn on a ridge above the path; other hours were spent warming her hands over a bowl of glowing charcoal, while the men who were lodged in an ancient church cleaned their weapons and talked about the past. The path became her "beat." Instead of the men coming to her, she would go to them. Every turn in the track became familiar to her, the smell of the decaying leaves, the sound of running water, a little wren foraging in the dead leaves for food, no matter how bad the weather.

Several times a week Flavio would come after dark to accompany her to the place where the shortwave radio was kept, to hear the BBC evening news in Italian. One evening, toward the end of January, she heard herself quoted on the news. There was a quiet round of applause from the crowded room smelling of male bodies. The next morning Flavio went on his first mission and was killed. She cried for the first time since the day that they had found her in a pile of leaves. She stayed in her loft throughout a long, gray afternoon, mourning the waste of it all.

Flavio was not replaced. There was no need for an orderly. Her closest companion was the Capo, who often walked the path with her. He wanted her. Why didn't she take him to her loft and let him make love to her? Next week, or the week after, the Capo might be dead. She should go to bed with him, but she could not. All she could do was to keep writing and try not to think about Paolo being dead. She knew she would never make love to another man again.

In early March the sun returned to northern Italy. The Axis was finally crumbling, and soon the spring offensive would begin. Perkins had spoken of the hope that there would be fifty thousand partisans in the field by then: There were already sixty thousand. It was warm enough to bathe, and Julia was assigned her own "facilities"—a pool beneath a waterfall that was off-limits to the men. There she was finally able to wash her filthy winter clothes and hang them out to dry, finally able to bathe in the numbingly cold water, lathering her hair with brown laundry soap. Afterward she lay naked on the rocks in the sun. Soon she was asleep.

"Signora, come, we have a spectacle." One of the men was calling from the trail above the falls.

Julia put on her still-damp clothes and trudged up the path to the trail.

"Come see. Carlo is back from Milano, and you must see what he has brought."

They followed the trail to the barn where the "intellectuals" lived. Julia walked along the sun-warmed earth in her bare feet, carrying her army boots. It was a big stone barn, on the edge of a field that had once been a pasture but was now overgrown with weeds. Spring flowers were pushing up among the dead weed stalks.

"You see. We're famous."

On the barn door the Capo had nailed posters torn from the walls in Milan. There were insane orders issued by Mussolini, threats of retaliation from the German commander, and a number of blown-up photographs of wanted "criminals" for whose arrest a reward would be paid. Their Ninth Brigade was well represented. A crowd of men pressed forward.

"Why, the lying bastards," someone said. "They claimed a year ago that they killed this one, and now he's being accused of 'heinous crimes.'" Julia pushed forward to where the men crowded around a poster. Big shoulders blocked her view, and all she could see was a piece of beard and two dark eyes . . . No! Don't start that or you'll go crazy! But she kept staring into those eyes, hypnotized, until she seemed to be surrounded by a white light and the men's voices and laughter had faded to a distant ringing in her ears. The eyes stared back at her and they said, believe, believe, if you only believe . . . She reached out and grabbed a shoulder for support.

"Scuzi, signora," and the man moved to make room for her.

She could see the whole face, and the name beneath it leapt out at her. She turned and took three unsteady steps and reached a stone wall just in time to keep from falling. She held on to it with both hands, and she could feel cold perspiration on her forehead. She mustn't let them see her faint.

When she felt steady again and the nausea had passed, Julia turned and walked out of the shadow of the barn into the spring sunlight. She stood for a long time in her bare feet in the meadow, ankle-deep in wildflowers. A rainbow glowed around the sun, and from the woods came the call of a song thrush, the sweetest of all bird songs. Paolo Danieli was alive.

Big drops of rain splattered against the windowpane, waking her. . . . She had been dreaming of Paolo. During the day she tried not to think of him, but she couldn't keep him from entering her dreams. He was alive, but the final battle was coming. How many more would be dead before it was over? If he were killed now, she would go out of her mind. Hope was the cruelest torture of all.

The wind bent the white trunks of the poplars outside the window and plastered the young green leaves against the glass. Julia drew herself into a ball beneath the down quilt. How nice it would be just to stay there forever. But her watch kept ticking. Every morning she dreaded the knock on the door that would mean it was all beginning. She looked up at the calendar she had made with a pencil on the wall: April 22. They couldn't wait much longer. It would be today, she decided. As if to confirm her thought, there was a knock on the door.

"Come in."

The Capo walked through the door. He was wearing a knitted wool cap, a submachine gun was slung over his shoulder, two hand grenades hung from his webbed belt.

"We're moving out."

"Yes, I know." She sat up and put her feet on the floor.

"We won't be coming back."

"Why not?"

"This is the end. Either we win or . . ."

" 'I will come back carrying my shield or carried on it'? A noble sentiment, but I prefer to stay alive." She stood up and began brushing her hair, looking in a piece of mirror nailed to the wall.

"Well, of course." She could see him in the mirror, looking at her body in the tight-fitting woolen underwear.

"When do we move out?"

"About an hour."

"In daylight?"

"We're going to fight now. We don't need to hide anymore."

She looked into his eyes in the mirror. She hoped he would make it through the next days or weeks or however long until it was over. And this time it would be over. When the Germans moved behind the Po, everyone knew it was their last stand in Italy. The greatest irony of all would be if Paolo lived and she were killed.

As they walked along the trail in the spring sunlight, armed men came out of the farmhouses and out of the woods to join them. The column grew until, by the time they reached the end of the camps, it was a small army. By midmorning they had reached the crossing where Julia had hidden, covered with leaves, more than five months earlier. She borrowed a pair of binoculars and looked down at Mussolini's villa on the far shore of the lake. There was no sign of life. The shutters were closed. But the column turned in the opposite direction and began the ascent of Monte Baldo. By sunset they were on the shoulder of the mountain, looking down on the Adige, a silver thread winding toward the plain where Verona was visible, and, beyond, the Po Valley. Columns of black smoke rose into the sunset. They slept in an open field that night.

The next morning it began to rain, and for all the next

day they trudged through the wet woods. They followed the Adige south. On the highway above the trail, German trucks and staff cars sped in both directions in twos and threes. There were no convoys, and they met no German units. The Allied bombers were not flying, but the sound of artillery could still be heard. That night when they camped, Julia was too wet and cold to sleep, as tired as she was. She drifted off sometime before dawn, just as the clouds were breaking up and the moon appeared. An hour later she was awakened by a partisan. The *comandante* wished to see her.

The Capo and his lieutenants were sitting on a large flat rock beside the river. He motioned to her to sit down. A map was spread out in front of them.

"Are you ill, signora?"

"No, just tired."

The Capo looked at her as if she were a piece of machinery. "Do you think you could march all day and all night?"

"I suppose I could, if I had to."

"We are sending out a mission this morning. We would like you to consider going with it."

"It's a little late for reporting, isn't it?"

"It's not for reporting."

"I didn't come here to fight."

He ignored that. "Tomorrow the American Fifth Army will cross the Adige. At the same time there will be a general uprising behind the German lines. My men will attack a number of objectives around Verona, the most important of which is the German divisional command at Malspina."

"Malspina?"

"They are headquartered on the Morosini estate. You know it well, I believe."

"Obviously you know."

"We want to take them by surprise, of course. Our chances would be much better if we had someone with us who knows the layout of the estate. But it's entirely up to you."

She felt as if her whole life had come down to these moments beneath the ancient willow tree. Perhaps it had. In

the first light of dawn, she could make out the broken
bench where she and Paolo had passed whole afternoons.
The form of the house began to separate itself from the
dark woods behind, first the columns, then the windows
and balustrades, the row of statues across the facade. Had
this splendid place really been her home? It seemed impossible, but then it seemed impossible that violence and death
hung poised over the tranquil, elegant image of the Villa
Serena. She looked at the Capo. She didn't even know his
name. His still-young sensitive face was now hidden behind
a mask of charcoal and grease. A song thrush began to
sing. How many mornings had she heard that song and
known that dawn was coming, turned over and into Paolo's
arms. . . .

A light came on behind shutters in the east wing. That
would be the small study where she and Angelo and Victoria and Bruno had dined on her and Angelo's first anniversary. She had left the table in tears, and afterward they had
talked about where fascism was leading Italy. Well, now
they knew. Another light came on. What were they waiting
for, those eighty pairs of eyes watching from the edge of
the woods?

The Capo rose to his knees, checking his gun. Then he
whistled and dark figures began to move out across the
lawn. She stood up beside him.

"Get down," he told her. "When the attack starts, run
back into the woods. You know this place. Hide somewhere. If it goes badly . . ."

She knelt there, unable to speak. He was going to
die. . . . She knew it. . . . "Don't!" She grabbed his arm.

"Get down, I said." The Capo pushed her to the ground
and moved forward.

A red flare arched overhead and landed in the gravel in
front of the main staircase. Suddenly gunfire came from everywhere. More lights went on. There was an explosion and
a pair of shutters leaped off their hinges as flames belched
out. Someone appeared at a window only to disappear as
gunfire tore away the window frame. A partisan ran across
the lawn toward the house and hurled something through

the window: another explosion and white flames. Now there was gunfire from the roof, and one of the men on the lawn fell. More explosions; roof tiles rained down on the lawn. Someone jumped from a window, his nightshirt billowing out like a parachute. Smoke was pouring out from all parts of the house, joining in a single black column that rose into the pink sky. The main doors of the house were flung open, and a dozen men in pajamas and nightshirts and parts of uniforms burst out only to crumple under gunfire. A body rolled down the stone staircase. The gunfire ceased. Now there was only the crackle of flames, as the Villa Serena became a pyre. The black-faced partisans assembled in front of the house. Julia did not see the Capo. She got up and ran across the lawn toward them.

"What's the count?" someone said.

"We lost four."

"Not bad at all. It could have been much worse, but of course . . ."

The Capo was one of the four. He lay lifeless on the gravel, the pink flame of the flare still sputtering beside him. One by one the men took off their caps, as did Julia. Her eyes filled with tears. She blinked them away and saw that the men around her with blackened faces were crying, too. No one said anything. What was there to say that would make any difference?

She looked up at the house. Through a gaping window she could make out the painted shepherd and shepherdess on the ceiling who seemed to look down in terror as the flames rose to engulf them. A part of the roof buckled and collapsed.

"Get back," someone cried. "Get back."

Another voice: "Move out, move out."

From that moment on, after so many months of inactivity, it was continuous motion. The countryside was in revolt. German staff cars were ambushed, patrols were wiped out. There was sabotage in every town and village. The German army began to pull back, but it was too late. The next day Verona fell to the Americans, and the day after,

Julia was on the road to Milan with a partisan convoy. The German army was retreating toward the Alpine passes, and the partisans had taken over the countryside. She had hitched a ride in a captured German troop carrier, loaded with armed men, and late in the afternoon it reached the turnoff to Lake Como, where there was a roadblock.

"What's going on here?" the driver said.

"A little problem. We'll have it cleared up in a few minutes."

"What kind of problem?"

The man at the barricade shrugged. "A band of our boys killed some Fascists—at least I hope they were Fascists. You know how it is with these kids. Shoot first and ask questions later."

"How long are we going to have to wait?"

"Five more minutes maybe. Just long enough to get their cars off the road. They were in a convoy, a lot of big Milanese industrialists, trying to make it to Switzerland. They stopped them here, made them get out of their cars, and when the lads made up their minds who they were, they gunned them down. Not half an hour ago. Well, that's what happens at the end. Discipline breaks down."

Someone was shouting from farther down the road. The man moved aside the barricade and the truck drove on. There had been eight cars in the escaping convoy, now riddled with bullets. The cars had been pushed off the road and the bodies rolled onto the shoulder. The car at the head of the line was a canary-yellow Bugatti, an old one.

"Stop!"

"Signora, why? You don't want to look at that."

"Stop, I said."

Julia jumped from the open car. She suppressed a scream. Two bodies lay together alongside the road. Bruno was face up, his mouth and eyes open; Victoria lay face down across him, the back of her lavender dress a large red stain. One of her matching lavender shoes stood in the middle of the road, as if it were in a shop window on the Via Condotti.

Chapter Twenty

TEN MILES OUTSIDE of Milan, where the highway crossed the main Milan-Venice railway line, a locomotive that had been hit by a bomb blocked the road. American Army vehicles were backed up three abreast. Julia got out and went down the line of tanks and trucks until she found a group of officers.

"Lady," a colonel said, "what are you doing here?"

"War correspondent. *Baltimore Sun.*"

The colonel grinned. "You're way out ahead of your competition."

"What's going on in Milan?"

"Milan's secure. We're just on our way to garrison the city."

"I need to get there. I'm supposed to interview the leader of the partisan Sixth Brigade."

"They're in Milan?"

"They were. Can I talk to your intelligence officer?"

"You'll have to show me your credentials."

"I don't have any. It's a long story. My name is Julia Howard."

Why were they looking at her like that?

"Not *the* Julia Howard?" a captain said.

"Yes, but what . . ."

"Big story about you last week in *Stars and Stripes*," the colonel replied.

"There was?"

" 'American heroine behind German lines,' " the captain added enthusiastically, "with a picture, and you're just as . . ."

"Sergeant," the colonel said, "go find Major Barnett."

"Yes ma'am," Major Barnett said, "the Sixth Brigade's in Milan, pretty much shot up, though. When the Germans were trying to get themselves in formation to put up a stand against us, the Sixth came down on them like a swarm of hornets."

"You know the name of the Sixth Brigade commander?"

"Danieli. I shouldn't be using his name, but since you're . . ."

"Would he still be in Milan?"

"He would be, if he's alive."

"Colonel," Julia said in as casual a voice as she could manage, "how soon do you expect to be in Milan?"

"Tomorrow sometime. We've sent for some heavy equipment to get this locomotive off the road. If there were still fighting going on, I'd send the tanks on ahead across the fields. But as it is . . ."

"Tomorrow, then."

"At best."

"Thanks," she said, and walked away.

"Hope you get your interview," the captain called after her.

Julia slid down the bank to the railroad tracks that led to Milan. She looked in both directions: nothing but the four empty rails running away toward both horizons. The sun was going down. She started walking. At dusk she could see the spires of the Milan cathedral catching the last rays of the sun. Five miles? Six? It didn't matter. She could go no farther. Sleep in the woods. She had done it before.

The path up the bank led through pine woods to a vineyard on a stretch of level ground that surrounded a farmhouse, like a small island in a green sea. The door to the farmhouse stood open.

Once she lit a candle Julia could see that the house had been the country place of some moderately prosperous Milanese Fascists. Nothing had been disturbed. A picture of

Mussolini still hung on the wall. She locked herself in a bedroom, threw herself across the bed, and descended into a sleep so deep that even the images of Victoria and Bruno lying in the road did not come to haunt her.

She was up at dawn, heading down through the dew-wet vine leaves to the railroad tracks. She began walking the last miles to Milan. The rails multiplied as she drew closer to the city. Then the bomb craters began. The railroad yard was a mass of wreckage, deep holes torn in the ground, twisted rails. The station was a ruin. The great iron-and-glass vaults looked as if they had been smashed by a giant hand from above. Inside the station, in the darkness and rubble, women and children scavenged in the ruins of restaurants and stalls. The big hall at the bottom of the stairs was empty. The sun poured through a gaping hole in the roof, making a pool of light on the broken floor, where thousands of tickets were scattered like colored confetti. At the entrance of the station a group of armed men lounged.

"Headquarters, Sixth Brigade?"

"Via Vallazze."

"Where is that?"

"Other side of the Piazza Loreto, if you can get there." The men laughed.

Julia ran down the steps of the station. The Piazza Loreto was not far, but the streets were crowded. People everywhere were shouting and singing and crying, *"Viva l'Italia!"* And the streets were choked with the remains of collapsed buildings, the burnt shells of cars. Milan had been so blasted by Allied bombers that Julia could recognize no familiar landmark. But after a few minutes she came out on the Piazza Loreto. Thousands of people milled about at one side of the big open square, like a swarm of insects. There was no singing, no cries of *"Viva l'Italia!"* As she came to the edge of the crowd she began asking, "Headquarters, Sixth Brigade?"

No one knew, and few bothered to answer her. They were all pressing forward like a crowd trying to get into a soccer stadium. And then she saw the bodies, eight or nine of them, hanging upside down by their feet from a metal beam over some gasoline pumps.

"What is it?"

"Don't you know?"

"Haven't you heard?"

"Il Duce, see?" A big man picked her up under the arms and held her high above the crowd. Mussolini hung like a side of beef, his hands nearly touching the ground. A woman hung beside him, her skirt modestly tied up with a piece of rope. The man put Julia back down on the ground.

"And his darling Claretta. You saw her?"

"Yes, I saw."

"Victory!" someone shouted in her face.

She pushed her way out of the crowd. She began to run toward the empty far side of the square. Victory. There was no victory, only a trail of death: Angelo, Francesca, French and Bauman, Flavio, the Capo, Bruno and Victoria. . . . She felt no joy over Mussolini's end. For God's sake, where was the Via Vallazze? There, someone said, pointing to a street half-filled with rubble. Two armed guards blocked entry to the street.

"Headquarters, Sixth Brigade?"

"What do you want?"

"I want to see the *comandante*."

"What for?"

"I'm the first foreign correspondent to reach Milan. He'll want to see me."

"Where's your identification?"

"I don't have any. I've been with the partisans on Monte Baldo."

"Sure you have. How did you get ahead of the Allied army?"

"I walked along the railway track."

"Maybe. But we have strict orders. You'd better move along now."

Julia reached inside her jacket and took out the worn brown envelope. "If you will take this to him, he will see me."

"What's in it?"

"None of your business. Now, please . . ." Her eyes filled with tears.

"*Bene,*" the guard said, embarrassed by her crying, "come along." He walked with her to the first building on the street that had not been destroyed by the bombing and stood in the entrance to the bomb-damaged apartment building while a boy ran upstairs with the envelope. Three men in boots, with guns, walked down the stairs and out into the street. Then the boy appeared at the landing of the stairs.

"The *comandante* says for her to come up alone." She followed the boy up three flights of stairs.

"Here."

A guard stood aside and she went through the door into a sparsely furnished room. A heavy man wearing glasses sat behind a desk.

"*Comandante?*" she said, shaking all over. But the man shook his head.

"Wait here," he said. He got up and went out by another door, leaving her alone.

The man's footsteps returned. The door opened. The first thing she saw was the book of sketches clutched in a man's hand. But it wasn't the same man who had gone out of the door. She looked up into the face of Paolo Danieli. With a cry of joy and disbelief, she threw herself into his arms.

They wandered through the rubble-strewn streets of Milan for an hour, holding hands, touching, stopping to kiss. People smiled at them, said words of encouragement. The scene would be repeated thousands of times in the coming weeks and months—a coming together of the lucky ones who had survived. Julia and Paolo looked like a couple of tramps, in stained ragged pieces of khaki uniform, Paolo with a dark beard and Julia with hair so dirty it was like a greasy mop. Finally they sat down to rest on a bench in a little park that was an island of tender spring green in the bomb-wrecked city. A blossoming pear tree arched overhead; the white petals floated down all around them.

"I feel like a bride," she said. Paolo was kissing her on

the neck, and she began to giggle from the tickle of his beard.

"You are. Three-and-a-half years and our marriage still unconsummated."

"Oh, that," she said, and laughed. "That comes later. And all of my pent-up desires will be taken out on you. . . . Paolo, stop that!"

"Why should I?"

They were almost falling off the bench, drowning in a rain of blossoms and laughter. "Because," she gasped, "I don't want to be molested until I've had a hot bath and washed my hair and, for God's sake, you've shaved."

"You don't like my beard?" His hands were under her field jacket again.

"No. Want you all smooth and clean and . . . Oh, Paolo, you're not dead. . . ." She burst into tears, and he held her close while she sobbed.

"It's all right now," he said. After a long cry, she wiped her eyes with a sleeve and smiled.

"You're lucky to be alive yourself. That was a crazy thing to do, sneaking into Milano on your own. The American Army is only a day away." He held the back of her neck in his large hard hand, as though she were a naughty puppy.

When she tried to speak, his mouth was on hers. The kiss was long and deep.

"Tell me, how did you come to have my notebook of drawings? You can't imagine what it was like to have it handed to me with the message that *una bella signora* had brought it."

"You can't imagine what it was like to think you were dead. I almost went crazy, my darling. The notebook was found in German headquarters in Rome. Some soldier had turned it in for the reward they were offering, claiming he'd killed you."

"So that's it. It was in a coat hanging in a closet. I wasn't even in the apartment when the gestapo raided. . . . Francesca was."

Julia began crying again, and he enclosed her in his

arms. A song thrush trilled from the tree above them. There was hope again, and already the Italian spring was beginning to renew the country.

"I love her still." Julia wept and wept. "But I have you, and always I will see a trace of her in your eyes. Oh, how awful it all is. Yesterday—I can't believe it—I saw Victoria and Bruno lying dead beside the road. Oh, where will it all end?"

"It has all ended. For whatever reason, you and I have come through on the other side."

"Yes," she said, sitting up and trying to pull herself together. "Yes, we have. It seems only yesterday that we met on the *Velonia*, but it's been fifteen years. Fifteen years, Paolo. What are you going to do with a thirty-seven-year-old woman?"

"And you with a forty-year-old man? But do you think I would have that twenty-two-year-old spoiled brat you once were back now, even if I could? I'm proud of what you've done. And you're the most beautiful thirty-seven-year-old woman in the world. . . ."

She put her hand on his face. "Paolo, darling, now you're crying. . . . Oh, my dear, I'm so proud of *you*. When the history books are written, there will be a place for you in the story of how fascism was brought down . . . and then they'll also mention that Paolo Danieli became the greatest name in Italian painting in the years following World War II and . . ."

"Julia, do you see that old church across the street?"

"Yes."

"That is the church of Sant'Ambrogio. Do you know how old it is?"

"No."

"Parts of it at least were standing before the barbarians overran the Roman empire. Somehow it has survived every invasion and war. It's like Italy itself, enduring everything that time has brought. I don't regret the fifteen years I gave to help it survive. I've done what I had to do and now . . ." He smiled. "You and I . . ."

The thrush flew from the pear tree, swooped down, landed on the roof of the church, and began singing again.

"Tomorrow," Julia said, "I would like to visit Sant'Ambrogio with you, have you explain every detail of it to me. Then we'll go to the Duomo. I've never been there. I don't really know Milan at all. I'll find a dress somewhere, and there must be, even in these times, some place that will serve two lovers lunch, and then . . ." She looked at him, waited for him to speak, her heart so overflowing with love for him that she could say no more.

"And then," Paolo continued. "we start over from the beginning."